BITING THE

D1150067

"Watch out! Watch g!"

All around us t me around had redisc vertical. Multiple thoughts streaked through my mind simultaneously. Not all of them made sense, but a skilled translator might put them in the following light:

Oh Jesus! Oh crap! Zombies! The Wizard's a necromancer. He could be around here somewhere, pulling their strings. So should I just run off into the night like some rabid raccoon and hope I luck into him? How stupid is that? Plus, it's not him. It's probably an apprentice. You know that. It may even be the mole. Is anybody murmuring a spell? How the hell can I tell? We are so outnumbered! Did Ashley just go down? My God, I think the semi is farther away than ever. Is that possible? Oh Jesus, was that Terrence's leg? Don't turn your head. I said don't—never mind. Holy shit, that's the barrel of a Colt .45 aimed right at your face.

The reaver, a live one, grinned wide enough to show the gap between his front teeth as his finger squeezed the trigger

" cking strai

BY JENNIFER RARDIN

Once Bitten, Twice Shy

Another One Bites the Dust

Biting the Bullet

Bitten to Death

One More Bite

Biting the Bullet

A JAZ PARKS NOVEL

Jennifer Rardin

www.orbitbooks.net

ORBIT

First published in Great Britain in 2008 by Orbit
Reprinted 2009 (twice)

Copyright © 2008 by Jennifer Rardin
Excerpt from *Bitten to Death* © 2008 by Jennifer Rardin

The moral right of the author has been asserted.

All characters and events in this publication, other than those clearly in the public domain, are fictitious and any resemblance to real persons, living or dead, is purely coincidental.

All rights reserved.
No part of this publication may be reproduced, stored in a retrieval system, or transmitted, in any form or by any means, without the prior permission in writing of the publisher, nor be otherwise circulated in any form of binding or cover other than that in which it is published and without a similar condition including this condition being imposed on the subsequent purchaser.

A CIP catalogue record for this book
is available from the British Library.

ISBN 978-1-84149-640-5

Typeset in Granjon
Printed and bound in Great Britain by
CPI Mackays, Chatham, ME5 8TD

Papers used by Orbit are natural, renewable and recyclable products sourced from well-managed forests and certified in accordance with the rules of the Forest Stewardship Council.

Mixed Sources
Product group from well-managed
forests and other controlled sources
www.fsc.org Cert no. SGS-COC-004081
© 1996 Forest Stewardship Council

Orbit
An imprint of
Little, Brown Book Group
100 Victoria Embankment
London EC4Y 0DY

An Hachette UK Company
www.hachette.co.uk

www.orbitbooks.net

For Ben . . . one of the world's greatest wonders.

I love you.

Acknowledgments

I want to express my deepest gratitude to all the pros at Orbit who work tirelessly to put Jaz Parks into the field. They include: Bob Castillo, Bella Pagan, Penina Lopez, Alex Lencicki, Katherine Molina, Jennifer Flax, and most especially my editor, Devi Pillai, who is an absolute freaking genius. Plus, she's hilarious. To my agent, Laurie McLean, whose astounding energy and absolute support let me know I am professionally blessed—thanks so much for everything you do. My readers have hung in with me once again, and if the beauty is in the details, much of what's lovely in this book is due to Ben Rardin, Katie Rardin, and Hope Dennis. And to you, Reader, it's so cool that we've shared this adventure! Shall we have another?

Chapter One

Gunfire boomed in my ears, the sergeant crouched next to me yelling with triumph as his target fell.

"You were right, ma'am," he told me. "They drop like stones if you hit 'em in the forehead."

I nodded, appreciating the fact that he'd listened. Not all of them had.

My boss, Vayl, and I had just finished unloading our supplies with the help of our three-person crew. As we'd watched our Chinook fade into the night sky the monsters had attacked.

The situation looked dire. We stood a hundred yards from the tiny white farmhouse at which we'd arranged to meet the elite troops who would help us complete our next mission. Most of our gear was still packed, including the new high-tech weapons Bergman had brought for the Special Ops guys — which would've come in pretty damn handy.

My gun, Grief, the Walther PPK Bergman had modified for me so it could take down humans or vamps, rode in my shoulder holster. I also carried my usual array of backup weaponry. A syringe of holy water nested in the spring-loaded sheath I kept strapped around my right wrist. I'd tucked three throwing knives up my left sleeve just in case, and a bola inherited from my great-great-granddad rode in a leather pocket that ran down my right thigh. Everything else sat in the worn black case I wore on my back. In other words—inaccessible.

Vayl held the cane he always carried, an artisan's dream that hid a sword as lethal as its owner. Though he looked a lot more vulnerable than I did at first glance, his opponents were never deceived for long. The tall, broad-shouldered vampire who'd been my boss for eight months and my *sverhamin* for two carried within him an arsenal so formidable it had allowed him to survive nearly three hundred years, eighty of which he'd spent with the CIA. That made my four-year pin look kinda pathetic. But if you consider what I've done in that time, I'd argue that you should count them in dog years.

As consultants, Bergman and Cassandra weren't armed, so we'd stuck them in the center of our small circle, which we'd completed with our newest recruit. Cole Bemont had joined our ranks when his private investigations business burned as a direct result of his involvement with one of our missions. Vayl and I provided plenty of muscle for this one, and Bergman supplied all the brains we needed, but Cole displayed a gift for languages none of us could match. It had come to him, along with his Sensitivity, after he'd drowned in the icy waters of his family pond as a young boy and been revived long minutes later by rescue personnel.

His Gift had made him indispensable on our last job, when neither of us spoke Chinese, and this one, when nobody knew Farsi. It also helped that he could shoot with the accuracy and icy calm of a sniper. His weapon of choice was a 9 mm Beretta Storm, which he'd pulled and held steady in his left hand. His Parker-Hale M85 still rested in its carrying case across his back.

"Night vision!" I'd yelled to him as the creatures came roaring at us from the blackness of the desert, their noise and the suddenness of their attack making them seem like an army. As Cole obeyed, I squeezed my own eyes tight for the couple of seconds it took to activate the special lenses Bergman had engineered for us. They corrected any problems we had seeing far away, up close, or in the dark. The extra visual acuity I'd already gained from donating blood to my boss on a couple of occasions paired with Bergman's green-laced eyeball enhancers to show me a chilling sight.

At least twenty men swarmed us from all sides, their tattered robes and sand-caked hair flying back in the breeze caused by their movements. The sharp black outline surrounding their forms clued me in to their identities as did the third eye blinking wildly in the middle of their foreheads. Part of me stomped, swore, and snapped, "Are you *kidding* me? Already?"

"Reavers!" I yelled, glad my curls were caught inside the black scarf I wore, unable to impair my vision. "Aim for their foreheads!"

Most of the members of the Special Ops unit had been standing outside the farmhouse waiting for us when we touched down. They'd begun moving toward us as we unloaded, and two of the guys were within ten yards when the attack came. They reacted with admirable speed, riddling the nearest enemy with M4 fire. They seemed to heed my command, but I realized quickly they weren't aiming high enough. Their shots were landing pretty much between the ears. Made sense on anything but reavers, which only backed up at the onslaught, didn't even go down.

"They're shielded!" I screamed. "Their only weak point is that third eye!" Then I was too busy to worry about the men. The reavers were everywhere. I suddenly knew what it was like to be a tremendously popular rock star. We were about to be stampeded. Smothered. Except this mob wasn't after autographs—they wanted blood.

I took a deep breath. No room for fear here, where every shot had to count. I pumped bullet after bullet into the monsters attacking us as Cole's gun echoed mine and Vayl slashed and parried so quickly his hands were a blur. Behind me Cassandra was on her knees, the abaya she wore puddling around her feet like an oil slick. Was she praying? Well, she'd been an oracle once. If she had any pull left, now would be a great time to call in her favors.

Beside her Bergman clutched big tufts of his lank brown hair with both hands, his sparse beard seeming to tremble as he yelled, "Give me a weapon, goddammit! A rock! A screwdriver! Anything!"

Suddenly the Spec Ops guys were beside us, holding off the reavers when they weren't actually taking them out.

"Fall back!" I heard the commander say, his voice so familiar in my ears I had to force myself not to turn and look. A massive black dude knelt in front of me and started firing, so I took advantage of the break to hand Bergman my knife and reload.

Slowly, fighting all the way, we backed into the farmhouse. At some point I realized the two men who'd been out in front of the rest were being helped along by their buddies. A couple more had taken damage as well. They'd all been raked across the arms and chests by the reavers' harpoonlike claws, but the body armor they wore under their light-colored thobes seemed to have averted total disaster.

As the medic attended them, the rest of us took our posts at the windows and the open door. The reavers bombarded the house with no regard to the lead we poured into their bodies. But they dropped pretty fast when I repeated my call. "Target the third eye!" I yelled.

The sergeant hunkered next to me, chortling as he dropped yet another one. "I love my job!" he said. He couldn't have been much older than me, a mid-twenties adrenaline junkie whose Asian ancestors had granted him an exotic beauty set off perfectly by his square-jawed American side.

"Me too, pal," I said as I took my turn at the window. There were only a couple left. I decided to leave them for the others. I'd only brought a limited amount of ammo and I was a long way from home. I began refilling my clip as my neighbor introduced himself.

"Don Hardin," he said, holding out his hand, "but you can call me Jet."

I shook it, doubting I'd experience a wimpy grip in his ten-person unit. "Nice to meet you," I said. "I'm Jaz Parks."

You know how they say silence is golden? Not always. At the moment I'd have colored it orange. The hue of those construction lights you see on the highway, warning you to hit the breaks before you clip the poor schmuck who's holding the stop sign.

The last shot rang out. The final reaver fell just as I said my name and the farmhouse fell quiet. I looked around. The single stone room wasn't lit. The troops wore their night-vision goggles. Vayl could see in the dark. The rest of us had Bergman's contact lenses. I suddenly realized how completely we depend on being able to see the expressions on people's faces in order to interpret everything from feelings to appropriate conversational gambits.

"Somebody cover the windows. Give us a light, Cam," ordered the commander in the gruff voice I was sure I'd recognized before. All of us made the necessary adjustments so we wouldn't be blinded as a tall, broad-shouldered woman closed the door and hung blankets over the window openings, and one of the guys across the room pulled the hood off a surprisingly bright lantern.

I blinked as the commander stepped forward, looming over me like Albert used to right before banishing me to the yard, usually for talking when I should've been shutting up. Once there, I was required to run laps until further notice. Generally he had to reseed a three-foot path all the way around our property line every time we moved, since I usually figured whatever I'd pulled was worth the punishment, my brother felt the same, and our sister, Evie, ran with us to keep us company.

Dave had grown since then, and I'd never seen him so fit. But I didn't think he'd appreciate me *ooh*ing and *aah*ing over his amazing abs in front of his unit. My suspicions were confirmed when he asked in a demanding and somewhat annoyed tone, "What're *you* doing here?"

That's the CIA for you. Don't even tell your partners who's coming until they get there.

I was tempted to strike a dramatic pose, hands on hips, hair floating on a well-timed breeze as I declared, "We have come to vanquish the Wizard!" But there would be no awed intakes of breath if I took that approach. According to our pentagon briefers, these guys had been chasing the bastard for a year. But he'd been killing long before that.

The Wizard had caused more U.S. and allied soldier casualties in the past decade than entire countries during official armed conflicts. He'd murdered thousands of innocents during terrorist attacks—his own people and ours. He made few distinctions. Anyone who denied his god, Angra Mainyu, as the Big Kahuna, made himself a target. And the Wizard, well, he didn't exactly call Angra Mainyu Daddy, but he'd begun to drop hints. Frankly, it did seem as if he had some divine assistance at times. He'd slipped so many traps locals said he ate shadows and drank starlight.

He also made the dead walk.

Which meant our training for this mission had included a crash course in necromancy that had left me with a bad case of the gag-a-maggots. Cassandra, of all people, had been our instructor. Pete had set us up in an empty meeting room around a scratched table with a fake wooden top on which she'd gently set the Enkyklios. The size of a makeup case, it held hundreds of years' worth of histories and lore gathered by Seers from across the world. Though I'd seen it work several times before, I still marveled at the unseen power that moved its parts, which resembled rainbow-colored glass balls. The kind hip women put at the bottom of vases. Don't ask me why. I've never been hip.

Bergman had still been buried in his lab, so only Cole, Vayl, and I had watched as Cassandra whispered, *"Enkyklios occsallio vera proma,"* triggering the marbles to change, rearrange, and reveal their zombie-making secrets.

Out of a grouping of orbs shaped like a bell came a hologram so clear I was tempted to reach out and touch the weeping woman wearing a faded flower-print housedress. She strode down a narrow dirt path, her sensible shoes raising small clouds of dust with every step. Her wheat-colored hair had begun to escape from the bun she'd arranged at the nape of her neck. Tendrils of it brushed across her shoulders, pointing down to the dead girl she carried in her arms.

She headed toward a thatch-roofed cottage, the garden of which was so wild and dark it looked like it belonged in a painting by van Gogh. When she got to the door she kicked it twice. "Lemme in, Madame Otis!" she cried in a harsh cockney accent. "I need your help! I'll pay, I will!"

After she'd kicked a couple more times the door flew open. "What—" A narrow-eyed, stringy-haired woman took in the scene before her and crossed her arms. "Go home and bury that girl," she said flatly.

"She's my only child," the mother replied, desperation making her voice crack. "I know you can bring her back."

The woman spat into the tangle of weeds and hollyhocks next to the doorway. "I won't." We exchanged interested looks around the table. Not "I can't," but "I won't." Madame Otis was a necromancer.

"I need her!" wailed the mother. "I can't live without her! You can't imagine the pain!"

"What's your name, woman?" demanded Madame Otis.

"Hilda Barnaby, and this here is Mira," she added, nodding to the burden in her arms.

"Don't imagine you're the first woman to fall to her knees under the crush of a child's loss," snarled Madame Otis. "What you're asking me will bring you horrors beyond imagination. Wrap up that child, shoulder your grief, and move on. Because, believe me, you cannot be rejoined to her on this earth without conjuring yet more pain and an eternity of regret."

The women stared each other down. Almost at the same moment Hilda got that *aha!* look on her face, we realized Madame Otis had experienced a much similar loss and a parallel reaction. With one exception. She'd become a necromancer so she could raise her own dead. The nightmare of that experience still played across her face, though instinct told us it stood many decades in her past.

The picture faded as Hilda's voice came in unrelenting monotone through the misty gray fog that replaced the images. "I convinced Madame Otis to raise Mira in the end. All it took was everything I had. And it seemed so little to give. Even though Madame Otis explained to me that Mira would not be the same, I couldn't bring myself to care. My little girl would walk and talk once more. I would be able to hug her. Cook for her. Watch her walk down the aisle." Bitter laugh. "I couldn't have been more wrong."

New picture now, of Mira lying on a bed of rose petals on the floor of Madame Otis's cramped living room. Hilda's job seemed to be to keep the wood stove in the corner packed full. Every few minutes she'd pull open the black cast-iron door and throw in a foot-long piece of maple. Hilda spoke again. "Looking back, I think most of this was for show, or just to keep me busy. The important part was something I never could have grasped and should have stopped before it began."

I could've keeled over when Madame Otis went to her knees beside Mira and began speaking the words Raoul had taught me. "I recognize that chant!" I said. "She's going to separate from her body!"

Within moments she proved me right, though I was the only one who saw her rise, a jagged red crystalline dagger shot with black hovering over her inert and uncaring body. An unearthly scream filled my ears, as if the first violinist in the New York Philharmonic had taken a saw to her strings as a tiny piece ripped from the whole of Madame Otis's soul. It shot straight into Mira's body, making it spasm.

Hilda screamed and ran to her daughter, snatching her limp hand off the floor along with a few stray petals. "Mira, baby! Speak to me! Speak to me!"

Madam Otis quickly recalled herself, grimacing deeply as her two halves reconnected. She sat hunched over for a good thirty seconds before straightening. The expression on her face when she finally lifted it made me shudder. I recognized it. Had seen it on a few of my foes when they thought they had me cornered. Pure evil triumph.

"She's my child now, Hilda. Get out of this house before I decide she needs to strangle you." She fixed Mira's mother with a malevolent glare, one that made Hilda shiver and sit back on her heels. But she wasn't ready to give up. Not when her darling had finally reopened her lovely blue eyes. Even if they were, well, vacant.

"Mira, mine. Come home now. We've got so much to do."

But Mira, the part that mattered, had already gone home. The bit that remained marched to the drum of a new master. That part opened its mouth wide, sank its teeth into Hilda's wrist. And *chewed*. Hilda screamed, shoving at Mira's forehead, trying to get her to release her hold as blood began to spurt from her deepening wound.

Mira growled with irritation as Hilda pushed her away, shoving her half off her tasty treat. She released the wrist but snapped right back to target. Hilda recoiled, but not fast enough. This time Mira had her by the hand. I glanced down at my own hands, marked forever by the talons of a pissed-off reaver. And that's when I really began rooting for the underdog.

After a brief tug-of-war backed by Mira's growls, Hilda's screams, and Madame Otis's delighted cackles, Hilda finally broke free. She ran out of the cottage, trailing blood as she went. Again the picture faded.

"From then on I spent all my time researching necromancy," Hilda's robotic voice informed us. "I discovered that the truly dead can be reanimated by the energies of the necromancer, but she must be choosy. Because though the soul has left the body something remains. A shadow that can become difficult to manipulate depending on how the person lived. Children and those who were obsessed or fixated in life are the easiest to control in this way, as long as the necromancer keeps visual contact with her subjects. I have just discovered there may be another, more insidious method of controlling the dead. But it requires much more sacrifice on the part of the necromancer, because the soul is trapped inside the victim's body. Therefore this method is rarely used."

A new, more energetic voice suddenly replaced Hilda's. "Before Hilda could complete her research she was killed. See eyewitness account by Letitia Greeley."

But when Cassandra tried to reference that account, the Enkyklios simply offered up a name—Sister Doshomi.

"What's that mean?" asked Cole as he popped a blue bubble.

"The Letitia Greeley story is in her Enkyklios," said Cassandra. "I'll have to contact her and see if she can send me a copy."

"Seriously?" marveled Cole. "There's more than one of these out there? I mean, I thought yours was, you know, *the* database."

Cassandra shook her head. "Even the Enkyklios is limited in what it can hold. If we were to lose one, we certainly would be devastated if we had no backups. And despite what you may think, it isn't easy, or even recommended, for one person with one Enkyklios to travel the world recording stories. And so"—she shrugged—"sometimes we find we must still share information the old-fashioned way."

"By telephone?" Cole ventured.

Cassandra rolled her eyes. "No, silly, by e-mail."

But Sister Doshomi had proven hard to pin down. In fact, she'd been mountain climbing when Cassandra tried to contact her and wasn't expected back until after we left Ohio.

While we'd begun the mission with an incomplete view of raising the dead, at least the Spec Ops guys had given us solid information regarding a meeting our necromancer would be attending. They knew the time, location—they'd even snagged a picture of their nemesis. The first ever and quite a coup for Dave's group. He'd probably still be basking in the glory if he hadn't simultaneously discovered his unit had a mole. The only one who suspected, Dave had tried to hand off the meeting coordinates, along with the job of exterminating the Wizard, to another unit. Instead SOCOM, with the direct support of the DOD, had requested that we team with them.

They knew the CIA had a consultant on staff with insider knowledge of the Wizard. They'd heard our particular department fronted a team of assassins that had never failed to nail its target. And they felt only outsiders like us could ferret out a mole while leaving the rest of a highly trained, incredibly valuable fighting element intact.

Problem was, these guys were tight. I could see them resenting our presence, especially since we'd been called in to finish the job they'd started. If we did this wrong, if Bergman pulled an attitude or Cassandra freaked somebody with one of her visions or Cole made a joke nobody laughed at . . . Hell, so many things could go wrong that if we got through this mission without crossing the path of any "friendly" fire I'd be amazed.

I played it absolutely straight and hoped that was how everybody in the room would take it. Meeting my brother's green eyes, the only part of him that made me feel I was looking in a mirror, I said gravely, "I know you're a lot more surprised to see me than I am you. But then, that's how the Agency works sometimes. Secrecy is the key to success. *You* know that."

He paled slightly and I mentally slapped myself. I'd been reunited with him less than ten minutes and already managed to remind him of the most painful tragedy of our lives. Because it had nearly destroyed our relationship, we'd never been able to confront it head-on. That's something I can manage with limited contact. Not so much up close and personal. I'd have to step lightly if I still wanted a brother when this mission was over. *Dammit, all this tiptoeing is already making my arches sore.* "Anyway, about eight months ago, I teamed up with Vayl."

"So . . . you're an assassin?" Dave asked incredulously.

"Why do I feel like you'd have used the same tone if I'd just confessed to being a stripper?" I demanded.

"Sorry," he said quickly. "I'm just a little surprised, is all."

"I'm very good at what I do."

Dave nodded, then shrugged. "They said they were sending the best."

"Well, then." My entire crew had gathered around me as I spoke, Vayl by my right side, Cole at my left, Cassandra and Bergman behind us in the gaps our shoulders made. I didn't like the formation. It looked too much like a defensive barrier. But that's how people break themselves down in any new situation. Get with the herd until you know the lions aren't going to pounce.

Dave's group, superior to ours in both numbers and weaponry, felt free to stay scattered across the room, though every one of them remained alert to our conversation, even the wounded. The medic, a sturdy, dark-skinned brunette with strong, capable hands, had patched two of her charges and was threading a needle for another while a fourth held a bandage to his bicep to help control the bleeding. That fourth, the same giant who'd saved me during the battle, gave me a considering look, cocked his head to one side, grinned, and winked. I couldn't help it. I kinda thought we were going to be friends.

I didn't have time to check out the other half of Dave's unit. He'd found yet another unhappy thought. At this rate, even a whole pouchful of Tinker Bell's magic dust would never get him flying. "There's something weird about this whole deal. Two people who've barely spoken to each other in over a year—"

"Sixteen months," I told him.

He barreled on. "—don't just whoops into the same mission. Especially when those people are twins."

That got his unit's attention. My eyes raked the room. Yup, amazement in all corners. *Geez, hasn't he told them anything about me besides my name? I mean, omitting the fact that you're a twin? How pissed do you have to be . . .*

I guessed I knew the answer to that.

The guy who'd uncovered the lantern sauntered over, rolling the toothpick he carried in his mouth from one side to the other. Cole twitched so hard he actually bumped me. A glance in his direction showed him biting his lip. Uh-oh. Our interpreter had something of an oral fixation, which he generally soothed with varying flavors of bubble gum. Unfortunately, he'd run through his entire supply on the trip over. I crossed my arms, jabbing him in the ribs as I did so.

Toothpick-chewer stopped beside Dave and looked up at him, nodding, just nodding, as a smile spread across his broad, pitted face. I liked him immediately as well, which didn't bode well for any mole-hunting I'd be doing in the future. *Come on, Jaz, you're supposed to be the neutral party here.* But this dude, you could tell he'd been through all kinds of hell. If the acne had been cruel, the shrapnel had been brutal, leaving a spray of scars across his forehead, cheeks, and neck that the beard and mustache only partially disguised. I also noted a ridge just in front of his ear that made me wonder if somebody had, at some point, been required to sew it back on. And still this immense humor danced in his hazel eyes, just waiting for the right moment to leap.

Like the rest of us, he was dressed in traditional Middle Eastern clothes, looking comfy in a flowing white thobe and shalwar pants to match, a maroon kufi resting on his brown hair. We would only wear these sorts of clothes while we traveled across the eastern edge of Iraq and crossed the northwestern corner of Iran. Once inside Tehran we'd change into the more commonly worn Western wear of the city folk. Button-down shirts and khakis for the guys. Hijab and pantsuits for the girls that involved a knee length, button-down tunic and comfy, elastic-waisted pants, covered by either a chador or a manteau—both of them dark and shapeless coverings—when we went out. Not that we meant for anyone to get a close look. For obvious reasons Vayl and I moved at night. Lucky for us, Dave's unit preferred the same.

"Cam?" said Dave as his sergeant continued to nod with a general air of amusement.

"Yeah?"

"You got something to say?"

"Well, sir, on behalf of everyone here I'd appreciate knowing if she's as big a pain in the ass as you are. Because, if so, we'd like to request double hazard pay and an extra week of leave after this one's wrapped up." Chorus of chuckles from Dave's team.

Our dad, the marine, would burst a vessel at such a breach of military etiquette. But it just didn't track among people so highly skilled they worked only the most top-level, skin-of-your-teeth, crap-down-your-leg missions available. In fact, it got in the way. However, since he'd put Dave in a helluva spot just now, I fielded the man's question. "That one's going to be tough to answer, Cam. As siblings, we're very competitive. Which means we could probably argue this issue all night long and never come to a satisfactory conclusion. Actually, though, if you'd ever met our dad, you'd probably agree that the award for overbearing, tyrannical, asshole of the century would have to go to him."

Which was when I realized how this little coincidence had been arranged. Albert Parks was a semiretired consultant to the CIA. He might have been able to pull enough strings to pair his kids on the same mission if he felt either one of us would benefit from it. But in order to do so he would've had to know about it. Yeah, he could've found out. I wasn't sure how, but with his contacts, I could practically see his hairy paw prints all over this deal.

"Jaz?" Dave asked. "Are you okay?"

Oh, absotively, brother dear. Well, okay, I want to thump our father over the head with a large blunt object. Like his ego. Because what the hell is he trying to prove? Interfering old poop. But other than that, I'm just peachy.

"I'm fine," I said. I sounded okay, too. *Good.* But to help bring myself back to center, and because I really did want to see his reaction, I said, "Did I tell you Albert bought a motorcycle?"

My brother's mouth fell far enough open that I had to stifle an urge to wad up the nearest napkin and try my rim shot off his upper lip. "You're shitting me!"

"Nope. He has a purple helmet to match the gas tank, which glitters in the sunlight like Mom's old bowling ball—I'm quoting him here. Also he bought a full set of leathers. I think Shelby—that's his new nurse," I reminded him, "has to spray him with Pam before he slides into them."

"How does he start it?"

"Push of the button. No kicking necessary." His knees weren't what they used to be.

Dave shook his head in horrified disbelief as he rubbed the back of his neck, maybe imagining our dad breaking his. "What the hell was he thinking?"

I shrugged. "He just became a grandfather. I guess he's trying to pretend he's not an old man despite all evidence to the contrary."

"You guys are making me squirm," objected Jet. "Colonel Parks is practically a god in my house. If my dad knew you two were talking about him like this he'd beat the shit out of *me*!"

Dave nodded toward my shooting buddy. "I guess Albert saved his dad's life a couple of times. You know how it is." I did. Jet's dad had probably spent more time with mine than *I* had. Even now, all grown up and taking care of myself, I couldn't help the spear of jealousy that skewered me when I thought of their relationship. They'd never struggle to understand one another. Never question each other's motives. Their bond was unbreakable. Sometimes I wasn't even sure Albert and I had one.

I shoved my hands into my pockets. My left forefinger brushed against the memento I always kept there. The engagement ring Matt had given me two weeks before he died had only lately begun to remind me of a relationship that hadn't made me want to pull my hair out by the roots. And that only because I'd finally accepted that now, sixteen months after his death, maybe Matt wanted me to be happy. Too bad my closest male relatives didn't always feel the same.

"Jaz? Are you sure you're okay?" Dave asked again.

"Yes." *Shut the hell up and leave me alone.*

He reached forward, pulled my hijab down, snagged one of the long curls that framed the right side of my face. Usually they're a vibrant red. I'd dyed them black for this mission. Except . . . "Did you have an accident recently?" he pressed.

"Why do you ask?"

He pulled the twirls of hair straight and stretched them across my vision. My lips went dry. "What," he demanded, "has turned your hair white?"

The first thing I did was grab another hunk of hair and yank it forward. Whew! It was still black. Only that bit beside my face had turned. The relief was so intense I laughed. Not so my crew.

During the moments of babbling, confusion, and near panic that followed I had to remind myself that I hadn't just been in a near-fatal car accident. Nobody had shot or stabbed me. We were just talking about some hair tintage here, folks. But you'd never have known that by the frenzy my crew fell into. And damned if they weren't getting me wound up all over gain.

"Ohmigod, somebody's gotten to her!" yelled Bergman, clenching his bony fists like somebody was about to take a swing at him. "She's probably caught some vile disease!" He hadn't forgotten the close call we'd had with a virus called the Red Plague that had been designed to wipe out ninety percent of those who were exposed to it. He scuttled to the farthest corner of the room despite the fact that it put him next to the woman who'd covered the windows—a six-foot-one-inch amazon with the face of a beauty queen.

At the same moment Cassandra leaned forward and said urgently, "I can help you fight whatever has possessed you." A courageous offer, I thought, since as soon as she touched me she'd be putting herself at its mercy, too.

"I'm not sick and I'm not possessed," I said, but my reply was muted by Cole's exclamation.

"It's this location, isn't it? I told you they've got all kinds of lethal crap floating in the air over here. Comes from all that nuclear testing and biological warfare and—"

"Enough!" Vayl bellowed. The sudden silence made my ears ring. I thought, *See what happens when you hardly ever raise your voice? You should take a lesson from this, Jaz,* though I knew I wouldn't. Vayl looked at me. "Are you all right?"

"Yes."

"Do you have any idea what caused this?" He curled the offending hair around his finger, brushing against my face as he did so. His touch, gentle and yet electrifying, made me hold my breath.

"Yes."

"Would you like to discuss it?"

I sighed. If I could say it had nothing to do with the mission I'd be off the hook. But it did. In fact, it had a whole helluva lot to do with why four good men were currently sitting on the floor feeling like the poster boys for Johnson & Johnson.

I met Vayl's eyes. They were the indigo blue that signified deep concern. I twirled Cirilai, the ring he'd given me, around the finger of my right hand. I don't know if it was that simple action or a stronger power from Cirilai itself that calmed me, but as soon as I thought of it, touched it, I relaxed. "I fell asleep while we were in the helicopter," I said.

"Yes, I know." Oh, so that had been his shoulder I'd been leaning on the whole time. Comfy. Anyway.

"Raoul came to me in a dream." You could almost feel the intensity in the room rise. It started with Vayl, who knew Raoul had twice resurrected me. Yeah, as in, *Lazarus, quit acting like such a stiff already.* He'd also, from time to time, offered me advice, usually in a thunderclap sort of voice that made me wish I'd bought earplugs.

The intensity spread to our crew when they realized, just from looking at our faces, who I must be talking about. Cassandra and Bergman had seen Raoul pull his first miracle on me via holographic replay. They'd filled Cole in later on. It wasn't something any of them were likely to forget.

Dave knew Raoul as well, and his team, keyed in on him as they were, reacted to his startled response with a little dance I like to call the bump and shuffle. It's a series of significant looks accompanied by shifts in stance and simple footwork that a very tight-knit group uses to let each other know something big is about to go down and everybody should remember their assignments. I didn't know what they expected me to do. Suddenly transform into a brain-eating siren? Mow them all down with the AK-47 I kept hidden in my undies? Burst into flame?

Vayl, noting the change in pressure, tried to put a spin on the release valve. "Jasmine is a Sensitive," he explained to the room at large. "Among her Gifts is the ability to travel outside her body. Raoul exists in that realm, and has had occasion to act as her Guide."

Dave gave his okay-whatever shrug. I got the feeling he and Raoul weren't quite on speaking terms. I believed the difference in our relationships with him had something to do with the fact that Vayl had twice taken my blood and left some of his power in its place. Those acts had left me with extra abilities Raoul found valuable. Plus, Dave didn't appreciate outside interference in his missions, no matter who assigned them. If not for the mole, I doubted Vayl and I would be here at all.

"Go ahead, Jasmine," Vayl said, "tell us what happened when Raoul arrived."

I cleared my throat. Looked around the room. "Well, he showed up during my bubble bath dream."

I love that one. It's always so warm and cozy and I wake up feeling practically boneless. Raoul had stepped into my little white bathroom, his green and black camo and impossibly broad shoulders making it seem more like a Chinese takeout box than a lavatory as he said in his Spanish-flavored accent, "I'm sorry, Jasmine, but there's no other way to do this. I've got to take you to hell."

Chapter Two

The trip from my rest room to what Granny May's minister used to refer to as Satan's Playground so closely resembled the blackouts I'd experienced after losing Matt and my Helsinger crew that I came to with a strong desire to run straight to my sister's attic, dive into the trunk she stored for me there, and resurrect Buttons, my old teddy bear. But since spineless wimps don't survive long in my business, I decided to go with Plan B.

I opened my eyes.

And that's when I started to swear.

"Hell is massive," I told my audience, who'd gathered around me like a bunch of kids at their library story hour. "Imagine looking through a telescope. Think of all the black space between the stars. It's like all that got sucked into an observable area that you somehow know is also an endless, infinite tract. But it's not empty.

"The ground is covered with rocks. Some sharp, some rounded. Most covered with mold, blood, or vomit. Raoul and I stood on a huge boulder just flat enough on top to hold the two of us. In the distance I could see a chain of mountains. Did I mention the rocks? The point is, you have to watch every step. Citizens of hell don't look up. Not unless they want to drag around a broken ankle or two. Some do.

"As a visitor, I felt free to explore. So I glanced up."

"Shit, Raoul, the sky's on fire!" I ducked, nearly pulling my hand

from his as I moved. His grip tightened, pressing Cirilai into the adjoining fingers until they throbbed.

"Whatever you do, don't let go," he warned me. "Hungry eyes are on us, waiting for us to break the rules."

"All you told me was that we couldn't be late and we had to leave when we were done!" I snapped. "If you're going to risk my life—"

"Soul," he amended.

"Oh, that's better."

Raoul fixed me with a drop-and-give-me-twenty look. Through clenched teeth he said, "We are allowed only a brief amount of time here. If they can separate us, they will. If we use our time trying to find each other, we have wasted the sacrifice it took to come here. Worse, if we're separated and can't find each other in time, one or both of us could be stuck here for eternity."

"Sacrifice?"

"You did agree."

"When?"

He grimaced at me, reached into the chest pocket of his jacket, and handed me a note, written in my own hand:

> *You had a meeting with the uppity-ups during your blackout. Someday you might remember, but there's no time to explain, and this is too important to screw up. In the end you'll agree this was worth the sacrifice. So shut up and listen to Raoul.*
>
> *J*

"So your hair," interrupted Bergman, "is that the sacrifice?"

"I doubt it," said the wounded guy who'd had to be stitched. He'd shed his turban to reveal a shiny bald pate that somehow made him resemble a rhinoceros, whereas any other white man would've looked like a cancer patient. I learned later his name was Otto "Boom" Perle, and before he'd become a munitions expert he'd been a wildass teenager who'd burned his eyebrows and half his hair off in a fireworks accident. After hearing that story, bald seemed brilliant. Otto motioned to his wound. "Seems like hell would want something more like this."

I agreed. In which case the sacrifice had yet to be made.

"So the whole place was just rocks?" asked another hurt guy whose rosy cheeks and light brown beard made him look a lot younger than he was. He introduced himself as Terrence Casey, father of five, grandfather of one, and biggest Giants fan of all time. I shook my head.

No, there was more. The plants that grew between the rocks were vicious. The vines tripped. The bushes stabbed. Only the trees seemed harmless. Then a sharp wind blew, and I realized the trunks weren't extra thick like I'd thought. Those were blackened bodies hanging from their limbs that now rocked and jiggled in hell's breeze. And the awful thing was, they were aware.

So were the walkers. Nobody within range of my sight sat and rested. They all moved among one another, never conversing, but often talking to themselves. It reminded me a little bit of a busy New York sidewalk, except everyone was looking down, watching the rocks.

Then I began focusing on the individuals and the sense of community dropped away. Right in front of us a woman continuously combed her fingers through her long blond hair. When she got to the tips she yanked hard enough to jerk her head sideways. Every few seconds she took the hair she'd pulled out of her skull and stuffed it into her mouth.

"Why's she doing that?" I whispered to Raoul.

He shrugged.

"Don't you know?"

"It's not like their sins are tattooed on their foreheads."

"Look at her. She's crazed. They all are." To our right a thin, black-bearded man bent down, picked up a rock, and began shredding his shirt

with it. When the material fell from his shoulders in tatters he began again, this time on his skin. I tried to swallow, but nothing went down.

My eyes moved to another man, the first I'd seen who'd paused in his forward motion. He looked straight ahead. For half a second his eyes cleared.

Everyone within a hundred yards stopped. Crouched. Let out a collective groan that knifed straight into my gut and twisted.

Flames shot from the sky, engulfing the man. As soon as he began screaming, the fire spread to the people surrounding him, as if a large demonic fist had reached down with a red plastic can and sprayed them all with kerosene.

I've seen more horror than I care to remember in my twenty-five years. But nothing had ever come close to this. Maybe I could've stood just the screaming. Or just the sight of fifty people burning. But not—"Raoul, the smell . . ."

He reached into a pack at his waist and pulled out two white ovular tabs that resembled smelling salts. "Stick these in your nose."

I did, and they helped. I wondered what else Raoul had packed in his Let's Go to Hell kit. Better not to ask.

Around the burning people, everyone else continued with their business.

A woman bit steadily on her middle finger. I noticed she'd already chewed her thumb and forefinger off at the first joint.

A man fell to his knees every few steps, leaving a bloody trail on the rocks behind him.

Two teens, identical twins, took turns lashing each other with branches they'd torn off one of those not-so-innocent trees.

Though I'd just come from a bath, I wanted to go home and shower. And watch Pollyanna. *And cuddle with my infant niece. Anything to be reminded that good still existed somewhere in my world.*

"I knew hell was like this," I told Raoul bitterly. "Insanity's last stop. Where there's no help. No relief. Just unrelenting madness."

"For you and these people, yes. For others, it's something entirely different."

"But everybody's in physical form here?"

"It's part of the punishment," Raoul replied.

As Vayl had mentioned, I'd traveled outside my body a few times. What a rush. But once I'd stayed away a little too long. Nearly all my ties to the physical world had faded. I remembered how hard it was to rejoin my flesh, how constrained I'd felt, almost trapped. I could see how, having once broken all earthly boundaries, being forced back into a body could make it seem like a prison. Even holding tight to my Get Out of Jail Free card, I was ready to leave.

"Can you tell me what we have to do here?"

"Our scouts have reported rumors of a conclave to be held there, beneath that guard tower." He pointed at the nearest hanging tree. Wait a minute.

"Raoul, what is hell to you? What are you seeing?"

Things I never wanted to witness again, his eyes told me as they met mine. "A POW camp," he told me hoarsely. "Torture, starvation, and deprivation all the way to the horizon."

Big reaction from Dave's people. Not surprise though. Maybe they'd suspected it all along. I searched their faces as I spoke.

"I wondered if that was how he'd died. But I hadn't known him long enough to ask. I had other, more palatable questions. Like who would be qualified to scout the activities of hell's minions? And what did any of this have to do with me? But according to my note, we didn't have time for chitchat."

"You said he was wearing camo when he came to get you," said a short, wiry man with a full black beard who introduced himself as Ricardo Vasquez. "Was that all?"

I knew what he was getting at. "No, he had a black beret with a Ranger tab on it."

Murmurs around the room. My savior solider, who'd taken

watch at the window, said, "You want to find the gates of hell? Walk into any POW camp and you're there."

"Damn right, Natch," the amazon agreed with a sharp nod of her head. Rage, that's what these people were feeling. I realized if I ever decided to storm the place, maybe stage a massive rescue, I could count on these folks to back me up.

I went on. "Raoul assured me the citizens of hell couldn't see us since we weren't of the place, only in it. And it sure seemed that way as we picked our way to a ring of footstool-sized rocks that surrounded a three-foot pit of golden-orange bubbling magma. The walkers kept away from the pit and the ring. Could they sense what was coming? No. They just didn't want to get hit by the streams of lava that came shooting out of the pit at random intervals. But it seemed to have some sort of rudimentary intelligence that allowed it to strike with agonizing accuracy every time."

"Remind me that these people are bad guys," I begged Raoul. "They deserve what's happening to them, right?"

He shrugged. "Most do. But remember the reaver, Desmond Yale."

"Who's that?" asked a guy I'd been trying not to stare at, just because he was that pretty. His name, he told me the first second he had a chance, was Ashley St. Perru. He came from Old Money, meaning his mom was a bitch, his dad was an asshole, and his sister couldn't leave a store without dropping three grand first. He'd left home in search of a family and found one in the middle of nowhere. Go figure.

"Cole's first official kill," I said, nodding toward our interpreter. Even without looking at him I could see the shadow that experience had left behind his eyes. It wasn't an overwhelming force anymore. Just a part of his past that made him older and wiser and, somehow, easier to be with. "But he wasn't a cinch for us to take down. He was a soul-stealer, like the ones we fought just now, only a savvy old pro. His job had been to nab the innocents and shove them into hell to suffer right alongside the deserving. Ultimately he and his buddies had come to help start a war."

"You know a lot about reavers, huh?" commented Dave, his eyes narrowing. *Are you putting my people in unnecessary danger?* that look demanded.

I decided it would be best to ignore him for now. I went on. "Just as Raoul mentioned Yale, the first of the attendees crawled out of the pit. As soon as I saw those clawed, skeletal fingers I knew this creature was the same one that had pulled the reaver's body through the doorway he'd created from the heart of a dead woman. When the creature had fully emerged my stomach lurched, she looked so much like pictures I'd seen of concentration camp survivors. Except her skin was the bright red of a poison ivy rash and a hump of flesh stood in place of her nose, as if her Maker had seriously considered endowing her with a trunk and then changed his mind very last minute. And then there was that third eye. Except when the lid opened, the socket glared red and empty. She moved to one of the rocks. More creatures emerged from the pit after that, one after another, so quickly I lost count until they finally all sat down."

"A dozen demons," I whispered to Raoul, "and not far removed from the artist's drawings I've seen looks-wise. How did they know?"

"Are you so sure of what you see?"

"What do you mean?"

"I see a military court. It looks to me as if there's about to be some sort of formal proceeding."

"So you're telling me my mind is supplying me with these pictures? That none of this is real?"

Raoul met my gaze straight on. "One thing I know about this place, this meeting, and your mission . . . nothing is as it seems. Remember that on everything you hold dear, Jasmine. Nothing *is as it seems."*

"Okay," I said as we turned our attention back to the conclave, "but if that's the case, how do I know what to believe?"

"Your instincts are excellent. Some of the best I've ever seen. Trust them."

One more creature had stepped out of the pit. Unlike the others, he didn't stagger under the weight of immense curved horns or inspire shudders with multiple sores oozing pockets of pus and slime. He had the fierce, lethal beauty of a wildfire. Stunning sweep of white-gold hair. Deep red skin drawn taut against an I-oughtta-be-a-god body. This stud yanked the Oooh baby *right out of the girl in me. Until I looked deeper.*

He came with his own special Fallen Angel vibe. I felt it because, as a Sensitive, I can pick up on certain otherworldly powers. For instance, vamps and reavers stick out in a crowd for me now that I've spent some time on the wrong side of life. So I was familiar with creepy, freaky, rot-scented types of beings. Had hunted a few and killed a bunch in my career. This guy gave off a psychic stench that made me want to scuttle into the nearest bomb shelter and play like a hermit crab. Somehow I knew the first time he'd pulled the wings off a fly he'd giggled like a schoolgirl. Serial killers tickled the crap out of him and mass executions left him rolling. The bastard loved to laugh.

Like the other demons he went naked, except for a belt, from which dangled a coiled black whip. He couldn't keep his hands off it either. Played with it during the entire assembly.

I didn't understand the talk, so Raoul translated for me. Since he thought he was watching a court proceeding, the words hardly ever matched the actions, but it ended up making an odd sort of sense. Especially when their most animated conversation conjured strong mental images that needed no translation.

Whip dude sauntered over to the last empty rock, which stood taller and flatter than the rest, and took a seat. "Who summons the court and its Magistrate?" he asked, folding his arms across his chest, although he still kept one hand on the whip.

Up jumped Skeletal Woman, the one who'd been the first to emerge from the pit. "I do," she said.

"State your name and case."

She wrung those bright red claws and blinked her eyes. The third one was out of sync with the rest, and the lack of an eyeball flipped my stomach sideways. Which surprised me. I've seen splatted brains, headless torsos, and spines glistening through the fronts of bodies. I really thought I'd reached my gross-out limit. Now I understood hell was going to slam those boundaries till they shattered. The realization made me want to curl up into a ball and tuck myself into Raoul's pocket until it was time to go home.

"I am Uldin Beit. My mate was murdered. I wish to Mark his killer."

"For the record, what was your mate's name?"

"Desmond Yale." Her voice cracked as she spoke. I could see his loss had devastated her. I shook my head, amazed that even evil soul-snatching scumbags could find somebody to love.

"And what was the nature of his death?" The Magistrate kept throwing out the professional questions, but he smiled gleefully as she forked over the gory details.

"He was shot through the soul-eye at the direction of a woman named Jasmine." Her words were accompanied by a visual of Yale with a gaping wound in the middle of his forehead. Several of the demons tittered. Uldin Beit resolutely ignored them. She said, "I witnessed this. The rest is information Sian-Hichan was able to gather when I brought him Desmond's body." She gestured to one of the seated beasts, who was covered with yellow, fist-sized warts.

At a nod from the Magistrate, she sat down and Sian-Hichan stood. "As you would expect in cases like this, I followed protocol and immediately probed Yale's mind to see if I could retrieve any vital information." That's sure not what Sian-Hichan's facial expressions and hand gestures were conveying, and his audience found his description damn entertaining. The reason, I gathered from the mental images he projected, was that he'd also put the corpse through a series of calisthenics in order to win a bet. Something having to do with rigor mortis. Geeeross. Uldin didn't seem to appreciate it much either.

I wished I could trade hells with Raoul. His seemed so much more precise and refined. Then I thought better of it. He was still crouched in a bottomless pit of doom and despair. His was just better organized than mine.

Sian-Hichan went on. "Jasmine seems to be a code name for a reaver hunter named Lucille Robinson. Yale lost two apprentices to her and fought her himself twice before being killed by her *student. Yale's gravest concern was that Lucille Robinson had gained the Spirit Eye." His speech brought forth an image of me. Not as myself—an underweight redhead helping a legendary vamp assassin eliminate threats to national security despite my mind-bending past. This me was bigger than life. A windblown supermodel standing on a summit surrounded by a crackling crimson aura, tricked-out gun in one hand, great-great-granddad's blade in the other.*

I'd thought the Spirit Eye would be an orb. Maybe a gigantic version of one of the Enkyklios balls. Maybe an actual eye, floating above my head like a halo. But I realized now it was more integral. An inner flame that burned away preconceptions and prejudices until I could really know, really see through the mask to the evil writhing underneath. The aura, I decided, must be its exhaust.

Even in my version of hell, impressed courtroom murmurs circled the ring. The Magistrate didn't have a gavel. Didn't need one. All he had to do was jerk his head and the demons quieted down. "If she has the Spirit Eye she will be more than a match for your Mark," he told Uldin Beit.

"The Eye is only partway open," Sian-Hichan told the Magistrate.

"Ahh."

The Magistrate nodded his agreement with this collective com-

ment, his mane of hair sweeping elegantly across his shoulders as he moved. "Are you prepared to pay, then?" he asked, stroking his whip so fondly I actually had to make sure his hand hadn't moved elsewhere.

Uldin Beit did a sort of full-body twitch. Then she nodded.

"And who is your sponsor?"

"Edward Samos." As soon as she spoke his name I received a mental image of him. An impeccably dressed businessman, his Latin heritage provided him with the flashing brown eyes, bronze skin, and shining black hair that had, no doubt, brought Vayl's ex to her knees. Uldin's memory of him had included a conversation where his personality had burst into full bubble, like a bottle of fine champagne. He'd sat back, laughing with genuine humor, his mouth wide open so you could see the fangs. But the threat you always felt with bared fangs, even Vayl's, Samos managed to refute by the simple I'm-your-pal look in his eyes. No wonder he was so hard to resist. I could feel the lure of his charm even through Uldin's imagination.

I wasn't surprised Samos had involved himself in her revenge project. He'd sponsored Yale as well. But damned if the news didn't steam me. I was so sick of fighting his underlings I could literally lean over and puke any time I thought of them. And the victims. Lord, the list read like a Civil War memorial, so extensive you wondered where to begin. Maybe at the end—with his last known kill—a tailor whose shop he'd used as a rendezvous point for important meetings. He'd hung the man up and gutted him like a deer. And now he'd set his sights on me.

"Jasmine, are you all right?" Raoul whispered.

"Sure? Why?" He nodded to his arm. Without thinking I'd dug my nails in so deep I'd made purple marks. I immediately moved my hands up to his biceps. "Sorry. I didn't realize."

"You did see Samos just now, yes?" asked Raoul. "That must be worth the sacrifice you made to come here."

Not knowing the parameters of the forfeit, I was hardly in a position to say. "I guess. I mean, it helps. But knowing me, just being able to ID the guy wouldn't be enough to make me give up something I cherished. I think there's something more."

"Perhaps the reason he has agreed to sponsor the reavers?"

I shook my head. "I imagine it's straight revenge, just like Uldin Beit." Samos must think I'd killed his right hand, his avhar, *an Asian vamp with a thing for pastel suits named Shunyuan Fa. I hadn't. But I'd had a near-death encounter with Fa, who'd lost his head during a failed coup later that evening. I didn't know what Fa had said to his* sverhamin *about me before going smoky, if anything. But Samos knew I'd taken out a rookie reaver on the same yacht where he'd placed Fa as his emissary. The evidence tying me to Fa was so rickety you wouldn't want to cross a steep gorge on it, but it probably worked for him. Shoot, most juries would hang me on less.*

"Come forward," the Magistrate told Uldin Beit as he stood and moved away from his rock.

The seated demons showed noticeable signs of excitement. Tongues hung out, eyes bulged, and, uh, other things as well as she obeyed a little unsteadily. As she knelt before him, he uncoiled his whip.

"Oh shit, Raoul, tell me this isn't happening."

"I wish I could."

I didn't want to watch but felt I had to. This was the price I was willing to pay her for killing her mate.

The Magistrate reared back, the whip flying behind him and then shooting forward as his arm fell. Uldin Beit's blood exploded into the air. I flinched. She screamed. And I knew no revenge could be worth this. Again and again the whip lashed, literally cutting the skin from the reaver's back, until the Magistrate held the strips up in one bloody hand.

"Here!" he roared. "The pound of flesh! Do you bear witness!"

"Aye!" the demons bellowed back.

"I've seen enough," I told Raoul. "Let's get outta here."

"That's when I woke up on the Chinook, ten minutes out from the LZ." I avoided Dave's eyes. He could probably tell I was lying. That I'd had a few more harrowing experiences before hell finally released me. But no way was I going to share those details with a room full of strangers, including an employee of the Wizard.

"So *you* brought these reavers down on us?" asked the amazon. Bergman decided he didn't care for her company and moved to the window next to Natch, the giant.

"I'm sorry, I didn't catch your name," I said.

"That's because I didn't throw it," she replied.

We stared each other down, neither willing to budge. "That's Grace Jensen," said the medic, who seemed to feel we girls should stick together in a predominantly man's world. Ignoring Grace's dirty look she added, "And I'm Adela Reyes."

"Nice to meet you," I told her. "You do excellent work."

She gave me a just-doing-my-job shrug. "These guys are tough. It's going to take a lot more than a few stitches to keep them down."

I nodded, hiding my smile as chests puffed around the room. "That's obvious."

"You didn't answer my question," snapped Amazon Grace.

I gave her a leisurely look, knowing it would irritate her, wondering how far I should push her. Could she be the mole? Trying to stir up conflict within the unit in order to undermine the mission? Hard to say. It could just be an honest reaction to us stepping on her turf and putting her buddies in harm's way.

"I gave you this information as a courtesy," I told her, "because I believe you'll function more effectively if you understand what's happening and why. But here's the deal, Grace. My boss and I have been assigned to kill a man and that's what we're going to do. You can be part of our team, or you can be a tool we use to get our job done. Either way we have success. You just have to decide if you want to be happy or miserable."

While Grace digested the fact that she'd just been outbitched, I went on, speaking to the rest of Dave's people. "When the Magistrate asked Uldin Beit the name of her sponsor, she responded by saying 'Edward Samos.' That doesn't mean anything to you, but it's hugely significant to us. Samos is the CIA's top target, an American-born vampire with aspirations toward world domination—the sooner we nail him the better. You have to understand that all reavers need an earthly sponsor. Somebody who can provide them with bodies to inhabit and souls to snatch."

This was all true. Now for the lie.

"We've also discovered that Samos has been watching the Wizard's movements with interest for quite a while. He intends to use his reavers to shanghai the Wizard's body and, as a result, his entire operation. At which point I guarantee he'll make the Wizard's past exploits look like a practical joke. So, feel free to be pissed that reavers have been sent after me. Just remember, as soon as I'm out of the picture, they're going after the big game."

The seed had been planted. Now we'd watch and wait. Hopefully the mole would find it necessary to pass this juicy morsel on to the Wizard. As soon as he or she tried to make contact, we'd close in. And then we'd have him. I looked at Grace. Or her.

Chapter Three

So," said David, after taking a few minutes to mull it all over, "here's my take. A pound of flesh has to buy more than a single raid. I figure we've got at least one more assault to throw back. And logic dictates it'll happen when we make the move to the truck."

The truck was a semi, returning empty from its Tehran-to-Baghdad run. Somewhat miraculously we'd found a driver willing to get us into the city in return for six visas to New Jersey for himself and his family.

"I don't know if I'll be any help to you during the actual fighting," Bergman said as he shoved his glasses up the bridge of his nose. For him, it was a brave moment, surrounded as he was by men much bigger and scarier than he. "But I did bring you a weapon I've developed that might make things a little easier on you." It was one of the main reasons he'd been allowed to come along.

After our last mission he'd flown back to his lab. And despite the fact that Cassandra had insisted he'd be needed on this job, when he'd called me a week later, I'd said, "Stay home, Miles. Work. Rest. You need a break from us. From this craziness. It's so not your thing."

"I need to come with you, Jaz."

"No." We were both remembering the last time out, when

Vayl had taken the bad guy's blood and part of his power. Even though Bergman couldn't explain it scientifically, Vayl had been able to call from within himself a bio-armor based partially on Bergman's own invention. It had blown Bergman's mind. That and Cassandra's ability to mask my looks with a magical amulet had hammered at his core beliefs hard enough to rattle him teeth to shins.

We sat silent on the phone while Bergman mustered his arguments. I looked at my watch. I'd promised to meet Cole at the shooting range. I was about to be late.

"I'm tired of being afraid, Jasmine. If I keep running and hiding . . . if I don't ever come out of my cocoon. Well, I'm never going to have a life."

"I thought you liked your life. I mean, you said most people irritate you, so you don't long for companionship. And you love inventing things—"

"Yeah, that part's fine. It . . . it's me." He took a deep breath. I could almost see his shoulders rise as he braced himself for the confession. "I get up in the morning and look at myself in the mirror. And I can't even meet my own eyes. I know this probably sounds stupid and old-fashioned to you. And, being a girl, maybe you won't even get it. But for me, it's not a matter right now of being a *better* man. I've just gotta . . . It's time to *be* a man."

O-kay. Hadn't really expected that one. Still. "I don't see how I can justify your presence. We don't really need your expertise on this one."

"Don't worry about it. I'll think of something." And he had. Still, I kept thinking he'd chosen the wrong venue to prove to himself, what, that he wasn't a coward? That he could somehow fit his own definition of masculinity? I mean, he was talking about really basic stuff. I wasn't sure you could even get to where he wanted to go in less than a few years. But I had to love his brass. Once he decided he wanted something, he just kept trucking till he figured out the right formula.

Bergman scanned the cramped little farmhouse for volunteers. "If some of you could just help me bring the boxes in?"

From the way their faces lit up you'd have thought Santa just hit town. At a nod from Dave, two of them went for the guns while my shooting buddy Jet and his friend Ricardo guarded them.

I took Dave by the arm. "These reavers have some unique physical properties you should be aware of. Let me show you what we're up against." I took him outside and we knelt over one of the bodies, while yet more troops watched over us from a distance. "You know about the third eye," I said. "That's used for containing the soul of the victim until the reaver can deliver it to hell." I grabbed the reaver's jaw, opened it, and part of its pink, spiked tongue unrolled onto its chin.

"There's something in its saliva that contains the soul, keeping it from ascending while at the same time absorbing it into that third eye."

"You really are an expert on these things, aren't you?" Dave asked.

I shrugged. "I know a lot more than I'd like to."

He stood up. I looked over my shoulder. We were alone. "There's something else I need to tell you," I murmured.

"What's that?"

"While I was in hell . . ."

"Yeah?"

I cleared my throat. There was no easy way to say this. "I saw Mom."

Dave immediately squatted back down beside me. "Tell me."

"It was when Raoul and I were getting ready to leave. We

turned around and there she stood, right in front of me. She said—"

"Jasmine?"

"Mom?" *I took a step back because she was—I shit you not—licking her fingers and trying to get a smudge off my forehead.*

"It won't come out." She wrinkled her brows with frustration.

"I'll get it later." I grabbed her wrist because she couldn't seem to stop and I was sensing the loss of several layers of skin in my imminent future. "What are you doing here?" I turned to Raoul. "What's she doing here?"

"Are you certain this is your mother?" he asked.

Oh, right, how could I have forgotten already? Nothing is as it seems. *But it looked an awful lot like her. Same curly, honey-blond hair. Same distant blue eyes. And surely I couldn't mistake all those smoker's lines around her lips? "How else would she recognize me?" I reasoned. "You said nobody could see us here because we weren't of the place. But* she *can, so it must be because she's my mom."*

We were distracted by the arrival of a couple of demons, who had apparently decided to take a stroll before they followed their brethren out of the pit. They were deep in conversation, one with his horned head bent almost double over the other's green, slimy one. Though Raoul didn't bother to translate, I still got the visuals.

A big, fancy office with a desk you could sail on and enough chairs in which to seat a jury. Samos and the Magistrate standing on either side of the desk as Samos's dapper male secretary laid two copies of a contract between them. Samos pointing to a particular section, shaking his head, an incredulous look on his face. The Magistrate, smiling like a saint, uncoiling his whip and flicking it against the shoulder of Samos's secretary, ripping his white shirt, his skin, leaving a bloody trail both men found überfascinating. Samos, licking his lips hungrily as the secretary's face transformed into Uldin Beit's and then back again.

The Magistrate pushed the contract toward him. Samos pointed toward the same spot, mouthed the word "sacrifice," and shook his head. When he said "sacrifice" I began to get another image. Something started to emerge from the shadows behind his open door. All I could see were the eyes. Glowing like embers in the darkness. They winked out when the largest of the conversing demons glanced up.

"Look!" he cried. "The Lucille is in our midst!"

Raoul snapped, "Is he your mother too? Or is it that everyone can see you because there's a Demon Mark on your forehead!" I had time to think, Oh, so that's what Mom was trying to rub off! *before he grabbed my hand and yelled, "Come on!"*

I still had my mother's wrist, so I shouted the same to her and we ran like mountain goats, leaping over rocks and dodging malicious plants as the demons raced after us.

"What have you done?" screamed my mom.

"I killed a reaver!" I yelled back. "But only because he ripped a woman's heart out and stole her soul!"

"But why did they call you 'the Lucille?'"

"It's my alias. I'm an assassin for the CIA." Wait, could I tell her this now that she was dead? And in hell? Holy crap did I ever need a Zima!

"How far?" I asked Raoul as we muscled our way through crowds of shocked self-mutilators, all of whom could see us now. He looked over his shoulder at the pursuing demons.

"They'll be on us before we get there. We'll have to fight."

"I'm armed," I said helpfully.

"Your weapons won't work here." And neither, *said his eyes,* will your hand-to-hand. At least not well enough to save you. Not on their turf. We're doomed.

Suddenly Mom ripped her arm out of my grasp. "Run, Jazzy," she cried as she leaped back at the demons. "Get free!" With a frenzied sort of charisma I'd only ever seen in my father, she mustered a unit of maybe twenty psychos who thought battling demons would be a great way to commit hari-kari, and together they attacked our pursuers tooth and nail.

I tried to go after her, but Raoul wrapped his arm around my waist and, lifting me bodily, rushed back to our original boulder. Somebody hit me on the back of the head. Though I blamed it on my Spirit Guide, he later told me it was simply the jolt of transition that had sent me, once again, into the Land of Blackout.

Dave considered me for a while, then turned his eyes to the reaver corpse. "It wasn't Mom."

"No?'

"Couldn't have been."

"Why not?"

He turned on me so sharply I almost cringed. "Our mother is not in hell!"

"Why!" I demanded. "Because you don't want her to be? Let's sit here and list all her redeeming qualities, David, starting with the fact that she only beat our butts on a *semi*regular basis!"

"So she was harsh. That shouldn't make her demon fodder."

Actually, I agreed. But that's because I was just as twisted as him, thanks, in large part, to our dear, departed mother. I suddenly realized I'd spent a lot of my life hating the people I loved. I wondered if that could become habit forming.

"Fine, so maybe it wasn't her," I said. "And even if it was, it's not like we could do anything about it anyway. Right?"

"I guess not." We both stood, refusing to meet each other's eyes, knowing neither one of us was convinced. But at this point we had no choice but to stick to our current mission.

"Do you think we should move the bodies?" I asked.

"Ideally we'd bury them," he said, "but I don't want anyone

caught outside when the next wave comes. And we don't have time to bury so many. We'll leave them," he decided.

"On the other issue," I said, as he turned back toward the farmhouse. He stopped, dropped his head. I knew the very idea of a traitor in his band tore him up. These guys were as close as humans could get. In forty years they'd still be in touch, still want to know how it was going, still need to share the memories. To know one of their number had betrayed them must have wounded him to the core.

"The trap has been set," I said. "Keep an eye out for an effort to make contact." He nodded, his eyes still on the ground, and went inside.

Chapter Four

Dave's crew had begun their love affair with the guns by the time we got back, exclaiming over Bergman's improvements on their M4s, including a shorter barrel for street fighting, a built-in silencer, and a well-armored computer sensor on the barrel that read return fire and gave you those coordinates, automatically siting you in if you wished. The biggest improvement was in weight, since Bergman had crafted the weapon from a new alloy he'd invented that was not only lighter, but also required less maintenance.

As Bergman handed out ammunition, he explained that the Manx, as he liked to call the small, ferocious weapon, was a multitasker: Sensors built into the butt of the rifle could sniff out a vast array of biological and chemical toxins. In addition, every third round was equipped with something he referred to as an infrared dye. Anything it hit was bathed in that light, allowing the shooter to see farther than his goggles or, in our case, lenses, would normally allow.

Bergman had actually brought a few pairs of his night-vision lenses along as well. "They'll only work if you have twenty-twenty to start with," he warned. "I didn't have time to check your prescriptions and make special ones. But if you like them, I'll customize some for you when I get back." The offer, a generous one from any perspective, surprised me. He must've had to make a lot of promises to get his skinny butt on our jet.

While Cam, Ashley, and Natch tried out the lenses, I decided to make some formal introductions.

"Dave, I'd like you to meet my crew." I led him to the corner we'd commandeered.

"Everybody," I said, "this is my brother, Dave. Dave, this is Cole. He's our interpreter." Cole had been leaning against the wall, chewing on the collar of his dark gray thobe. Like me, he'd dyed his hair black for this mission, but it still ran wild, sticking out from under his cap in every direction as if directly reflecting his stress over popping his last bubble nearly twelve hours ago. He spat out the collar and shook Dave's hand.

"Pleased to meet you. Do they give you guys gum in the army? Chewing tobacco? Anything like that?" He looked at me. "What?"

"Shut up," I mouthed.

Dave frowned at me. "An interpreter seems redundant. Otto speaks Farsi."

I raised my eyebrows. *He's only redundant if Otto's not the mole.* Dave got the message. Out loud I said, "Cole is also in training. He'll be going solo after this mission."

Cole dug out his most charming smile. "Plus, I have somewhat of an insider's knowledge of Tehran. I dated a girl whose parents were born there. They left to study in America and never went back." He looked at me. "She really dug tea."

"Why'd you leave her?" I asked, knowing it hadn't been the other way around.

"Couldn't hack all the praying. We have arthritis in the family, you know. I'd have had to get knee replacements before I was fifty."

I turned to Dave. "He grows on you."

Vayl stood beside him, his hand wrapped firmly around the head of his cane. Somehow he managed to look as if he belonged, as if he'd been chiseled out of the same stone as the walls of the farmhouse. His short dark curls were nearly hidden beneath his turban, which accentuated his winged brows, fine Roman nose, and full lips. Those lips had brushed mine once and nearly sent my heart tumbling out of my chest. But I could never forget they hid a pair of fine, sharp fangs. Yeah, you had to be careful about Vayl's unseen qualities. Those were what would kill you.

He turned to face us fully as we approached. Can nerves tighten? Mine felt like fishing line. The kind with an obese accountant on one end and a nine-hundred-pound tiger shark on the other. I cleared my throat. "This is my boss, Vayl."

Dave didn't quite stand at attention, but he pulled his shoulders way back and totally blanked his face, the way he does when something's made him deeply uncomfortable. "You, uh, you're not human, are you?"

Total silence fell in the room behind us. I couldn't believe Dave was so out of touch with his Sensitivity. What the hell did he use it for?

"No," Vayl said. "I am vampire."

I did a half turn so I could monitor Dave's people. They hadn't moved yet, but they sure looked interested in the conversation. I searched their faces for animosity. Nothing. They'd donned the same mask as Dave. Their eyes were schooled to blankness. But in his, the question I dreaded: *Your fiancé was killed by vampires, Jaz. How* could *you?*

I could because I knew, just as well as Dave did, that not all vampires were evil. He and I had worked closely with two vamps on our Helsinger crew. I was surprised he didn't have one in his unit right now. Obviously he'd changed more than I thought since the days of our youth.

"The vulture responsible for Matt and Jessie's deaths"—I paused when I said Dave's wife's name, but he didn't motion for me to stop, so I went on—"for killing our Helsingers, Vayl destroyed him two months ago. Vayl's one of the good ones. He doesn't hunt. He doesn't turn people. He's been working for our side since Granny May was a little girl." Why did I suddenly feel so defensive? It wasn't like everybody was going to grab a torch and have at my boss like some crazed mob. These were highly disciplined troops. They'd at least wait until Dave gave the order. Still, I had to fight a sudden urge to leap in front of Vayl and yell, "Back off, bozos!"

Dave and Vayl had a long staring match, during which Cole moved from his collar to his fingernails and I tried to decide if I might actually be forced to choose between my brother and my *sverhamin.*

Cassandra came forward, emerging from the shadows like a guardian angel. She'd discarded her hijab, and her hair hung in a long black curtain to her waist. Somehow, even in her abaya, she managed to resemble an exiled African princess. Her usual compliment of glittering gold jewelry helped with the illusion, but really it was the way she held herself, tall and confident with just a touch of listen-up-punk in her attitude that made you pay attention when she spoke.

"Jasmine has become very precious to me," she said, the combination of kindness and command in her voice forcing Dave's eyes to hers. "It is such a pleasure to finally meet her twin. My name is Cassandra." She held out her hand, and before I could prevent it, Dave slid his into hers.

I wish I'd known Otto a little better. I'd have said, "Hey, Boom, do me a favor and set off some C4." I'd have bet a month's pay neither Dave nor Cassandra would've noticed the blast. Some other kind of explosion had gone off in their brains and they both looked slightly dazed from the fallout.

"Do I . . . know you?" Cassandra finally asked breathlessly.

Dave shook his head, his free hand going to the back of his

neck, as if checking to make sure he hadn't just been clubbed. "Would you like to?" he asked; then he slammed his mouth shut. He couldn't seem to believe those words had escaped it.

Behind him his crew agreed. Amazon Grace and Jet exchanged amazed glances. Cam mouthed the words "Is he flirting—with a girl?" to Natch, who replied with a stupefied nod. The rest of the unit seemed equally stunned, except for Adela, who was new enough not to realize how monklike Dave's existence had been since his loss. She kept her attention on Vayl, and though she made no outward sign I sensed, of everyone in the room, she was the unhappiest with his presence there.

The sound of a distant engine broke the silence.

Dave dropped his hand. The smile he gave Cassandra was the first I'd seen since before Jessie died. "I'm glad Jaz has someone like you on her team." While I totally agreed, an aggravated Puerto Rican chica stomped to the front of my brain and screeched, "Someone like *who*, you testosterone-crazed hunk of beef? You ain't known Cassandra more than ten seconds!"

I was just wondering how much more complicated this whole mess could get when Dave turned to his team. "Okay, let's pack it up," he said calmly. "Our ride's nearly here."

Within two minutes we were all ready to board the truck, which was just now slowing to a stop in front of the farmhouse.

"Stay inside until Mehdi opens the back doors," Dave had ordered, so we waited and watched while the driver parked his rig, hopped down, and walked around to the back of the truck. He carried a flashlight, which trembled as he trained it first on the road, then on the back of the truck. He never flashed it at the farmhouse. Maybe he'd been told not to. After some fumbling, he threw open the doors.

"All right," Dave whispered into the small headset he and his team all wore for communications. "Let's go."

It wasn't far from the farmhouse to the road. Maybe thirty yards. Of dirt. Yeah, I know. It sucked. No trees to hide behind. No little outbuildings. No cover whatsoever. But it worked in our favor too: We'd see anyone coming well before the bullets could hit us.

Dave had set Terrence and Ashley at the windows to guard our move. Terrence operated their SAW, a lovely light machine gun currently set on a tripod for maximum stability. Ashley, not willing to entrust this duty to his new Manx, held his M4 ready.

Dave led us out with Cassandra by his side. I hadn't been sure about mixing my people with his so soon, but I could trust this pairing. So too, the next one.

Natchez, who'd told Bergman his real name was so embarrassing he'd legally changed it to his birthplace, hadn't stopped asking him questions about his inventions since he'd broken out the guns. They'd discovered a mutual interest in weapons engineering that I figured would at least carry them through Iraq before Bergman said or did something that made Natch want to rip his face off.

Jet came next, followed by Adela. Moments later Ricardo left the farmhouse. Grace hung back, probably to keep an eye on me. Cam lingered as well. I got the feeling he wanted to make sure she behaved. And Boom decided he too could bring up the rear with Vayl, Cole and me.

With the exception of our doubled teams, everybody walked out on his or her own, advanced a few feet, stopped, crouched. Stared into the darkness. Strained to see beyond the blackness and got ready to shoot. The idea was for the guy behind to move forward, tapping the frontrunner on the shoulder as he passed. In this way we meant to leapfrog to the semi.

The first two groups had reached the truck and Mehdi had helped them inside when the reavers attacked.

They were better organized than the last bunch, coming at us almost in formation from the north side of the road. The distant whinny of horses told us how they'd arrived so quick upon the heels of the last group. They were also better armed than their predecessors. When I heard pistol fire followed by an agonized scream my heart stopped for an anguished moment as I tried to place the voice. "Doc!" somebody yelled from midpack, and then all hell broke loose.

Chapter Five

I'm still not sure how we all didn't kill each other that night; bullets were flying so fast and furious during that battle. The reavers rolled into us, firing seemingly at random. But there was a method to their madness. Reavers operate by strict rules. I didn't know what the punishments entailed, but they must've been extreme, because even the old gnarly ones wouldn't break them. The main no-no revolved around killing. Reavers were only allowed to eliminate people who'd been Marked for murder. In other words, me. Everybody else had to survive. So while the reavers had to take me out, they only wanted to take everybody else down.

What they didn't count on was the supreme skill and professionalism of their foes. Though they outnumbered us at least three to one at the start of the attack, within sixty seconds we'd whittled their numbers to fifteen.

Our guys had taken a couple more hits. One second Otto had been crouched near to me, a half grin on his face, saying, "If I had a wheelbarrow full of dynamite I'd blow these fuckers to Mars." The next second he lay writhing on the ground, trying not to scream, his hip shattered. As I stood over him, nailing reavers when I had a clear shot, pulling up when I realized I'd just aimed at one of my own, I saw Ricardo drop beneath a mass of monsters. Grace had made little progress toward the truck, and was bleeding heavily from a facial wound. Still, I thought we had them.

Then two more groups appeared, coming from both our flanks. These didn't have firearms, but we already knew the power of their claws, and several swung swords. Terrence and Ashley fired into them, but they didn't have the right angle to get more than one or two head shots per burst.

"Form on me!" yelled David.

Our guys from the farmhouse joined us and we tried to keep moving, but they swarmed us. Terrence went down under a reaver's claws. Vayl, seeing him fall, took the reaver's eye with his sword and pulled the wounded man to his feet. I holstered Grief and grabbed his machine gun. Switching it to three-round burst mode, I fired into the crowd of reavers coming at me, their tongues lolling in anticipation of tasting my soul.

"Jasmine!" called Vayl. "Do not stop!"

Easier said than done. I inched forward, almost tripped over a body, ducked quickly to avoid a neck-ripping swipe, and nearly screamed as the corpse between my legs lurched to its feet. I managed to mute the scream into a squawk as I jumped back, banging into Cole in my rush to avoid the rising reaver.

"Son of a bitch!" he cried. "I missed!"

"Watch out! Watch out!" I yelled. "The dead are rising!"

All around us the reavers we'd defeated the first time around had rediscovered vertical. Multiple thoughts streaked through my mind simultaneously. Not all of them made sense, but a skilled translator might put them in the following light:

Oh Jesus! Oh crap! Zombies! The Wizard's a necromancer. He could be around here somewhere, pulling their strings. So should I just run off into the night like some rabid raccoon and hope I luck into him? How stupid is that? Plus, it's not him. It's probably an apprentice. You know that. It may even be the mole. Is anybody murmuring a spell? How the hell can I tell? We are so outnumbered! Did Ashley just go down? My God, I think the semi is farther away than ever. Is that possible? Oh Jesus, was that Terrence's leg? Don't turn your head. I said don't—never mind. Holy shit, that's the barrel of a Colt .45 aimed right at my face!

The reaver, a live one, grinned wide enough to show the gap between his front teeth as his finger squeezed the trigger.

"Vayl," I whispered, my eyes somehow tracking straight to his in my final moment.

"Jasmine!" He lunged toward me, too late. The gun boomed and I went down almost at the same time. Except the horrifying pain I expected never split into my brain. A zombie had tackled me, its puppetlike efforts to take off my head such a welcome relief to point-blank murder I actually giggled. I know. Inappropriate. That's pretty much how it happens with me.

The zombie's weight left me as Vayl picked it up and threw it at least twenty feet. I took the hand Vayl offered and remembered to grab the SAW as he jerked me upright. Ahead of us Cole lifted Terrence onto his shoulder. Two reavers came at him, one living, one dead. Somehow the zombie missed our guys and clawed the living reaver instead, taking out most of his face. When he turned toward us I took out his legs with my machine gun.

"What is it with these zombies?" I asked Vayl. "Not that I'm complaining. But you'd think they'd come from two-thousand-year-old corpses the way they're behaving."

"Maybe their master is new to the art."

"Huh."

"Aaaah!" I spun at the sound. The zombie behind me clutched at the gaping hole in his chest. A living reaver had circled back to the farmhouse door. Had taken a bead on me. Somehow the zombie had gotten between us.

I took aim at the zombie. Hesitated. Moved my sites to the reaver. It yelled at the zombie. Gestured for it to clear the line of fire. Instead the zombie shambled straight toward the living reaver.

What the hell?

I glanced over my shoulder, hoping for some confirmation from Vayl that he'd witnessed this bizarre event as well. He was with Otto, lifting him off the ground. Grace and Ashley were already limping away ahead of them.

I looked back. The zombie had reached the living reaver. Grabbed the gun. Moved clear. I took the shot. The reaver fell dead. I waited for the zombie to make its next move. It hesitated. Appeared to study the gun as if it wasn't sure what to do with it and, in the process, managed to blow its own head off.

"Jasmine!"

"Coming!"

I ran to join Vayl and Otto, guarding them the rest of the way to the truck. I had to take out three more zombies. More a matter of immobilizing them with leg shots than actually destroying them, since you can only turn them off by distracting or killing the necromancer whose spirit moved them in the first place.

Multiple hands reached out and helped us into the back of the semi.

"Jet," Dave said, "you ride with Mehdi for now."

With a sharp nod, Jet jumped out. "Everybody set?" he asked grimly.

"Yeah, close the doors," Dave told him.

Moments later we were sealed inside, speeding away from a battle that really had been my responsibility. Maybe I should've aborted the mission when I woke inside that Chinook with the taste of hell still fresh on my tongue. But I just couldn't see the Department of Defense saying, "No, really, Ms. Parks, we don't mind taking it up the wazoo because you were disturbed by something you saw in a dream."

Unfortunately not all of my truckmates saw it that way. As soon as Dave lit the lantern, I encountered the blood-stained glare of Amazon Grace. She clearly wanted to slam me against the wall and pound me purple. I gave her a courtroom stare—no emotion whatsoever—and moved my gaze onward.

Most of the group was busy with the wounded. Special Ops folks cross-train like elite athletes, so while each has his or her specialty, they can also back each other up in a pinch. Cam and Natchez took turns laboring over Otto and Ashley, Cam with a couple of syringes that I assumed held painkiller, Natch with antibacterial spray, gauze, and tape.

Dave crouched beside Ricardo, who'd been shot in the arm and—"I know," he muttered. "I'm never going to hear the end of it."

"I keep telling you to keep your ass down," Dave said. The bullet had gone clear through his right butt cheek, leaving his pants soaked with blood.

Dave glanced over at the medic. "Adela," he said, "how's Terrence?" The native New Yorker was by far the worst of the wounded. His ankle had nearly been torn off by a close-range shot. She'd tied a tourniquet around it, but nobody was sure he'd be able to keep his foot. He'd also suffered gaping wounds across his chest where, after repeated hits, the reaver's claws had sheared through his body armor.

Adela shrugged. "They all need to be evacuated," she told him. "The sooner, the better." Her eyes darted to Vayl's and then away so fast you'd have thought she had a crush on him. Until you saw the sign she made with her right hand.

Since I was sitting beside him it was easy to lean against his shoulder, give him the sideways nod. *See that?*

The slight raise of his chin signaled he had. It was an ancient gesture made popular recently by a bunch of girls who'd achieved CNN status by declaring that a coven of vampires had tried to bewitch them over to the dark side. They said they'd saved themselves by using the sign to ward off evil. Called mano cornuto, it's a gesture originated in Italy where the index and pinky fingers of the left hand are raised while the others are curled into the palm. So apparently if you're a Texas Longhorns fan, making this gesture gets you both loyalty *and* protection from evil.

As soon as these teenyboppers opened their mouths I knew a couple of things for sure. The vampire community, the ones trying to blend, to live in peace with humans and other supernatural beings, were probably laughing their asses off at the girls' choice of verbiage. Vamps don't organize into covens. Nor do they do any bewitching. Hypnotizing, yeah, but not bewitching. And they probably agreed with me that the dark side is mainly reserved for people who need to replace their lightbulbs.

I also knew life wasn't going to improve for Vayl or *others* like him while people like Adela were running around forking their fingers at them. And that was just the mild stuff. Before we'd boarded our Learjet for Germany, FOX News had reported that a group of drunken rednecks had lynched a woman in Alabama. They'd accused her of practicing black magic, hexing one of their buddies so that he couldn't perform in the bedroom. And who knows, maybe they were right. Problem was, although the hanging had been carried out in broad daylight on the courthouse lawn, nobody would step up and point out the perpetrators.

It's an old story, I guess. People get away with murder all the time. In the end it does matter who you know, how much money's in your account, and who gives a crap about you. It shouldn't. But it does.

On this mission, it would help a ton if our team of backup ass kickers felt friendly toward us. But sentiment seemed to be leaning hard in the other direction as the wounded sat stoically, staring at the ceiling, trying not to cry out as their comrades patched them up.

Bergman joined Cole, Vayl, and I at the far corner of the semi, closest to the doors. Cassandra moved toward us as well, lost her balance, and nearly fell. Dave half rose and caught her, his hands steadying her at the waist as she found her equilibrium. "You okay?" he asked kindly.

She nodded, but her lips began to tremble, and moments later tears rolled down her cheeks. She hid her face, turned to go, but Dave pulled her into his arms. He rubbed her back tenderly. Whispered into her ear. She made some soft reply. I strained to hear, wishing my enhanced Sensitivity involved audio. It didn't. I'd just have to worm the information out of Cassandra the old-fashioned way.

I looked around the truck, gauging reactions to the chick flick. Most of the guys had decided to pretend it wasn't happening. Adela flicked another warding gesture at Cassandra. How original. And Amazon Grace looked thunderously pissed. Only Cam and Natchez exchanged grins.

Vayl bent toward me to murmur, "Amazing, is it not?"

"What?"

"How effortlessly some slip into love."

I snorted. "I'd hardly call it that," I whispered, trying to keep the sibilance out of my voice. I didn't want him to know his comment pissed me off. "They've known each other for what, five minutes?"

Vayl put his finger under my chin, lifting my face to make sure I met his eyes. It was only the second time he'd touched me in weeks. I'd tried to forget how the simple brush of his skin against mine could zap me like an electric wire. It disturbed me, made me feel like I spent most of my time operating on standby. Like I was only fully functional when I was aware of how much Vayl could rock my world, if I let him.

"Love knows no boundaries," he said, his eyes that soft amber hue I'd begun to equate with the finer emotions.

"Neither do horses," I drawled.

He dropped his hand. Sat back. "What do you mean by that?"

"You lead them to a barrel full of oats, they'll eat till their stomachs burst. You put them in a pasture, they'll run off if you don't fence it. They don't even go to the same spot to crap every time so you can manage their manure."

So much for amber. Vayl's eyes hardened to blue, which was how I could tell I'd affected his emotions pretty much the way I'd attempted to. He said, "I assume you have a point to make with this semihysterical outpouring."

"Just because something doesn't have boundaries doesn't mean it's good. Or right. Or even possible."

"What is your problem with Cassandra and David?"

"David just lost his wife. He's not ready for a serious relationship."

"It has been well over a year, Jasmine—"

"He's not ready. End of story."

But Vayl wouldn't let it go that easy. He gave me his sternest gaze. "Whose feelings are you describing now, really? Your twin's? Or your own?"

Chapter Six

Sometimes I get songs stuck in my head. I had one playing right now, even as I snoozed. It was that Kenny Loggins hit "I'm Alright." And I knew why. When we were seventeen Dave and I had snuck off to a Van Halen concert. Ordinarily he'd have gone with a group of his cool friends. But it was summer, we'd just moved to town, and he hadn't had a chance to make a name for himself as a stellar running back, or point guard, or pole vaulter.

In my dream we were closer to the stage, near enough to piss off Security if we decided to throw something more life threatening than panties. The opener, a band called Ringgs, was covering the song and doing damn well. The lead singer, an anorexic mike swallower who thought he was stud enough to go shirtless, sang, "You wanna listen to the man? Pay attention to the magistrate."

I glanced at Dave, swigging his beer, flirting with the girl dancing next to him, and wished I could get to know people that easy. When I looked back at the stage everything had changed.

One by one, the band members ripped off their outer skins, revealing the same demonic faces I'd seen on my visit to hell. Uldin Beit pounded the drums, her flayed back oozing as she flew through the song. Her fiendish pathologist, Sian-Hichan, fingered the bass guitar. A huge, broad-shouldered demon with the horns of a ram played lead guitar. And center stage, his voice tearing at my heart, stood the Magistrate himself.

I pinched myself. Nothing. Gave my cheek a slap. Looked around. The scene remained the same. "Dave, wake up!"

"Dude, I'm fully conscious!" he yelled, rolling his eyes at me as he dropped an arm around Neighbor Girl's shoulders.

The Magistrate finished the song, raised both hands above his head, like he wanted to catch the wave of thunderous applause and throw it over his shoulders as a mantle. When he lowered his arms, he pointed both forefingers at me. "Come."

I rose into the air, as if some roadies had attached wires to my belt while I was buying my ticket.

Oohs and *aahs* from the crowd as I gulped down a scream. I'd looked up. And seen fire. This was no dream. Somehow I was back in hell. Without Raoul. My only comfort was that I'd also seen the golden cord that connected my soul to my body. Small comfort however, in that none of the other cords that bound me to my closest friends and relatives were visible. Worse, something green and slimy had encased the cord. I could almost feel it, like an infection on my heart.

The "wires" broke about ten feet above the stage. I landed and rolled the way I'd been taught, sustaining no damage because I wasn't in a real body anymore. On my feet again, I felt for weapons. But of course I'd come with nothing corporeal. The Magistrate laughed heartily.

"What a little spitfire you are!" he cried as he approached me. I backed to the edge of the stage. Thought about jumping. But he'd just pull me up again.

"How did you bring me here?" I demanded, sounding a lot braver than I felt.

He poked a finger toward my forehead. I jerked back before he could touch me. "You're Marked, little girl—Uldin Beit's blood has bought you a spiritual tatoo. And do you know what that means? I can find you anywhere. I can take your soul anytime I please."

He grinned. Gorgeous freaking demon, he could've made the cover of *GQ* twelve months running. And yet my only response was a wave of terror so huge I felt it freezing my brain, numbing my senses. And I knew I was quickly becoming the victim he wished me to be.

I curled my fingers into fists. Though Cirilai was just the ghost of a ring, I still felt it warm on my finger, reminding me of who I was. Of who believed in me. The wave subsided just enough to allow me to hear my own voice, desperate, strident, practically hoarse from trying to be heard over the fear. *Come on, Jaz, if he could really take your soul, he'd have done it to start with. You've been in bigger trouble. Not often. But you survived. Just stay on your toes and don't, for God's sake, do not freak.*

"You can't make me stay here," I said.

"I am the Magistrate," he crowed, throwing his hair back as if he knew just how beautifully it set off his profile. "I can do anything I like." He pointed out to the audience. "See?"

My neck creaked as everything in me wished I didn't have to turn. To look. But I did. The adoring screams had changed while my eyes moved from him. As I stared outward I wished I had the means to vomit. They'd been crucified. Every one of them, nailed to crosses that spun like windmills. Except my brother. He was gone. What did that mean?

That you have some control.

I tested my cord. I should be able to travel right back to my body along its length. But the stuff covering it acted as a roadblock. I'd have to figure out a way to blast it off before I could get back to my body. And soon. Already the gold had begun to fade. If I waited too long I'd lose that line and never be able to find my way home.

I stared at the Magistrate. *Which was your plan all along, wasn't it, asswipe? Just keep me here until I had no other choice.*

"I like your hair," said the Magistrate. I ignored him, concentrated on moving up my line, but force would not remove the glop that encased the cord. "You know what that shock of white tells me?" he inquired. As if we were having a polite conversation, he went on. "It says you have a very close relative in hell who touched you on your last tour."

I looked at him then, narrowed my eyes, barely bit back a threat. Anything I said could endanger my mother.

He giggled with delight. "You two will have such fun together."

"I'm not staying," I said. I closed my eyes. *Raoul, I'm in deep trouble here. Any ideas?*

No reply. I didn't really expect any. Hell was probably way out of Raoul's calling area.

Another chorus of screams opened my eyes. They came, not from the audience, but from the band. A group of fighters had rushed the stage from the back. Dressed all in white, including masks that covered everything but their eyes, they attacked the demons with weapons that glittered so brightly it was hard to look at them.

I wished Cole was with me so he could verbalize what I was thinking. He'd pop a big old grape bubble and say with childlike wonder, "They are like ninjas from heaven."

Two of them swung on Uldin Beit with curved swords carved with runes that glowed in turns, as if the sword itself was somehow speaking as its wielder fought.

Uldin responded with surprising speed, leaping from her stool and spinning her sticks like nunchakus. With each spin the sticks grew, until she held a couple of mallets with round heads sprouting sharp points. Medieval weaponry fans would've called them morning stars. I thought they looked too evil for such a pretty name.

Two more light-coated warriors swarmed Sian-Hichan. This

duet carried swords as well, only they were straighter, bulkier, built for heavy lifting. Sian-Hichan swung the guitar over his head, slammed it against the stage. Instead of scattering Gibson parts as far as the eye could see, he pulled back holding a double-headed battle axe. And damned if he couldn't swing that thing like Paul Bunyan on a bet.

The third demon had already fallen by the time I glanced at him. His three opponents were still beating him with what looked like miniature silver telephone poles. The Magistrate had uncoiled his whip in readiness to rescue his fallen bandmate when he was attacked himself.

Built like a heavyweight boxer, his single foe didn't seem to need or want assistance. He rammed into the Magistrate, making his eyes do a dance I called the oh-shit-blink-and-pop, widening the way they will when one has just encountered a force of nature. The two went down, trading punches, wrestling for control over the whip.

The white fighter clocked the Magistrate solidly to the nose. Blood went flying as both it, and the Magistrate's grip on the whip, broke. The fighter rolled free, armed now, and apparently well versed in the offensive capabilities of a tightly braided length of steel-tipped leather. He cracked the whip against the Magistrate's side as he rolled to avoid the hit. Got him in the back too before the Magistrate caught the whip on the third strike. A brief tug-of-war followed, during which the whip broke.

The Magistrate screamed in fury, a sound echoed by Uldin Beit as her attackers overwhelmed her, one of them skewering her as the other lopped off the lower half of her arm.

Sian-Hichan still held his own, fighting with the mindless rage of a berserker. His axe blurred as he swung at his attackers, its bloody edge and their wariness both witness to his effectiveness.

The wet slap of fists on flesh brought my attention back to

the Magistrate and his opponent. Now they fought hand-to-hand, throwing kicks, blocks, and punches with a speed that astonished me. Honestly, you just don't see fighting like that in the world. At least not outside of a movie screen. It looked almost—choreographed. The Magistrate jumped and spun, his kick just barely missing the white fighter's skull. Only a late block by the fighter followed by a flurry of kicks to the ribs kept him in the game.

The Magistrate tried a knife hand to the neck, missed high, and instead ripped the mask off his opponent, who looked at me with such alarm you'd have thought I was about to turn state's evidence against him.

My knees folded like the paper fans my sister, Evie, and I used to make from Granny May's church bulletins. I don't guess I hit the stage gracefully. That would've been too much to ask. I did land on my ass, and since I wasn't corporeal it didn't hurt. It wasn't pretty either. But my mind had no room left in it for that kind of thinking. It was full. Brimming over, in fact, with the discovery I'd just made.

My late fiancé was a ninja from heaven.

Chapter Seven

Some things you just know. I'd stood at Granny May's bedside as she'd drawn her last breath. I'd watched her eyes empty, and I'd known she was gone. Where she went, well, that we could debate all day long. But she'd left our realm, of that I was certain.

So at my core, where I absolutely refused to bullshit myself, I knew this moment was too good to be true. But I wanted it so badly that the rest of me took some convincing.

"Matt?" I whispered.

He didn't have time to reply. The Magistrate had closed in, whacked him good with a combination of punches that backed him up several paces. But by then his comrades had finished with their demons. They joined him, turning the tide, whaling on the Magistrate with their various weapons until he sprawled on the floor, looking like an autopsy photo.

A sick, weak feeling stole over me. I checked my connection to physical me. Uh-oh. "I have to go," I murmured.

Within moments I was surrounded. I stood. Looked into Matt's eyes and wished I could weep. It wasn't him. Someone had created an excellent facsimile. But one thing I knew, just like I'd known about Granny May. When we did reunite, Matt and I would burn white-hot with the kind of flame that either eats you up or changes you forever. That's the kind of love we shared. That's what was missing from this Matt's eyes.

The white fighters joined hands, raised their heads toward my fading golden cord, and sang. The cord immediately started to vibrate, to try to make its own sound, the song that made it unique to me. The slime that covered it hardened, cracked, began to flake off. The fighters sang louder and my cord responded. This time it was successful. I heard my own tune, weak but clear. I rose, following it toward my body slowly, almost hand over hand as the shell that had stranded me fell away. I picked up my pace, refusing to look over my shoulder, to thank my rescuers because I wasn't even sure that's what they were. I speeded back to myself. Trying not to think. Trying to outrun my breaking heart.

I took a swift look around to reorient myself before I entered my body. It hurts like hell and I needed to know just how much teeth gritting would be required. A lot. The room was full.

We'd arrived in Tehran before dawn and set up in the building our people had rented for us the week before. A new construction, the white, four-story hexagon with dark brown trim housed three fairly luxurious apartments built right on top of a parking garage that could fit five cars and a midsize RV.

Only the downstairs apartment had been furnished, so that's where we'd crashed. Not all of us. We'd stopped once, just before crossing the border, to transfer our wounded to a helicopter along with Adela, which was a shame, since she was the only team member besides Dave who I knew couldn't be the mole. She was just too superstitious to work with a necromancer.

She hadn't expected to go. The helicopter crew had brought a doc along with them and, for obvious reasons, units like Dave's kept their medics close at hand. But Dave had made it an order.

"I know how you feel about the vamp and the Seer," he'd told her quietly as the healthy guys helped the wounded aboard the chopper. "That's not a problem I need on this mission. I'm sending you back to Germany. Once there, you'll be reassigned."

"I don't understand," she'd said, anger beginning to stir behind her dark brown eyes. "I've done excellent work here." She gestured to the guys. *See? All alive.*

Dave cocked his head to one side. "Six weeks ago my best connection to the Wizard was killed in an ambush. In her efforts to save him, my medic gave him CPR. He was a werejackal. Tell me, Adela, could you have put your mouth on his and blown your breath into his lungs?"

The eeww-gross expression that sped across her face before she could blank it out told the story. As soon as she knew she'd been had, she dropped the facade and let 'er rip. "Those creatures are evil. Every one of them should be put down." The scorn in her voice infuriated me. As if God himself had given her the necessary moral superiority to decide the fate of anyone different from her. I didn't realize I'd taken a step toward her. That my fists were clenched and I was prepared to swing until Dave grabbed my arm. But he couldn't shut me up.

"Those creatures have been living on this earth as long as we have. Some would argue that, even now, we survive only because a few of their most powerful leaders know it's in their best interests to live alongside us, even with us, rather than without us."

"They're monsters," Adela snapped.

"Keep thinking that," I told her. "Pretty soon you'll find yourself scrubbing toilets in some veteran's hospital. And you know what? When I bring my dad in for his colonoscopy, I'm sure he'll have to take a piss right before, and I'm not going to remind him to lift the lid."

"Jaz!" Dave didn't need to say another word. I knew by his tone I'd gone too far. Again. But, dammit, I was getting so sick of this shit! Most of these bigots had never met a supernatural being in their lives and were operating either from family-held superstitions or media-hyped fears. To be fair, lots of vamps and weres and witches were scary bad. Otherwise I'd be out of business. But then, so were plenty of humans.

With nowhere to go but backward, I joined my crew on the road and let Dave's team say their goodbyes. It had been an emotional parting for them, tough to watch by its very lack of tears and bear hugs. Vicelike handshakes with the second hand clutching a shoulder or elbow. Tight-jawed promises to "See you as soon as we get back" and demands to "Take care of yourself." And from Terrence, Ashley, Ricardo, and Otto, of all things, apologies. "Sorry I let you down." "I hate like hell to miss this." "I'm so sorry, man." I finally had to turn away.

"It is not your fault these men are hurt," Vayl told me as we walked back to the truck. When I didn't reply, his hand, startlingly warm on my shoulder, stopped me. He turned me to face him. "Jasmine?"

"I could say it's Uldin Beit's fault," I told him miserably. "Or Desmond Yale's. I could mention the fact that these guys knew the risks when they signed up. And maybe I'd even be right. But *I* feel responsible for their wounds. Their pain. If I'd just—"

Vayl ran his thumb across my lips. Usually I'm not that easy to silence. But suddenly I couldn't think of a thing to say. "They will be all right," he whispered.

He'd leaned in to speak the words. If I rose up on my toes, my lips would just brush his. And why in the world would I think that would be okay right here, right now? *Because you want it that bad. Admit it, at least to yourself. If you thought your heart could handle it, you'd lay this vampire down.*

I took a deep breath. Focused on the job. Let it pull me back from the edge yet again. "Maybe we should send them all back. Do this thing ourselves, like we should have all along."

"Their unit would still be compromised."

"You think the mole is still with us?"

"I would say the chances are excellent."

"About that. Did you see anybody signal from the farmhouse before the second attack?"

"No."

"Me neither. But those zombies didn't just come out of nowhere. And the mole wouldn't have known they'd be needed until after the first attack."

"I agree. Therefore, they must have set up quite an imperceptible means of communication."

"I'll ask Bergman about it. Maybe he'll have some ideas."

That proved difficult, however, since the semi, and then the apartment building, provided hardly any privacy. And when we did split up to sleep, we'd gone boy-girl, so Cassandra and I shared a room with Grace. Her wound had turned out to be superficial. Where was the fair in that?

Exhausted from our battles and a long night on the road with hardly any shut-eye, we'd slept until two, when Dave had mustered his troops and my crew. The exception, of course, was Vayl. He remained in his light-impervious tent, which he'd pitched on top of an ornate, gold-rimmed bed upholstered in blue and white fabric that looked to have been designed for a queen. Or, um, a king. Who happened to be a vampire. Anyway.

For the past hour we'd taken turns showering and eating, each of us finally wandering into the high-ceilinged living room, which had been plastered and painted a cheery buttercup. Recessed lights pinpointed a modern fireplace, forget the mantel, and a chocolate-brown floor with a large triangular inlay that was probably cheaper than it looked. In this room the rugs had been hung on the walls, with thinly cushioned chairs lined up underneath like hotel lobby afterthoughts. The center of the room had been left empty in case, I don't know, we wanted to play a quick game of shuffleboard?

"Cassandra," I said to my friend, who was pretending not to notice Dave was pretending not to notice her. Ick. "This room sucks. Let us lay some rearrangement on it, shall we?"

She nodded hard enough to make her braids bounce, making me realize this little mutual crush between her and my brother might actually have its humorous points, and we set to work. With six bored guys only too willing to jump in and help, we turned the place into a passable representation of an American family room in no time. Of course, we had to steal some rugs off the floors of other rooms. And a couch out of the guys' bedroom. But we felt a lot more comfortable afterward.

Cassandra, Cole, and I landed on the couch with me in the middle, facing the fireplace and David. Bergman took one of the two chairs to our left. Cam and Jet, who absolutely refused to hate me, took the next-largest piece of furniture, which we'd placed across from the chairs. A love-seat-sized brown leather piece that had been stuffed until it looked ready to pop, it held five white furred pillows that turned out to be quite popular with the guys.

Natch, who'd kept up a dialogue with Bergman during the entire semi trip that ran the gamut from night-vision equipment to deep-sea diving, took the chair to Bergman's left. At the moment he was entertaining Miles with a story that seemed to involve Harleys and topless biker chicks. Grace hung to the back of the room. I didn't like that I couldn't keep an eye on her, but I noticed Bergman glancing at her every so often. For once, I thanked my lucky stars for his natural paranoia.

Dave launched into his speech. It was supposed to be a morale booster. We needed it after losing four guys and our medic. So it was a real shame I missed the vast majority of it. About all I caught was "The good news is Ricardo, Terry, Ash, and Boom are going to be fine. As soon as this mission is over we're headed back to Germany. Yeah, we'll be training like new recruits during the week, but the weekends will be ours. And we won't leave that country until our unit is whole again."

It had come on me without warning. And, really, what would I have done if I'd felt queasy? Or faint? Are you kidding? Surrounded by some of the toughest people on the planet? I'd have probably sat right in that spot if a meteorite had burst through the ceiling and landed on my lap. And that's what my body did. Sat there, breathing, blinking, looking like it gave a crap about Dave's message while the Magistrate sucked my soul straight to hell.

Dave had nearly finished talking when I returned. His audience looked somewhat cheered. Except for me. I seemed pale. Slightly blue around the lips. Cassandra had begun to look at me with concern. Time to dive in.

I managed not to yell. Just barely. Couldn't help sucking in my breath though. I buried my fingernails in my thighs. God, it felt like all my organs had jumped a foot. And, folks, those puppies are not meant to riverdance.

Cassandra leaned toward me, reaching out, whispering, "Are you all right?"

"Don't—" I hissed.

Too late. Her hand landed on mine, just a moment, before it jerked away. Wide, horrified eyes stared into mine. I imagine I looked a little peeved. I wanted to jump up and down, toddler-style, and yell, "Stop touching me!"

Dave was too good a commander to interrupt his speech to confront us just then, though his glance told us we'd been had. "So let's review the plan," he continued. "As soon as it's dark we'll scout the location. Remember not to speak to anyone. With Otto gone, only Cole knows Farsi well enough to pass for a native. And even disguised, he looks foreign enough that most folks won't be fooled."

"Are you kidding me?" Cam interjected, motioning at Cole with mock disgust. "He looks like his high school drama teacher went nuts with the spirit gum and the sheep wool!"

"I'll have you know this is the real deal!" Cole said, tugging at his beard. Then he grinned. "I do look like I should be selling pot out of the back of my love van, don't I?"

Even Dave laughed at that one. "If you are cornered," he went on, "remember you're Canadian students with relatives living in Tehran. You all have your passports and ID papers to prove it. Don't lose them. Natch, is your camera ready?"

Natchez patted the pocket of his brown plaid shirt. "Yeah."

"Good. We'll want as many pictures as possible. We'll be re-creating the interior of the location on one of the upper floors so we can practice the takeout when we get back." He didn't need to tell them they'd only have one chance at this. They couldn't make any mistakes. However, with a mole in the unit, he also couldn't tell them they'd be scouting a false location and practicing the wrong moves for a bogus meeting. Only Dave, Vayl, and I knew the real time, date, and spot of the Wizard's rendezvous with destiny. If we unearthed the mole before that time, Dave's unit would join our hunt. If not, Vayl and I would be on our own.

Chapter Eight

Once the meeting disbanded, I gave Dave and my crew the come-hither nod and they followed me to the bedroom where Vayl slumbered. Without breathing. Helluva trick, yeah? One of the reasons I find him so fascinating.

Before anyone could talk I held up my right hand, pointed my left at Bergman. He pulled his wallet from his pocket, slid an item the size of a credit card from it, and replaced the wallet. Holding the card flat in one hand, he slid his thumb along its length. A whirring sound preceded the release of small wings that unfolded from each edge of the card, making it resemble a miniature saw blade. He flung the card into the air, Frisbee style. It flew on its own power, circling the room in ever-tightening circles. When it had completed its scan, it zipped to a spot next to the bed, where a white-shaded lamp sat on a round golden table.

I nodded to Cole. *Check it.* While he looked for the bug, the card moved on to a cherry valet with a built-in seat. It dropped to the floor there, so we must only have two devices to worry about. I found what I was looking for in a hollow inside the leg.

I motioned for Bergman to come and deal with the bug. He pulled a small tool kit from his back pocket. It contained an eye dropper with a plug on the business end. He pulled off the plug and bathed the bug in the liquid it contained. Cole had found his nasty, so he did the same lamp side. "Okay," Bergman sighed as he replaced the plug, the dropper, and the bug snooper. "We're good to talk."

"Won't the mole find it suspicious that his bugs died just while we were in the room?" David asked.

Bergman shook his head. "I just doped them with"—he glanced at me, his nose and upper lip pinching in his nunya-bizness-Jack look—"let's just call it a robotic component that makes it seem as if the bug is picking up conversation. The listener will think he's picking up words and snatches of phrases, but it's all preprogrammed gibberish. The fault will be blamed on technical difficulties, not us."

"You're good."

Bergman beamed. I hated to cut off his ego-feed, but, "So's our mole," I cautioned. "We've made it a point to keep an eye on Vayl all day, since he's an obvious threat to the Wizard. Nobody's been in here without one of us. But I guess we knew we were dealing with a smooth operator. And right now, that's not at the top of our priority list." I described the incident with the Magistrate. "He said he could find me anywhere as long as I had this Mark on me." I resisted rubbing my forehead. Barely. "I'm sure the same is true of the reavers. And Raoul and my"—I stole a glance at Dave, noticed the way his brows were lowering, and decided to omit the fact that we might have a close relative in hell—"well, Raoul said I needed to get it off. So. Anybody have any idea how you remove a demonic Mark?"

Bergman looked at Cassandra. "Do you want me to get the Enkyklios?" Everybody took a second to stop and stare. I think for all of us that was the moment we realized his desire to break out, be more, was genuine. Was, in fact, going to take him places he'd never dreamed of going before. Three weeks ago he wouldn't have touched Cassandra's library with a welder's glove. But even he was willing to admit that if any information existed that could help me, the Enkyklios probably held it. Cassandra shook her head.

"Thank you, no, I . . . I already know what to do." Biting her lip, she walked to the window and pulled back the heavy blue drape. A sliver of sunshine framed her hands and face, highlighting the droop of her lips, the crinkling between her exquisitely arched brows.

Cole and I, having witnessed that expression before, understood the drill. He grabbed a pillow from the bench that sat at the base of the bed and handed it to her. I put my arm around her shoulder and patted gently. As she held the pillow to her chest, struggling with memories that might, or might not, bring on a torrent of tears, we stood close enough to speak privately if we all chose to whisper. Everyone did. At least to start with.

"You look pretty spooked," I said. "What's up?"

"I have lived a hundred lives. I suppose it's inevitable there would be a few I'd prefer to forget."

Bergman entered our circle. "You don't have to whisper, you know. My bug stunners aren't prototypes." Bergman's new innovations tended to fizz out or blow up unexpectedly.

Cassandra sighed. "That's not—" She shook her head and smiled at him. "You are an original." She looked over his shoulder at Dave, standing alone and somewhat forlorn in the middle of the room. "Come," she said after a moment's thought. "Join us."

He nodded, melded with our little group as if he was the last kid to find base in a game of tag.

Cassandra looked deep into his eyes. When her own filled with tears, she dropped her gaze. "During the fifteen hundreds I lived on an island near Haiti. It was small. Privately owned by a merchant farmer named Anastas Ocacio." Her jaw jutted, as if her teeth must shovel the words over her tongue. "Ocacio fancied himself an aristocrat. Despite the heat he wore stockings with garters and a floor-length gown. He oiled his hair, which was thick with dandruff and stank so badly we used to draw straws to see who would serve him supper. The first time I came to his table he pulled me down and whispered in my ear, 'I must have you.' The stench of his rotting teeth nearly made me faint."

She shrugged, as if to rid herself of his grasping memory, but it hung on. "My circumstances being what they were, I had no choice in the matter." She fell silent, giving us time to make the leap. It took a while. Even four hundred years ago women could often throw a glass of wine in a sleazy guy's face and kick his ass out the door. But a black woman? I could only think of one situation where her choices might have been so severely limited.

"Cassandra," I whispered, "were you a slave?"

Her nod resembled one of Vayl's. Barely an acknowledgment at all.

Dave immediately took her hands. The anguish on his face seemed to bewilder her. "I'm so sorry," he said.

"You had nothing to do with it," she said.

"We're white," I told her grimly. "We can't help it that those assholes were the same color as we are. But we're ashamed of it just the same."

Cassandra stared at each of us for a moment before she finally nodded. "After that first night, I swore I would die before I let him touch me again." Even now, centuries later, the memories made her ill. Cole put out a hand to steady her and she gave him a grateful look. "I knew how to summon demons. Back in Seffrenem — my country," she added for Dave's benefit, "we had often fought demonic cults. You cannot combat them successfully without knowing their methods."

"What did you do?" asked Bergman.

"I gathered together a short list of ingredients, common items you can find in most pantries. When it was mixed and ready, it resembled a small bowl of brick-colored concrete. I sat inside a protective circle and painted the Mark around my eyes. Then I pricked my finger and let the blood drip all around me as I spoke the words of summoning."

"What came?" I asked, half suspecting she'd describe the Magistrate.

"A demoness. I have rarely seen such beauty. And yet she horrified me. Does that make any sense?"

"Oh yeah."

So Cassandra made a deal with the devil, who took Anastas Ocacio for a long, bumpy ride that left him screaming for mercy. "It took them three days to find all the pieces of him," Cassandra finished. "And by the fourth I had found my way off the island. I had also found a holy man."

"So he removed the Mark?" Dave asked.

"No. But he blessed the water that I washed my eyes with. And he gave me a special prayer that protects me against the demon's return. As long as I do those two things every day as soon as I wake, I'm fine."

"Wait a second," said Cole. "Do you mean to say you've been washing your face with holy water for the last four centuries?"

"Yes."

"Without fail?"

"Yes."

"Or else the demon will come get you?"

"Yes."

"Wow. I'm trying to remember the last time I did anything for even a month straight."

"You shave."

He scratched at his beard. "Usually."

"You brush your teeth."

"That's true."

"It is that routine for me."

"You know what? I think I'll avoid demons anyway."

Cassandra nodded, the ghost of a smile flitting across her face. "It's probably for the best."

Bergman said, "So it sounds like Jaz just needs to wash the spot with holy water. Except"—he looked at me—"do you even know where the spot is?"

I thought of the Magistrate poking a finger at my forehead. And my mom rubbing my noggin raw as she said plaintively, "It won't come out."

"Yeah," I said, "I believe I do."

Chapter Nine

After a brief intermission during which I anointed my own forehead, learned Cassandra's prayer, and felt suitably guilty for not summoning a minister to oversee the whole shebang despite the obvious danger it would've caused her—I moved on to the next order of business.

"So, now that the Magistrate can't come after me, why do you think he let me go the way he did? Why make me think Matt rescued me?"

"It depends what he knows about you," said Dave. "Looking at it from a military perspective at least, you've got to wonder what he stands to gain from your release if he thinks you're just some girl as opposed to—"

"A Sensitive who has died twice and been brought back twice by Raoul. To fight for Raoul."

"So, assuming the Magistrate somehow has access to your background, how much do we really know about Raoul?" asked Dave. We looked at each other. Not a lot. There was that undercurrent that, when you started to translate it into words, began to erode. And made you look idiotic for trusting it. All we really knew for sure was that he was a force for good in the world. That we worked for him. And now I might be in trouble as a result.

I reached into my jacket for my cards. I wished I could shuffle them, but for now it would have to be enough just to hold them in my hand and pace. "Okay, let's put ourselves in the demon's head if we can. What do they always want?"

"Souls," everybody chorused.

"He could've had mine easy. I was good and stuck, but he let me go."

"Bait for the bigger fish?" suggested Dave.

"As in Raoul?" I asked. "If I thought Matt was working for Raoul in another capacity, would I go running back to him, demanding an explanation? Yeah, maybe. Even if it meant certain death for me. In which case, the Magistrate could easily follow me, because of the Mark. He could grab Raoul while he was sitting there with his defenses down and, no doubt, take me along with him."

"Should you warn him?"

I frowned at my brother. "Don't *you* two ever talk?"

He suddenly found the curtain rod fascinating. "This is the job I was meant to do. I figure if he has a problem with my performance he'll let me know."

Okay. So maybe Dave was more of a consultant. Like Bergman. And Raoul was waiting for just the right time to access his skills. Which might take forever if they had to actually talk. Because communication is such a two-edged sword for guys. On the one hand, they almost always mean what they say. Refreshing, I know. On the other hand, getting them to actually say it can be like coaxing a corpse to tap dance. Not that it can't be done. But it's so freaking exhausting. Not to mention the cost in heavyweight fishing line and Savion Glover videos.

I sighed. "Yes, I'll speak to him. By the way, Grace isn't your mole. Vayl and I have been taking turns watching her almost since we arrived. We found her behavior the most . . . suspect," I told him, feeling slightly apologetic now I knew she was innocent. An ass, yes, but a loyal one. "She hasn't been in this room at all."

"So who do we have left?" Dave murmured sadly. "The mole is either Cam, Jet, or Natchez." He went to the bench and sank down onto it, clasping his hands between his knees, staring at the ornate carpet. Cassandra followed, sat beside him.

"Can you tell us more about these men?" she asked.

"What about you?" he snapped. "Why can't you just tap them and tell who's betrayed me?"

She flinched, almost as if he'd hit her. "I'm sorry," he said instantly. "I just can't believe . . . you can't imagine what we've been through together."

"Our original plan was for me to try to divine their purposes," Cassandra assured him. "Unfortunately, something happened to me the moment I touched you. I was afraid to speak. And I wasn't sure until I linked with Jasmine just now. And nothing happened. Then I knew. I've gone muddled."

I guess we were all kind of gaping at her like seals at the zoo, hoping for a jaw full of fish. Tears sprang to her eyes. "It's not something over which I have any control. One doesn't plan for these things!"

"What do you mean by muddled?" I asked.

Cassandra tended to play with her hands when nervous. Since she wore multiple rings on her long, slender fingers, it was a wonder little golden circlets weren't popping off her knuckles like tiddlywinks. She darted one glance at Dave and then refused to look at him anymore as she told me, "Sometimes a Seer who is overwhelmed by a strong emotion becomes so inundated by all the wonderful possibilities that emotion opens up to her that she can See no other visions. That is what has happened to me."

It took me about a half a second to get it, and then, oh baby, did I! "You mean—"

"Yes," she interrupted, "exactly."

"I don't get it," said Cole. He moved to sit on the valet chair. His costume looked odd to me, though his beige-and-white-striped shirt and olive-green pants weren't that different from any of the other guys'. Then I realized I was missing the red high-tops he typically wore. "Are you, like, too scared to See?" he asked her.

"No."

"Then what is it?" asked Bergman.

Cassandra gave me a pleading look.

I shook my head, too unsure of how I felt about the event to actually describe it aloud. "I think you're going to have to tell them," I said.

"Now?"

Dave took Cassandra's hand in his. Her eyes went wide and a bemused sort of half smile spread across her face as he said, "Look, I'd appreciate anything you can do. Wondering which one of my brothers stabbed me in the back is pretty much killing me."

"I *want* to help." Cassandra ducked her head. "I just can't right now." She shrugged, spoke in a voice so low I think only Dave and I heard her. "Maybe love really is blind."

Dave stared at her for a couple of beats before his whole countenance lifted, as if a plastic surgeon had slid a computer printout in front of his actual face and said, "See, I can make you look ten years younger!"

Before our newest couple could get with the romance, I turned to Bergman. "We need to figure out how our traitor is contacting the Wizard. Nobody left the farmhouse, but either the Wizard or one of his apprentices knew to raise those zombies. What's that tell you?"

"The mole was probably carrying a bug. Or, more likely, had planted it on somebody else. So the Wizard knew all about the reavers. But he still had to signal the necromancer to raise the zombies, because he wouldn't have risked coming close enough for you or Cole to sense him." Bergman looked at Dave, who couldn't seem to keep his eyes off Cassandra, who suddenly found the bedspread fascinating. "Yo, Romeo." Bergman waved his hands, like a flight deck crew member clearing his pilot for takeoff.

"Uh, yeah." Dave smirked in a way I hadn't seen him do since he was eighteen. Good grief, what had happened to our badass military man? Had he truly been taken down by the blurry-eyed psychic?

"I'm thinking silent signal," Bergman went on, eyeing the couple doubtfully. I wasn't sure they were listening either. "There are a couple of different methods they might have used. We can test for them if you want. Of course we'll have to fly to Mars for the equipment, but I'm sure we'll be back in time for supper."

Bergman raised his eyebrows at me as Dave glanced at Cassandra and nodded. "He's got it bad," Miles whispered.

"And vice versa," I replied.

"What're we going to do?" Cole muttered. "We need Dave in his right mind. After all, he's kind of in charge."

Actually, if you wanted to be anal about it, Vayl was in charge. But I wasn't in the mood for technicalities at the moment. I took a second to observe my twin as he leaned toward Cassandra, whose hand he had not relinquished, and murmured into her ear. For a second I couldn't place his expression, it had been that long since I'd seen it.

"He's also happy," I told them. And I realized, whether Vayl had been right or wrong about my reaction to it, I had to back off and let this relationship run its course. "Let's give him that, at least for the next few minutes." I was pretty sure neither one of them noticed when we left the room.

Chapter Ten

Cole, Bergman, and I reconvened in the girls' bedroom. After a repeat of the flying card trick, we discovered no bugs. Not surprising. Still, we all huddled on the silver-framed bed and spoke in the hushed voices of those who are about to tell some truly gruesome ghost stories.

"Okay," I said, "we have three suspects who we need to learn a lot about in a short amount of time without them realizing we're doing research. Any ideas?"

"Get 'em all drunk and hire some strippers," Cole said immediately. "You'll find out everything you need to know in twenty minutes."

"Nice plan," I drawled, "in Miami. However I feel there might be a shortage of strippers in Tehran. And I believe you informed us the preferred drink here is tea."

Cole, having run out of fingernails, began gnawing on the button of his shirt. He spat it out immediately. "Plastic sucks," he said. "Dammit, I need gum!"

"I'm out," I replied. "Here, chew on this." I shoved up the sleeve of my light blue tunic, unbuckled the sheath I kept strapped around my right wrist, laid the syringe of holy water on the bedside table, and handed him the rest. "I imagine it tastes like old shoe, but the leather's probably good for your teeth. Plus, maybe it'll help zap your brain back to reality." I shook my head. "Booze and strippers. Geesh!"

Bergman tapped me on the knee. "I've been thinking about the ways the mole might be contacting the Wizard."

"Go on."

"He's carrying a transmitter on him, no doubt about that. But it may even be embedded under the skin, so I wouldn't recommend searching for it as your first means of digging him out. He's got to have a way to either power it up or key it to send messages. So we need to watch for odd gestures that don't seem to fit with what he's saying or doing at the time."

"That seems easy enough," said Cole. He began touching himself in random places. "These are my dad's old baseball signals," he told us as he pressed his thumb to the side of his nose, tugged his left earlobe, and slid the side of his hand across his chest. "I'm telling you to bunt, run like hell, and then if they throw you out at first, go to the concession stand and get me a Dr Pepper."

"I hardly think it'll be that obvious," said Bergman.

"You never know," Cole insisted. "When a guy's scratching his nuts, they don't always itch."

"Okay." I held up my hands. "No more testicular discussions. No more baseball. Though I can see how you got from one to the other pretty quickly, Cole, I am now certain the heat that built up inside that semi trailer during our ride here has boiled your brain. Bergman, anything else we should look out for?"

He began fiddling with his bootlace. "It seems stupid when I think about saying it now."

I wasn't sure how a guy with a genius the size of a small country could still worry about looking foolish in front of his buds, but I was beginning to think his troubles would drastically reduce if he could just find himself a good woman. Somebody to give him a daily dose of feel-good whether he needed it or not. I sure didn't have the patience for it. "Dude, spit it out. If we laugh, you can punch us both."

"But not in the arm," said Cole. "I'm still sore from all those shots they gave us before we flew over here. You can punch me in the stomach, but give me time to get ready. Houdini died because some guy didn't warn him first, you know."

I regarded Cole with the thinning patience of a kindergarten teacher who has neglected to take her Zoloft. "What the hell is *up* with you?"

"I am experiencing a deep-seated need to blow a bubble," he informed me.

I took his right hand, which held my syringe sheath, and shoved the leather in his mouth. It was like giving E.J. her pacifier. Instant relaxation of the facial muscles. Full-body quiver, as if a wave of stress had just exited his epidermis. And yet, at the back of his eyes lurked a tight black ball of tension that promised to explode the second he stopped chewing. Nope, Cole wasn't just stressed about the lack of bubble gum. Something much bigger had him twisted like a pretzel. I could probe, but I'd never get anywhere with another guy in the room. It was part of their Code. I didn't understand it. But I respected it. Like demanding silence while using the urinal. Some things men just wouldn't say in front of other men.

I turned to Bergman. "Go on."

"You guys are Sensitives, right?"

"Right."

"Well, it seems to me the mole might be an *other*. He could be communicating with the Wizard through telepathic or other nontraditional means. In which case one of you should be able to sense him."

"But we haven't," I said.

Bergman nodded. "All that could mean is that he's somehow shielded himself. In which case, you might be able to sense the shield."

Cole and I looked at each other doubtfully. In the short time we'd known each other we'd learned our Sensitivities differed quite a bit. We could both detect vampires. But only I could tell when reavers were around. Cole was better at picking out witches and weres. And the powers our Sensitivities gave us differed greatly as well. The fact that so far neither of us had noticed anything amiss among David's crew didn't do much for Bergman's second theory. "I guess it wouldn't hurt to give it a spin," I told Cole.

"So what do we do?" he asked. "Walk right up to them and give them a sniff?"

Sure, I thought, turning my card deck in my hands, *three highly trained Spec Ops troops aren't going to suspect a thing when we start nosing around their business. Especially after they start comparing notes*. I had just opened the flap so I could get the cards out when an idea hit me. The ideal way to study our suspects without them ever wondering why we were giving them the once-over. "Cole," I said, "why don't you go see if everybody's up for some poker?"

Chapter Eleven

Iranians dine on the floor, so, since we didn't have a table handy for poker, we sat on the living room rug in front of the fireplace. It reminded me strangely of Girl Scout camp, when we'd play Snap and Crazy Eights inside our tents after the marshmallow toasting and song singing had run its course. We formed a circle, most of us cross-legged. Only Dave and Cassandra were missing. They'd chosen to spend the afternoon in the kitchen, drinking tea and gabbing like a couple of beauticians. In any other situation I'd have needled Dave so hard he'd have resembled a coke addict. But in front of his crazy loyal crew I bit my tongue and filed it all away for future use. He'd be home for Christmas one of these days and then, *whap!* Watch that boy squirm!

"Okay, what do you say to this?" I asked as I removed my deck from its somewhat limp and discolored holder. "Dealer calls the game and the wild cards. Ante is seven thousand, nine hundred rials." We'd all been issued plenty of Iranian currency before we left. I'd just told the guys it would cost them about a buck apiece to get into the game. They'd been around this part of the world long enough to know exactly what I meant.

Everybody seemed agreeable, so I split the deck and bent the halves, thumbing the edges toward each other as I'd done tens of thousands of times. The cards flipped out of my hands like they'd grown springs.

"Very funny," said Cam, the twinkle in his eye making light of the sarcasm in his tone. "Tell us, Jaz, just how *do* you win a game of fifty-two-card pickup?"

Everybody laughed. But me. *Okay, don't panic. Your fingers probably just spasmed. Maybe you're not getting enough potassium.* I gathered the deck together and straightened it.

Okay, concentrate. Pretend you're just learning. Like Granny May is sitting beside you, patiently mapping every detail of each move. I watched my fingers begin the familiar motions that had become a balm to me, a rare and precious soothant to my savaged soul. They stopped working right around step three. As if they'd taken some major muscle damage while I wasn't looking.

At least my poker buddies didn't laugh this time. Maybe they noticed the look on my face. I tried to school in blankness, but my inner bitch wouldn't allow me to deny the awful, dawning truth. She sat on her customary bar stool, nursing a whiskey sour, checking her reflection every minute or so, swinging a black-stockinged leg just enough to make the guys around her hope her red leather miniskirt kept riding up.

"You dumb bimbo," she spat, adjusting a stray hair as she spoke, her silver earrings sparkling like daggers. "I can't believe *this* is the sacrifice you made to get into hell. And for what? Fair warning on the reavers? Big whoop. That helped you diddly squat. Insight into Mommy's whereabouts? As if you hadn't already guessed. A good look at the Raptor's face? Like one decent reporter won't scoop that story when Samos feels the time is right. You been screwed, little girl. And not in the kick your legs up and squeal kinda way, either."

I looked at the cards, strewn across the vibrant red tulip that anchored the rug on which we sat, and felt like I should draw a chalk line around them. Call their next of kin. *Wait, that's me. Oh God, this sucks.* I watched my hands gather up the deck, knowing

I would never find comfort in the *whoosh* of a perfect bridge ever again. Fighting the urge to weep.

No boo-hooing, I commanded myself. *No panicking either. Think.*

No way would I relinquish the sweet relief shuffling cards had given me for any of the reasons my inner bitch had listed. There had to be something more, something I'd missed when Raoul and I had traipsed through Satan's playground. Something key. But now was not the time to replay that visit. Work called. *Time to ferret out the mole*, it said, its whisper even more seductive than the brush of aces against deuces. I'd survived losses much worse than this. I'd get through. As long as I had the job.

I handed the cards to Cole, who sat to my left. "Shuffle for me, would you?" I sat back, letting my hands rest in my lap. Amazon Grace, sensing vulnerability, leaned her back against the fireplace wall and smiled lazily. "Your reflexes are catlike," she drawled. "I can see why they picked you for this hit."

Too bad you're not the traitor. I'd love to rip you in half and feed you to the town rats. I took my time replying, trying to measure how her comrades would react to anything I said. I decided they'd appreciate me rising above. "Well, my instructors figured out pretty quick they'd better teach me how to kill with my feet as well as my hands. It's a good thing they were so thorough, don't you think?"

That got a laugh, which pissed off Grace just enough that I felt better.

Cole handed me the cards. I called a game of five-card draw, one-eyed jacks wild, and everybody anted up.

The great thing about poker is people expect to be given the eagle eye on a regular basis. So for the next hour, Cole, Bergman, and I got away with shameless snooping right under our quarries' noses. Jet loved to talk, so we found out quickly that his mom and dad had met in Vietnam and now lived in California. His big sister taught violin at the local college and his little brother played drums in a rock band. He hadn't met the right woman yet, but when he did he planned to leave the service and start a pizza place because "Pizza is the best food in the universe. Am I right?" High fives all around as we were forced to agree. Jet played aggressively, winning and losing big, bluffing when he should fold. But, damn, he was fun company.

Natchez and Bergman, already mutual admirers, found even more reasons to respect each other. Bergman folded about sixty percent of the time, so he was usually all ears when Natch launched into another wahoo tale. Apparently, when he wasn't working along a tightrope, he lived on the edge. Every story, whether it ended with him being chased into a lake by a grizzly, BASE jumping off the Perrine Bridge, or freeskiing down Crystal Mountain on a virgin slope, made Bergman gape with awe.

"So there we were," Natch said as he tossed the equivalent of three bucks in the pot and threw an arm onto the cushion of the obese love seat behind him, "snorkeling in water not three feet deep when this ten-foot bull shark comes racing right at us. We found out later people had been feeding sharks in the area, so, who knows, maybe she was jonesing for a handout."

"Tell them what she got," said Cam as he threw down his hand in mock disgust.

"A face full of knuckles," Natch said, miming a slow-motion roundhouse. "Luckily she wasn't in a fighting mood, so she took off even faster than she came."

Bergman, who sat between Natch and me, just shook his head. "Natch went mountain climbing in Turkey on his last leave. Can you believe that?" he asked me. "You want to know where I went?"

"A software convention in Delaware?"

"Exactly!"

"Dude, you can't be comparing your life to mine," Natch said, clapping Bergman on the back hard enough to make him cough. "You're a damn genius. Do you think if I could make a gun like that little beauty you brought us I'd be dragging my sorry ass up some rock on my free time? Hell no! I'd be locked in my lab with my Bunsen burners on full blast, spreading beakers and whatnot across my tables and rubbing my hands like a maniac at the thought of what kinda wild shit I was going to come up with today!"

The image Natch's little monologue brought to mind fit Bergman so well that, despite the loss of my shuffling privileges, I had to laugh.

Another hour passed. Nobody tried any weird gestures, at least none that couldn't be explained. Natch scratched his chest a couple of times. But, hey, if mine was covered with hair, I'd expect some itching too.

The most interesting thing that happened was a three-way showdown between Cole, Cam, and Natch. As the dealer, Grace had decided on Texas Hold 'Em. Only the three guys had continued to bet after looking at their first two cards. Cole let me peek at his. With a suited king, ten, I figured he was right to stay in.

Grace dealt the flop, one of which was a king. Cole bet. After chewing on his toothpick for a few seconds, Cam did too. Then he sat back against the chair behind him and said, "Natch, I think you should fold, buddy."

Natch raised his eyebrows with amusement. "Why's that?"

Cam pointed a blunt-nailed finger at his own face. "See these scars?"

Natch rolled his eyes. "Here we go."

"These scars are for you, man. I took a grenade in the face just for you. You owe me."

"I bought you dinner."

"You think a steak is going to make us even?" Despite the

heavy growth of beard I caught the hint of dimples as Cam didn't quite succeed in hiding a grin.

"I think that time I carried your lard ass on my back for ten miles after you broke your ankle does."

"That was *before* the grenade!"

"You ate a whole box of donuts the night before!"

"I want to win this pot!"

"Not if I can help it!"

And it was on.

They razzed each other until they'd each managed to bet every bit of money they'd brought. And then Cole won.

Collective groan, as if one of them had come back from the shooting range without ever having hit the target. Then they all started talking at once.

Grace and Jet: "Somebody should tell those two how much they suck at poker." "Are you kidding? Think how much we can win from them next time we sit down!"

Jet and Natchez: "You know he's going to hold that grenade thing over your head forever." "I know. I should've jumped on the damn thing when I had the chance."

Cam and Cole: "You look like such a nice guy. I should've known you were a con artist." "I'll give you ten bucks if you keep me supplied with toothpicks for the rest of this mission." "You're on!"

Bergman and me in a low, low whisper: "God, but Natch knows how to live. That's how I want to be, Jaz! He's not afraid of anything!" "He's got some admirable traits, yeah. But don't forget, he's found a lot to admire in you too."

The deep, booming sound of the door knocker shut us all up. Dave and Cassandra rushed into the room.

"Were you expecting company?" he asked me.

I couldn't resist. "No, David. All my Iranian pals are busy this week."

"Smart-ass. Cole." He jerked his head for our Farsi speaker to take the lead. "Everybody remember, we're students," he hissed, "so quit looking like badasses in costume." Almost everyone took a seat on the piece of furniture he or she had been leaning against during the card game. Dave motioned for Cassandra to join Bergman on the couch. I followed him and our interpreter to the door.

My hands itched to pull Grief from its holster. But having a gun in your hand, though it's hidden behind your back, can prevent you from playing a scene cool. I settled for resting my palms against my thighs, where the fingers of my right hand could feel the reassuring outline of my bola. Dave stayed behind with me in the entrance to the living room as Cole went down three wide wooden steps into the foyer.

With a bench to one side and a gleaming vase full of red silk flowers to the other, the room had barely been built to house one full-grown man, much less the additional couple he let into the house. Even as the gentleman caller introduced himself, the three of them trooped up the stairs to join us.

"Hello, hello, I am so very glad to meet you. I am Soheil Anvari, the caretaker of this apartment building and this is my wife, Zarsa. We saw you arrived right on schedule. The owner asked that we should stop by to make sure you were finding yourselves comfortably placed. Is everything all right, then?" Soheil beamed. A lean, mustached man of maybe forty-five, he exuded goodwill like worms crap compost. And I'd have bought it, by golly.

Except for the wife.

She went heavily veiled. Inside, where it wasn't required. It wasn't quite as bad as the old pictures of women wearing blue tents with eye slits. But she'd come damn close. And that yellowish purple hue around her right eye couldn't be the latest craze in makeup. It looked to me like Soheil had been making free with the domestic violence.

My temper's got a fuse, and Soheil had definitely started a slow burn. Slow because I knew I couldn't afford an explosion anytime in the near future. But when the moment was right . . .

I met Zarsa's eyes. The depth of misery I saw in those dark brown orbs put me in mind of burned beds and poisoned coffee. Desperate measures taken by terrified, trapped women. I wondered if Zarsa had already reached her limit. If Soheil would "accidentally" slip in the shower and break his neck in the fall before I had a chance to exact some vengeance on his wife-beating ass.

"Everything is excellent, thank you so much," said Cole.

"You are students, yes?" asked Soheil.

"Yes," Cole agreed, "here to perfect our Farsi. May I try my hand on a native speaker?"

Soheil held out his arms as if to welcome Cole to the Farsi family, and they launched into a five-minute conversation interspersed with bursts of hearty laughter. Finally Soheil said, "You will do very well, I expect. I am so happy you have chosen to study here. And in your free hours, you must visit my shop! It is just down the street." He motioned south, no doubt toward the market about six blocks away.

We'd passed it on the way in, while the stores were still shut tight, their glass and cement facades reminding me so much of home that their brightly colored banners bearing odd, squiggly writing almost startled me. It had been close enough to dawn that the street sellers were already setting up in the alleyways, heaping homegrown goodies on large round trays that sat on the boxes they'd carted them to town in. We'd seen men wearing ball caps and jeans pushing ancient wheelbarrows full of turnips to the edge of the sidewalk while women cloaked in black crouched next to crates of apples, dates, and peaches, their backs resting against stone walls painted with glyphs of blessing from the goddess Enya.

Soheil went on. "Ours is the glass-fronted store with the large yellow signs all across the top. You cannot miss it. We sell only the best in clothing and shoes. And my wife does readings in the back. She is quite popular with the students."

Here we go. Definitely time to act all interested and girly. "What kind of readings?" I asked. I went for breathless and wide-eyed and figured I succeeded when Cole smirked at me behind our visitors' backs.

"She will tell you of your future. All you need do is let her touch the palm of your hand. She can also help you recover what has been lost. Or, if you prefer, guide you toward true love."

Huh. I wondered if Zarsa belonged to Cassandra's Sisters of the Second Sight guild. I was thinking . . . not. "That sounds wonderful!"

Soheil said something to Zarsa in Farsi. Obediently, she pulled a small brown square of heavy paper embossed with gold writing out of her pocket. "In case you get lost," he explained with his charming grin. "Just show this to anyone on the street and they will direct you to our shop."

"Thank you!" I said, taking the card from Zarsa's outstretched hand. I avoided touching her. All I needed was for her to divine the real reason I'd come to Iran. Even in her present state, she'd probably still feel obliged to turn me in to the authorities. Eventually Albert might put up a tombstone for me, but my epitaph would probably read "And She Was Never Seen Again."

They left shortly after that. After a communal sigh of relief, Natch announced it had to be time for chow.

"Hey, we're pretending to be regular people, ya mook," said Cam, "and regulars don't say 'chow.'"

"They do if they're Italian," Natch replied, for which he got a punch on the shoulder, which erupted into a three-man wrestling match once Jet joined in, with Amazon Grace officiating.

She didn't have many rules. As far as I could tell the only things she wouldn't allow were eye gouging and spitting. In the end she declared herself the winner and made the men carry her to the kitchen.

Dave shook his head at his crew, but the look he gave me as he followed them out of the living room spoke volumes. *How can one of them be the enemy when it's so obvious they love each other like family? Why can't I be wrong about this whole, horrible situation?*

But he wasn't. Someone on his team had telegraphed their position to the Wizard six weeks ago, which was why his informant, the werejackal, was dead today. Dave definitely had a mole. But neither Cole nor I had picked up any signals during the game that made us suspect one man over another. All we'd done was find out how much we liked and respected all three.

Chapter Twelve

The party continued through supper, just rations we'd brought with us, and moved into the kitchen as we transported our mess back to where it had originated. The room surrounded us with a cozy, college days feel despite the white-tiled walls that tried to make it resemble an OR. The sink and appliances, all stainless steel, surrounded a tile-topped island that had been furnished with four stools. These were covered with bright yellow material that matched the cabinet doors and transformed the room from nauseating to cheerful.

Cole was hunting soap for the dishwasher, Cassandra was scraping plates, and Cam had just begun to tell the story of how Dave had led the raid that netted two of the Wizard's top men, when my ring sent a shaft of heat up my arm.

He's awake! Alive! Whatever! Okay, calm down. How old are you anyway? Geesh! I looked down at my right hand, trying to distract myself from the rush of excitement that made it hard to deny how much I'd missed my boss for the past twelve hours.

I nearly whispered the ring's name. Not because I knew it meant "Guardian." But because I loved the way the word sounded coming off my tongue. *Cirilai.* Like a long, soft kiss. And I valued both the craftsmanship and power Vayl's family had put into the gold and ruby masterpiece that protected his soul. And my life.

I used my thumb to turn the ring, watched the gems snatch the light and throw it out again, a thousand times clearer and more beautiful than it had been to begin with. I wished I could do that with my life. So much confused me lately. I rarely went through a day knowing anything for sure. Maybe I could at least discover something concrete about Cirilai. Even if Vayl couldn't—wouldn't—fully explain the relationship it symbolized.

Oh, I knew the basics. In the Vampere world we'd be considered a couple of some sort. His *sverhamin* to my *avhar.* Certain rules applied, only a few of which I knew. He had to reveal anything I wanted to know about his past. In return—well—pretty much, I had to make sure he didn't turn into a towering asshole, take over some small country, and eat his neighbors.

But deeper complexities existed within our bond that Vayl had promised to reveal over time. He said if he gave it to me in one lump my circuits would melt. I suspected if I knew the whole story I'd run to the nearest airport, crash the pilot's lounge, and promise the first uniform I met my life's savings if he'd get me out of town, like, yesterday.

And yet even if I was coward enough to run, I knew I'd return. Because something more lasting and powerful than gold and rubies connected us. Blood. Once in Florida and again in Texas Vayl had set those soft, full lips against my skin and sank his fangs into my throat. The first time I'd been offering him a chance to survive. The second he'd been giving me the ability to save countless lives. But, more than that, we'd found in those moments a bond so basic and pure that, while we silently acknowledged it, we never spoke of it. As if to do so might curse it.

Cam's story distracted me from my thoughts. "So here I am thinking this is the easiest takedown of all time, when Dave steps up to the Wizard's right-hand man to ask him a question. And this guy, JahAn, goes ballistic. Starts screaming at Dave, who's kind of smiling, playing it nice and cool. After all, what can the guy do, right? He's tied up nice and tight. But somehow his buddy, Edris, has wiggled free, and he's the one we should be worrying about. But he's staying nice and quiet in his chair. At least that's what we think."

Cam looked around the room, stretching the tension just enough to make even the guys who'd been there lean forward with anticipation. "JahAn is practically foaming at the mouth he's so pissed. Dave is asking him how long he's worked for the Wizard when Edris jumps him. Goes straight for the throat, and though we pull him off quick, there's a ton of blood under Dave's hands, which he's crossed over his larynx. Plus he's been knocked out."

Cam shook his head, his eyes dimming as he remembered their fears. "Lucky for us, he came to right away and most of the blood turned out to belong to Edris. He'd scraped his wrists raw getting free. Turned out he'd just nicked Dave with a fingernail. I've seen worse paper cuts. The actual impact caused more damage. He had a hard time talking for a couple of days after that. Most peaceful forty-eight hours I ever spent in the service," Cam said, chuckling.

The appreciative laughter trickled off quickly when Vayl entered the kitchen. I kept my seat, but I was practically the only one. As soon as he opened the fridge and pulled out a plastic bag full of blood the room cleared like an elementary school during a fire drill. Clatter of tableware. Mumbled excuses.

"Don't worry," I called after Dave's people as they ran for cover, "we'll do the dishes." Apparently Spec Ops types don't mind seeing blood coming out. Or being the cause of it. But going in? Different story altogether.

Within five minutes of Vayl's entrance, my crew and I had the place to ourselves. Even Dave had left. Feeling guilty for sitting out the card game? Maybe. *Or*, my conscience, a country-club regular with flawless makeup and 2.5 child-star wannabes goaded me, *does he just hate to be reminded of who, and how, Jessie might have been if you hadn't staked her?*

And suddenly I was back there, in the townhouse I'd shared with Matt. Barely moving. Barely breathing, three days after his death, dragging my butt to the kitchen because some ass would not stop knocking. I checked to make sure my gun's safety was engaged before flipping on the light. I threw open the door. Took a big step back.

Jessie stood on the threshold. "Let me in," she begged, looking over her shoulder as if she'd met the bogeyman and he was actually scarier than her.

"No."

"Jasmine, please. They're going to experiment on me! They're going to do tests and shoot me full of chemicals like I'm some kind of lab monkey!"

I believed every word. She'd been turned by Aidyn Strait's nest, and he loved his weird science. I said, "Jessie, go away. Don't make me keep my promise."

Her eyes flickered. Maybe the change had made her forget the vow we'd made. We had both believed that to become vampire meant one agreed to relinquish her soul. And the only way to get it back . . .

"Let me in," she commanded, holding my gaze. It might have worked before the battle. But already I had changed. The Sensitivity had kicked in and vampires could no longer hypnotize me. I aimed the modified Walther PPK Bergman had made for me at Jessie's heart. I'd already disabled the safety. Pushed the magic button. The bolt I sent into her chest flew true. I held her eyes until the very last moment, but I'll never know if I saw relief in them. Or if I was just wishing.

I looked at the gun in my hand as the smoke from my best friend, my late sister-in-law, wafted away in the cold November breeze and told it, "You give me nothing but grief."

The clack of Vayl's porcelain mug against the tile of the countertop brought me back to the present. "What are you thinking?" he asked.

I searched his face. "I'm wondering if it's always right to keep your promises."

"Yes." He said it so instantly I felt stunned, as if he'd unexpectedly thrown something and hit me with it before I could catch it.

"Aw, come on," said Cole, "not always."

"Always," Vayl insisted. "This is one of the reasons I have made you my *avhar,* Jasmine. A promise is a sacred bond, never to be breached."

"You sound like a third grader," Bergman said, adjusting his glasses as if he couldn't believe what he was seeing.

Vayl made one of those irritated noises unique only to him. Like a huff, but more masculine. "Perhaps because children know how important trust is. Only when they are repeatedly betrayed by adults do they finally give up believing they can ever find it in even a single person."

These were the times I liked Vayl best. I could've set my chin on my hands and just watched him talk for hours. Usually I didn't see squat behind that statuelike facade. The only peek I often got into the turmoil of emotion that I suspected he barely kept in check was the changing hues of his remarkable eyes. But every once in a while the mask would crack and I'd see how important he thought it was, not just to be human, but to be good. Hokey, I know, but the dude's nearly three hundred. He's allowed.

"What?" he asked me.

"I don't know. I . . . I guess I'm glad you feel that way. It makes me feel better about a promise I kept."

"Good. Now, tell me what I missed today."

Between the three of us, we filled him in. I finished with, "Something funny's going on. Think about it. Those zombie reavers didn't hurt a single one of us. All they did was get in the way of the new reavers. Is there any reason the Wizard would want to be helping us?"

"Oh, yeah," scoffed Bergman, "he's all about aiding and abetting his own assassination."

"But—"

"I believe Bergman is right, Jasmine," Vayl put in. "The Wizard wants us eliminated. End of story."

Yeah, but . . . I itched to take the picture of the Wizard Pete had given us out of the pocket of my tunic and study it for the hundredth time. Something about *it* bothered me too, but I'd never say that out loud. Dave and his team would probably get medals for discovering that priceless bit of intel along with the cell phone number whose intercept had ultimately led to this mission. As they should. So who was I to say that the man with the graying beard and wide, brown eyes who stood before a tall green door with his arms around his wife and smiling daughter reminded me more of my sweetheart of a neighbor, Mr. Rinaldi, than any of the mass murderers I'd ever encountered? I'd be the first to tell any group of innocents never to base your trust on looks. *Okay, so no dice on the Wizard.*

"Then what about the Magistrate?" I asked. "Why all that hocus-pocus with fake Matt?"

"You don't like the trapping Raoul theory?" Cassandra asked.

Not when you pair it with the weird zombie reaver theory, I thought, but since that had already been shot down I just shrugged.

"I do not see how it matters since you have found a way to protect yourself from detection," said Vayl.

Yeah, but I'm not going to be happy washing my forehead with holy water every morning while praying. I mean, God and I . . . I guess we're on decent terms. But we don't talk a lot. I'm sure every time he hears me pray he does a double take. So the morning baptisms just seem . . . hypocritical. And irritating. I'm going to need to figure this one out.

Apparently now would not be the time, though, because Vayl had other things on his mind.

"Tell me more about this Seer," he requested. So we went back over the visit from Soheil and Zarsa. This time I added my impressions while Vayl listened intently, sipping from his mug as we spoke.

"I must visit this Zarsa," he decided. "Does she speak English?"

Cole thought about it while Cassandra gave me an intent look that said I'd better be having a private chat with her soon. "She didn't while she was here," Cole finally said.

Vayl's brows lowered. You could see his desire to talk to a Seer war with his need for privacy. Desire won. "You must come with me, Cole."

My teeth tried to clench, and while I was making my jaw relax my hands curled into fists. "What am I supposed to do while you're gone?" I demanded.

He shrugged. "Clean Grief? After I return, you and I will attend to our other business." Meaning we'd scope out the café where the Wizard would, according to the late werejackal, be celebrating his birthday with several close male family members tomorrow.

Though I wanted to argue, the wild wiggling of Cassandra's eyebrows forced me to press my lips together. "Fine," I said. I couldn't help adding, "As long as you're handing out assignments, what about Cassandra and Bergman? Any interesting jobs for them to do while you're gone?"

Vayl, within minutes of exploring the depths of a new psychic's powers for news of his lost sons, remained blissfully immune to my sarcasm. "Actually, yes. I thought the idea of a shielded *other* within our midst was rather brilliant. Perhaps the two of you could work on a way to reveal that shield, or lower it, so we could at last pinpoint our partners' betrayers."

Bergman, the buttons of his bland brown shirt practically bursting from Vayl's compliment, jumped off his chair. "We'll get right on it." He was halfway out the door when he turned back to Cassandra. "Well? Are you coming?"

"Of course." She nodded at the men, gave me a get-your-ass-in-here stare, and said pointedly, "We'll be in the girls' room."

Vayl clapped Cole on the shoulder as if they were headed out for a beer. His sudden camaraderie, coming on the heels of so much suspicion and even downright jealousy, made me want to demand a DNA test. Or at least stand up and yell, "Stop acting so damn weird!"

"Ready?" Vayl asked.

"Uh, are we going to have to pay her?" Cole wondered. "Because I lost most of my money playing poker." A lie. He had, if anything, come out a couple of bucks ahead.

"Ah, yes, compensation," Vayl said. "I will be right back." He practically skipped out of the kitchen.

As soon as Cole was certain he couldn't hear us he whispered, "Vayl and cheerful do not mix. It's just creepy."

Yeah. And depressing. Because it's for the wrong reasons. I realized *I* wanted to put that dimple in his cheek. His eyes should always be hazel. I liked it when he twirled his cane like he was leading a really great band. And all that would disappear the moment Zarsa told him she couldn't See Hanzi and Badu any better than Cassandra could.

"Pay close attention to what happens in there," I told him. "There's a reason this feels wrong."

"Speaking of which, I really need to talk to you."

"Okay." I'd been expecting this. Should've sought him out sooner. Because now that the two of us were alone, he'd let his guard down. And the pain stood clear on his face. "What's up?" I asked softly.

He stepped closer. Looked deep into my eyes. Hesitated a millisecond, and then dove in. "I think I'm falling in love with you."

Oh. No.

"Cole—"

"I know how you feel. About me. About him. I just wanted you to know—we could be good together. We could have a life. Kids. Vacations. On Sunday mornings I could serve you breakfast in bed." He gave me his I-know-you-find-me-irresistible grin. "And then I could make you something to eat."

"I—"

"No. Just tell me you won't commit to him until you've considered me."

I didn't know how to answer that. Because deep down I kind of thought I already had. Plus, I understood this was so the wrong moment to yell, "I *like* you, idiot! I have, maybe, three friends in the world and you may have just messed that up for me! You're only the catch of the century. You could do us all a favor and fall for one of the hundreds of women who've lined up for you. But, no. You've got to declare for me. And now things are going to be all awkward and strained between us. You ass."

Or, even more appealing, I could just punch him in the gut and run off, cackling, into the night. However, considering his eight-year-old mentality, he'd probably take that as a sign of affection and the next thing you know we'd be engaged. I opened my mouth, hoping something intelligent would pop out, and then clicked it shut again when Vayl breezed back into the kitchen. His manner blew my worries about Cole to the back of my brain. Something about the way he glanced at and then dismissed me worked on me like a time machine, took me right back to my childhood.

I was fourteen. And I'd just been dumped by Ellis Brenner. I'd had to tear off all the covers of my notebooks so I'd no longer have to look at the elaborate drawings I'd made that variously said Jasmine Elaine Brenner, Mrs. Jasmine Brenner, and Jasmine and Ellis Brenner. I managed to keep it together until I got home from school. And then I lost it. I saw myself now as if I was my mother, standing at my bedroom door, watching teenaged me draped across the lavender bedspread in the room I shared with Evie, sobbing hysterically as I clutched Buttons the Bear to my chest.

"What's up with you?" Mom had asked, still manning her post, as if entering my room might be noted by the door generals, who could have her shot for dereliction of duty.

It took me a while to get the words out. Saying it aloud made it so real. Which made it hurt more. Which made me cry all the harder. "E-huh E-huh Ellis d-huh-dumped me!" I finally wailed. I curled into a ball with Buttons at the center, as if he'd become the wounded little girl I needed to soothe and protect. I longed for my mother's arms. Though, by now, I knew better than to expect that comfort. We didn't hug. Not even when we were delighted with each other. Which hadn't been for a very long time.

"Who's Ellis?" she asked.

That stopped me. The way sometimes an explosion will put out an oil fire. I sat up in bed. Wiped my eyes and nose on the hem of my shirt. "How could you not know? I've only been talking about him every minute of the day for the last month! He was my *boyfriend*, dammit!"

"You watch your mouth, young lady!"

"Get out of my room!" I screamed.

Rolling her eyes, she backed into the living room. "You should be onstage with those antics," she said just before I slammed the door in her face. I cried most of the rest of that night. Evie helped me through it. But I never told her the worst part of my grief was the realization that Mom really didn't give a crap about us.

Indifference. That's what she'd shown me when she'd said, "Who's Ellis?" That's what I saw on Vayl's face when it should have been clear to him that I was tied up in knots after my conversation with Cole. That I was upset about his choice to talk with Zarsa. I knew that if I stepped up to him right now and said, "Vayl, I need you. Please stay," he wouldn't. He'd let me down. Just like my mother had all my life.

Well, I'd had no choice with her. But I sure as hell wasn't going to let Vayl get away with it.

Chapter Thirteen

I really didn't think I could sink any lower than I had the day I'd motored through Corpus Christi on a 1993 moped. Apparently I'd been mistaken. "This is it," I muttered to myself as I crouched on the roof of Soheil Anvari's business, the second floor of which was his home. "I am officially a stalker."

I'd been trying to justify following Vayl to Anvari's for the past half hour. *He's treated me like crap*, I told myself. *So the second he's done with Zarsa I'm grabbing him by the short hairs and shaking till he whimpers for mercy.*

But it's tough to lie to yourself when nothing is happening to distract you from your own insanity. I'd set out behind Cole and Vayl with the idea that, once they were done with the reading, I would intercept them. Initiate a confrontation. Force Jaz-interest back into Vayl's eyes.

Now I had to admit I might just be nutty-bar jealous. Because my strongest current impulse was to drop through the ceiling and kick Zarsa in the teeth for putting that spark of hope in Vayl's heart and then leading him into her den so she could crush his hopes and dreams. What made it worse was that I could see her torturing him even now. Because these people had a skylight. It pissed me off, actually. What, did they just trundle off to the Home Depot when they discovered Zarsa didn't have enough light to break her clients' hearts by? In Tehran? Gimme a break!

He was taking it well. But he would. Vayl would hardly flinch if you filled him full of lead and accused him of kidnapping the Pope. On the other hand, Cole clearly needed a quick getaway followed by an all-nighter with a bowl full of Bubble Yum. He'd already chewed three toothpicks to shreds and was halfway through his fourth. Zarsa would run her finger along Vayl's palm, say something, and Cole would practically jump out of his chair before translating.

"Okay, I've had enough," I said for the eighth time. "I'm going in." But with what excuse? I couldn't think of one thing that wouldn't bring the full fury of a psychic-deprived vampire down on my head. I should've asked Cassandra for some ideas before I left. She certainly had good insight into his current frame of mind.

As soon Cole and Vayl had departed I'd run up to the girls' room. Cassandra had practically thrown me in a chair she was so anxious for my attention.

"Listen to me," she said. "Vayl is in danger."

I jumped up. "Is it the reavers? Did you have a vision just now?"

"No." She shoved me back down, which was when I realized how serious the situation had become. She really did know better than to push me around. "Vayl is a sober, reasonable creature except when it comes to his sons. And then he cannot be made to hear anything he doesn't want to hear. Do you understand?"

"He's obsessed?"

Cassandra knelt by my knee while Bergman sat on the bed, unpacked his tools, and pretended not to listen. Actually, I hoped he was all ears. He could be just as obtuse as Vayl at times. "Please promise me you will never repeat what I am about to say."

I thought of what Vayl had said about promises. Looked at Bergman and raised my eyebrows. He nodded. "I promise," I said.

Cassandra looked over her shoulder.

"Me too," he said.

She'd been clutching my tunic, almost begging for my word. Now that she had it, she dropped her hands to her lap and began. "Many of my Sisters have sought Vayl's sons for him over the centuries."

"So he wasn't exaggerating?" I asked. "They really have been reincarnated?"

"Yes. Some of us have seen the possibility of the three men meeting, but always our visions end in disaster. Vayl is not ready to reunite with his sons. He has let their deaths immobilize him in some vital way. Until that changes, any encounter between them will lead to all of their deaths."

"Holy crap." I knew one thing. Even if everything turned out great, if Vayl transformed his whole world and pulled off a happily-ever-after, this was one particular promise I'd be taking to my grave.

Now I watched Zarsa murmur something that made Cole squirm in his chair as Vayl nodded eagerly. "What if she tells him?" I asked myself for the fifteenth time. "Naw." Cassandra had already made it clear how particular Seers were when it came to moral issues. Cross the line and you can forget ever working in the field again. Nope, Zarsa would be breaking Vayl's heart any . . . minute . . . now.

He got up. Gave her some money and that half smile that drives me wild when I let it. Walked out the door. Whistling.

Oh. Shit.

My first instinct was to rush back to the house. Dive right into damage control. Then I remembered Vayl telling me another Seer had predicted he'd meet his sons in America. That's why he'd emigrated from Romania, or wherever he'd been living at the time. I wasn't actually sure. Anyway, he certainly wasn't going to be joining them until we'd finished this mission, so I had some time. And I really needed to use it to calm down.

Because I kinda wanted to kill him.

Never mind the fact that he should be . . . we should be . . . well, it's about time for fireworks between us and he's taken off with the lighter. Not to mention we're planning a major hit in enemy territory and his first choice is to go trotting off to visit a psychic! I fumed. *How stupid is that?*

Not stupid. Desperate. After all this time, he's still a grief-stricken father. Really, what would you do if you thought you could be with Matt again?

But that's just it. I can't. I accept that now. We had our time. And it was glorious.

But if he came back today?

My mind wouldn't go there. But Vayl's had, almost right away. So I had to wonder, for his sake, what do you do when it's over before you're ready for it to be over? Do you chase that relationship, that role you assumed, for the rest of your existence? Was Vayl looking for his sons because he couldn't give up fatherhood? Because it made him the person he wanted most to be?

I had asked him about Hanzi and Badu once. "So you want to meet them? Make friends? Be . . . a father to them?"

"I *am* their father!" he'd snapped. "That is the one, incontrovertible truth of my existence."

If so, what did that mean for us? Somehow I knew other women before me had stood in the dust of his wake as wagon, horse, stagecoach, and train bore him away on yet another wild chase for his boys.

"No," I murmured. "Not me. I'm not losing another one." I barely heard myself as I descended from the roof. On such a badly lit street, it was easy to keep to the shadows, avoid detection, as I shadowed him.

Which was why I sensed the reaver long before he could get a bead on me.

Something at the entrance to my sinuses went, "Holy crap, that's just disgusting!" Though it wasn't as much an odor as an awareness that something monstrous had entered the neighborhood. I peered over my shoulder. There, unmistakable, that black outline. He loped down the narrow street behind me, one hand flopping at his waist as if he'd been running for miles. The other held a cell phone to his ear. Every few seconds the flop hand reached up and swatted at something that seemed to buzz around his head. I eased into the gap between a hand-lettered sign that had been tied to a storefront and the smooth, weathered stone of the building itself. I figured to let him go. He couldn't nail me now that I was protected. And I couldn't risk the mission by outing myself, even if it was to rid the world of a soul-stealing monster. Maybe after we were done I could come back. Do some cleanup.

I'd just begun working out the logistics in my mind when the reaver passed me. "I'm telling you, Samos," he growled into the phone, "we followed her to this area and then she just disappeared." Up went the flop hand. Swat, swat, though no bugs had bothered me the whole time I'd been outside. "We thought we could catch her using this one body, but it's going to take some time to find her now. We need more." He jerked his eyes left, right, left again. "Shut up," he growled, as if to invisible listeners. "I'm telling him, aren't I?" Either the guy had multiple personality disorder, or . . .

I slipped out of my hiding place, following him as stealthily as I could. Though he was so distracted by his phone call and the need to flail every few seconds I don't think he'd have seen me if I'd walked past him naked.

"I don't care what you have to do!" the reaver snapped. "You're the Sponsor and we need bodies. This form was not made to hold six reavers at once. Its brain is shorting out. You wouldn't believe what it's starting to see!" He listened for a few more seconds. "You're the one who's lost an *avhar*," he finally hissed. "If you want your revenge on the Lucille, you're going to have to do better than that!"

My hands itched to grab that phone. God, if only I was free to follow this lead! I might be able to pin down Samos's location from the signal.

"Channel Fourteen?" said the reaver, "Yes, this body is familiar with it." He listened intently, and from the way his shoulders relaxed, liked what he heard. "You're sure they'll be receptive?" Short pause, shorter nod. "Excellent. I'll contact you when it's done." He ended the call, pocketed the phone, batted at his unseen pests, and changed course.

I stood in the shadows, debating. Maybe it would be better to take him out after all. Right now he seemed to be in a weakened condition. If I waited until later, he'd have infested five more bodies, and it was hard enough to kill one of them.

Okay, not so tough when you have Dave's kick-ass colleagues in tow. But I doubt we'll be able to sail through Tehran with our Manxes on display when we finally have time for a reaver hunt. Plus, there's the phone to consider. No. I've got to do this now.

I reached underneath the shapeless black manteau I'd thrown over my inside clothes. Began to slide my bolo from the pocket of my sky-blue pants as I stepped into the street. I stopped immediately, my forward progress suddenly blocked by a broad-shouldered, white-bearded man dressed in a black pullover with elaborate embroidery around its V-neck, matching black pants, and sandals. It was the words he said as much as his imposing physical presence that shut me down.

"Please do not kill the reaver tonight, Jasmine." He pronounced my name Yaz-mee-na, just like Vayl does. "The mahghul may not have come for you, but they will take you if you spill blood in this place this evening." His gesture invited me to scan the rooftops, but I took a good look at him instead.

He towered over me, his royal-blue turban probably putting him close to six and a half feet tall. His droopy eyes and long nose gave him a despondent air. Kinda like a Persian Eeyore.

"How do you know me?" I demanded, glancing in the direction he'd pointed. Even with my night vision activated I couldn't see anything moving above us.

"This is my home. It is my business to know who comes and goes here."

"Actually, in this case, no. It's not."

When he smiled his whole face joined in, from the crinkles in his forehead to the curls in his beard. He held out his hand. "My name is Asha Vasta."

I declined to shake. "How do you know about reavers?"

I found his sigh eerily familiar. It so closely echoed the one Vayl put to use after I'd lost my temper. Usually it was followed by words like "How can you stare through the scope of a rifle for three hours without saying a word and yet, as soon as you hit traffic, begin yelling? Like that. Can you be sure that man is an idiot? Maybe he has low blood sugar. And that woman you just compared to a female dog. Perhaps she just learned her husband is in the hospital and she is rushing to be with him."

I'm sure the cosmos has a greater purpose for surrounding me with patient people. But mostly it just makes me want to scream. Like now, while I waited for Asha Vasta to get the lead out and make with the explanations. While he pondered his reply I took another look upstairs, past the drab, window-filled walls of an old apartment building. There. A blur of movement out of the corner of my eye, but nothing more concrete. "I've never heard of the mahghul," I said.

"I am not surprised. Though quite ancient, they have been confined by their creator to this land alone." I thought he was going to go into more detail about the mahghuls' maker, but he just shook his head sadly. "I am afraid they have found abundant fodder from which to feed and have, therefore, thrived when otherwise they might have perished."

"So what are they?"

"They are parasitic fiends, seen by humans only when their blood has run. They can smell a murder coming days, sometimes even weeks, before it occurs. They flock to the rooftops, waiting, watching. But more than that. Making the husband think, *My wife has looked at another man*. Making the business partner suspect, *The books are unbalanced because I am being cheated*. Making the daughter believe, *There will never be an end to my misery. I might as well die*."

"You can't seriously be telling me some sort of otherworldly ambulance chaser makes people kill each other. Or themselves. Whatever happened to freedom of choice?"

"Certainly their suggestions would never work if people's minds were not already open. If they were not already willing to listen." Asha shook his head. "You would not believe how many are."

I glared up into the darkness. "Why can't I see them?" *After all, I'm not quite human anymore*. And then, to soothe the savage tear that thought put in my heart, *at least in the ways that don't matter*.

"It is easier if you know their favorite roosting spots. There. Right at the corner of that roof, where it juts out slightly. Do you see?"

I couldn't have without the extra visual acuity I'd gained by donating blood, and gaining power, from Vayl. And even then I got more of an impression than an actual photo image. Cat size. Bat wings. Alarming foot speed, aided by four muscular legs accentuated by impressive talons.

"What are those spikes beneath their eyes?" I asked.

"Their most terrifying aspect. In the moments of murder, the mahghul drive the spikes into the brains of both the victim and the murderer, and through them feed off the fury, the terror, all strong emotions such violence invokes. They leave no memory of their own attack. And so they can follow a murderer for years before the authorities put an end to their frenzy."

"How do you fight them?"

"With you it is always the fight, is it not?"

"How—"

He held up a finger, signaling he hadn't finished his thought. "Sometimes the best way to win a brawl is never to begin it in the first place."

"Yeah, sure," I said. "People are so good at that."

"I can see why Raoul chose you."

I took a step back. "You know Raoul?" I grabbed his shirt and yanked him into the recessed doorway of the nearest store, a bakery that looked like it had been plucked out of the thirties, with bare bulbs hanging from the ceiling and day-old breads displayed in the dusty window. Within seconds I'd pulled my bola and stuck the tip of the blade to the base of his throat. "You're working for the Magistrate, aren't you? What's your plan, huh? Do you really think Raoul gives a shit whether or not one of his peons bites the bullet? He's got thousands like me." Well, at least one that I knew of.

Asha's eyes, colored a sickly green by my night vision, rounded with alarm. "The mahghul," he whispered. The flap of wings, the scratch of claws on concrete, confirmed his warning. "Jasmine, do not bring this plague upon yourself."

"What makes you think you'll be spared?"

"I am Amanha Szeya."

"What's that mean?"

"They sucked me dry long ago."

Chapter Fourteen

I guess Asha and I stood in that darkened doorway another minute before I sheathed my knife and the mahghul retreated. He hadn't tried to fight. That counted in his favor. So did the long-suffering expression on his face. Mostly, though, it was the thunderous voice in my ears, Raoul's, shouting, "BACK OFF!" Okay, so I'd pulled a knife on one of the good guys. Did he have to yell?

"Sorry," I muttered. "I've never drawn on an innocent before."

Asha's lips drooped into a sad smile. "I cannot remember a time when I was pure. But thank you."

I rubbed my eyes. Looked to the rooftops and realized the mahghul weren't just moving. They were gathering. "Hey. That's Soheil Anvari's building."

"Yes."

"I knew it! The minute I saw her face. She's going to kill him out of self-defense, isn't she? Or is he going to beat her to death? Either way, isn't there something we can do?"

When Asha didn't immediately answer, I looked him in the eye. He seemed . . . confused. "You are talking about Zarsa and Soheil, are you not?" he asked slowly.

"Yeah."

"They are very happily married. Deeply in love, in fact, with four wonderful children. Neither would dream of lifting a hand against the other."

"But I saw her tonight. She was veiled, but I still caught the black eye."

"Oh, that." Asha chuckled. "Yes, she was sitting on the floor with her youngest son on her lap, reading a book to him. When she turned the page the picture frightened him. He sat back quickly, knocking his head into her eye. She did not want people to think Soheil had done such a thing, so she went veiled."

"But, Asha, she *was* miserable. You can't fake that."

"Yes, something has happened to change her. Something vile and traumatic. The mahghul have sensed it. I fear she will take her own life."

I leaned against the glass of the storefront and thought, *Wrong again, Jaz. Grace wasn't the mole. Asha wasn't a bad guy. And Soheil wasn't beating Zarsa. Hey, what do you say we go for four out of four and just assume this whitewash on your demon Mark is going to work forever and ever, amen?*

"Why does Zarsa matter so much?" I asked.

"The future she chooses could change the course of this country."

Oh, is that all? "Do you want me to go talk to her?"

He regarded me with those basset hound eyes. "I think, perhaps, it would be more helpful if you spoke to Vayl."

Where have you been?" Vayl wasn't angry. I could tell by the gleam in his eye. The twitch in his lip. Any other man would've danced me across the floor when I walked through the door.

"Scoping out the neighborhood," I told him. "I didn't feel comfortable not knowing how to get in and out of here." I hated lying to him so much that I promised myself I'd do some actual scouting the minute I had time.

"We must talk." He led me to the sofa.

"Where is everybody?" I asked.

"Cassandra and Bergman are in the kitchen, working on the project I gave them. Cole went with David and his team to scout the Hotel Sraosa in case they need an interpreter. Do not worry, we can talk freely. Bergman has carded the entire house."

"Did he find any more bugs?"

"No." Vayl brushed off my question as if it was inconsequential and gestured for me to sit down. "I have exciting news," he said as he joined me.

"You do?"

He draped one arm over the back of the couch and folded his left leg so he could sit comfortably sideways, facing me. I'd never seen him looking so . . . casual. It gave me the willies.

"Zarsa says my sons are here. In Tehran!"

"She . . . she does? But I thought you were supposed to meet them in America."

"So did I. And she says they spent time in America. But they are here and she told me she could take me to them!"

"When?"

"After I bring her over."

I felt like someone had cut open my chest and poured ice water directly onto my heart. "She . . . wants to become a vampire?"

"Yes."

Cirilai began to burn on my hand. But I didn't need the ring to warn me how close Vayl stood to disaster. And how none of us who cared for him could avoid the fallout if this backfired.

"How long does something like that take?" I asked.

"The longer the better. Ideally it takes a year. But with the proper preparations we can do it in a week."

"Have you already, you know, taken her blood?"

"No, not yet."

"Ah."

Vayl suddenly seemed to focus. "You do not seem pleased. I thought you would be happy for me."

"Well, sure. I mean, finding your boys is vital to you. And I want that for you. When nobody has to get hurt in the process."

"I will not hurt her."

"Do you mean before or after you kill her?"

"She has asked for this!" he thundered.

Another sure sign Vayl had gone over the edge. He so rarely raised his voice that when he did I jumped in my seat. Now doubly pissed, I didn't bother to keep the irritation out of my voice when I asked, "Since when does a Seer require such a massive payment for such a small service?"

Vayl jumped to his feet. "This meeting means everything to me!"

I stood too, wishing I was taller so I could go nose to nose with him. "Which is exactly why you're completely off square! Don't you think if your boys were in Iran Cassandra would've told you?"

"Cassandra is useless! Look at her! She cannot even find the mole!"

Complete silence as we both realized she must have heard us. Vayl stalked out of the house, slamming the door so hard behind him the panes in the side panels broke. The crash of glass brought Bergman to the doorway.

"I'll get a broom," he said, heading back into the kitchen.

"Leave it," I called. "He broke it. He can damn well clean it up." I trudged after him, thinking, *That went so well, I should become a diplomat. Then they could assign me to some political hotbed like, oh, I don't know, Iran, and hey, maybe I could get the whole world blown up!*

"I'm not going to make any excuses for him," I said as I walked into the room and caught Cassandra dabbing tears from her eyes with a cloth napkin. "That sucked what he said about you." I caught her gaze. "Grief can make you crazy, you know?"

She nodded and gave me a crooked smile.

I sat on a stool. It creaked as my butt came down on it. If anything, I'd lost weight in the past few weeks. I kept forgetting to do lunch. But it reminded me of how I'd missed my morning run, and would continue to until we left the country. How the hell did women stay in shape around here?

For a while I just stared at my hands, clasped in front of me as if they alone were praying for an answer.

"Have you ever seen Vayl like this before?" Bergman finally asked me.

I shook my head. "But I haven't even known him a year. In vampire time that's like a couple of seconds." I watched Cassandra absently stroke the Enkyklios. I asked her, "When a person goes to a Seer with a request like Vayl's, what's the typical payment?"

"It depends. For the Sisters in my Guild, we request only a contribution to the Enkyklios."

"You mean, a story."

"Well, not just any story. One that would add to the knowledge of our world and the creatures that inhabit it."

"So most of your Sisters have day jobs?"

"Yes. We have found, over time, that to use the Sight for personal gain is a good way to lose it. So we must be careful who benefits from our visions and why."

"Did you hear what Zarsa wants in return for her visions?" Cassandra and Bergman both nodded. "So what do you make of that? Is she even the real deal?"

Cassandra shrugged. "I can't say without touching her. And since I met David, that probably won't work."

I decided to change the subject. "I met a man tonight. Okay, not a man. Something *other* that snuck right up on me. His name is Asha Vasta and he says he's Amanha Szeya. He knew my name and Vayl's, and he knew about Raoul. Frankly, the only reason I let him go was he promised me we'd meet again." I sighed. "He's obsessed with Zarsa and I'm not going to be able to let this thing with Vayl go. So we'll probably be falling over each other in the dark for the next few days while we try to figure out how to stop their idiot plan."

I felt a sudden, unreasonable surge of anger at my father. It was his fault I'd been given this damned assignment. If not for him, I'd never have known I was capable of stalking my *sverhamin*. *Rein it in, there, Crazy Horse. It's not really stalking. It's more just following him to make sure he doesn't cause himself or anyone else—me, for instance—permanent damage.*

Are you sure? The inner bitch was at it again, demanding the full truth whether I wanted to face it or not. She leaned over the bar, showing so much cleavage you could've planted a shrub down there, and said, *Admit it, toots. The thought of him sinking those lovely fangs into her neck, resting his lips against her velvet skin, drives you nuts. And the idea that he would turn her, link her to him for all time, makes you want to scream. That's a permanent blood bond, baby. All you've got is a measly little ring and the blood equivalent of a couple of one-night stands.*

"Anyway," I said quickly, "do me a favor and find out what Amanha Szeya is. I've gotta go find (*not stalk!*) Vayl."

Chapter Fifteen

In another life, in another world even, Vayl would've been a spectacular teacher. It's not enough for him to *know*. The longer we're together, the more I realize he can't help himself. He's got to share what he's learned. And since I'm usually the only one around, I'm generally the beneficiary, like it or not.

Often it's been not.

There was the time he decided my table manners lacked a certain, shall we say, appetizing flare.

"Did you just burp?" he asked me one evening as we sat at a table covered in white linen and real silver.

"Excuse me," I said. "Wine gives me gas. Plus it tastes like road kill. Don't they serve any beer here? There's the waiter. I'll ask him."

"No! Jasmine . . ." Vayl caught the hand I'd raised and lowered it quickly to the table. "Obviously we need to talk."

Thus began an intense month of table etiquette lessons and, right along with them, my growing loathing of eating in restaurants. Thanks to Vayl I can fake my way through a seven-course meal alongside an army of French food critics without raising a single suspicion that I can't wait to run home, throw a burrito in the microwave, stuff it down my throat, and fart my way through an episode of *South Park*.

My latest, and by far most appreciated bout of training, had involved a much more valuable skill. From the start, Vayl believed my Sensitivity would allow me to find and follow vampires. On our last mission he'd proved himself right. I could track reavers too. Presumably, as I developed my abilities, I'd be able to sense and find even more *others*. That's what I hoped, anyway.

I don't think he ever believed I'd use my ability on him, at least not in this way. But here I was, stalking (no, no, sneaking—like they taught us to do in spy school) down the streets of Tehran, chasing his scent and hoping it wouldn't lead me to Zarsa.

It didn't.

It meandered around for a while, turning back on itself once or twice, making me think he had no particular destination in mind. He was just trying to walk off some steam. I got a great tour of the city, which included some lovely frescoes, a major boulevard that reminded me of downtown Chicago, and a building so ancient I could actually feel the history radiating off its arched doorways and crumbling columns. At last Vayl's path straightened, headed north.

Our safe house sat on the southwest edge of the city. The longer I followed Vayl's trail, the more convinced I became that he was traveling toward the café where he and I were supposed to complete our mission the following evening.

"How nice of you to join me," breathed a voice from behind me.

I whirled. "Vayl! How—"

He regarded me with narrowed eyes as he leaned both hands on his cane. "You are *mine*, Jasmine. When I wish to know where you are, I have only to open my mind."

After an oh-shit-what-have-I-done moment, I managed to pull myself together. "Yeah, about that. I've agreed to look out for your soul, not sit in your closet between your Armani suit and your Gucci shoes. So stop acting all proprietary there, Ricky." As a fan of the *I Love Lucy* show, he should get the reference.

He put the heel of one hand to his forehead. "I did not mean it that way. Ach, this would be so much easier if you had lived even a hundred years ago. Now everything that comes out of my mouth can be construed as an insult, when I only intend . . ." He shook his head. "I fear there is no way to explain without further offending you." He turned away, whipping his cane forward every other step like he was striking at ghosts from his past. I walked after him. The silence spun between us like some sticky web neither of us wanted to touch. But I wanted to look at it even less.

I held my watch out in front of him.

"What?" he asked gruffly.

I pointed to the dial. "Pick a time," I said.

"Why?"

"Come on, play along."

Long-suffering sigh. "All right. Midnight."

I looked at the watch. "Okay, it's about eight thirty now. So you can say anything you want to me for the next three and a half hours and I promise not to get angry about it."

"You do?"

"Hey, quit sounding so cynical. You know I always keep my promises."

"All right, then. You have lovely hair. Red is my favorite color, so I hope you never dye it again, though I know you will."

"Vayl! That's not what I meant!"

"Are you angry?"

"No!"

"You sound angry."

"No. I'm just . . ." *reeling from a sudden desire to lay a big fat kiss on those luscious lips of yours. When I'm supposed to be pissed. Because you've been rejecting me like one of those damn bill-changing machines. Too many bent corners and wrinkles that I just can't iron smooth. Maybe if I died. Yeah, then you'd definitely chase me all over the freaking countryside. Okay, Jaz. Stop thinking. Because you're starting to sound really. Really. Whacked.* "Tell me what you meant before," I said a little desperately.

He shrugged. "It is hard to explain when you have never lived in the world of Vampere, or even in a time when it was all right for people to belong to each other."

"Try me."

"An *avhar* is an extension of her *sverhamin*. Not a possession, but a beloved . . ." He paused, pressed his lips together as if he'd like to take that last word back. He shook his head. "If you cannot understand how dear you are to me by now. How high I hold you in my esteem. How deeply I depend on your insight, your wit, your temper, your *humanity*" — his eyes glittered in the moonlight — "we might as well call this whole relationship off."

We'd stopped in a residential area. The houses peeked at us over their walls like curious little brothers. I wished I could tap them on the shoulder, ask them if they'd just heard Vayl pour on the praise. It was so out of character, I really felt I needed third-party confirmation.

"So, I'm kind of leading a double life," I said. "The CIA pays me to be your assistant. But as your *avhar* —"

"You are my partner. My companion. My . . ." He exhaled, letting the last word die on the breeze of his breath. And I wanted too badly for it to sound like "love" to trust my ears when they told me I was right.

"Cool," I whispered, allowing myself a moment's relief. The break I feared hadn't yet begun. He still cared.

We began walking again. For a few minutes neither one of us spoke. We became just another couple out for an evening's stroll. In one way we could've been ambling down any city street in America. The road to our right was wide and well-paved, lined with lovely green oak trees. The buildings to our left looked to have been built in the seventies of light brown brick. But the streetlights betrayed our location. Most of the cars looked like they'd become classics a decade ago, and while the men who crowded past us wore typical Western clothes, the women—well, they reminded me of really depressed ghosts.

Even that wouldn't have bothered me. I figured, if they wanted to slip tents over their heads every time they went outdoors, that was their right. But I wished they'd have chosen more vivid colors for the chadors that hid the clothing that would've betrayed their real personalities. I wanted to see cloaks in hues like those reflected on the signs above the businesses we passed. Vivid blues, greens, and yellows that grabbed you by the cheeks and shook, like a fat old aunt who hasn't seen you in years.

What did shake me was the furtive sense of mistrust I felt coming off the people we passed. Not just for us, though we obviously didn't belong. But for the police, present in surprising numbers on street corners and patrolling on motorcycles. And for one another, as if at any moment someone meant to yank an Uzi out of his backpack and mow down everyone else. It felt as if all the pedestrians had been apprised of the plan and all that remained was for them to get a glimpse of the gun and duck.

I turned to Vayl, trying to form my impressions into words. They shattered when he murmured, "I wonder if my sons are students here."

Geez, Vayl, why don't you just slam me on the back of the head with a garbage can? That way I can have the worst mood swing ever. I mean, we can move me from feeling terrific about my job performance and my relationship with you, not to mention being überthankful that I was born an American, to wanting to gouge my eyes out with a couple of grapefruit spoons in, like, two seconds!

I didn't say a word. I figured he'd already broken glass over my comments earlier this evening. The next step was probably my neck. But apparently he didn't mind an unresponsive audience, because he charged on. "That would be ironic, would it not? Our cover being their actual purpose for traveling to Tehran? I wonder, as well, if I will recognize them. You know, if something in their eyes will remind me . . ." He trailed off, his voice husky with emotion.

I wasn't sure how Zarsa could bring herself to commit such an atrocious act on someone, but I did know I'd never been so pissed in all my life. She'd taken a magnificent creature like Vayl, a vampire who inspired fear and loathing in every corner of criminal society, narrowed in on his single vulnerability, and stabbed.

Well, she hasn't gotten away with it yet, I told myself. *And if she thinks she's going to take advantage of my* sverhamin, *she can just see how much she likes eating supper out of a straw for the next six weeks.*

I was half inclined to march right back to Anvari's and beat the hell out of her right then and there. The mahghul wouldn't mind, as long as I left her alive. Then I saw them. Just blurs at first, out of the corner of my eye.

"Vayl." I pointed to the nearest rooftop. "Do you see those?"

"Yes, I do," he said. "What are they?"

Time for another lie, because I sure couldn't tell him I'd met somebody who'd filled me in on the backstory while I was spying on him. "I don't know. Let's follow them and see where they're going."

He might not have agreed, except they were moving in our general direction anyway. The farther we walked, the more we saw, as if an army was gathered somewhere near the heart of the city. At last we came to an enormous plaza. When it was empty, I supposed it stretched the equivalent of three or four blocks, an expanse of gleaming white concrete set in a complicated cylindrical pattern, echoing the rugs the country was famous for. Benches and streetlights marked the edges of the plaza, which abutted high-rise office buildings on three sides that glared down at a collection of restaurants and luxury-item merchants on the other.

A one-way street circled the plaza, giving cars a way to enter and exit the area, but it had been cordoned off for the safety of the two thousand or so men and women who'd congregated there. For what purpose I couldn't quite guess. They didn't broadcast the upbeat excitement of a party crowd. They didn't seem to be in religious mode. I'd place the vibe closer to lynch mob. Which explained the mahghul. And the absence of children. And—*oh shit, we are so in the wrong place at the wrong time*—the gallows.

It stood at one end of the plaza, a long, flat stage like the mobile judges' stands small towns erect for their parades. Of course there were a few additions you'd never see in Mayberry, including a sturdy crosspiece from which hung two nooses, a couple of trapdoors, as well as an open space under the stage so the audience could see the bodies fall.

I stuck my left hand in my pocket, closed my fist around my engagement ring, glad to have something of Matt's I could touch. I carry another, less tangible token of his love with me wherever I go as well. But the ring gave me the solid comfort I needed just now. And as I clutched at that collection of gold and jewels, what I remembered was not the day Matt had given it to me, but the day he'd told me about his first job.

We were sitting on the front porch of a plantation house we'd just cleared of predatory vampires and their human guardians, trying to blow the stench of death out of our nostrils as we cleaned our weapons. Our crew of Helsingers, newly formed and just beginning to gel, was scattered among white wicker chairs and matching porch swings. Ten ass-kicking twenty-somethings (with the exception of our two loyal vamps) who'd just given the government their money's worth.

"I gotta tell you, Jaz," said Matt as he wiped down his shiny black crossbow. "I had my doubts about your ability to lead a crew like this when I first saw you. Do you fool a lot of people with that sweet little redhead act?"

"Only till she opens her mouth," said Dave from his perch on the railing.

Appreciative laughter, even from me. I sat back in my chair and slid my gun into its holster. "So what branch of the military were you in?" I asked Matt.

"Is it that obvious?"

I shrugged. "I wasn't trying to insult you. I can tell good training when I see it."

"I was a SEAL."

"Why in God's name would you put yourself through that?" asked Jessie Diskov, who, like me, had come to this job pretty much straight from college. She sat close enough to Dave that, if he concentrated any less on his task and any more on her lovely indigo eyes, he might just end up shooting himself in the leg.

"My mom and dad asked me the very same thing when I gave them the good news," Matt said. "You want to know what I told them?"

I sure did. And when Jessie didn't immediately reply, I thought I was going to have to reveal my more-than-professional interest in the broad-chested young stud with the wicked smile, stellar ass, and bedroom eyes. Finally Jessie decided the vanes on her bolts were all in good enough condition to warrant a division of attention. "Yeah," she said. "I do."

Matt glanced at me, smiling a little to see he had my attention, before he replied. "I just said, 'Some people gotta fight for what's right. Even when most everybody else thinks it's wrong.'"

Matt would never have allowed that scaffold to stand in *his* country, that was for sure. But this one seemed to have bred all their Matts right out of the population. Or maybe killed them off in previous wars. Because no one protested when a dozen brown-uniformed men climbed the stairs to the stage, escorting the condemned, who were chained hand and foot.

Vayl and I exchanged a look. Knowing I wanted to speak he leaned in close, so no one who stood near the back of the crowd with us could overhear. "Women?" I hissed, clenching my teeth to keep from screaming. "They're hanging women in the public square?"

Vayl shot me his give-me-a-break look. "Come now, Jasmine. You, of all people, should know that women are capable of some of the most heinous acts imaginable."

So true. I struggled to control my temper. I'd jumped to conclusions, just because I'd identified with them. Major mistake and one that might, at some point, get me killed. I didn't even know what they'd done. Maybe they'd killed their kids. In which case, they did deserve to die.

The younger one had begun to cry. The older woman was comforting her.

An officer with so many medals pinned to his chest, if he jumped in a pond he'd probably sink right to the bottom, stepped to the front of the stage and read a proclamation. The crowd reacted with angry murmurs that escalated to shouted demands. I wished Cole was around. I wanted to know the details. Especially when the older prisoner started shouting back.

The uniform standing closest to her slammed her so hard on the side of the head that she slumped to the ground. Cheers from the crowd. The younger woman tried to go to her but was forcibly restrained.

All of this visibly excited the mahghul, which covered every rooftop, signpost and power line around the square. They stood shoulder to shoulder, bouncing up and down on their muscular legs, craning their necks, stretching those long wings with a whispering sort of rasp I couldn't believe no one else heard.

The uniforms approached the younger woman guardedly, as if she might tear through her bonds and jump into the crowd. She stood absolutely still, and I thought she was going to take it lying down. But just before they pulled the hood over her face, she shouted a name.

"Who's FarjAd Daei?" I asked.

"I have never heard of him," said Vayl, who kept up with world movers and shakers even better than I did. The crowd sure had. Many of the men took the time to spit beside their shoes when they heard his name. But a few made a gesture so casual I wouldn't have noticed if one man, about my age, hadn't caught my attention. He drew the thumb of his right hand across his thigh, then turned his hand, palm outward, toward the doomed woman. When he caught me staring he nodded once and mouthed the word "Freedom." I raised my eyebrows at him and he nodded again before melting into the crowd.

The young woman went through the trapdoor with a mahghul draped over her head like a second scarf. Already its comrades had begun to feed off the uniformed men, some of whom watched her body swing while others stared off into the crowd as if this execution had as little to do with their lives as a classic-car auction.

When the second woman dropped, her chador came off. She'd pinned a picture to the white dress she wore underneath. I couldn't see the details, couldn't read the bold black captions above and beneath the photo, which covered her entire chest. But those in the crowd who stood closest to her shouted in outrage.

The crowd surged forward, their screams encouraging those behind them to join in, and within seconds the bodies disappeared beneath their tearing hands.

"Time to leave," Vayl murmured. I could feel his power rising to shield us from watching eyes as he took me by the arm and steered me out of the plaza.

Behind us the rest of the mahghul had joined their brethren, sweeping down on the rioters, shrieking joyfully as they fed on the violence.

Vayl and I didn't speak as we rushed away from the scene. Within five minutes we arrived at our destination. As soon as we saw the place we reached an unspoken agreement to put the nightmare of the plaza behind us, at least temporarily. Duty called. As usual, it surprised me.

I'd expected the Oasis to present me with a dimly lit throwback to the 1860s. A MEN ONLY sign on the front door. Cigar smoke so thick you'd have lung cancer by the time you sat down. Dancing girls entertaining the high rollers in the back room.

What I found was a thirty-year-old, white-block two-story building housing an Internet café, with single booths stationed around the perimeter of the room, each holding a PC, most with an avid user glued to the blocky, fifteen-inch monitors. In the middle, tables with red-cushioned chairs invited customers to sit and chat face-to-face, rather than online. Either way, it made no sense to me.

Why would the Wizard, a guy who'd sent a letter to the BBC stating that "America is the infant England should have aborted," agree to party in a café surrounded by reminders of the very country he despised? Okay, so it's the World Wide Web. The whole concept of freedom of information is so American it practically square dances.

We sat down. Since the place had signs in both Farsi and English, we felt free to reveal our foreign natures. At least to some degree. Vayl lapsed into his accent to order us both tea. And when the waiter inquired as to our countries of origin, Vayl told him we were from Romania, attending a family funeral. I didn't speak at all until the waiter left.

"Nosy, isn't he?" I whispered.

Vayl's eyes followed the waiter as he cleared a table across the room. "He could be freelancing for the government. You never know."

Too true. "Listen, do you really think we've got the right location?" I shared my doubts.

"Perhaps that is why he has never been caught," my boss replied. "By maintaining continual unpredictability he has evaded the authorities for nearly twenty-five years."

"I guess," I said. I badly wanted to study the photograph Dave had given us again. Ask it questions neither one of us could answer.

Vayl nodded his head behind me. "This is a modern building. They actually have public restrooms. Given the rate at which tea passes through the system, I would say our best shot at the Wizard will be any one of the three to five times he goes to the bathroom during his visit here."

"So you want to set up in there?"

Vayl stood. "I will go check it out." I watched him leave, wishing oddly that I could stop him. *We shouldn't be here*, I thought, sitting back and casting my eyes casually around the room, hunting for the source of my unease. As usual, I couldn't match it with a familiar face or a psychic scent. Couples, most of them under thirty, sat chatting and laughing over bowls of thick soup and plates whose predominant ingredient seemed to be long-grained rice. No threat there. So what the hell?

It's this whole damn mission. Everything about it's got me flinching at shadows. Or maybe it was my double trip to hell that had done it. Either way, I wanted badly to click my heels together three times because, by God, there really was no place like home.

Vayl returned in a reasonable amount of time. "There is a window big enough to crawl through if it comes to that. We are—how do you say—set."

I smiled thinly as the waiter brought our tea. Vayl began to talk, or rather gush, about Zarsa. And I meant to listen, honest I did. But Raoul chose that moment to drop in. His way of grabbing my attention is to reach into my brain and squeeze until either I tune in or black out. It had taken a while, but I'd finally learned to listen.

"Let me guess," I said in the mental drawl I reserved only for him, "you were the fifth of eight children and your mother had you all very close together. Am I right?"

CLOSE ENOUGH.

Figures. "You probably shouldn't even be talking to me." I told him about my return trip to hell and gave him my fake Matt theory. When he didn't immediately reply I said, "So, what do you think? Is he gunning for you?"

MAYBE. And that's really as specific as Raoul would probably get at this distance. It wasn't the ideal way to communicate, but hey, considering we were operating on entirely different planes, I probably came off sounding like a talking mosquito to him.

"Actually, I have a great number of preparations to make this evening," said Vayl as I snapped back to my reality. Which currently sucked.

"You do?"

"If I am to turn Zarsa without injuring her, I must make sure everything is in order."

Okay, this is the point where a reasonable (sane?) person would back off. Because clearly this train was headed straight over the cliff and there wasn't a damn thing I could do to stop it. Still. I raised my hands to the table. Was not even slightly surprised to see both of them curled into fists.

"What exactly do you mean by 'in order'?" I inquired acidly. "Are you doing an HIV test on her before you dig in? Having her line up a nanny in case you goof and leave her children motherless? Is there a liability-free form her hubby has to sign before you can kill the woman he loves and turn her into a creature who will be forced to watch every single person *she* loves die?"

Vayl leaned forward. Shot the word at me like a bullet. *"Stop."*

I met him halfway. Not a smart move for anyone facing a pissed-off vampire. But anger generally puts me beyond smart moves, especially when it comes to Vayl. Knowing he could sense all of my strongest feelings, I wrapped them in a flaming ball and threw them at him with two simple words. "You first."

Chapter Sixteen

Vayl left me at the door to the Oasis with a mumbled, "I am sure you can find your way home from here," and disappeared into the night. I watched him go, depressed on every front, including the one where I had to admit he was right about getting back to base. I didn't even need a map. (One of the perks of my Sensitivity.) What I did need was to talk to somebody who could help me unravel this coil. Usually Vayl was my go-to guy. But since he'd caused the biggest tangle, I was left with little choice. Too dangerous to contact Raoul. Too risky even to talk to Dave. That left the old man.

I pulled out the new stealth-communications device the DOD had issued us before leaving on this mission, stifling a pang of guilt at the pleasure that flashed through me as my fingers caressed the sleek black case. I love technology almost as much as I adore fast cars and strong, mysterious men. I opened the case, took out the trendy new eyeglasses it contained, and put them on. As soon as they settled on my face a robotic arm grew out of the earpiece. Having watched the live-action version before we left, I knew a tiny receiver was blooming from its tip, and within moments the arm would stick it in my ear.

In the meantime, using visual commands to work the menu shining across the top of my lenses, I placed my call. Then I covered my mouth with my hijab so no one could see me having a conversation seemingly with myself.

"Parks residence."

"Shelby?" I was surprised. Usually, well always, Albert answers the phone. Finding his nurse on the other end of the line was a bad sign. Dammit, I needed to talk to my dad!

"Jaz? Did your work finally track you down?"

Shit, shit, shit. Stop talking right now, Shelby. I do not want to hear what you have to say. "No."

Long pause. Big breath on Shelby's end. "Jaz, your dad's been in an accident." When I didn't immediately reply, he added, "He's alive. But he's in critical condition."

I kept strolling down the street as if part of my head hadn't just floated off into the stratosphere and my heart hadn't just burst. I didn't cry or call out, because that would have brought attention to me, and I was on the job. Such the professional. *Yo, Pete, I didn't blow it when my dad's nurse told me he was near to death. Give me a fucking bonus, will ya?*

"What—" I cleared the croak out of my throat. "What happened?"

"He was riding his motorcycle down the street not two blocks from here when a woman hit him from behind. He flew back into her windshield; then he rolled forward onto the pavement. Luckily there was a cop right on the scene. He had somebody pulled over, giving them a traffic ticket. So he nailed the driver right away. Had an ambulance on the spot within three minutes. It probably saved his life."

"But he's still bad?"

I could hardly bear the sympathy in Shelby's voice. I wanted him to growl like Albert. That would make me mad. Then I wouldn't want to cry. "He's a sixty-one-year-old diabetic. Admittedly he's in better shape since I started taking care of him, but he has multiple fractures, including a couple in his back that may be very serious. They won't know for sure until the swelling goes down. There may also be issues with his kidneys. A young, healthy guy is going to heal up pretty fast. Your dad does have a couple of strikes against him. But he's also the most stubborn, mule-headed bastard I've ever met."

We laughed. "Me too," I said.

"If anybody's going to beat this, it'll be him," Shelby assured me.

"Shelby." I swallowed a sob. *Breathe, Jaz, breathe.* "I can't come home. I'm overseas."

"They told me."

"Have you been in touch with Evie?"

"She's at the hospital right now."

"Okay. Tell her I'll call as soon as I can and I'm sorry I'm not there." *I'm sorry I'm never there.*

I walked the rest of the way back to the house in a stupor. Since my mind kept shying away from Albert's situation, all I could think was, *Who am I going to call now? Who's going to tell me what to do now that the mahghul are stalking Vayl?*

When I got back to base the door was locked. Too tired to retrieve the key from my pocket, I reached through the nonexistent side pane, unlocked it from the inside, and went in. Cassandra and Bergman had moved their research to the living room. They'd taken over the love seat and were nearly bumping heads as they whispered over the Enkyklios. Though the marbles kept moving, forming myriad shapes, the pictures that projected from them made little sense to me, probably because they were so small.

I shucked my shoes, climbed over the back of the couch, and sank down into the cushions, wishing desperately for a comfort I'd never again experience. Still, I pulled my old card deck out of my pocket and ran my thumb across the tops. *Thrum.* What a beautiful sound.

Cassandra came to sit beside me, leaving the Enkyklios to wind down on its own. "What happened?"

"You want the bad news or the worse news?"

That got Bergman's attention. He eyed the cards. "Maybe you should pick up another habit, Jaz. I heard about these ball bearings—"

"Naw. I think I'm just going to start drinking."

Long silence while Bergman and Cassandra tried to decide whether or not I was joking. Why does nobody get me? Finally Cassandra said, "Tell us everything."

So I did. And when I was done, I'll admit it, I was glad our consultants had come along. No matter what else they contributed to the mission, they didn't make fun of me when I cried for the dad I barely got along with and only loved because I had no other choice. And they didn't protest when I declared I was going to stop Vayl's lame-ass turning-the-Seer scheme if it killed me. Which, to be honest, it very well might. But they didn't want to help me plan how. They had something else on their minds.

"We think we've figured out how to detect the shield," said Bergman, jerking his thumb toward the Enkyklios with barely checked excitement.

"Yes," Cassandra agreed. "And it has to do with your acquaintance, the Amanha Szeya."

I thought of sad-eyed Asha and actually felt some remorse at nosing into his business. But not much. When a guy keeps me from taking out a reaver, he'd better expect some payback. "So, you have a record of his kind?" I asked.

Cassandra nodded. "He is a Nruug Stalker."

"And what's a Nruug?" I asked tiredly.

"An *other* who's abusing his or her Gift."

I threw up my hands with relief. "So we're set! I found him

outside Zarsa's house. She's obviously abusing. He'll take care of the whole deal."

"Not necessarily," cautioned Bergman. "According to some of the histories we saw in the Enkyklios, many Nruug Stalkers won't step in until after somebody's actually died. They have that mentality where it's not a crime until the deed's done."

"Well, shit."

"But you can certainly talk to him," Cassandra encouraged me. "And when you do"—she and Bergman shared a gleaming look of anticipation—"maybe you can tell him about Bergman's idea."

"Well, it started with Cassandra," Bergman said graciously.

"But Bergman made the leap," Cassandra added.

I held up my hands. "Okay, enough with the lovefest. I almost liked it better when you two were slamming each other. At least we were more efficient."

Cassandra nodded to Bergman, who sat forward eagerly, his chapped hands each clutching a bony knee. "We realized the only way to detect a shield of the type we suspect is to use a really finely tuned tracker." He tried to pause for dramatic effect but was too worried about being yelled at to work it for long. "Like you."

"But—"

He held up his hands. "I know, you and Cole didn't feel anything during the card game. But think. Every time Vayl has taken your blood, he's left some of his power behind and it's increased your own Sensitivity. The reavers even have a name for it."

"My Spirit Eye," I said.

"Exactly. We think if you were able to soup up your Sensitivity again, you might be able to see the mole. Or at least the shield he's using to hide behind."

"One problem," I said.

"What's that?"

"Vayl's pissed at me."

Cassandra shook her head. "We aren't suggesting you donate any more blood to Vayl. We don't think he'd take it if you offered, now that he's fixated on Zarsa. We think you should talk to Asha."

I slumped so far down the couch my butt hit the edge of the cushion. Oh yeah, this was going to be a blast. Because I was sure whatever exchange they were suggesting involved some major vulnerability on my side. And, frankly, if I had to crack open the shell I'd begun to build the moment I heard about my dad, I would never make it through this mission.

A clatter at the door that led into the apartment from the garage signaled the return of Dave and his crew. I straightened. Pulled myself together. No way in hell would I let Amazon Grace see me looking pitiful and forlorn. She'd get off on it way too much.

They joined us in the living room. Natchez dropped next to Bergman on the love seat. Grace settled by the fireplace with Cam. Dave sat on the couch with Cassandra and me. Jet and Cole took a detour into the kitchen and came out minutes later with drinks for everyone.

"How did it go?" Cassandra asked Dave.

"Pretty well," he replied. "We've got the location scouted and photographed so we can make a mock-up on the second floor and do some run-throughs with Jaz and Vayl later tonight." I looked around the room, expecting satisfied nods. But they all looked pretty grim and stoic to me.

"What happened?" I demanded, shelving my own bad news until I heard theirs.

"We ran into some trouble," Dave said. "We'd probably be in jail right now if not for some quick talking on Cole's part."

Now the nods came, along with several toasts. Cole accepted them with his usual good-humored grin.

I looked at my recruit and raised my eyebrows. "Well?"

He sauntered over to Cam, held his hand out, received a toothpick and a salute before taking his place center stage. "We'd finished the reconnaissance and were headed back when the police stopped us and herded us into this huge square. They made us join a group of maybe thirty men. I asked an older guy if he knew why we were there, and he told me we were all suspected of inciting a riot that had happened earlier that evening."

"I think we were there," I said through lips that had gone numb. "Two women were hung, right?"

Cole nodded in surprise. "That's what he said."

"I thought the riot started when the older woman's chador came off."

"According to the old man, it was a combination of the picture pinned to her dress and what the people in the crowd were shouting."

"Tell me."

Cole scratched his beard as he gnawed at the toothpick, both sure signs of distress. "The picture was of her daughter, who'd been buried to the waist by her uncle and then stoned to death by him and some other male family members for trying to divorce her husband."

Though Dave's crew had already heard the story, they still looked sick. As new partakers of this information, Bergman, Cassandra, and I kept looking at each other, not knowing how to react. We had no common ground from which to pull a story that started, "Oh yeah, I had a crazy uncle once who . . ." Nope. The worst thing my uncle Barney ever did was get so drunk at my cousin Amelia's wedding he thought he could limbo with the young guys. He threw his back out and missed work for a week.

I tried to comprehend the mind-set that would make the leap from divorce to a death sentence. No dice. My mind, already overloaded, attempted to step out. I felt as if I was watching our impromptu meeting from somewhere near the ceiling. "And the crowd?" I heard myself ask. "What were they yelling?"

"I guess the mother became a dissident after that," Cole said softly. "They were shouting things like 'Women Deserve Life,' and 'Laws for Women,' which drove the entertainment seekers crazy. I guess they tore up the bodies pretty badly."

"Why . . ." The word didn't come out right, sounded more like a wail. I coughed. Tried again. "What crime were they convicted of?"

Cole shoved his fingers through his mass of hair. Right now I thought its wild tangles perfectly reflected all our feelings. He said, "The old man told me that she and the younger woman had been executed for fomenting rebellion against the government."

So. The ladies hadn't murdered their kids after all.

My mind took me back to that moment at the plaza and drew me a parallel. Big stage. Expectant crowd. A show that made you feel you'd stepped into hell on earth. And in actual hell, the Magistrate putting on his own show. Acting out his own murder scene. Staging my spectacular rescue.

On earth the mahghul had descended like a flock of evil mutant pigeons and fed on the hate, fury, and fear of every single person in that crowd.

The Magistrate was no different. No better than a parasite, he wanted to feed on something that he could only get to while I was in ephemeral mode and rocketing toward Raoul. But what? I had a feeling there was only one way to find out.

But now was not the time. Cole had continued his story, explaining how he'd sweet-talked the old man into faking a heart attack. The resulting diversion allowed them to slip away.

Dave slapped his hands on his thighs. Guy-speak for, "So let's get on with the stuff we came to do, shall we?" "Cam, have you still got the DVD?"

He nodded. "It's in my pack."

"Okay, then, let's head upstairs and tape off a mock-up of the hotel. If we work quickly enough we can get a couple of run-throughs done before daylight." He looked at me, playing his part to the hilt. "You guys are gonna have time to do this tonight, right?"

"Sure," I said enthusiastically. As if I had any idea where Vayl might be at the moment. Or if he'd even be in the mood to pretend we were still working with the Spec Ops folks after the blowup between us.

They turned to go.

"Wait," I said. They all looked at me. Great. The last thing I wanted was an audience. "Dave, can we talk a second? About family stuff?"

"O-kay." His tone told me I'd better have a damn good reason for delaying him when he had important work ahead. I led him into the kitchen. Once we were facing each other across the island I dove in.

"Dad's had an accident. Shelby said a woman hit him while he was riding his cycle and he's pretty torn up. He's in intensive care."

I stood there a full thirty seconds. Waiting for something. Anything. But he didn't react at all. Except to scratch his neck until I wondered if he was going to make it bleed. Finally he said, "Okay. Let me know if you hear anything else." And he walked out.

"Wow, that went so well," I murmured. "I wish I had more bad news for him. Maybe I should call home. See if his storage unit's burned up. Or if somebody's stolen his identity." I squashed the urge to chase after him, shake him until his teeth cracked together, and yell, "What the hell is wrong with you!" He was a grown man with his own well-developed ways of coping. And as the Queen of

Denial, it was hardly my place to tell him they weren't going to help him sleep any better at night.

I entered the living room in time to see Dave clap Cole on the shoulder. "Good work tonight," he said. "You want to join us?" He jerked his head toward the door at the end of the hallway, which stood open and led to the upstairs apartment.

"Sorry, Dave, I already have plans for him," I said.

Cole polished his nails on his shirt. "Obviously I'm going to have to start charging more for my services."

Both men laughed and Dave gave him another slap on the back, which made Cole cough. I waited until I could hear Dave's footsteps on the floor above us before I said, "Cole, I need you to come with me." I headed for the front door.

"Where are we going?" he asked as he trailed after me.

I looked over my shoulder, letting him see the steel in my eyes. "Hunting."

Chapter Seventeen

Cole and I perched on the roof of Anvari's, peering over its edge at the dimly lit street below. The thin sliver of moon helped not at all as we searched for the tall, gaunt form of Asha Vasta. Or, better yet, the purposeful stride set off by the tiger-carved cane that was unmistakably Vayl. As I explained to Cole, Asha was my quarry, Vayl his.

"You want me to follow the boss?" he'd asked, as if I'd just told him to bait a grizzly with a rib eye while doing an Irish jig through the clover.

"He can feel me," I explained. "And I've got to keep tabs on him. The second he makes contact with Zarsa again I need to know." He shook his head. "Oh, come on, Cole. You know if he turns her it's going to be a disaster for everybody involved, especially her kids."

"Oh, I'll do it," he assured me. "I just can't believe you have the nerve to ask without offering something in return."

I bit my lip as I recognized the look on his face. This was hard-ball Cole, and I wasn't sure I wanted to know what was on his mind. But I had no other choice. "What do you want?"

"A date. With you." He glared at me, like I was already trying to weasel out of it. "A real one, where you wear a dress and I ogle your butt when you're not looking."

I sighed. "Cole—"

He took my hand. "I know you have major reservations about us. And Vayl's making you crazy. Whatever. Just give me this." His grin turned evil. "Or I won't play."

Well, shit in a stovepipe, Jaz. Now you're really going to be in a bind. But what choice do you have? "Okay." We shook on it. I called him a blackmailer. He told me my ass belonged in a picture frame in the Metropolitan Museum of Art. And we decided to look somewhere else for our prey.

Since Vayl was my highest priority, I took Cole back to the Oasis. From there we followed his trail for miles, along wide, well-lit boulevards lined with cypress trees and narrow brick-paved streets where you couldn't see your hand in front of your face. We strode past billboards advertising Chanel No. 5 and hand-painted signs of the Statue of Liberty with a skull where her face should be. Our trail took us past high-rises and ruins, soccer stadiums and mosques. The juxtaposition of modern against ancient was so extreme it actually lessened my surprise that the country found it so difficult to plot a middle course toward any goal. Finally we reached the edge of the city, where a dilapidated auction barn packed mostly with sheep, goats, and donkeys sprawled over an area roughly the size of a city block.

We crouched beside the fence of an outdoor pen in which three groups of five or six camels each stood or laid according to their preferences. "Oh my God!" breathed Cole. "This is our chance!"

"What are you talking about?" I whispered as I tried to figure out what Vayl would want with a sheep or goat. *Sacrifice,* my mind whispered. I told it to shut the hell up. Zarsa probably just needed to ride a donkey around the house three or four times as part of some symbolic journey to her new life. *Yeah. Sure.*

"You've heard of cow tipping?" asked Cole.

"I'm from the Midwest," I answered. "What do you think?"

"Well, I'm thinking we put a Middle Eastern twist on it and do some camel tipping tonight!"

"Cole, I hate to burst your bubble, but—" He was already inside the pen. "Cole!" I hissed. "Get back here!"

He rushed over. "You got any advice for me?"

I looked into his sparkling eyes and thought, *Aw, screw it. He wants to believe, let him*. "They're supposed to be asleep," I told him. "You see any sleeping camels out there?"

He took a good, hard look. "Yeah." He nodded excitedly. "A couple. You gonna come help me?"

"No. I'll stay out here and keep watch. Now, you just tiptoe up to one of those sleeping camels, nice and quiet so you don't wake him, and give him a hard shove on the shoulder. Basically what happens is he'll be so startled when he wakes up he'll fall right over on his side. Cool, huh?"

"Awesome!"

"Now, don't let him kick you, because he'll for sure kill you."

"Do I look that stupid?"

I stared at him until his feet started to shuffle. "Okay, no."

"Good answer. Now, come on, woman. Some support for the big, brave man going off to have the adventure of his life!"

I shot my fist into the air. "Go for it!"

Cole leaned in. "I was thinking more along the lines of a long, juicy kiss."

"Before our first date? What kind of girl do you think I am?" We shared a grin, remembering our first meeting and the fact that it had ended with a spectacular lip-lock. One of those spur-of-the-moment things neither of us would have attempted in any other situation.

I watched Cole kick it into stealth mode like an off-duty ninja and had to stifle a giggle. The camels observed him approach with the bored attention of animals who're too damn tired to give a crap. Only the ones lying down were asleep, but Cole decided a big female standing in the center of the pen was enjoying forty winks. He snuck right up to her, planted his hands on her broad side, and gave her a huge shove.

She swung her head around, looked him right in the eye, and spat in his face.

"Oh, very funny," he said when he got back to the fence and found me laughing so hard I kept snorting every time I stopped to breathe.

"You have a brand-new stench about you," I noted, my face beginning to ache from the size of my smile. "What do you call it?"

Though by now his face was clean, he wiped his sleeve across it again. Then he wrinkled his nose. "How about Gagfest?"

"Yeah, I think that describes it pretty well. When we find Vayl, I suggest you stay way behind him."

"Can we just get out of here?"

"Okay. But I'll never forget the look on your face. Not as long as I live."

"Me! What about her?"

"You mean the camel?"

He nodded. "Seriously. I don't think she even knew she was going to hawk a loogie until it crossed her lips. Did you see her blinking at me with those enormous eyelashes of hers? I'm telling you. She was as surprised as I was."

I couldn't help it. Despite the absolute gravity on his face, I let out a hoot of laughter. Within moments Cole had joined me and we stood there, in the middle of one of the most dangerous countries we'd ever entered, tee-heeing like a couple of best girlfriends.

And that was all it took. "Cole, I've got it!"

Total bewilderment. "You do?"

"It was what you just said. About the camel? About her not being aware of her own actions? I'll bet that's the same deal with the mole! Think about it. Dave can't imagine who'd betray him. And we haven't been able to pick anyone out, either. Because the mole *himself* isn't aware."

Cole considered my idea. "It makes a lot more sense from a Spec Ops standpoint too," he finally said, warming up to my theory. "I mean, you might get some treasonous types in the general military population, but once you get into the elite groups, I don't see it happening. Especially not in this case."

"So let's work this out," I said as we began tracing Vayl's path back toward town. "The Wizard is a necromancer. How does he get control of one of Dave's men?"

"Well, I guess he kills one, does his mumbo jumbo, and sends him back to the unit."

"That's some amazing power," I replied. "Every one of them seems pretty vital. I can't imagine one of them being dead. Except—" The words froze in my throat. I stopped walking. Cole got ahead of me, realized I wasn't beside him, and came back to stand in front of me. He peered down into my face.

"Jaz? Are you sick?"

I nodded. *Actually, yeah, I'm feeling pretty queasy right about now.* "David's dead. Or undead. Or, I don't know, something other than alive," I whispered. "He told me it happened on a training run. But maybe it didn't. Maybe that's just what the Wizard wants him to remember. He sure doesn't get very choked up about it when he tells the story."

"What else did he say?"

"That he's working for Raoul. Only . . ." I thought back to the conversation we'd had after his first medic had been killed. "He already knew all the details about my visit upstairs. So the Wizard could've implanted a false sense of purpose too." No, wait a minute. The first time Raoul and I had met face-to-face in his high-roller suite in Vegas, I'd asked him if David had come to the same place. But he hadn't given me a straight answer. He'd said, "In a way."

Oh man, oh man, oh man. Did something go wrong while Dave's soul was winging across outer space? Did Raoul have him and somehow . . . I don't know, lose his grip to the stronger, meaner pull of the Wizard? How does that work anyway? Or—could it really be that Dave was given a choice in the matter and he preferred the Wizard's work? No. Impossible. There must be some logical explanation.

Honest to God, if I didn't have to wear a damn hijab I'd have pulled my hair out. I couldn't imagine a worse possible scenario. Because if I was right. If my brother was the victim of the Wizard—I leaned over, put my hands on my knees as I felt the bile begin to rise—that meant as soon as the son of a bitch was done with him, David would die for good.

Chapter Eighteen

Ask any warden of any prison facility in the world. There's something about isolation. You think you're a pretty tough cookie. You think you can take being cut off. Having no one to share your thoughts with. No one to turn to. Until you find yourself curled up in the corner, crying like a baby. I'd gotten close to that once. Losing a fiancé. A sister-in-law. A crew of close, personal friends and the steady support and affection of a twin. Yeah, I had a damn good idea how it felt to be alone. It'll make you crazy, that's what.

To say I didn't relish the thought of facing that prospect ever again in my life was a massive understatement. Along the lines of mentioning that Pamela Anderson's had some work done. Or that TV news agencies occasionally slant their stories to interest viewers. But as Cole and I trudged toward an ancient temple where my stunned brain could no longer deny that Vayl had probably stopped to do a number on the animal he'd taken from the auction yard, I realized I might just have to walk down that long, empty road again.

What if I'm wrong?

Raoul's voice came back to me, his words a lot more significant now, especially since he'd spoken them to me in hell. *Nothing is as it seems.* Ha! Apparently that included my old reliable Spirit Guide. He'd told me to trust my instincts then, and instead, encouraged by my distracted *sverhamin*, I'd been ignoring them. The time had come to face the music. Problem was, they were playing a dirge.

Damn, damn, damn. I am so screwed. Because neither Vayl, Pete, nor anyone at the DOD was ever going to believe my new theory. Which went like this.

The Wizard picks the commander of a Spec Ops crew, unbeknownst to the man himself, as his inside guy. Why?

To make sure we come after him.

This, of course, is where I lose my willing audience and any support I might hope to gain from my bosses. And why, if I didn't play this just right, I could lose my job. Which I love. More than cookies and milk. Or shuffling cards. Or any movie starring Will Smith. No, it's not even close to that sort of comfort and joy. My work is my life. It's kept me breathing. Literally.

I gulped back a massive wave of the boo-hoos and went on with my internal hypothesis. It made all the other weird stuff that had happened up to now line up. The fact that, after all these years of batting a total zero, we'd finally found a picture and information leading us straight to the Wizard. Those zombie reavers who just happened to get in the way of the attacking ones, making sure most of us survived to continue with the mission. Even Zarsa's presence, distracting Vayl from the job so any suspicions the mole's twin might raise would be ignored. I figured Cassandra's psychic blowout was just a lucky break for him. I certainly don't think he'd planned on her coming. But I'm sure if she had kept her senses, he'd have found a way to kill her before she could communicate her findings to anyone.

"That could be the connection," I murmured.

"What?" asked Cole.

I looked at him out of the corner of my eyes. "I really shouldn't say. What I'm planning has PROFESSIONAL SUICIDE stamped all over it. Believe me, you don't want to be standing too close when this all goes down."

Since he'd lost his first career due to his connections with me, Cole had no problem buying my line. Still, he said, "Use me, Jaz. I may be new at this game, but I'm a good agent. I'm also a grown man. Stop feeling like to have to protect me all the time."

I nodded. Weak, I know. But in the end I couldn't face being alone again. "Soheil Anvari said he was the caretaker of our building. Now I'm wondering who owns it."

"Why?" I gave him my theory. "So you think maybe it belongs to the Wizard?" he asked.

I shrugged. "It makes sense to me. How else does he know to put Zarsa in Vayl's path? Maybe he even had those bugs planted before we got into the house, and that's why we never saw who put them there."

"But they were only in the men's bedroom," Cole objected.

"Have you forgotten where we are? Why would a guy like the Wizard, a guy who put the X in extremist, give a crap what the women were thinking?" Which made me revise my theory slightly. Zarsa wasn't meant to distract Vayl from me. I wouldn't be expected to pull any weight at all. She was just supposed to keep him from focusing on anything that didn't have to do with the mission. Like, maybe, the pesky little mole-hunt the DOD had sent us on in the first place. At least, he wasn't supposed to worry about that until after he turned Zarsa, which would definitely be post-hit.

For a second I wondered how innocent Zarsa was in this whole drama. Then I decided I didn't care and moved on to the main issue. "Why would the Wizard want us to kill him?"

"Maybe he's got terminal cancer," Cole murmured as we mounted the temple steps.

"Suicide by cop?" I replied. "Come on, you can do better than that. Think of what he had to do to put this whole deal together. It must have taken months, if not years. So why does the U.S. military's number-one enemy and the bane of his own people orchestrate this elaborate plan where the end result is his own assassination?"

"Maybe he wants to make himself a martyr. I don't think his god's very popular among the civilians. Too creepy-looking. He's got, like, three heads, you know? And one of them's a snake. But if the big bad U.S. kills Angra Mainyu's most loyal fan, maybe there's some sort of uprising in reaction. Maybe it starts a whole wave of religious fervor and the Wizard gets to be a god like he's always wanted."

"That's a lot of maybes," I said. But it made more sense than anything else I could come up with on short notice. The Wizard's top men always filled their we-did-it videos with plenty of preaching after each of their attacks. And they always referred to the Wizard as their god's mouthpiece. Martyrdom would certainly get him the kind of attention he never had in life.

The temple's front entrance was lit by torches. I only had to take one look at the twenty-foot-high figures carved along the facade—a parade of rabbits, tigers, and wolves halfway through their transformations into jackals, deer, and badgers—to realize who the temple honored. It was Ako Nogol, goddess of change. Even *her* place of worship had turned out to be too hot for Vayl to handle. He'd left a goat tied to the front door latch. The animal had taken a crap right on the threshold, which I didn't think Ako Nogol would much appreciate, before settling down for the night with its legs tucked under itself as if the night was too cool for its little hooves.

"Vayl brought the gods a goat," Cole said.

"Goddess," I corrected.

"He could've at least dressed it up."

"How do you mean?"

"Pink tutu. Floppy hat with flowers. You know. The usual." I elbowed him, but it didn't keep the grin off his face. "Your boyfriend's completely lost it," he murmured in my ear, not bothering to keep the delight out of his voice.

"Shut up and follow me," I growled as I went back down the steps. "He spent some time here." Not praying. That probably would've fried his brain. Meditating maybe. Or chanting some arcane spell. "We're getting closer."

We caught up to him about a mile north of the temple. I saw the mahghul first, loping along the elaborately trimmed rooftops, their presence a chilling reminder of how much was at stake. I held Cole back as I recognized the long, purposeful stride of my *sverhamin* ahead of us. "This is where we separate," I said. Cole nodded. "Just keep an eye on him," I warned. "He can sense strong emotions, so stay cool. And don't get cocky. If you lose him, go back to the house and get cracking on that research. I want to know who owns the place by morning. You got your funky glasses on you?"

"Yeah."

"Okay. Call if something goes wrong. And don't forget this whole city is the danger zone, okay?"

"Okay! Geesh! Are you sure you don't have some eggs you need to hatch somewhere?"

"Sorry. Old habits. Still, be careful."

Exasperated sigh. "Get *out* already!"

I left. By now my feet felt like a couple of cooked meatloaves. I was surprised they weren't smoking. But I had farther to go, so I went. Clear to the storefront where I'd first met Asha Vasta.

I didn't expect to find a visual sign of him, so I wasn't disappointed when the whole street was empty. What I hoped for was a trail, like the one Vayl had left. I stood in the shadows of the bakery's doorway and opened my mind. Nothing beyond a hint of the reaver I'd allowed to pass unharmed.

"He went to Channel Fourteen," I murmured. "Gotta remember that." Right now Uldin Beit's team was out in force, pretending to be reporters and cameramen, trying to track me down. While I, on the other hand, couldn't find one large and rather conspicuous looking *other*. Well, if I were him, would I want to be found by a woman who'd held a knife to my throat? Hardly. By golly, I'd be covering my tracks like they used to do in the old Westerns, with a well-branched limb and a roundabout path home.

Wait a minute. The knife! I pulled the bolo out. Pressed the point, which had touched Asha's throat, against the tip of my nose. And drank in his scent. With no *others* around to distract me, I was able to mentally tag the unique identifier that surrounded him wherever he went. Call it an aura. Or charisma. The essence that gave a person presence—so even if no one heard or saw them enter a room they still knew they'd been joined—had lingered on the steel of my blade.

"Gotcha," I breathed. I sheathed the blade. Took another breath. Concentrated, narrowing my eyes to focus the trail, and moved.

Chapter Nineteen

I found Asha at a black-fenced cemetery, the stones of which all laid long and flat like legless benches. I liked the idea. This way there was never any debate about whether or not you were stepping on hallowed ground. He perched on top of a gatepost like a gigantic statue, watching a group of people huddled together inside.

"Were you going for an übercreepy vibe?" I asked as I came up to him. "Because, actually, it's working. And how do those guys not see you?" I pointed to the group of half a dozen black-suited men gathered around the candlelit, petal-strewn tombstone maybe fifty yards in.

Asha hopped down. "They are too busy with their own business," he said. "Note the gentleman standing between the two largest candles."

"I see him. Is he . . . signing?" I looked at Asha. "He's a medium, isn't he?" All *others* who could communicate with the truly dead were deaf. Many were mute as well.

He shook his head. "This word. Medium. Does it mean the same thing as Spirit Bridge?"

"Yup. So is this a séance?"

"Of a sort. These men have just lost their father. And they wish to talk to his spirit to find out why he committed suicide."

"That seems reasonable. Except you're here. Which means this particular Bridge isn't nearly as upright as he seems."

Asha stared at me like I'd just announced that the city fathers had agreed to allow a Gay Pride parade down the main thoroughfare of Tehran the next morning. "You know what I am?"

Was he pissed? Or just extra depressed? At this point, I didn't really care. I was here to get what I needed from him and to hell with his feelings. "I have an idea. And I need to talk to you about how, being who you are, maybe you could lend me a hand with a little (*huge!*) problem I have when you're done here."

"All right." He moved toward the gate. Paused when he realized I hadn't followed him.

"Aren't you going to stop this first?"

"What do you mean?"

I could feel my anger rise. Though some clinical part of my brain understood it was closely tied to my worries over whether or not my dad would ever wake up again and if my brother would survive past tomorrow, it still managed to focus purely on Asha. "I thought you were supposed to police the *others*. Isn't this guy committing some sort of offense?"

"Yes. In fact, he is telling the men their father's spirit is here, speaking to him, explaining that he could no longer stand the pain of his cancer and the knowledge that he would soon become a complete invalid."

"And that's not true?"

"I doubt it. If the father's spirit is present, it is howling. Because one of his sons, one of these men, killed him."

Okay, Jaz. The shaking is not a good sign. Usually that means you're about to hit something. Or somebody. And you need this dude's help. So don't break his nose. At least not until after you get the favor. I really should listen to myself more. I often have good intentions. But when I opened my mouth, the words that came out were "And you're *leaving*?"

"Would it be better to reveal the truth? To let these brothers kill their own kin even as the mahghul drink their emotions like the finest wine?" Did I detect a trembling in his voice when he mentioned the murder monsters?

"Are you afraid of the mahghul, Asha?" Pressing his lips together, he turned his back on me. Strode out of the cemetery. I hurried after him, my mounting rage burning my brain like a fever. "So you're letting a charlatan help a man get away with murder. Wow. I'm so bummed I left my autograph book in America," I drawled. "I bet you've decided to let the whole Vayl/Zarsa travesty play out too, haven't you? Because you're afraid to step between them. Scared Vayl will get violent and the mahghul will want to join the party before you can dive for cover."

"You have no idea what it is like!" he hissed, his pace increasing so much I had to trot to keep up.

"Tell me!" I demanded.

He didn't. Not right away. We walked until I was so damn tired I just wanted to lie down. Even the gutters began to look inviting. Then he stopped in front of a six-foot-high arched gate painted salmon to match the wall that fronted the two-story house behind it. The house was well enough lit outside that I could see many of its accents, including balcony railings and window trim, also painted salmon, which complemented the natural stucco color of the rest of the place.

Asha keyed open the gate. As I stood on the sidewalk, wondering if I'd just blown my only chance to save this mission, not to mention David, he finally turned to meet my eyes. "Six hundred years ago I was a different creature. I pursued wrongdoers with a singularity of purpose that would allow no deviation from my goal. I dealt with the Nruug as I had been taught by my predecessor."

When he fell silent I said, "And how was that?"

"Usually a draining of the Gift. Either temporarily, or

permanently, depending on the severity of the crime. But sometimes even that was not enough. Sometimes only a Nruug's death would protect his next victim. You understand this?"

I nodded. *Only too well.*

"It was during one such battle that a powerful Nruug brought the mahghul against me. He was a sorcerer, steeped in dark powers, and his influence had spread over the land like a poisonous cloud. I killed him. But the mahghul remained even after the battle, covering me like a blanket. Their fangs sank into the skin of my back, my legs, my chest, even my skull. I imagined I could feel their tongues like probes inside my brain, sucking out every last emotion until, when they finally left me, nothing remained. I laid like a husk for days. Perhaps I would even have died, but an old couple found me and took me in."

He gazed at me with his forlorn eyes and asked, "Do you know what it is to feel nothing? I did not miss so much the anger or the hate. But I found I could barely move without the hope."

"You're moving now."

"Yes," he said, almost eagerly. "Eventually I realized the Council of Five must soon replace me. All I had to do was write the names of the Nruug in a book for the next Amanha Szeya. He will be filled with the passion I have lost. He will fight the mahghul and win."

Oh, for chrissake. I need a nuclear reactor and what do I get? A dead battery. "When's he coming?" I asked.

"Soon," Asha replied.

I shifted on my feet, which badly wanted a hot bath and a massage. "Can you get any more specific than that?"

"Only a year. Perhaps two at the most."

That is it! "I haven't even got a *day*! Now, you listen to me. I'm already pissed that I allowed you to talk me out of taking down that reaver when he was vulnerable and carrying around five of his buddies in his head. I'm still seriously considering dragging your ass back to the cemetery so we can nail that murderer, because two wrongs do not make a right, and frankly, I've done nothing right since I hopped the plane for this country. Though I should, I'm *not* going to ask you to pull Zarsa off Vayl. I can take care of him myself. But I *am* going to stand here, right in your face, and call you a fucking pussy!"

Oh boy, did that bring the blood to his face. Apparently the mahghul hadn't drained Asha of all his emotions. I raced on, so enraged by his lack of action and my own bottomless well of shit that I didn't give a crap how he reacted to what I said. "Your job is to protect people from *others* who abuse their powers and you are failing miserably!"

He started to speak, but I held up my hand. "Don't even try to make excuses. I don't give a damn what the mahghul did to you. The Council of Five didn't send someone to replace you after that battle, did they?"

He shook his head.

"So there was nobody else. In fact, there's been nobody since. You're it, Asha. You're all that stands between innocent people and criminal *others* in this city. And all you've done for the last—how long?"

"One hundred years," he murmured.

"Oh my God, for the last century your only effort on the people's behalf has been to write the bad guys' names in a book? No wonder the place is a cesspool! You know, I came to ask for your help. You're a Power, and I was hoping you'd share just a little of it with me. Just enough so I could do my job, stop a guy who's killed hundreds of your people and mine, and hopefully save my brother's life in the process."

I paused. Had to. The tears that crouched at the back of my throat, waiting for me to consider the men in my family, had to be swallowed. When I'd gulped them down, and then taken a second to marvel that Asha hadn't slammed his gate in my face but stood rooted to the sidewalk, his mournful eyes glued to mine, I said, "But I can see that's a waste of time. You decided a long time ago just to sit on your power like a gigantic ostrich, bury your head in the sand, and wait for somebody else to show up to do the hard work."

The sound of squealing tires distracted me. I turned to look as a van hurtled onto the street. Though it was still maybe five blocks away, the light reflecting off the satellite dish attached to its roof revealed its identity. I'd bet my next paycheck when it pulled up to Asha's gate the sticker on the side would translate to Channel Fourteen.

As soon as I saw the van I felt an ache between my shoulder blades. Confirmation that the vehicle contained one, if not all, of the reavers. How had they found me?

I looked at my watch. "Shit! It's a new day!" I slapped my hand to my forehead, as if that could cover up the Mark. I felt my arm for the syringe of holy water I usually kept there. But it was gone. I'd given the sheath to Cole to feed his oral fixation and had stored the syringe back in my weapons case.

"What is happening?" asked Asha. His eyes had moved from the van to the rooftops and gone as round as campaign buttons. The mahghul were gathering.

"The reavers are coming for me. Remember that one you wouldn't let me kill?"

Asha nodded, wincing at the bite of my tone.

"Well, his sponsor is a mortal enemy of mine who found him a bunch of willing bodies working at a local TV station. Now he's dumped the demons he was carrying in his head into those bodies, and at least a few of them are in that van." I took a second to think. No way could I fight off the reavers if, indeed, all six of them had piled into the van for this showdown. I was about five miles from home base, so no time to run for cover. Cirilai would've told Vayl I was in trouble, but he'd never get here in time to help. And Asha. Well, we'd already established his status.

I turned to him. "Do you have a car?" I asked, as I looked over my shoulder. They were two blocks away now. I could see reavers in the driver and passenger seats as well as one glaring out the front window between them.

"A car? Yes. But . . . I rarely drive it. I mean—"

"Good." I pushed him inside the gate, slammed it shut, and barred it from the inside. "I need it."

We ran around to the back of the house. Asha opened the garage door while I pulled Grief. I thumbed off the safety as I heard the van screech to a halt in front of the house.

"In here," Asha whispered. I followed him into the garage and stifled a whistle as he opened the driver's side door of a black BMW 3.

Sweet. He handed me the keys, shielding his face from me as we made the transfer. Still, I caught the glint of tears on his cheeks. *Aw, for—are you kidding me?* The guy could probably kick my ass into the Persian Gulf while juggling the reavers with three fingers if he wanted to. But I'd called him a name and made him cry. And now I felt bad. Because the truth is I do have a big mouth that I absolutely need to learn to keep shut, and he did have an excellent reason for avoiding the mahghul. I was just so desperate, at this point I'd smack the angel Gabriel upside the head if I thought it would make him mad enough to get down here and yell at me for three days. Because sometime within that span I'd need backup, he'd be there, and voilà. Problem solved.

I slipped into the driver's seat and closed the door. Asha reached through the open window and poked the remote attached to the visor. The back gate began to roll open. I started the car. "I'm sorry, Asha. I was a real shit to you back there, and here you are, lending me your wheels."

He leaned down, his sad eyes nearly level with mine. We couldn't hear the reavers, but they were coming. My back muscles spasmed, as if at any moment they expected the reavers to jump up from the rear seat, rake the meat off my spine, and yank out my still-beating heart.

Asha wiped the tears off his face with both hands. "Here," he said gently. "Take them." He cupped my cheeks. I sucked in my breath as the moisture burned into my skin.

"Asha."

"Now go!"

He made a commanding motion and of its own accord my foot slammed the accelerator.

Chapter Twenty

I believe in miracles. E.J.'s my main proof. I can't look into those wide green eyes, feel those perfect little fingers wrapped around mine, realize this complete little girl with her own personality, made of my sister and her husband and a little bit of me, shares my world, without knowing our family recently experienced a miracle. That's a biggie. Sometimes God throws me small ones too. Like the fact that I didn't crash Asha's BMW as I took a sharp right coming onto the road out of his back gate despite the fact that most of my attention was on the rearview mirror.

Four reavers had come after me. Two of them ran after the car. One actually jumped onto the trunk, but flew off as soon as I turned the corner. The other two had entered the garage to confront Asha, and I felt my chest tighten with fear for him. I'd just decided to turn the car around when I saw the reavers fly out of the garage and the door thump down. Then I was on the street, wailing down the asphalt like a bank robber, heading back to base through choppily lit, third-world-looking neighborhoods on roads that were often so narrow I wasn't sure how vehicles passed each other during the day.

I'd made it maybe halfway back when the TV van caught up with me.

It tried to ram me in the rear end, but I gunned the engine and pulled far enough ahead to wonder if I was giving them too good of a shot at my back tires. I took the next left before I could find out, watched the van nearly roll in its attempt to follow me, and decided a zigzag course might be the best way to keep them from flattening any part of Asha's ride.

As we raced through the eerily quiet streets of the city, I debated whether or not to call the team. I'd put it off because, although I knew the Wizard would want them to defend me from the reavers and would, therefore, let Dave help me, I didn't want any of them hurt because of me. More important, I didn't want the local authorities to get wind of our operation. Something they were bound to do if the neighbors heard gunshots.

I slammed the brakes, spun the wheel hard to the left, accelerated almost before I straightened out again. Behind me the van's tires squealed in protest and a glance in the mirror showed me reavers being thrown around the interior like balls in a batting cage.

"Dammit, would you monsters wreck already?" I headed down a narrow alleyway, watched the van throw sparks as it squeezed past the buildings that flanked it. "I need Vayl. Come on, Cirilai." I rubbed the ring against my thigh like it was Aladdin's lamp and if I wished hard enough Vayl would just waft out of one of the rubies, sink onto the seat beside me, and calm me with that ultracool demeanor of his even as he and I worked out our battle plan.

Vayl was out, though. The closer I got to the house, the surer I was of that fact. "Shit! Why didn't I tell Cole to chew on his own holster? Then I'd still have that holy water on me and this Beemer and I could've disappeared into the city like a couple of street tramps."

As soon as I said the words "holy water" I got an idea. At the next intersection I swung the car back toward the temple.

The van dogged me all the way there. But it didn't attempt any more quick turns. And it didn't run up on my bumper, for which

I was grateful. If I trash another car this early in the year, I kind of thought Pete would have a heart attack.

I drove right up to the steps, dove out the passenger door, and raced to the temple's huge entryway. The goat raised its head with interest as I stopped at the threshold.

The van screeched to a halt and reavers piled out like it was on fire. The mahghul crowded onto its roof and the adjoining satellite dish, watching eagerly as the four of them came at me.

I stepped inside the temple. They stopped on the other side of the door, prohibited from attacking me, as I'd hoped, by the sanctity of the place. At a temporary impasse, we stared each other down.

The original reaver, who was no longer slapping imaginary flies, had found himself some real winners to help him take me out. Beside him, panting like he'd just run to the top of the Sears Tower, was a sweaty, fat man who reminded me of a puffy Jason Alexander. He leaned hard against his neighbor, a tiny old dude who barely looked capable of holding himself up, much less a creature six times his size. The fourth reaver was so thin you could actually see his skull through his skin.

But though they looked pathetic, underestimating these creatures would be a huge mistake. I could still see their shields, framing each of them in black. And every one of them stared at me from a third eyeball centered in the middle of their foreheads.

"Where's the rest of the gang?" I asked the original.

"Somebody had to stay back at the station," he said. "We're a twenty-four-hour-a-day operation, so you know what that means."

"I do?"

He grinned, his spiked tongue wagging out of his mouth like a bird dog's. "That means we can wait you out, lambie pie. As long as it takes. Eventually you'll have to leave here. And then we'll have your heart. And your soul." His three amigos giggled. They reminded me of the hyenas in Disney's *Lion King*. You're laughing with them on the outside, but inside you know those sons of bitches mean to eat your favorite cubs and it makes you want to puke.

Ignoring a sudden urge to run to the bathroom and heave into the toilet, I said, "What's your name, Reaver?"

He smiled graciously, his three eyes blinking at a steady, four-second beat, as if he had a timer attached to his eyelids. "You can call me Prentiss Cairo."

"Well, P.C., here's the thing," I said, flavoring my voice with enough camaraderie that he looked puzzled. "You can take the Magistrate every single one of my organs, tie up my soul with a pretty pink bow, and he's still not gonna pat your fanny and send you to the showers with a bonus."

When they all looked at each other with the confusion you often see on guys' faces when women start discussing the pros and cons of home hair tinting, I decided to be blunt and hope to God I'd guessed right in forcing this confrontation.

"Have you boys been in touch with the boss recently? You remember him, don'tcha? Pretty boy hauling around a pound of Uldin Beit's flesh? The reason I ask is, *I* have. And I can guarantee there's been a change in plan. Your sponsor, Samos, may still want me dead. And I'm sure Uldin Beit hasn't changed her mind. But the Magistrate has developed a whole new strategy where I'm concerned. And he is the guy with the whip, after all."

The four of them huddled, all of them talking at once. "I *told* you we should have checked in when we hit this plane!" whined the Jason Alexander clone.

"She's lying!" declared the old man.

"If we mess this up he's going to kick the crap out of us," declared the skinny guy.

"Shut up!" yelled Prentiss, glaring at me over his shoulder. I shrugged, gave him a hey-it's-not-my-fault-you-can't-control-your-stooges look, and stuck my hands in my pockets. The left brushed past my engagement ring. Instant comfort, as if Matt was standing beside me, his hand on my shoulder, his whisper warm in my ear. "You're doing great, Jaz. I'm proud of you."

The other slipped over the hilt of my bolo. The mahghul stirred with excitement as my hand wrapped around the handle. Gave it a slight pull. Several of them dropped off the van. Crept up behind the reavers.

"So what do you say, P.C.?" I inquired, resolutely ignoring the mahghul. "You want to kill me and put yourself so deep in the Magistrate's doghouse, instead of souls, you'll be chasing cockroaches for the next couple of hundred years? Or do you want to make a deal?"

Prentiss narrowed all three of his eyes. Eeeww, freaky. "What do you mean?"

I shrugged. "Leave me to the Magistrate. I get to survive another day. Uldin Beit gets what she wants in the long run. And you guys don't get your asses reamed by the bossman. Seems like a win-win to me."

New huddle, much whispering accompanied by a few violent gestures compliments of Prentiss and the old fart. A few moments later they faced me, united and decided. "We'll do it," said the old guy. He held out his hand, expecting me to shake on it. Which was when I realized I was screwed.

I know a little bit about dealing with the devil. Or, at least, his minions. The CIA presents a whole course on it. People in our line of work, well, we get tempted. A lot. Rails and sates, adversaries and siordents, they've all been known to throw our agents an offer they couldn't resist. So, in order to make sure none of us rookies got dragged off to never-ever-laugh like the famous Drew Telast, who'd thought it worth risking his soul to get the dirt on Premier Khordikov, the Agency had organized a class. As a result, I knew no servant of the Great Taker would ever make a bargain with a simple handshake. If he'd really meant to seal the deal, both of us would've had to get bloody.

I stared at the outstretched hand. Wished I had just one ally guarding my back. Then realized I had an entire temple.

I stepped forward, shoved my palm into Old Fart's, and grabbed hard with the other hand as well. Throwing all my weight backward, I swung him around and through the doorway. He screamed as he burst into flame—*whoosh*—as if he'd been dipped in lighter fluid and thrown into a bonfire.

"Sarif!" screamed the anorexic guy, momentarily stunned into stillness as his comrades attacked.

With no time to draw my gun and fiddle with the safety, I went for my knife. It felt heavy in my hand, which was when I realized a mahghul had wrapped itself around my forearm like a giant sloth. My skin burned where it had bitten me. I tried to shake it off, but only succeeded in making it latch on tighter.

Fine, I thought, the rage rising in me. *I'll take care of you later, you little bastard. And if I torture you some first, just think of it as payback.*

The part of my mind that had gained extra protection when my Sensitivity first kicked in understood that my thoughts were no longer quite my own. The mahghul was ratcheting up my killing instinct even as it ate my fury. But I didn't have time to concern myself with petty details right now. Prentiss and the fat reaver were charging me. Though the mahghul on their backs slowed them some, they still came faster than humans, and only my training allowed me to shove the bolo through Fat Guy's third eye before spinning clear of P.C.

I threw a kick at Skinny Dude's head before he could completely recover. His shield protected him well enough that it only staggered him, but that gave me time to draw Grief. I shot twice at Prentiss, missing the sweet spot both times.

"Shit!" Now mahghul weighed down both my legs. I felt teeth in the small of my back as well. I wanted to shoot them. But this was no time to waste ammunition.

The reavers looked like mutants as they moved toward me, so completely had they been overtaken by the murder monsters. The sight made me feel slightly crazed. I felt as if the mahghul were stealing something vital from me by draining my victims. The pleasure of the kill? The delight of seeing real fear in their eyes? Suddenly shooting the reavers seemed too quick. I wanted them to die more slowly. So I could enjoy it.

I slapped myself across the face. "Get a grip, ya loon!" I aimed Grief at Skinny Dude. Shot him almost point-blank. He went down hard, disappearing beneath the writhing forms of the mahghul like a prey fish caught inside the net of a piranha feeding frenzy.

Prentiss punched me in the chest so hard I thought for a second my heart had stopped. I staggered backward, hit the frame of the temple's doorway, and spun on into the building. A chorus of screams rose from the mahghul, nearly deafening me. They pulled away, smoke rising from their skins as they ran out of the temple. The last one didn't make it in time. He didn't burn like the reaver. He exploded.

I covered my face with my hands, and when I raised it again, realized it was the only part of me not covered in gore. If I'd been in my right mind just then, I might have lost it completely. But the mahghul had drained so much of my vitality that I simply didn't have any freak-out left in me. I struggled to my feet, knocked the ick out of my gun barrel, and stepped back outside.

Prentiss looked like a gorilla with mahghul swarming all over him. Something, maybe seeing mine explode, had made him realize he was under attack. He was trying to pull them off. But they held tight, like a pack of enormous, excited ticks.

"Help me!" he screamed just before one stuck its small paw down his throat. His next bout of begging came out as a series of indecipherable glugs. My first instinct was to run back into the temple. Grab a torch off the wall. I was betting it doubled as holy fire. I had a feeling that might make the parasites loosen their hold.

Except as soon as they did, P.C. would try to kill me some more.

So instead I took steady aim at that extra eye, the one the mahghul seemed intent on avoiding. It widened. Began to blink rapidly as the gurgling sounds rose to a fearful peak.

I squeezed the trigger gently, part of me happily amazed the mahghul avoided me as I finished off the reaver. Maybe the smell of their brethren on me was enough to keep them at arm's length. Had I happened on a new pesticide? Should I give Asha a buzz? *Hey, buddy. Great news! All you gotta do is spread mahghul guts all over your bod and you can go back to busting humps just like in the good old days!*

As the remaining nasties slunk away I tried to plan my next move. But it wasn't easy to think past the I-couldn't-give-a-shit that had stolen over me. I knew those who'd bitten me had left a mark deeper than the bloody imprints of their fangs. Impossible to pinpoint among the emotional scars that crisscrossed my soul, marring it just as deeply as the welts on Vayl's back, these wounds were already festering. Soon even the core of me, still clear-eyed enough to be biting its nails to the quick, wouldn't be able to fend off this pervasive sense of hopelessness.

"I need a cure," I whispered. I looked down at myself. Covered in drying blood and body parts, I should be puking, gagging, swearing. Jesus, I should at least be trying to get it off! But I just stared. *I'm doomed.*

A single tear escaped the corner of my eye, burned its way

down my face, and dripped onto my hand, which still held my bolo. I watched it sizzle on my skin for a moment, as if it were a drop of grease in a pan.

"Ow!" I rubbed my hand, surprised at the pain a bead of moisture could cause. Certain the Amanha Szeya had affected more than my tear ducts when his hands had cupped my cheeks. Pleased at the white spot I'd cleared with that small effort.

I wiped my face off too, before it could get any hotter. Took a look at the gook my hand had removed.

"A shower. That would make me feel better." Just knowing I'd entertained a positive thought allowed me to move to the vehicles. No way would I sit my disgusting ass in Asha's beautiful black sedan. So I got into the TV van, started it up, and drove home.

Chapter Twenty-One

Being a girl, I enjoy the dramatic entrance. Having all eyes on me, preferably admiring and male, as I sashay to my table. Or, better yet, to the podium to accept a major award. My hair, makeup, and gown the most perfect combination any woman has ever put together in the history of the world.

But in my line of work, if that happens, I've just screwed the pooch. So when I opened the kitchen door, after parking the TV van in the garage and thanking my lucky stars its high ceilings just barely accommodated the satellite dish, I experienced a flash of guilt when every eye in the room turned to me and widened in a united moment of shock. I couldn't hang on to the feeling though. In fact, no emotion seemed to stick for longer than a few seconds before it fizzled beneath the mahghul tumor that grew inside me, spreading its tentacles into every part of my being.

"Hard night?" asked Cole in a lame attempt at humor.

"You could say that," I replied, taking stock of my audience. Everybody had bought a ticket. Except Vayl. "Where's the boss?" I asked Cole.

He hesitated, then shrugged. "In the guys' room," he said, "meditating. Apparently you have to achieve nirvana before you can turn a human into a vampire, and he hasn't quite made the leap."

Anger flitted through me. Cirilai would've warned him of my

danger. Normally he'd have come dashing to the rescue. Even if he'd thought I could handle the situation, he'd have hovered nearby. Stood on the sidelines and cheered me on. Nothing on earth would've stopped him from backing me up. Until now.

"Jaz." Dave stepped forward from his spot by the stove, where he'd been talking with Cassandra. "What happened to you?" He reached out and I backed up, my heel banging into woodwork before my shoulders could hit the wall and leave a big red splotch.

"Don't touch me. I . . . the things that attacked me leave a residue. I don't want you hurt." *And I don't want you to know that I know. Somehow I think if you touch me the Wizard might get a whiff of my suspicions. And that'll be the end of us all. Oh Jesus, Dave, how am I going to save you?*

"Are you infected?" demanded Amazon Grace, jumping off her stool and heading for the living room. She grabbed Jet and Cam, tried to drag them with her, but they didn't seem interested in budging. "She's going to give you guys some fatal disease," Grace warned them. When they still refused to stand up, she snarled something unintelligible, let go of their shirts, and stomped out of the room.

"It's not something you can get through the air," I told them. "Probably not even by touching. I think you have to actually kill somebody."

"Which you obviously did tonight," said Natchez, his upper lip curling at the sight I made.

"I'll fill you all in, I promise. Just let me get a shower first, okay? Actually,"—I turned to Cassandra—"what I really need is some holy water."

Half an hour later, anointed and bathed, realizing I should feel tons better and feeling a fat lot of nothing instead, I headed back toward the kitchen. I passed the guys' room on the way. Vayl had closed the door, but I could sense him behind it. The anger came again, and before it could leave I grabbed it. Held hard to it, though it tried to wriggle out of my hands like the slick little eel it had become.

I threw open the door and strode into the room. "Where the hell were you?" I demanded.

He sat on a beautifully crafted blue and white rug within a circle of stones, his hands resting in his lap. His expression, serene as a Buddhist monk's, didn't change when I barged in. But his eyes, already a troubled oceanic blue, darkened to purple. Any other time I might've taken a second to wonder why Vayl, sitting alone, preparing for an event meant to lead to the fulfillment of a centuries' long quest, had reason to be upset about anything. But the clock was ticking on my wave of anger and I had more urgent business to deal with.

"What do you mean?" he asked smoothly. He stood, I think because he didn't like looking up at me as I glared down at him.

Stay mad, I told myself. Not an easy order to obey considering my circumstances. And the fact that Vayl had already changed for bed. All he wore was a pair of white silk drawstring pajama bottoms that left very little to the imagination. And mine had kicked into overdrive.

I resolutely kept my eyes on his as I said, "While you were out playing Turn the Seer, four reavers nearly killed me. Not to mention twenty or thirty mahghul. You're supposed to be my boss. You *said* we were partners."

"What are mahghul?" Vayl asked, allowing his eyes to wander to the bed, which already held his sleeping tent. He didn't even seem interested.

"We saw them at the hanging!" I informed him hotly. "They attack killers and their victims. They suck away all your emotions and leave you fucking numb, Vayl. They were on me. You wanna see?" I turned around and lifted my tunic, gave him a good five seconds to survey the damage. When I felt the tips of his fingers brush my back I jerked my shirt down and spun around.

I didn't want to recognize the expression on his face. In my opinion, you shouldn't have to see that kind of grief on a person more than once in your life. David had worn that look sixteen months ago when he'd walked into my kitchen just in time to watch me destroy his wife.

"What have you done?" he'd yelled, running to the spot where she'd stood only seconds before, begging for entry. So she could tear my throat out.

"She made me promise," I told him through chattering teeth. I'd begun to shake head to toe. I put my newly named gun on the table before I accidentally shot myself in the foot and hugged myself. "We vowed to each other that if one of us turned, the other would smoke her."

He stared at me, his eyes wild and disbelieving. I could tell he wanted to lean down, touch what remained of her clothes, her being, but his broken ribs barely allowed him to stand. His doctor had only consented to release him for our team's funerals if he'd promise to stay with a family member. Since I lived closest to the cemetery, he'd chosen me.

"You're lying!" he cried. "Jessie would never make that kind of deal! She'd want to live no matter what!"

"No." I tried to shake my head, but all it would do was jerk. I swallowed reflexively. No longer just trembling now, I was seizing. Having some sort of convulsive fit that made me feel like I was standing on top of a jackhammer. I clenched my teeth together, forced myself to talk through them. "*You* want her to live no matter what."

"You're such a fucking hypocrite!" David yelled. "If Matt had been standing on your threshold, asking to come in, you'd have thrown open the door. Hell, you'd have slit a wrist for him!"

I didn't say a word. Useless to tell Dave that Matt and I had made the same deal as I'd had with Jessie. What did it matter anyway? If he wanted to be mad at me, if that helped him get through this nightmare, let him. It was the least I could do.

I dug my fingernails into my sides, sank them deep and concentrated on the pain. It helped. Kept me from taking the next step, which was walking over to the wall and banging my head against it till I passed out.

"I can't stand the sight of you for another second," he said, spitting the words like venom. "I'm getting out of here."

I nodded, too wounded by my own terrible losses to let this new hurt do more than take its place in line. While he went to his room to pack, I took a few minutes to pull myself together. Then I gathered up Jessie's remains. They made a pitifully small pile for such a bright, vibrant woman. I put them in a cedar-lined box that Granny May had given me when I was a little girl and handed it to Dave on his way out.

"It's what's left of her," I said. "You can keep it or bury it. Whatever you want." Tears sprang into his eyes as he took the box from me. "I loved her, Dave. I loved them all."

He nodded. "You may have. But you were in charge. So it's your fault they're dead."

I'd nodded. *Yes. My fault, my fault, my fault . . .*

Later he'd sort of apologized for that last remark. But he'd never really forgiven me for Jessie. And I still didn't blame him. I guess I'd never pursued another real conversation about her with him after that because I hadn't wanted to see that expression on his face again. But here it was, plastered across Vayl's visage like a movie on a screen.

"Cirilai did not warn me," he said.

"Vayl, this ring is better than a hotel wake-up call. You must've felt *something*. It's been zapping me left and right about you."

He dropped his head. Shook it a few times. When he looked up again, his whole face seemed to have tightened, as if a decade's worth of worries had suddenly dropped on his head. "What do you think this means?"

"Why are you asking me? It's your ring. You should know why you've become disconnected from it." *From what it represents. Come on, pal, isn't it obvious?*

He threw back his shoulders. Determined, it seemed, to soldier on despite the growing evidence against the wisdom of his current course of action. "It does not matter. You are obviously fine. Our mission is still on course for completion. And Zarsa will be ready for the turning by week's end. Everything is on track." By the tone in his voice, I thought he was trying to convince himself more than me. Normally I would've grabbed him by the shirt and shaken some sense into him. But at the moment I couldn't find one give-a-crap bone in my body.

"Okay," I said. I turned to go.

"What did you say?"

I looked over my shoulder. Why would he be mad? I'd just agreed with him. "I said fine. You're right. Now if you don't mind, I'm going to—"

"I most definitely *do* mind!"

I turned back to face him, always a good choice when dealing with a madman. "Vayl," I said gently, so as not to push him clear off the deep end, "what is it that you want?"

"I want you to yell!" He stopped, looked surprised at himself, rushed on. "You have been"—he searched for the words—"on my case, how you say, in my face, ever since I took up with Zarsa. Frankly, it has infuriated me to no end!"

"Uh-huh. And now that I've stopped, you want me to start

again? Aren't you kind of undermining yourself here just a little bit?"

"Yes! But when I fight you, I do not have to listen to my own doubts."

Ahhh. "Well, sorry, Charlie, I don't feel like sparring anymore." I tried out a smile, realized I couldn't quite hack it. "Come to think of it, I don't feel anything anymore."

Vayl closed the distance between us so swiftly my eyes barely followed his movements. He pulled me into his arms almost violently. It was a me-Tarzan-you-Jane kind of embrace. And Jane liked it fine.

His eyes transformed as they stared into mine, changing from amethyst to emerald in a couple of dizzying seconds. "I find I do not like this new, mahghul-inspired you," he said, running his fingers through my wet hair. He spent some time on the bit that had turned white, twining it gently around his thumb. And I let him.

Hell, if he'd wanted to give me a full-body massage I'd have hopped on the nearest table and invited him to dig in. His powers percolated at their usual level, so I knew he wasn't using any hocus-pocus on me. But I still felt hypnotized, captivated by his touch, the fascination in his eyes and the possibilities they hid.

"I don't like it either," I whispered. "But I seem to be stuck with it."

"I disagree," Vayl replied softly. "Creatures who feed on emotions leave a void that can be filled again—over years, with a great deal of patience. Or all at once, with a strong dose of emotion. The trick is to find the proper sensation." As he looked into my eyes, Vayl smiled. Not his regular lip twitch, which made him look more cynical than amused. Not even his full-faced, ferocious grin. This smile was new. Because it managed a sweetness I'd never seen in him before.

"Vayl?" I never got a chance to ask the question forming in my mind. It couldn't have been that important anyway. Because the moment Vayl lowered his head, captured my lips with his, I forgot it.

I'd fantasized this kiss a few hundred times since the last time Vayl's lips had brushed mine. And I've got a terrific imagination. But I still hadn't prepared myself for the rush of desire that tore through me as Vayl's arms tightened around me, pulling me so close I thought for a second I could feel his heart beating in my own chest.

I know, I know, it was just a kiss, right? Nobody's ever really heard violins. The only people who've been blinded by passion were the ones who couldn't see that well to start with. I've heard all the clichés and called them crap myself. That was before I met Matt, before I learned what a difference real love could make. But, while I knew paradise existed, I'd never really expected to visit it again.

Especially not on the wings of a single kiss.

Still, it was Vayl. Who'd brought me out of the darkness. Who'd stuck with me despite some spectacular screwups on my part. Who'd given me his ring, his trust, his innermost secrets. And who had nearly become a stranger in the course of a few days. That last bit had terrified me more than I realized. And it made our kiss all the more breathtaking. Because it meant he was back to stay.

When I finally came up for air, Vayl drew his head back and said, "How do you feel?"

Realizing for the first time that my arms were around his neck, I let them drop to his chest. His body felt so incredible, my hands just wanted to keep wandering, but I forced them to keep still. I smiled lazily. "Delicious."

"Excellent." He slapped me on the butt. "Now, off with you. I still have a great deal to do if I am to turn Zarsa before week's end."

I watched my hands curl into fists. And if I caught some chest hair in the process, tough. "What the hell did you just say?"

He chuckled. "Just checking to make sure your temper is intact."

"Oh, believe me, it is. In fact, right at this moment, I feel perfectly capable of taking your head off!"

"Then perhaps I will just let this whole pact with Zarsa fall by the wayside."

"You're damn straight you will!" I was still pissed, but not so much that I didn't catch his look of regret as he leaned over and began gathering rocks into a pile. I said, "I am sorry though. I know finding your boys means everything to you."

He stood, let the rock he held slip from one hand to the other and back again as he watched it thoughtfully. Finally he said, "You must know that I will never give up the search. I *have* to find my sons." He met my gaze. "But I will never again let that desire come between us. What we have . . ." His eyes warmed to amber. "I cannot imagine losing it. Not for anything."

Chapter Twenty-Two

I never really pegged Vayl for a sweet talker. But damned if the words he said didn't make me want to jump on him and smother him in smooches. I'd just taken a step toward him, watched his eyes crinkle with pleasure as he realized my plan, when Cole cleared his throat behind me.

"Jaz, I thought you'd want to know," he said roughly, "I found the home owner."

I turned around, my Lucille smile firmly in place. My alter ego would know how to deal with Cole without hurting him, whereas Jaz would just be blunt. Maybe even mean. "Cool! Who is he?"

"A businessman named Delir Kazimi."

"Have you got a picture?"

"I'll print one up for you."

"Great. Thanks!"

Cole and Vayl traded stares. If they'd been any other species of male, the next step would have been a full-on charge. I started to shake my head. *How do I screw things up so expertly in such a short amount of time?* I asked myself. *I really thought I'd settled things with Cole. That he understood I didn't want a relationship. Then, the next thing you know, he's professed his love, we're camel tipping in Tehran, and I've let him blackmail me into a date. And that's going to thrill Vayl like a stake through the heart.*

Meanwhile, the vampire in question, perhaps realizing Cole

was no threat, had turned his attention to me. "Why do you want to know who owns this house?" he asked.

I explained my theory that the Wizard had taken control of David and that, perhaps, he even owned the building in which we currently resided.

"I suppose it is possible," said Vayl, "but the motivation for doing such a thing makes no sense. Why would someone with his power and reach set himself up for assassination?"

"We haven't quite figured that out," I admitted. "I think first we need to prove Dave is the mole. Then we have to figure out how to make sure he survives this mission."

"Jasmine," Vayl said gently, "you know none of us has the power to do that."

"Then I'll just have to talk to Raoul."

"Won't that be dangerous?" asked Cole, still sounding somewhat belligerent. "I thought after your showdown with the Magistrate you'd decided to avoid Raoul." He'd relaxed enough from his stare-down with Vayl to lean against the doorjamb. But he'd managed to bite the ever-present toothpick in his mouth in half, and was now searching his pockets for a replacement.

I looked him in the eye as he patted himself down, wishing I had such an easy-to-fix habit. The need to shuffle was practically burning holes into my palms. But all I said was "That was before my brother's life was on the line."

Vayl said, "I want to be convinced, and yet . . . if David did not die in training, how do you think the Wizard killed him? I would assume he was always with one of his men, even on leave. Unless he is a complete loner?"

I thought about it. Reluctantly shook my head. "No, he'd never take off on his own. He always hung with his friends. And in a place like this, even on leave, it would be too dangerous to wander off by yourself."

"Which means," Cole put in, "this dude would've had to kill Dave, plant some sort of control device, and bring him back right in front of his men, without any of them ever realizing it had happened."

"Are we sure there is a device?" asked Vayl.

"According to the Enkyklios, the Wizard either has to see his zombies to control them, or he has to implant something inside them that allows him to control them from a distance," I reminded him.

That implant would give off some sort of psychic signal, which was why Bergman had sent me to Asha in the first place. Flash of guilt as I realized I still hadn't clued Vayl in as to his existence. Well, hey, we weren't married. I didn't have to tell him every little detail of my day. *Except*, I reminded myself, *when it has some bearing on the job*. But I found it harder than I expected to admit to Vayl that I'd met somebody while stalking him. That the guy was so powerful he knew Raoul. And that he'd shared some of his go-juice with me. I let it be, hoping I'd find a better time and place. Or at least more courage if the timing turned out crappy.

"Maybe we should ask the guys in Dave's unit," Cole finally suggested. "One of them would probably know what we were talking about right away. It would've had to have been a time when he was at least injured, right? I mean, you can't kill a guy and bring him back without leaving some trace."

"That's it!" I cried. "Cam was just telling us the story! How they captured two of the Wizard's cohorts. How one of them went for Dave's throat, left massive amounts of blood all over the place, and Dave without the ability to talk for a couple of days."

"That's right!" Cole said. "And come to think of it, doesn't he scratch his neck quite a bit?" The signs Bergman had told us to look for. They were right under our noses all the time. I hadn't sensed David's uniqueness because I'd accepted it to start with. I'd thought he was one of Raoul's fighters, like me. And I hadn't noticed his tells because, by bringing up his suspicions about a mole, he'd turned those doubts completely away from himself.

"All right," said Vayl, nodding slowly. "I am convinced. And yet, I still wonder. Why? What is to be gained by arranging for two CIA assassins to come and kill you?"

We offered him our theories, which he refused to swallow. "I do not believe he wants to die. Especially not at our hands. That would be the height of dishonor for him. So let us assume he wants to live."

"Maybe he wants to go straight?" Cole hazarded. "Make it look like he's been killed, when in reality he starts a new life somewhere completely different?"

"And so he has set us up to kill—who—his double?" Vayl asked.

We nodded. It happened all the time. Bad guys sent their patsies in one direction while they went the opposite in the hope that whoever was chasing them would follow the patsy and drop the J-DAM on his head.

I fished the Wizard's picture out of my pocket and stared at it, feeling a whole new level of bummed for the ladies it portrayed. No way would the gentleman who held them willingly give up his life with them. Which meant he was being coerced. Shit. Not only couldn't we kill him, now we had to rescue his family before the Wizard's people found out the game was up, got pissed, and lopped off their heads. At the same time we still needed to locate the Wizard.

Time for Bergman and Cassandra to chime in.

It wasn't easy to separate Cassandra from David. They'd become kind of indivisible. Like prime numbers. Which broke my heart. And here I'd thought it was already totaled.

In the end Cole told Cassandra I had girl problems and nobody in the kitchen was interested in hearing any more about it. He lured Bergman out of the room by informing him Pete was on my special specs, something about a glitch in his translator hardware that had caused an agent's hair to catch fire.

When we were all gathered in the boys' room with Cole guarding the door against snoops, I gave our newbies the lowdown. Bergman took it well. Cassandra swayed a little, but she refused help as she walked to the bench, where she sat still and staring. I sat beside her, talking fast.

"I'm going to see Raoul as soon as I can," I told her. "I will work this out."

"If it's possible," she said, her voice distant, strangely calm. She'd had to dig deep for this strength. Almost to the other side of the world.

"Cassandra, you should have more faith in me," I said. I sounded composed, but my insides were quaking. The consequences of my failure were so extreme I could hardly bear the thought of them. So, of course, I didn't. "Did I not save your life on our last mission, despite the fact that you'd had a vision of your own death?"

Momentary pause. "Yes."

"Shouldn't that count for something now, especially considering the fact that you haven't had a single vision since you touched my brother thirty-two hours ago?"

It took a while for her eyes to focus on me. When they did, they managed a smile. "Yes," she said.

"Well then." I left it there. Moved on. "We think the Wizard's link to David is in his neck." And that's where I stopped. I looked at Vayl, suddenly helpless. If I had to say another word I'd burst into tears and ruin every bit of credibility I'd gained over the past five minutes. Because I could only pretend my twin being a zombie was no big deal for so long. And then the horror of it would overcome me, leave me speechless.

During these times I almost wished Vayl hadn't rescued me from the mahghul poison. What a relief to have cared less. Kept a distance from the pain. But I couldn't have functioned then. I'd have been left, like Asha, standing on the sidewalk, scribbling names on a notepad as if I thought that might make some difference in my worthless, blasted world.

Vayl nodded slightly, raising an eyebrow to ask if I'd be okay. I shrugged. He said, "We need a way to track the connection between the device in David's neck and the Wizard. We thought perhaps, between the two of you"—his glance took in Cassandra and Bergman both—"perhaps you could find a scientific and/or magical means to do that *without* alerting the Wizard that his plans have been compromised."

"That might be difficult on my end," said Cassandra. "David and I have been spending such a lot of time together. He might become suspicious when I begin to stay away."

A definite point. I said, "Then I think we bring in Cam. He can decide if the rest of the team can keep this kind of secret without letting Dave in on it. And they can divert him when you're busy."

We agreed to let Cole recruit Cam while I tried to contact Raoul. Bergman took my place on the bench. He and Cassandra immediately began discussing strategies while I went to stand by Vayl at the window.

"How do you want to do this?" he asked in a low voice.

"I'm not going out-of-body yet," I told him, trying not to shiver at how easily the Magistrate had trapped me last time. "But if I have to—" I bit my lip to keep myself from saying goodbye. You have to believe you're coming back. "It might get rough," I said. I twisted Cirilai on my finger. Gave it a tap. "You may need to send help." I paused. "If you can."

He nodded, the relief in his eyes making me wish I could hug him. "Yes. The ring and I are on speaking terms again."

Whew! In dire circumstances, Vayl could share his power with me through the ring. It wasn't easy on either one of us, but if Cirilai told him I was in trouble, he might be able to assist me. Having been through one battle without that fallback, I was doubly glad to have it now.

"All right, then," he said, "go ahead and talk."

I looked out the window. *Raoul? Major problems here below.*

I'M LISTENING.

I sketched out the details. *So, what do you think?* I finally asked. *Can you save my brother* this time? I emphasized the last two words, letting him know I remembered our brief conversation about Dave on my initial visit to his headquarters.

Long silence, during which I realized it had begun to rain. I gazed down at the small courtyard behind the house. It looked as bare and forlorn as my life would be without Dave in it.

Raoul? I don't think you're understanding the severity of my situation here. We need to talk face-to-face.

TOO DANGEROUS.

For you or for me? Because I gotta tell you, if my brother dies when I think you could've saved him, neither one of us is going to be very effective at our jobs for a long, long time.

HE IS GOVERNED BY EVIL.

So's practically everyone in this country! Come on, you're smart enough to tell the difference between a victim and a bad guy! Look at Dave's history, for chrissake. He's an angel compared to me! I paused to check my tone. No sign of whining, thank goodness, but a definite on the desperation. Screw it. I'd worry about my pride later. *I don't know why he ended up where he is. Or why you never told me. But I do know my brother. He'd throw himself on his own grenade rather than betray his comrades and his country.*

Another pause, which I used to remind myself to call my other sibling. Evie must be frantic by now, worried about Albert and unable to contact me or David. One thing at a time though. If I tried to think about everything I had to accomplish in the next twenty-four hours I'd shatter. *Save my brother*, I told Raoul. *You want to make some kind of sweet deal with me in return for that favor, I'm all about it.*

GO TO SLEEP.

I understood immediately. We operated on such different planes, communication was never easy. He couldn't speak to me at length in my head without frying my synapses. I couldn't visit him at home without dying first. If I left my body the Magistrate would pounce. My dreams were the happy middle ground.

Okay. Give me a few minutes to wind things up here.

Bergman opened the door to Cole's knock. He strolled in with a fake grin on his face. "Hey, Jaz, you'll never guess what Cam and I found in that TV van you stole."

Cam followed closely and Bergman shut the door gently behind them. They carried two portable cameras and a sheaf of papers Cole said were government taping permits.

As soon as Cam heard the catch click behind him, the easygoing smile left his face. He set the camera he carried on the floor and walked over to where I stood, still half gazing out the window, trying to marshal my arguments for my next go-around with Raoul.

"You got any kind of plan that's gonna save my commander's life, I'm in," he said flatly.

"It might call for some major acting skills," I warned him.

"Part of the reason they chose us for this job is because we can blend in. Become anything but soldiers. You need me to prance across a stage wearing a tiara and tights, I can pull it off so convincingly the audience will be screaming for more by the end of the show."

I swallowed a smile. "Well, it might be extreme, but you should be able to keep your pants on throughout."

He nodded, the twinkle in his eyes letting me know his humor might be squelched, but it would never die.

"What about the rest of your team?" I asked.

"You can depend on them," he said instantly.

"No. *You* can depend on them." I looked him in the eyes. "I don't trust Grace."

"She'd die for David."

"She's as territorial as a bull moose. Think about it, Cam. Her commander is no longer fit to lead, only nobody can tell him that. So we've all got to make him think he's in charge while somebody else calls the shots. Mission-wise, that somebody is Vayl. He's still overseeing this job. He's the one who's responsible to take down the Wizard. But where David's life is concerned, I'm the boss. I believe I know how to save him. I've begun that process. If Grace has different ideas, her instinct will be to take the lead. I won't allow that. You need to make her understand—if she can't fall in line on this, I won't argue. I won't hesitate. I'll just kill her."

For just a second I let the veil lift, allowed him to see the cold-blooded murderess I kept hidden from my family, my crew, even myself most of the time. She's not pretty or desirable. In fact, she's so freaking scary my instinct is to keep her bound and gagged, locked in a sarcophagus, and buried in the deepest tomb I can find. But I need her. She keeps me and my country strong. As long as I keep her leashed. So far it's worked out okay. But I know I'm playing with dynamite. I just hope I'm smart enough to exorcise her before she explodes.

Cam backed up a step, realized what he'd done and held his ground. He nodded crisply, his lips pressed into an uncharacteristically grim line. "Grace won't be a problem."

"Good."

"I'll spread the word."

"As far as the Wizard is concerned, we will continue with the original plan," Vayl told him. "However, Cassandra and Bergman have been assigned a new project. David will have to be kept from her when she is working. We would like your crew to make sure he does not suspect he is being separated from her deliberately."

"No problem." Cam looked at me, the concern so thick in his eyes it seemed to cloud every other thought. I could tell he wanted to ask if my strategy had a chance of working. But he'd been around too long, seen too much to believe I could give him a comforting answer. So he simply nodded, turned on his heel, and left.

When we were all alone in the room again, Bergman said in a small voice, "Would you really kill Grace?" I let the window curtain drop and fully faced my crew. I looked them each in the eye.

Bergman, his thin shoulders hunched against every fear he'd ever felt or imagined, peered at me through the lenses of his glasses as if they could shield him from whatever reality I might throw at him. Cassandra, with her classic bone structure and clear dark skin, would never look more than twenty-eight. But the weight of centuries of pain and hardship had somehow given her the air of an ancient goddess. Cole gazed at me with a frank acceptance that could become addictive. Vayl stood at my shoulder, not touching me. And yet I felt the solid strength of his support. After having lost it, even briefly, I realized how much it meant to me. That scared me. But not enough to let it go.

I talked to Bergman, though my words were for everyone. "Yes, I'll kill her if I think she's a threat. I'd do the same if I thought anyone was a danger to any of you. I learned a hard lesson with my Helsingers. It's not one I'm going to repeat. I won't lose another crew member if there's anything I can do to stop it. And I do mean anything."

I suddenly imagined Raoul, waiting for me to dream as he lounged on his black leather recliner, overhearing my last words. "Hmm, anything?" He'd take a look at the list he'd made on the legal pad in his lap, jot a couple of notes, turn the page, and begin writing in earnest.

Oh boy.

Chapter Twenty-Three

"I can't believe I can't sleep!" I wanted to punch something. The glass and brick facade of the business I currently walked past seemed a likely candidate, its broad, dirty windows revealing an enormous black machine that looked to have been attacked by men wielding baseball bats. It seemed like a helluva plan, but Vayl's hand, cool on my neck, deterred me from adding to the destruction.

"This is not helping."

"I'm just so pissed off!"

He nodded. It had been a god-awful hour. You think your plan is marching along like a band in the field, all the sections moving to their appointed places at the appropriate times. Then somebody falls on his ass and the next thing you know there's a clarinet player stuck in the sousaphone.

I'd just settled into bed when Cole had come to me with a picture of Delir Kazimi, the house owner. He looked almost exactly like our Wizard photo. But there were differences. A sharpness to the nose and chin. An emptiness in the eyes. This guy I could believe was a three-headed god-worshipping terrorist. His address was in Saudi Arabia, so I went back to Vayl's room and we called Pete to get the clearance to go after him. Since he couldn't discuss the deal without his DOD cohorts chiming in, we hung up while he took fifteen minutes to find them. In the meantime I called Evie.

"Hello?" Well, she didn't sound tearful.

"Evie?"

"Jaz? Where are you?"

"I'm in Germany. My company's merging with a pharmaceutical firm over here. And when I had a chance to meet with some execs to explain our marketing techniques, I jumped at it. Dave's on leave, so I'm actually hanging with him right now."

"That's wonderful! So you guys are getting along?"

"Pretty well. I mean, we haven't talked about Jessie at all . . ." I stopped. If Dave died with that matter still unsettled between us, I'd always regret it. I didn't think I could ever make him understand I'd done what I had out of love for her. But maybe . . . "Evie, I'm so sorry you're alone right now."

"No, Tim and E.J. are here. It's just, I was really worried about you when I couldn't find you." Now the tears. It seemed like every time I called my sister she ended up crying. How do you make up for that?

"I'm sorry." Nope, that wouldn't cut it. Try again. "Is there something I can do?"

"Come home."

Oh crap.

"Not now," Evie said, before I could even formulate a decent lie. "As soon as you can. I'll take care of Dad until then. But here's when I really need you. Easter is April fourteenth this year, and that's when Tim and I are getting E.J. baptized. Dad should be well enough to go . . ."

Or dead, we both thought, but neither one of us would say it.

"And I need you there with me."

"Why?"

"You're her godmother."

"I am?"

"You said you would."

"When?"

"When you were ten! Jaz, you promised!"

Oh my God, leave it to Evie to remember a vow I made fifteen years ago. It was probably during one of those rainy days when she'd forced me to play dolls. I could just see her, rocking her Betsy Burps Up while I sat on the floor beside her, looking longingly out the window at my limp and dripping basketball net.

"I'll be the mommy and you'll be the godmother just like when we're grown-ups," she would've said in her sweet little girl's voice.

And I'd have said, "Yeah, okay."

I switched the phone to my other ear and wondered how she couldn't see what a horrible choice she'd made. But she was my sister, and I'd abide by her wishes even if it meant I had to grit my teeth through piano recitals and school plays and awards banquets until my fillings fell out. "Of course I did," I agreed. "And I'm honored." Which I was, but she and Tim had better live to be a hundred. "And I'll be there. I will. And I'll tell Dave too. Maybe he can get away. Who knows?" I said brightly, although those last words tasted like ash on my tongue. In less than a month Evie and I might have buried our two closest male relatives.

No, nuh-uh, not if I have any say in this and, by God, I do. We will, every one of us Parkses, be there. Bitching about how uncomfortable our clothes are and feeling unworthy to be related to Evie and her precious bundle of bald, reflux-ridden joy.

I went on. "So now I feel horribly guilty for not asking right off, but how's Albert?"

"His leg is broken in two places, and they were worried about his back. But it's okay. He was wearing a helmet, thank God. You should see it. Anyway, he had a major concussion, so they're really concerned about him. And the diabetes isn't going to speed any healing. But he's been awake a few times and they're cautiously optimistic that he'll be okay."

"How does he look?"

She took a moment to think. "Shrunken. How does that happen, Jaz? He always seemed so huge to me. Like a T. rex just about to tear my head off. And now he looks like a little old man. I think his hair has turned whiter in the past couple of days too."

I pulled at my own strand of white and realized I'd either have to dye it or come up with an explanation for it. Maybe I'd just tell everybody it was a desperate cry for attention. Kinda like my belly ring, only visible.

"You know what might make him feel better?" I said. "A visit from one or two of his old Marine buddies. Why don't I call Shelby and—"

"Not from Germany, you won't," said Evie. "I can't imagine how much *this* is costing you. No, that's an excellent idea, but I'll make the calls. You just enjoy your time with Dave and make sure your little fanny is in my house on Easter Sunday. Got it?"

"Holy crap, you have turned into a bossy little Bertha!"

"I know." She laughed. "It's the mom in me. I think it's only going to get worse too!"

Despite Albert's precarious health, I actually felt okay when Evie and I hung up. Then Pete called. On the line with him were General Merle Danfer, our DOD liaison, and General Ethan "Bull" Kyle, commander of SOCOM.

"Gentlemen," Vayl said, "we have good reason to believe our target has lured us into this situation." He explained our suspicions without revealing who we thought the mole was. No sense in damning Dave until we had a way of saving him. "We believe the Wizard owns this house. Cole has faxed you his photo and address. We are trying to confirm his identity through his connection to the mole. If we can do that, we can continue the assignment as planned," Vayl finished.

Pregnant pause, the kind that makes you uneasy because you

thought everybody should've jumped right in and agreed with you from the start. "I think maybe you people have this all wrong," said Danfer. "It seems to me the Wizard set you up, not to kill him, but so he could kill you." Before we could poke any holes in his theory he rushed on. "He's been on the run from our Spec Ops people for over a year. His mole has certainly let him know we've sent our best assassins to take him down. Nope. It looks to me like he's just figured out a way to take the pressure off himself and make our military look like a duck trying to hump an emu. I say you continue with the assignment, only with the understanding that you'll be walking into a trap and will therefore need to take the necessary precautions."

"But, sir—" I began.

"Young woman, are you any good at what you do, or not?"

"I've never failed a mission."

"Then get off your ass and kill that Wizard! Or are you just trying to make me look bad?" *What the hell?* I spent about three seconds floundering in confusion and then the light dawned. I'd heard rumors that Merle Danfer had his eye on the Oval Office. Bagging the Wizard would certainly send whole waves of voters his way when the time came. Was his ambition blinding him to reality?

"Sir, if you're wrong we'll be killing an innocent man."

"How dare you question our intel!" Danfer roared. "People died to gain that information! Pete, what the hell kind of backwoods ingrates are you hiring over there? Maybe you should cull the herd before everybody's infected!"

When Pete didn't immediately leap to my defense my throat completely closed. No breathing allowed in the panic zone. I shot a save-me look at Vayl, who gave me a reassuring shake of the head. *No one is going to fire you,* his expression said.

You can't guarantee that, mine replied.

He knew I was right. Which was why his only answer was to drop his eyes.

"Jasmine, this is Bull Kyle speaking."

"Yes, sir." I sat up straighter. Couldn't help it. That deep commanding voice, accompanied by a storied career that included enough medals to cover one wall of my living room had impressed me despite the fact that he'd served with Albert and was still a close friend. That put him in the same category as Jet's dad, meaning he deserved either the cold shoulder or a punch in the face, whichever my career could handle. At this point I couldn't even muster a mild snub.

"How's your father?" General Kyle asked.

Do. Not. Cry. "The doctors are cautiously optimistic, sir."

"He's a good man. Better than you give him credit for." *Huh.* How did he know?

"The daughters are always the last to find out, sir."

He laughed appreciatively. "Yeah, well, maybe you should give mine a call." His voice changed, took on a certain timbre that made me think I'd better be listening carefully because I didn't want to miss a word. "This Wizard is a slippery character, isn't he?"

"Yes, sir."

"Hard to tell what he's up to until after he's taken credit for it."

"That's true."

"Make sure you get *him*." He emphasized the word just slightly. Paused to let me know he agreed with our assessment of the situation but couldn't officially set us on the track we wanted to take. He finished with, "Not the other way around."

Easy for General Kyle to say. He wasn't sitting in a rental house in Tehran, wondering just who would dig his career out of the Dumpster if he killed the right guy, but was never able to prove it. The Wizard's henchmen might continue his work, use his name like he was still calling the shots and no one would be absolutely sure he wasn't. I'd be lucky to get a job scraping gum off the undersides of the desks at Roosevelt Middle School.

Vayl and I looked at each other, and I could tell we were both thinking the same thing. Better to follow General Danfer's directive. Take out the double. Maybe I'd been wrong about him and he hadn't been coerced into this situation. No, he was probably a highly placed lieutenant, responsible for arranging or executing many of the atrocities the Wizard had committed over the course of his career. Okay, so we wouldn't end up eliminating our true target. At least they couldn't fire us for following orders.

But the whole deal sat wrong. It was the picture, dammit. The man in my hip pocket with his arms around his family. Nobody had ordered us to kill *him*. We weren't certain he'd committed *any* offense deserving of assassination. Which was why I still couldn't grab onto the sleep I so desperately needed.

After the phone call I stalked back to the girls' bedroom. Tossed and turned for fifteen minutes. Gave up, got dressed, and sought out Vayl. He was still in his room. Sitting on the bench at the end of the bed, his hands on his knees, staring at the carpet.

"I can't sleep!" I announced as I marched in. "I'd be snoring now if not for those calls! I'm going to build a time machine, go back to visit Alexander Graham Bell, and kill him before he invents the telephone!"

Vayl mustered a smile. One of the twitchy ones, which told me he was nearly as disturbed as I was. But he'd lived a lot longer, so he knew better how to go with the flow. "We have already hashed this out from every conceivable angle, Jasmine," he said. "I cannot see an alternative to deviating from our original assignment that will not gravely jeopardize our careers."

"I know, I know. But I still can't sleep. And I *need* to!" I think the desperation in my voice finally registered, because Vayl slapped his hands on his knees and stood decisively.

"A walk then," he said. "To cool you off and cheer both of us."

I almost asked him what he had to be depressed about, that's how tangled up I'd been in my own junk. But one look at his face reminded me of what he'd given up when he'd agreed not to turn Zarsa. I searched my brain for a way to make him feel better about not seeing his sons right away, but it was so raw from its recent bombardment it just moaned and curled into the fetal position.

So far the walk hadn't done either of us any good. Of course it probably hadn't helped that I kept bringing up our intolerable work situation and Vayl wouldn't stop talking about Badu and Hanzi.

A red glow in the middle of the street several blocks ahead of us stopped me in the middle of my current rant, which effectively saved General Danfer from the maw of the Sarlaci from *Return of the Jedi*. "Do you see that?" I asked, grabbing Vayl's sleeve and pulling him forward as I spoke.

When he didn't immediately comment I looked up at him. The expression on his face threw me because it was so intense. "Vayl? What's wrong?"

He jerked his arm away from mine and stopped cold. "That red flame is outlining a plane portal. I can see it because I am *other*. And because I have had occasion to battle creatures that emerged from similar portals elsewhere. *You* see it because your Spirit Eye has obviously gained power enough to open farther than ever before. But that power did not come from me." His eyes sparked their own shade of red in the shadows of the street. "What vampire has taken your blood, my *avhar*?" Somehow he put a wealth of meaning into that last word.

"Okay, first of all, you've got some kind of nerve throwing that double-standard crap at me after what you were just planning to do with Zarsa," I snapped. "And second, I was trying to do my job by finding the mole. I needed to boost my Sensitivity and you, my *sverhamin*, had made yourself about as scarce as it's possible to be without actually falling off the planet!"

"Who. Is. He?"

"Not a vampire," I said, hating the fact that, despite my righteous stance, I still felt guilty. "He's an Amanha Szeya."

Vayl's brows shot up. He looked around the street, his fiery gaze taking in the locked shops, the quiet sidewalks, the arched doorways and window frames that gave everything its wonderful Persian flare. I decided he expected Asha to jump out of the nearest alley, at which point they would bicker over who had the most right to sink his powers into me.

"I take it you recognize his race," I said, mostly to fill in the uneasy gap his raging silence left.

"I thought his kind had died out aeons ago."

"He was after Zarsa for the deal she'd made with you," I said, conveniently omitting the fact that Asha hadn't meant to take any action to prevent the turning. "We met on her roof."

Vayl pinned me with a look so piercing I put my hand to my chest to make sure there weren't any smoking holes in it. "What were you doing on Anvari's roof?"

I cleared my throat, switching stances uncomfortably. I suddenly wanted to pull my gun. Not to aim at anybody. Just for the comfort it would give me. I had so little left. But hey, if Cole could find a substitute for bubble gum, surely I could pick up a replacement for shuffling. Something soothing both in its repetitive nature and in the way it sounded as I took it through its motions. An idea struck me. Just as suddenly I ditched it. How was I supposed to fit a guitar into my jacket pocket?

Realizing I couldn't put off this confession any longer, I put up my hands in mock surrender. "Okay, I admit I might have been keeping an eye on you. But I really had good intentions," I assured him as his entire face tightened in his version of an oh-boy-did-you-ever-blow-it scowl. "I didn't trust Zarsa and I wanted to make sure you were okay . . ." I let my voice trail off. It sounded so stupid when I said it out loud.

"So, you followed me then as well?"

I nodded. Just a little.

"Jasmine, are you stalking me?"

I closed my eyes. Why, oh why, was there never an alien abduction team around to whisk you off to Neptune during these horribly embarrassing moments? "Stalking is such a harsh word," I said weakly, looking at Vayl's shoes since I couldn't bear raising my gaze any higher.

"What would you prefer to call it?" he asked, his voice still hard. His fingers lifted my chin, forcing me to meet his relentless stare. And that was all it took. My temper, rarely long at rest, woke from its short nap, stretched like a hungry lioness, and immediately riveted on my boss.

"How about babysitting?" I inquired, cringing only slightly when his eyes narrowed dangerously. "I mean, though you repeatedly told me how much my opinion meant to you, and how much you trusted me, which was why you gave me Cirilai in the first place, you wouldn't listen to a word I said. You just dogged Zarsa like some kid after a tasty treat. Frankly, stalking you was turning into the least of my worries. I thought I was going to have to kill her."

Vayl's hand dropped to his side. "Would you have done that?" he asked.

I couldn't tell from his expression what answer he wanted. So I gave him the truth. "Yes. Because Cassandra told me ethical Seers don't ask for any payment for their services, other than maybe a good story for their Enkyklios. I already knew from Asha she was misusing her powers. So yeah, if I couldn't have come up with any other way to pry her claws out of you . . . Plus . . ."

"What?"

Dammit, Jaz, why can't you shut your mouth before you get yourself in trouble? "Nothing." I hoped he'd let it go, but somehow he knew.

"No, tell me."

Goddammit. "And I would have killed her because I sensed that turning her would have caused a big rift between you and me." Not a good enough reason for assassination by itself, but paired with the first one, it worked for me. Even if I'd have had to deal with the guilt for the rest of my life.

Vayl took a step toward me. I licked my lips in anticipation. Then his phone rang. Which, since we were both wearing our stealth specs, meant he just got this faraway look on his face and started talking to invisible people.

"What?" he rapped. He listened for about five seconds, said, "We will be right there." He grabbed my hand, nothing romantic in that gesture, damn-it-all, and strode back toward the house.

"What's the deal?" I asked.

"That was Cole. He said we should come back right away. Soheil Anvari is there. He is yelling like a madman. And he has a gun."

Chapter Twenty-Four

We arrived at the house with less than half an hour until dawn. Not a comfy way to end Vayl's day, especially considering the fact that Zarsa's hubby was waving an AK-47 around with his finger inside the trigger guard as he spoke. I scanned the living room to see if he'd already shot somebody accidentally, but everyone seemed to have all their parts.

The entire crew was present. Jet, Bergman, and Natchez shared the couch. Cole stood behind the love seat, on which sat Cassandra and Zarsa. Dave, Cam, and Amazon Grace stood in front of the fireplace. All of Dave's people, plus Cole, carried some sort of concealed weapon. And I could tell by the way Grace had her arm behind her back that she held her firearm in-hand, though Soheil was too distracted to notice. They could take him out any time if they were willing to take damage and make noise. But that might put the kabosh on our mission. So while that possibility remained on the table, Vayl and I hoped for a peaceful alternative.

"There you are!" cried Soheil, as we came through the door. He swung the gun on Vayl.

"Now, wait a minute," I said, stepping between the gun and its target. *Stupid*, I realized immediately. Those bullets wouldn't kill Vayl, but they'd certainly do me in. Amazing what places your instincts will take you. I stepped back to my original position. "I think we have a huge misunderstanding here," I said.

"What makes you think I would listen to a woman?" Soheil spat. "I have been betrayed by one!"

"That is not so!" Zarsa cried, jumping off her seat.

"Sit down!" roared Soheil. Zarsa dropped to her butt so fast you'd have thought he slapped her.

And that's when I really began to worry. Soheil, the adoring husband, seemed to be so far beyond reason no one could reach him. I wasn't sure anyone would leave the room alive. And the mahghul seemed to agree. They'd begun to pour in through the windows Vayl had broken. No one saw them but Vayl and me. I tried not to stare, but I kept seeing them out the corners of my eyes, perching on a shoulder, crouching in a corner or on the lip of a vase. A room full of ghouls just waiting for the violence to commence.

Vayl sent out a wave of power, just a brush of cool breeze that swept through the room, taking the edge off the fever pitch, making Soheil blink. "Cole said you came to see me," he told Soheil gently.

"My wife, she says you two have made the deal."

Vayl nodded. "We had spoken of a matter involving my sons, who died many long years ago."

Soheil shook his head. He obviously didn't care about that part. "She tells me I no longer have to worry about her getting sick. She says after you are finished, she will live forever. But first she must die." His eyes widened with horror as he delivered this news. "But that is not the worst. She says then she must spend many months with you, learning your ways, so that when she returns to me she can use her powers to mend the wrongs that have been done to our family. This I cannot allow."

A sob from Zarsa. She clapped a hand over her mouth.

"You have defiled my wife," Soheil announced. "Therefore I must kill you."

"No!" cried Zarsa. "Never!"

"How exactly did he defile her?" I asked, stepping up to Soheil, getting into his face, forcing him to deal with me. "By making the agreement?"

Soheil pointed at Vayl dramatically. "He took her blood!"

I turned to Cole, knowing it could only have happened on his watch. He winced as he met my eyes and we shared our first unspoken conversation.

Cole?

I couldn't tell you. You would have just thought I was trying to get you to hate him and like me. I'm sorry, Jaz.

No. It can't be.

I faced my *sverhamin*. "Vayl?" I asked, forcing my voice low so the screams I felt building wouldn't accidentally release. "What do you say to that?"

He lowered his head just slightly. The gesture acted like a hatchet, burying in my heart. "It is true. We had begun the turning."

I spun back to Soheil. "Go ahead, shoot the son of a bitch."

He looked at me, round-eyed with surprise as Vayl said, "Jasmine, you must understand. I was not in my right mind then."

"Oh, I know exactly where your head was at!" I yelled, stomping up to him with the idea of punching him right in the nose. But Albert had raised me to hit people in self-defense, not vice versa, so I went back to Soheil. "What are you waiting for, Hot Stuff? You wanted to shoot somebody, there he is! Tell you what, why don't you aim for the gut? I hear it hurts more and it takes them longer to die."

However, the more I ranted the less Soheil seemed interested in gunning down the vampire who'd bloodied his wife. But now I was just as pissed at her as I was at him. I marched over to her and yanked her to her feet. "You've got a lot of explaining to do, woman."

Her eyes went wide as I touched her, which let me know she wasn't a pure fraud. Generally I'd have dropped her wrist like it was on fire, but this time I held on. Let her have her visions. I hoped they gave her nightmares for a year. Finally she ripped her arm free. "What kind of monster are you?" she blubbered, rubbing her wrist like it had been in manacles. I looked at Cole. He quickly translated.

Wrong thing to say, missy. I closed on her, because she'd backed away when I'd let her go. "The kind who's going to kill you, your husband, and all of your children if you don't confess, right now, to every single crime you committed against that man." I pointed back at Vayl, looking as fierce as I possibly could, hoping she wouldn't call my bluff. I'd never kill a kid. But Zarsa didn't know that.

She covered her face with her hands as she began to cry. But she started talking too. "You must understand, I had my reasons. I . . . I had good reasons!" she wailed.

"Confess!" I roared.

She cowered from me and I felt like the worst kind of jerk. But, dammit, I wasn't the one still waving an automatic weapon around the room.

With Cole translating almost as quickly as she spoke, she began speaking. "I have visions, yes!" she cried. "I See when I would rather be blind! But I cannot stop them. And they tear at my soul. When I touch a woman, I see her father's fist crashing into her cheek. I feel her loathing at being forced to submit to a husband she did not choose for herself. And I know I cannot change these things. I am only the witness."

I darted a look at Cassandra. She nodded gravely. *Oh yeah*, said her look. *Been there; tried to forget that.*

Zarsa went on. "But always I find a way to hope. I have Soheil and my children. Life is not always bad. And then a man comes to

Soheil. He is the owner of this house. He hires Soheil as the caretaker and says for us to come here. To invite you to a reading. We are happy to have the extra income. Until the day I am cleaning and I pick up the key he has left us."

Oh shit, Zarsa, stop! I wanted to yell. *The Wizard's watching you right now!* But I couldn't warn her. Couldn't make a move without betraying what I knew. So I sat tight and hoped for the best.

"The vision I have from holding this key is of a horror before unknown to me. I See doom for my people. Brothers strangling their sisters only to make their corpses walk again. Murderers lopping off heads like they are halving melons as their bodies writhe with parasitic monsters. Women setting themselves afire. My own children crying as they are forced to watch an endless procession of hangings. And behind it all someone laughing and laughing. It"—she held her hands out, almost pleading with us—"how can I tell you of the despair I felt afterward?"

Zarsa dropped her head as if it was just too heavy to hold up anymore and shook it. Every eye in the room was glued to her. No one spoke as she pulled herself together.

"That night I dreamed," she said in a small voice. "A man came to my door, power rolling before him like thunder. I knew all I had to do was open my arms and it would be mine. I could take it, mold it, and use it to transform myself. To fight the vision of the key." Though her arms still covered her stomach and she rocked on her knees like a mental patient, her eyes were dry. "This is why I must turn," she said, her voice little more than a rasp. "I must have Vayl's strength, his magic. So I told him he could meet his sons."

"Even though it will kill them?" I asked. A pang went through me at breaking my promise to Cassandra. I'd probably go straight to hell for it. Spend eternity eating my hair and arguing with my mother. Oh well.

I could tell the question shocked Zarsa. She gave me such a

how-did-you-know stare that Cole didn't even bother with a translation.

Vayl came forward, his shoulders hunched as if someone had set a crate full of lead on them. "Meeting Hanzi and Badu . . . will lead to our deaths?" he asked.

She met his eyes squarely. "Sacrifices must be made to prevent the horror," she said flatly.

"No, Zarsa," I said. "You can't prevent the horror by becoming one." I glanced at Vayl. "No offense meant, boss."

"None taken," he replied.

"And look what this plan has done to your marriage," Cole urged. "You don't want to lose something so fine and rare, do you? Or do you enjoy putting your husband in such a crazed state?"

"No! Of course not!"

"And what about your children?" I asked.

"I act for them!" Zarsa exclaimed fiercely. "This world I saw, it is possible because too many have already failed to fight! Because fear is a weapon this man wields like a bully's club. If I do not stand, my children will be crushed! I cannot, I will not allow that!"

I glanced at Soheil. The AK-47 hung at his side, nearly forgotten in the surge of pride that had washed away his previous rage at his wife. "She's a pistol, isn't she?" I asked him.

He nodded, his eyes shining with admiration. "I have married a tigress."

I turned back to her. "Listen, I know you're hell-bent on this course. And I met a sort of prophet on the street outside your house yesterday who told me you *are* destined to change the world. But *without* Vayl's help."

Her expression asked me why she should believe me. "What was his name?" she inquired.

"Asha Vasta."

I'd never seen such an emotional quick-change in my life. Zarsa went from a cynicism heavily dosed with agitation to absolute awe. "You have met the Amanha Szeya?"

I cleared my throat, let my eyes roam the room. Amazon Grace still hid her gun behind her back. David scratched his neck, probably sending a video straight to the Wizard. Cam rolled his toothpick back and forth like it tasted of chocolate. Everyone else looked riveted. Except the mahghul, which began to file out of the room.

"Um. Yeah." I didn't realize the dude was so famous.

"There are legends, but we had thought them just that. No one has seen or spoken to him since the time of my great-great-grandfather. Can you take me to him?" she asked eagerly.

Whoops. I suddenly felt like Pandora and, unable to close the box up tight again, wanted only to backpedal until nobody could tell I'd been the one whose hands had been on the latch. "He's uh, well, hah." How could I tell her he'd probably been standing right outside until a couple of minutes ago, but that he was only going to disappoint her?

"Do you know where he lives?" Vayl asked me.

I tried not to squirm under that cool blue gaze. "Maybe."

Again with the eyebrows. Well, hey, I told myself, if he hadn't been such a jerk none of this would've happened. "You have been inside his house?" Vayl asked, his voice only slightly less frigid than an ice cave.

"No. Only his garage. He lent me his car so I could get away from those four, uh, *guys* I told you about."

"Where is this vehicle? I thought you drove some sort of truck back. No, it was a—"

"Um, can we talk about this later? When we don't have company?"

Vayl nodded shortly and turned to Soheil. "I deeply regret anything I have done to offend you or injure your relationship with your wife. I was momentarily blinded by the hope that I might be reunited with my sons, whom I have been too long without. Obviously you and Zarsa have much to discuss. If, at the end of that time, you wish to visit Asha Vasta, my colleague here will be happy to guide you to his door."

Vayl shot me a look over his shoulder that warned me not to say a word. I'd already done enough. My nonvocal reply said, *You too, Mr. Obsessive.*

Soheil threw the AK-47 over his back by its sling and helped Zarsa to her feet. He looked around the room, trying to formulate the right apology for taking a bunch of people hostage on the mistaken assumption that they could somehow stop their vampire associate from turning his wife into a blood-sucking immortal. "I have not the right words," he finally muttered. "I am so very sorry." They left quietly.

Chapter Twenty-Five

Raoul met me in my restroom again, minus the bubble bath dream. This time I was standing fully dressed in the tub, armed with Grief and a wickedly curved blade that I might gut myself with if I wasn't careful.

"What took you so long?" he demanded, his accent very Antonio Banderas in the extremity of his irritation.

"Couldn't sleep," I said shortly, remembering that last few minutes before Vayl had turned in with a grim, plodding-through-a-parade-of-blow-dart-shooting-pygmies sort of feeling.

Somehow our good moments were always so fleeting. The two times he'd taken my blood. That kiss. Spectacular. And yet the job had intervened, as usual. And in the end we'd said our good nights with the distant friendliness we reserved for airline attendants and taxi drivers. I don't think he minded so much about the stalk — uh, tailing — I'd been doing. But keeping my knowledge of Asha from him had been a mistake he wouldn't instantly forgive. Plus, I think he was still reeling from the idea that if he met his sons now, they'd all die.

And on my end, I felt like he'd cheated on me by taking Zarsa's blood. Not that we'd had the exclusive talk yet. And if we did, shouldn't it be about who we dated, not whose veins he drained? See, it was still just too confusing for me to relax into another kiss.

So when he said he had to turn in, he didn't give me the walk-me-to-the-tent look I'd have anticipated pre-Soheil. For my part, I barely glanced up from the card game Dave's team had begun. Cam had snagged a box of poker chips from the Hotel Sraosa before they'd left. Apparently the big spenders spent a lot of time in the "meeting room" playing no-limit Hold 'Em. Anyway, he was teaching me how the pros shuffle their chips while they decide what to bet. I couldn't do it without making a huge mess, but Cam kept encouraging me. He made it look easy too. Halve the stack, lift, combine, and blend. Oh man, I loved the sound too. Yeah, I was hooked. When I couldn't keep my eyes open anymore, he let me take a handful of ones to practice with. Gotta love that guy.

Raoul, on the other hand. Not so cuddly. In fact, I thought he resembled a pissed-off timber wolf as he towered over me, his crew-cut practically shooting sparks as he said, "You asked for this meeting. You would not believe what I had to do to be here. You know"—he put a fist on his hip and ran the other across his head in a gesture so much like my dad's I had to stifle a laugh—"I don't just sit around waiting for you to call! I am trying to find out what the Magistrate wants with you. You do remember him, don't you? Tall, blond demonic type? Likes to tear the skin off people with his whip?"

"Yeah, Raoul, your description rings a bell." *Okay, Jaz, drop the sarcasm. Right. Now. As far as you know, this guy is the only one who can save David. For once in your life, do not piss off your last chance. Even if he did foul up Dave's transition and let the Wizard . . . No, you're not even sure of that. Quit judging, keep an open mind, and don't screw this up.* I sighed. "I'm really sorry. It's . . . this mission is just insane. Things keep happening and I honestly couldn't fall asleep when I wanted to. I tried. I really did."

Raoul's expression softened. "Let's go somewhere else to talk," he said. "Your bathroom makes me feel as if I'm buried alive."

Gee, thanks. Now I'm going to have that lovely image playing in my head every time I have to pee. But I didn't say a word. Just followed Raoul out the door and into my living room.

He didn't complain about its size, but he should've. It wasn't even cozy. I just . . . I don't really know how to make a place seem like home. We moved so much when I was a kid, and now I spend so much time in rented rooms. I guess I feel more comfortable in a hotel atmosphere.

The white walls were bare. The brown suede couch and chairs matched; they just didn't look like anyone had sat in them in the past five years. I use an ottoman for a coffee table. It was empty. The only redeeming feature of the whole room was the fancy maple rack behind the couch that held my prized possession. In her will, Granny May had specifically stated that I should receive her Amish quilt, a gorgeous black, red, and green creation that played on your eye like a classic piece of art. Someday I'd display it that way. But only when I'd found someplace permanent.

Raoul settled on the couch. I sat beside him. "Have you thought about what I said before?" I asked. "Give it to me straight. Does Dave have any chance at all? I mean, I can't let the Wizard control him much longer. When we pull the plug, so to speak, what will happen?"

Raoul sat forward, his hands clasped between his legs. "He may have a chance. But before you start the party, let me explain." Deep lines appeared between his brows. "No. Let me apologize." He met my eyes squarely, because that was how he'd been trained to face things. "I am forced to follow certain rules that strictly govern how much I may"—he grimaced—"interfere. Which is why I could not warn you. Couldn't immediately send you to his aide. Even now I must be careful what to say."

I stifled the urge to shake him. To get in his face and yell, "This is my brother we're talking about! Tell me everything you know, dammit!"

Raoul went on. "When a person is murdered at the order of a necromancer, great powers are stirred in order to strap the soul into the body and bind it into service. One with the strength of your brother cannot be completely restrained. A part of him, almost what you would call a shadow, escaped. That was what came to me. Ever since then I have been trying to find a way to free him."

Okay, so Dave *was* the second kind of zombie. The kind necromancers rarely messed with. The kind Hilda the expert had died trying to find out more about.

"But . . . this assignment. I thought it was engineered by the Wizard."

Raoul nodded. "And yet, even seeds need nourishment to grow. So if I made a few suggestions as he dreamed . . ." He shrugged. "You're here. And yet we still walk a thin line. David's soul is incredibly vulnerable. Freeing it could be the worst possible scenario. Because we believe—"

"Wait a minute. We? Who's we? Does that include Asha Vasta? I mean, is he part of the we?" Because if he was, maybe he could help Dave if I crapped out on Raoul.

Raoul sat back, his eyes troubled. "What was the Amanha Szeya doing when you met him?"

"Talking me out of killing reavers."

Raoul shook his head. "And so it goes." He sighed. "Asha is not part of my—how would you understand it?—my regiment. The 'we' to which I was referring are the Eldhayr. Like you, we once lived as human beings. And now we fight to protect our kind. Asha was never human."

"So how many of you Eldhayr are there?"

Raoul shook his head. "Some details are better left unknown."

I recognized that face. That was the you-might-get-tortured-so-remain-ignorant-please expression Pete always got when he sent us into anti-American territories. "Okay. Fine. So did you tell your Eldhayr buddies what an excellent recruit Dave would make? He already thinks he's working for you, so obviously he's cool with the idea. Plus—"

Raoul held up a hand. "Jasmine, there is no need for the sales pitch. Of course we'll invite your brother to join us if he can. But it won't be as easy for him as it was for you."

I gulped. When your Spirit Guide compares your neck-breaking experience to anything and calls it easy, his next news ain't gonna be pretty.

"Why not?" I asked, clearing my throat to hide the quiver in my voice.

"We believe the problem is directly related to your last experience with the Magistrate. The fact that the scene was a concert was no coincidence." He stopped. Said, almost to himself, "How to explain this so you'll understand?"

So suddenly that it startled me, he jerked around to face me fully. "Since we're in your dream, this shouldn't hurt. Here." He held his large, broad-fingered hands out to me. They made mine look like a little girl's when I slid them into his. He closed his eyes for a second and I felt a tingle coupled with a sudden desire to throw him down on my couch and see just what hid under that starched blue shirt of his.

I pulled my hands away. "Oh, hey, that's not fair!"

He grinned. "Relax, Jaz. It's just chemistry, as you like to say. And I rearranged yours momentarily to help explain what I mean. That feeling you just had? Well, you felt it with Matt, didn't you? And now it's growing in you for Vayl. Am I right?"

"Uh."

"Okay, too personal. But when you hold your niece or hug your sister, also there are good feelings, correct? Feelings of connection and belonging."

Where the hell was he going with this? Should I take notes? "Sure," I agreed.

He gave me a good-girl nod. So far I was getting an A in his class. "Those feelings are actually songs. Part of the music of the universe. Everyone has their own tune, and when they find someone whose music harmonizes well with theirs, a link is made. Sometimes for a few weeks. Sometimes forever."

Okay, now I'm getting it. "So when I go out-of-body, those golden cords that connect me to everybody I'm close to are . . . what?"

"The songs the two of you make as members of a relationship. They allow you to find each other across time and space. That's one of the reasons why, when you die, your soul knows where to go."

"And this has what to do with the Magistrate?" I asked.

Raoul dropped my hands. "While he had your cord frozen, his song was playing against all the songs of the cords connected to you. We believe you were right that he wants you to leave your body again. But not to lead him to us. We think he heard something unique in David's tune. Something that makes him valuable as a prisoner of hell."

I stared at my bland beige carpet, trying to put it all together in my head. "So you're saying, as soon as we take the Wizard's control away from Dave he dies again. But that leaves his soul vulnerable to the Magistrate."

"Exactly."

I met Raoul's eyes, but the pity in them made me feel like bawling, so I went back to the carpet. When had I spilled Coke on it? "I can't let my brother continue to be a zombie. He'd despise that. But I can't let the Magistrate get him either. Well, this sucks like a frigging leech."

"I agree."

I leaned back on the couch. Switched my gaze to the ceiling.

Boring white tiles that did not work to distract me like I'd hoped. "I'll have to figure out a way to fight the Magistrate."

"Not in this form," Raoul reminded me. "You haven't yet developed the ability."

"Okay. There's a couple reavers left. I could probably get one of them to deliver him a challenge. Have him meet me in Tehran. But he might kick my ass since Asha's tears didn't really give me the boost I was hoping for, physically speaking. Maybe Vayl—"

"Jasmine, the Magistrate is *nefralim*. That means the only way he can enter your world is to be summoned. Wait, what did you say?" asked Raoul. His voice, sharp with command, caused me to sit up straight like when I was seven, at the dinner table, and Albert had just ordered me to finish my lima beans.

"Well, Vayl's kind of pissed that I didn't tell him about Asha right away. But he'll probably be over it by sundown. If he takes my blood again maybe I'll—"

Raoul shook his head so hard I thought I heard his eyeballs rattle. "No. No, before that. Did Asha share his tears with you?"

"Actually, I kind of had to guilt them out of him. And then they burned. And then nothing. Except I did see this flaming door, which Vayl said was a plane portal. I didn't learn much more about it because Cole called to say a guy was threatening to kill our people, so we had to get back to the house. And then Vayl was mad at me about the Asha thing. So . . . what was your question?"

Raoul smacked a hand on his thigh. "That may be the answer."

"Okay." I waited, and when no information was immediately forthcoming said, "Raoul. Spill. Before I have to beat you. Which I'm kind of sure is a major sin."

"Asha's tears have given you the ability to see the portals. But more than that, they have allowed you to step through them. Into neutral territory." He was leaning so far forward he looked like he was preparing to take off, as if he'd just received an emergency call that required his unique skills. "This means you can meet the Magistrate physically. Anywhere. You can fight him using your abilities. Your weapons. All right, not the gun. But definitely the sword." He looked at me, gave a sharp decisive nod. "You could beat him."

Chapter Twenty-Six

I woke with the afternoon sun slanting through the windows, feeling as if I hadn't slept at all. But also as prepared as I'd ever be to face an opponent who might well kill me.

Cassandra and Grace still snoozed on their pallets, giving me the chance to sneak my new toys into the bathroom without having to deal with a lot of diversionary tactics. Once Raoul had given me the correct words to say, I'd made a physical trip to his headquarters during the post-dawn hours of the morning using the portal I'd seen while walking with Vayl.

Beyond the fact that I was actually alive this time or, well, as near as I'd ever get to it again—nothing much had changed from the way I remembered his place. The suite made me feel underdressed in my shapeless black manteau and pants. At least I matched the bar stools to the right of the front door, which lined up neatly under a sleek black counter backed by a mirror that ran the length and width of the wall behind it. But I looked like I should be running a vacuum over the plush white couches, arranged just as I recalled in the center of a room made even more elaborate by white satin curtains and marble floors with rich pink veins. In the back corner of the room, a lovely ivory dining set with six high-backed cushioned chairs completed the mood.

Raoul had been standing by the bar when I walked into the room. "How was your trip?" he asked politely. "Any problems?"

"No. Should there have been?"

He smirked. "With you, I'm never sure. May I take your coat?"

"Please." I shucked the awful thing, watched him hang it on the elaborately curved black wall rack by the door. "That's one depressing piece of clothing," I told him. "Makes me feel like a mortician."

"Well, I think I know just how to lift your spirits."

He led me past the bar and the dining table toward a door I assumed led to the bedroom. It didn't. It was a hall. A long one that, as we walked it, branched into several others, making me wonder just how big Raoul's penthouse really was. The door we finally stopped at looked no different from any of the others. Rimmed with elaborate white molding it held the kind of lock you expect to see in a hotel. But Raoul didn't slide a card into the slot. He leaned down, pulled a knife out of his boot, and quickly slashed his forearm. Gathering a generous amount of blood on the blade, he then transferred it to the lock, letting it drip the whole length of the slot. When the light turned green, he opened the door.

"That's some security system you've got there. I'm guessing you don't access this room very often."

He sent me a smile over his shoulder. "Since I met you I'm doing all kinds of things I haven't done for years."

He was right about the room cheering me up. When you're in my biz and you walk into an arsenal, something inside you springs to its feet and starts yelling, "Yipee!" The place could've come straight out of a medieval castle. Swords, axes, lances, spears, anything that could hold a blade and prove fatal graced three and a half walls of a room roughly the size of Raoul's living space. The last half held built-in drawers, which I soon discovered held armor. But this was modern. Stuff you could wear under your day clothes, probably even move comfortably in. And yet I imagined it outperformed even

Bergman's famous dragon armor, which, since we'd rescued it from its kidnappers on our last mission, was still undergoing testing at White Sands.

The armory's floor space had been kept completely clear. For sparring? I kind of thought I was about to find out. Raoul strode across the battered wooden floor to one corner of the room, lifted from its moorings a sheath holding a curved blade similar to the one I'd been clutching in my dream. Prophetic, huh?

"This shamshir was forged by an Amanha Szeya," he told me as he pulled it free and handed me a shining silver blade that felt like it had been made for my hand. As I marveled at the balance he said, "That means it can kill a *nefralim*."

He moved to the drawers next, taking from them a suit of black body armor. It weighed almost nothing. But Raoul assured me it could stop a bullet, though the force of the impact would still throw me to the ground. "Not that you have to worry about that from the Magistrate. It's the cut of his whip from which the suit will protect you. I fear, however, you may still feel its sting."

I could've said something cocky at that moment like, "I'm no stranger to pain." While true, it just seemed stupid to throw fastballs at karma, knowing how much she enjoyed shooting them right back at you. So I just nodded my thanks.

"How good are you at swordplay?" Raoul asked as he took a blade similar to mine off the wall.

"Better than I used to be." Having nearly lost major body parts to Desmond Yale, I'd spent the time I could spare between missions honing my skills. That meant two hours a day with the best coach I could find.

Vayl was a patient teacher, but a strict one. By the end of week one I was sick of hearing "Watch your form."

"Vayl," I said once, wiping sweat out of my eyes in exasperation. "What the hell? I'm not training for the Olympics here!" Here was the gym a retired agent owned and allowed us to rent during his off-hours.

When I saw red spark in his eyes, I realized I'd pissed him off. But I didn't much care at that point. I was hot, sweaty, and, yeah, frustrated that it wasn't for any of the fun reasons. Never mind that it had been my choice. And that I should respect Vayl for giving me the space I thought I needed.

Having no idea as to the real source of my unspoken frustrations, Vayl addressed my vocalized ones. "Correct form allows you to find the balance you need to fight. It keeps you from tiring too quickly. And it prevents you from telegraphing your moves long before you make them."

"Oh."

Vayl and I had never fought with curved blades, but I figured the basics he'd taught me would still serve me well. I stood en garde and moments later Raoul and I were hard at it. Every minute or so he'd stop. Say something like, "Look, if you'd turned the blade this way you could have disarmed me on that swing." He showed me some moves unique to the blade, and within half an hour I felt like I'd been born with it in my hand.

"You're a fast learner," Raoul said when he finally called for a stop.

"It's more of a defense mechanism than anything else," I replied as I sheathed the blade. "Since my parents were my first teachers, and things always escalated to yelling if we didn't catch on fast, we figured out quick how to listen and learn."

I saw the thought on Raoul's face, though he was kind enough not to say it out loud. *No wonder your mother's in hell.* Yeah. And he didn't even know the half of it.

"Get your armor," he said. "I have one more item to give you before you go." I grabbed my goodies and followed him to the Charm room.

It resembled a jewelry store, with multiple racks of necklaces, bracelets, and enough other sparklies to keep a serious accessorizer busy for days. He took me straight to the back, where a locked glass display case backed in red velvet held some fine old pieces. As he unlocked it he said, "You must remember never to let the Magistrate touch you. We're not sure how he managed to pull you out of your body the first time, but we know it was at great expense, both in terms of power and time. That's why he'll want you to do most of the work yourself the second time around. Since you haven't willingly left your body, he'll find a way to trigger that exodus if he can. But he won't be able to if he can't physically touch you."

"Or kill me."

Raoul gave me a you-could-have-gone-all-day-without-saying-that look. "Obviously." He pulled a delicate, octagonal bluish white stone out of the case and handed it to me.

"It's gorgeous," I said.

"It's best worn near the center of your body," he replied. "In ages past, men and women wore it on a long chain beneath their clothing. But since you have a rather convenient piercing, I took the liberty of mounting it for you."

"Cool!" As I replaced the gold stud I currently wore in my navel, I said, "What's it do?"

"It protects the soul during flight. It will shield you from any sort of attack the Magistrate may launch should the worst happen."

"Thanks. Really."

Raoul nodded. "I wish I could do more." He stopped. Shook his head. Looked at me through hooded eyes that said, *If I were the man I should be, I would do more.*

"Rules are rules," I said simply. "I don't understand them all yet. I don't agree with half of them when they're explained to me. But I know sometimes they're all that separate me from the guys

Pete sends me after." I gave him the straight stare he'd earned. "I appreciate your help. But I don't expect you to do my work for me. Or to stick your neck out so far it snaps." Okay, considering the way I'd died the first time, maybe that was the wrong metaphor. We looked at each other for another three seconds. And then we both smiled.

"You're amazing," Raoul said.

His words warmed me, deprived as I was of genuine compliments. I let them carry me back to the house. Played them over and over in my mind as I prepared to face the Magistrate, strapping the sword to my back with a special belt Raoul had given me that was completely hidden under my bland brown tunic and black hijab.

"I'm amazing," I told my reflection in the bathroom mirror. It didn't seem convinced. Maybe it was too busy trying to remember that first visit to hell. Not the part about Mom. That was just too disturbing. The before, when Uldin Beit had presented her case to the Magistrate and his court. Something about that scene, I thought, had inspired me to give up my card-shuffling acumen, which I was desperately wishing I had back at this very moment. Something I'd missed had required that sacrifice.

Now I thought maybe I'd witnessed the secret to the Magistrate's downfall. Not that I wasn't pretty confident in my sword-fighting abilities. Especially after Raoul's high praise. But it never hurt to have an edge. (Ha! Jaz made a sword pun! What a gas.) So I played the scene over and over again in my head. Trying to remember details I'd registered only with the back of my mind. For some reason instead of lingering on the Magistrate it kept jumping to Samos and those strange glowing eyes I'd seen behind his office door.

That's not going to help. What's the Magistrate's weakness? What did you see?

I headed to the kitchen, still racking my brain, which was starting to ache from the unaccustomed just-woke-up-dammit strain. "They were sitting in a circle," I murmured. "There were twelve ugly-ass demons plus supermodel Magistrate. They talked. Then the whipping. But the whole event was about Marking me."

I gave up. Let my subconscious chew on it for a while. Maybe it would regurgitate something useful while I choked down some toast and juice. And wondered why nobody else was stirring. I finally decided the card game had gone on well into the morning. Figuring they might not make it through the next night, Dave's crew had probably stretched their time together as far as it would go before they began nodding off into their poker chips.

Cassandra and Bergman had used their distraction to retire to the guys' room, where they'd worked till God knows when on what they now called their save-Dave device. I hoped they'd made ample progress. Because I planned on needing it soon.

"It's quiet in here," I told the cabinets, which stared back at me stoically. I scanned the kitchen. The room should've cheered me. But I hadn't felt this bummed in a while. Going off to fight your battles alone, without a friend or loved one to see you off, sucks. And if I didn't come back, they'd never know what happened to me.

I thought briefly of leaving a note:

Off to kill the Magistrate. Raoul taught me how to find neutral ground on another plane and summon him there. No biggie. Just a life or death struggle that may slightly muss my hair and call for a new manicure when all's said and done. Oh, yeah, there is that bit about the risk to my soul. But don't worry. My new belly gem should have that covered. Maybe. Of course he didn't mention that it would protect any of the other souls connected with mine. Nothing to fear, however, I'll be back in a flash. Or, alternatively, a pool of blood. In which case, tell Vayl . . .

What? That I wished he hadn't turned into a complete ass on this job? Because after that kiss I'd thought we were right for each other. Only now I wasn't so sure. A man who will forsake you for his obsession, which includes taking a stranger's blood, is not one who'll treat you well anytime soon. I caressed the ring in my left pocket. I'd had the right kind of man. One who'd known what I was worth. I could never settle for anything less.

I walked out the door, the windows beside which Vayl had temporarily mended with some slats of wood he'd found in the garage. People glanced at me as I made my way down the street. Most of them seemed simply curious. But a couple—purely hostile. Though I'd darkened my hair and skin, I was clearly not a native, and two gray-bearded men didn't approve of me walking around unescorted. But I wouldn't be alone long.

The portal hadn't moved since I'd glimpsed it the first time and then used it to visit Raoul. People walked right through it as if it didn't exist. Well, it didn't for them. Because they didn't have the Spirit Eye to see it. Didn't know the words to open it. I did.

Raoul had told me no one would notice when I walked through. The portal itself would shield my passage, actually project an image of me walking into the nearest store, though the proprietor inside would never even see his door open.

Chanting the words Raoul had taught me, I tried not to flinch as the flames framing the door flared, and its black center melted in every direction to reveal . . .

"A football field? Are you serious?" I asked as I stepped out of the street and into the stadium. Well, Raoul hadn't lied. Things definitely weren't what they seemed. Maybe the Magistrate would observe an entirely different setup when he arrived. A gladiator's ring. A matador's arena. Or, more likely, a reeking pit lined with burning skulls.

My mind had come up with the old RCA dome as neutral territory. A little tip of the hat to my brother-in-law, the rabid Colts fan? Or just a wish that I could revisit Indy, hang with people I loved. With whom, I suddenly realized, I'd come the closest to finding a home.

I shook my head. The time to ponder had passed. And what a relief it was, in a way, to let go of all those thoughts zooming around in my head like child stars hurtling toward their first DUIs.

I shucked my outer layer of clothing, which left me in a white T-shirt and a pair of loose black pants. Drawing the sword, I made the specific motions in the air Raoul had taught me. He'd called them *atra*-cuts, and explained they were symbolic of me slicing through the planes between us in order to bring the Magistrate to me. You could do them with any blade, and though by themselves they didn't affect any change, coupled with the words I spoke they worked to bring the *nefralim* onto the field.

When I was still working solo I had a job in L.A. where I happened to see Keanu Reeves lunching with, well, who gives a crap, right? Say what you want about the guy, he's easily the most hell-yeah gorgeous dude on the scene today. The Magistrate left him in the dust. And, shame on me, there was a very American part of me that wanted badly for him to be good because of it. Surely somebody whose eyes, cheekbones, chest, ass made me want to stand up and applaud couldn't be pure evil.

Okay, can we all just take a minute to remember high school, please? Good. Now, back to business.

He wore, well, that whip. And that was all. Disconcerting.

Because I have, believe it or not, never fought a naked man before. Which, while he was not a man, he was certainly built like one, and that could be a distraction. Or a hindrance. Because, despite my chosen profession and my tendency to leave a trail of bent and broken bones behind me, I try to avoid injuring the man parts. They're just so damn vulnerable. Plus, Dave once explained to me in excruciating detail exactly how it feels to be kicked there. Which is why I totally understand now why guys cringe just seeing it happen on TV. Give it any name you want. My definition is torture, and I just haven't gotten to the point where I'm willing to cross that line.

On the other hand, this battle had everything to do with saving my brother. Keeping that thought firmly at the front of my mind, I knew I'd do damn near anything to keep the Magistrate from grabbing his soul when the moment came for him to climb that rainbow-colored cord to Raoul.

As the Magistrate loosened the whip from his belt, sauntering toward me from the visiting team's locker room, I had maybe thirty seconds to consider whether or not Raoul and I had calculated correctly. If we were right, this would be a quick, aggressive fight. Like most of my opponents before him, he'd assume I was weaker, slower, and more likely to give quarter than take it. The very fact that I was standing there showed it never hurt to be underestimated.

"You annoy me, little gnat," the Magistrate snapped as he strode toward me, uncoiling his whip with a whoosh of air that sounded painfully lethal. "Summoning me away from my duties as if I were some sort of common rail."

A rail, as I'd learned on one of my previous missions, was a hell-servant. I'd thought they were higher up the hierarchy. Like reavers, and with the same ultimate goals. But apparently the Magistrate saw them more as clean-the-toilet and mop-up-the-puke sorts of demons.

Raoul had advised me, "Do what you do best." So I taunted him. "And yet you're here. So who really has the power, huh? I'm thinking the skinny redhead with the kick-ass Spirit Eye."

Oh, that brought the purple to his face. He charged me like a blitzing linebacker, belatedly remembering the whip. He swung it around as I brought my sword through and the weapons clashed. My blade bit into the leather-wrapped handle of his whip. And stopped. Whatever hid under that overlay was as strong as steel.

I jumped back as he reached out to grab me, slashing at him with the knife I held in my left hand. At the last minute, Raoul had found me a long, thin dagger. Not a one-blow killer, but a cutter, nonetheless. And, baby, did the Magistrate bleed when I strafed that blade across his chest.

"Bitch!" he screamed, spraying spit, jumping backward, giving me just the room I needed to swing the shamshir again. He turned just before the blade bit into his heart, catching most of it on his left shoulder. Though it disabled the entire arm, it didn't put him down.

Quicker than my eye could follow, he lashed at me, his whip cracking across my upper back. The armor took it a helluva lot better than the T-shirt, which split in two and dropped to the ground. The impact staggered me, and as I struggled for balance he struck again. Twice. The first blow hit me across the upper chest and neck. Though only the tip of the whip touched skin, it felt like a cowboy had pressed a brand to my jugular. Blood began to stream from the wound.

I didn't have time to figure out whether or not it was serious before the third blow landed, the hardest so far, striking me across the thighs so suddenly and painfully I looked down to make sure my legs were still attached. The whip had wrapped around them. The Magistrate yanked, taking me to my knees.

I countered by rolling away from him, out of his coil. As soon as he attacked again I lunged forward. If I'd been a hair quicker, I'd have buried the sword in his abdomen. As it was I left a three-inch slice that bled freely down his leg and brought another obscenity from his lips.

"Where did you get that sword?" he demanded.

"I have friends in high places," I said as I jumped to my feet. Afraid to give him any more room to lash me, I rushed him, forcing him to use the handle of the whip to parry my attack. I could see in his eyes he didn't want to deal with me anymore. Wasn't prepared for this kind of fight. Hadn't expected me to be able to hurt him. Hadn't dreamed I'd be able to withstand his weapon.

I pressed my advantage, slashing at every vulnerable point I could reach with the dagger as he blocked my sword swings. Within seconds his chest and good arm were covered in red, while the blood he'd lost from his left shoulder trailed down his back like a wet cape.

"You're going down," I whispered triumphantly.

He kicked at me and I jumped back, giving him the distance he needed to bring his whip back into play. For a fleeting moment I saw him consider it. Realized he meant to go for my face. Blind me if possible. It was a good strategy. I moved in, hoping to ward it off by being too close for the strike to hit me clean when it finally came. Then the Magistrate surprised me.

He wheeled around and ran back the way he'd come, his injured arm flopping against his side until he finally grabbed his wrist to keep it from moving.

"Oh no you don't!" I sprinted after him, tasting the win like dark chocolate on my tongue.

"Jasmine!"

What the hell? Still running, I glanced over my shoulder. It was Asha, standing on the sideline, waving his arms like he wanted me to call time-out. I looked back at the Magistrate. He'd almost made it off the field. If I let him out of this plane, I figured he'd go back to hell. And I didn't have anything left I was willing to sacrifice to follow him there. "I'm busy!" I yelled.

"Please! The need is dire. I wouldn't have come otherwise. Thousands of lives balance on our swift actions."

The Magistrate was gone. Too fast for me, even with all the wounds I'd inflicted, he'd split the battlefield and run home to nurse his wounds. Get better. Raise an army. Come back and flatten my ass.

I strode over to Asha, getting more and more steamed with every step. "*Now* you decide to interfere? *NOW?* When I'm on the verge of saving my brother's life? I should do the world a favor. Split you in half this instant! Why didn't I get mahghul guts all over the inside of your car when I had the chance?"

"I have no idea," said Asha as he grabbed my elbow, hustled me to the portal, which, from this side, looked like a gigantic metal door. The kind you expect to see on the loading dock of an aircraft carrier.

"Could you, for once, quit sounding so kind? I'm deeply pissed at you!"

"Rightfully so. And I promise, if there is anything I can do to make it up to you, I will. But right now, we have an emergency situation."

"No," I said, as the metal sort of fizzled and we walked through the resulting hole into the streets of Tehran. "*You* have a situation that, once again, you are unwilling to handle all by yourself. It's a character flaw, Asha. I'd think you'd want to work on that. Build up your backbone, so to speak."

"I am," Asha insisted. "Which is why I came to get you. If this country loses Zarsa, nothing I do will make any difference for the next five hundred years. But why should she listen to me? All I have done is stand around and let her get herself deeper and deeper into the mess in which she currently finds herself."

"What mess?" I demanded as we walked toward Anvari's. Actually it was more like a two-legged race. I was dressed so unacceptably that I could easily be arrested in the time it took for us to cross the few blocks from the portal to Zarsa's door. So Asha had yanked off his turban, wound it around me the best he could and then held me close, hiding the rest of me with the proximity of his body. As I struggled to match his long stride I said, "We straightened it all out last night. The deal's off. Vayl's not going to turn her. Soheil doesn't think she's having an affair. End of story."

"Not quite," murmured Asha as we reached the back entrance to the store. He opened the door and let me in. The smell of kerosene made me gag. Instantly I knew Zarsa had not accepted our solution to her terrible dilemma and had instead come up with her own fiery plan.

Chapter Twenty-Seven

Asha and I rushed into Zarsa's little back room, where she stood against the wall, a burning candle in her hand, her hair and clothes wet, limp with the fuel she'd poured over herself. I expected to find Soheil on his knees on the worn red and gold carpet that covered the floor, begging her to blow the candle out. But he and the children were conspicuously absent.

A letter sat on the round table that dominated the room, which Zarsa had used for her readings. The shop was in the front of the building. It was closed, which told me she'd been minding the business alone. The family lived upstairs. And though I knew Zarsa had never experienced such despair, I couldn't believe she meant to burn down her family's home and sole means of support. So she must be psyching herself up to take to the street. Make that final dramatic statement with a self-inflicted funeral pyre.

"Asha, you are a complete idiot," I whispered out the corner of my mouth. "You have brought an assassin to talk a woman out of suicide. You couldn't have made a worse choice if you'd gone back in time, plucked Cleopatra, Sylvia Plath, and Marilyn Monroe off their deathbeds and brought them here with orders to cheer Zarsa up."

"Please," he begged. "You have immense powers. I can feel them flowing over you like waterfalls. Must they all pertain to destruction? Surely one of them can be directed toward *saving* a life?"

"Oh, you're a fine one to talk, ya big . . . skinny . . . procrastinator!" Now that it had become glaringly obvious I was out of good insults *and* a hypocrite—because all I wanted to do was put off dealing with this anguished, crazed woman—I gave up and joined the let's-save-Zarsa team.

I stepped forward, holding up my hands slowly so Zarsa could see that . . . whoops. Still armed. I gave Asha my weapons. "Don't lose those," I ordered. "They're not mine. And translate fast. All she has to do is pull that candle four inches toward her and we're going to be scrambling for the fire extinguishers."

"You are not a student," she said flatly, taking in my blades, my state of dress and, I supposed, the trail of blood leading from my neck to the apple-sized blotch on my chest. "I felt it when I touched you. You are—"

"A student as far as anyone needs to know," I replied firmly, my eyes telling her to keep my damn secrets as I touched my throat warily. I looked at my fingers. Fairly clean. Well, at least I'd stopped bleeding. We should celebrate. With cake. But no candles, thank you very much. "So, you're looking like hell," I said. "Is this the new Iranian spring fashion I've been hearing so much about? Little bit of a you-suck to the government for their ridiculous women's apparel crackdown?"

She shook her head.

"Okay, Zarsa. Talk to me. I'm not here to stop you." *Liar!* "I just want to know why."

She leaned against the wall behind her, one hand braced to help her legs hold her upright. "I can hardly breathe," she said, her eyes suddenly hidden behind a veil of tears. "My husband. My children. I know I should be happy to have them. I am a blessed woman. But that is why my soul weeps. To love so deeply, with every atom of your being, is to know what they can lose. To realize how horror awaits them around every corner now that my last hope is gone." Her smile reminded me so much of Vayl's twitchy-twitch I had to suppress a shudder.

"But, I thought you had new hope after we talked last night. Remember? About the Amanha Szeya?"

"I did," she said. "Until I dreamed of him."

Uh-oh. "What, uh, what happened in your dream?"

"The same atrocities I described to you yesterday. All of them under the unwavering gaze of the Amanha Szeya. He alone can change nothing for me and my people." She jammed the heels of her hands against her eyes. "And now I see the visions constantly. Everywhere I look it is as if the killings have already begun. Even you"—she pinned me with her desperate stare—"seem little better than a walking corpse to me."

Now I understood the immensity of her pain. And her problem. With Vayl a no-deal and Asha unable to weight the balance, she had no place left to turn. So her desperation loomed, taking all the air out of the room, all the hope out of her heart.

For a second I couldn't imagine how to help this woman. But I figured she'd already come up against a brick wall. She didn't need any company in the helpless/hopeless department. So I said, "Zarsa." I waited for her eyes to clear. For her attention to center. Knew that anything I said might not mean squat if she'd truly counted down to self-destruct. "Your original vision. What makes you think it was wrong?"

"I . . . there was a man. I thought Vayl . . ."

"So you weren't sure who would partner with you in this rise to power?"

"I didn't see him clearly. That is, Soheil was with me, but there was another."

"So you got greedy. Decided now's the time when maybe you should have waited a week. A year. Until the right person came along. Whoever that was."

"There *is* no right person!" Zarsa insisted hysterically, the candle shaking so badly I was afraid she'd drop it on herself accidentally.

"Seriously? You haven't heard of anybody that open-minded Iranians like you and Soheil look up to? Some sort of underground ass-kicker who knows how to get people stirred up without resorting to blowing up shoppers and schoolchildren—"

"FarjAd Daei," she whispered.

That name. Where had I heard it before? I had to hammer at my memory banks for a second before it came to me. The young woman who'd been hanged. She'd cried it out just before they'd executed her. "Who is he?" I asked.

"I have only heard rumors. He speaks in common places. Markets. Teahouses. He talks of peace. Of treating women as partners, not cattle. Changing our minds. Changing our times."

"Yes!" said Asha, finally finding the courage to speak for the first time. "I overheard two men who were planning to go and hear him tonight. He's speaking at the Oasis."

I grabbed Asha's arm. "Where?"

When he'd repeated the name back to me twice, I knew there was no mistake. "Do either of you know what he looks like?" I asked, digging the picture out of my pocket that I'd carried since our initial briefing.

Zarsa shook her head, but Asha nodded. "I have seen him. And heard him. That is why I was so interested in tonight's talk. He is a teller of stories, you know."

"You mean a liar?"

Asha snorted. "No. A master storyteller. Someone who can weave plot and character into a fascinating tale from which his listeners not only identify, but learn."

"Is this the guy?" I showed him the picture and when his eyes lit in recognition, I could no longer put the two items I'd just discovered off to coincidence. FarjAd Daei was the man in the picture. The man scheduled to appear at the very café Vayl and I had scouted as our assassination scene yesterday evening. Knowing what I already knew about Dave's link with the Wizard, I could only come to one conclusion. Iran's most notorious terrorist had just set up the CIA to blot out its brightest hope for deliverance.

Chapter Twenty-Eight

You don't bring someone back from the brink in a couple of minutes. We talked to Zarsa for hours. At least we convinced her to shower early on, and we did open up the house so the fumes could exit the premises before the kids got home from school and started asking awkward questions. In the end, having an important task to do was probably the key to turning her face away from the grave.

"Such a vital thing you ask of me," she said for the third time. "Are you sure I am capable?"

I looked her over and thought, *No, not even close. You're so strung out it'll take you weeks, maybe months to recover the kind of inner balance you need to function properly. But sitting around biting your fingernails and obsessing about your last stupid move is going to drive you even crazier. So*—"Absolutely. But if it's not safe, or if Soheil doesn't feel comfortable with our plan, make sure you leave your outdoor lights off. Got it?"

She nodded. Then she jumped up. "The house is a mess from last night! I must make it ready! Oh—" She looked at us, realizing suddenly that she was being a terrible hostess. Then she got this confused look. Did the host/guest parameters even apply in cases like these?

I stood, more than ready to rescue her. "We have to go anyway. I have quite a few preparations to make myself."

She wanted to hug me goodbye, but I told her with a smile that I try to make it a practice not to touch Seers. She understood, and made a sign over my head that ended with her blowing me a kiss.

"What was that?" I asked.

Zarsa said, "The blessings of Aranhya, the Great Mother Spirit."

"Cool. And for you . . ." I did a succession of quick-march moves followed by a complicated salute. "My brother, sister, and I made it up. We always did it for our dad before he left the country, usually to fight in some conflict or another. And he always came back in one piece, so it's gained a sort of mystical good-luck quality in our family over the years." Which was why Dave and I did it for Evie right before she and Tim got married. I guess we might've chosen a more appropriate setting than the altar. But it did crack everybody up, and set the tone for a really fun wedding. Plus their marriage was still going strong. So what the hell.

Zarsa seemed to like it as well. We left her smiling, something I wouldn't have bet a penny on at the beginning of our visit.

"The sun is beginning to set," Asha noted as we paused outside Anvari's so I could do up my last button. Zarsa had lent me clothes to allow for a hassle-free walk back to the house. But I wasn't looking forward to it. Vayl would be up soon.

"Yeah. I'd better get going," I said.

"Is there anything more I can do?" Asha asked.

"Just stick to the plan and make sure Zarsa doesn't get hurt for taking part in it," I replied. She ought to be okay as long as the Wizard thought we were still going to kill FarjAd Daei. But just in case . . .

He nodded. I watched him walk away with a sinking heart. If everything went according to that plan, General Danfer would be so pissed off that he'd probably find a way to pressure Pete into firing me by morning.

When I got back to the house, Dave and his crew had commandeered the living room, taking up all the furniture and most of the floor, prepping their weapons for the night's "raid." Looking at him as he sat with his back to the fireplace wall, his M4 in pieces on a sheet of plastic he'd found in the garage, I felt a horrible ache press against my chest. Because if this all went to shit, I'd never see him again. And we still didn't have our past straight between us.

"Um, Dave? Can I talk to you for a minute?"

"Sure." He jumped to his feet and headed toward the kitchen, so I joined him there, sitting next to him on a stool that I wished had a back. It was suddenly taking all my energy just to sit up straight.

"I was just thinking, this assignment's going to be over soon," I said, choosing my words carefully so I wouldn't betray myself. "And then we'll go our separate ways again."

He nodded, tracing a random pattern with his forefinger onto the countertop of the little island we shared. I looked down at my own hands as I said, "I was just . . . you know, people shoot at us all the time. Eventually somebody's going to have good aim. And one of us won't come back. Which was why, now, I wanted to explain about Jessie."

Though I wasn't looking at him, I felt him stiffen. He didn't raise his hands to stop me. Didn't even shake his head in vehement denial. But I felt a wave of don't-go-there come off him and very nearly caved. I didn't, only because I thought I'd never be able to muster the nerve to talk about it again, even if I got the chance.

"You know, she believed deeply in heaven. And she wanted to

go there. But she didn't think she'd be able to if she became a vampire. She also understood the lure earthly immortality would have for her, especially after she married you. She knew you'd never agree to smoke her if she turned. So she made me promise. And she did the same for me."

"Promises were made to be broken," he said, his voice hoarse with suppressed emotion.

I looked at him then. "I wish you could forgive me. Jessie said you might not be able to."

"She . . . she thought it that far through?"

"We were battling vampires almost nightly. I'm surprised you didn't do the same."

He shrugged. "I never figured on losing."

I spread my hands out on the countertop. The left one now bare. The right sporting a glittering reminder of how many battles I'd won. "I didn't think about it much myself until Jessie brought it up. And then what she said made a lot of sense. She was just doing what she thought she needed to in order to save her soul, Dave."

As I spoke, his lips drew back farther and farther, as if he'd bitten into something rancid. "She was my wife. And yet she didn't trust something that sacred to me. If only she'd explained—"

"Could you have let her go?" I whispered. "Could you have stuck a crossbow in your wife's chest and released an arrow into her heart, knowing the alternative was eternal life, right here on earth, with you at her side? Come on now. I could barely bring myself to do it, and I was only her sister-in-law."

He rammed both fists onto the counter. "Why are you bringing this up now? I have to be sharp for tonight and you're tearing my damn heart out!"

Why did I suddenly remember all those afternoons we'd spent pounding Play-Doh into pancakes in Granny May's kitchen? Evie had wanted to play house, which was hilarious in retrospect, since not one of us knew how a normal family functioned. I'd reluctantly agreed, but Dave had taken one look at our yellow, blue, and red clay breakfast and decided to transform it into a sport. Five minutes later we'd transformed the pancakes into Frisbees and set up a course with Granny May's Tupperware bowls that would've impressed an Olympic committee.

I said slowly, "In case something goes wrong at the takedown, I wanted things to be straight between us."

"Are you asking me to forgive you?" Dave asked. I thought he sounded more grieved than aggravated. But when he scratched his neck, I was reminded I still couldn't speak freely.

"No," I said, surprising myself just as much as him. "I just needed to explain how it went down. And to tell you I'm sorry."

"Why?" He didn't bother to hide the bitterness in his voice. "Jessie knew you'd keep your promise and you did."

I bowed my head. "You gotta have a big streak of ice running through your heart to follow through on a vow like that," I told him. "I'm apologizing for being that cold."

Dave nodded. "You did what Jessie wanted. And if she was right, I should be down on my knees, thanking you. I know I should . . ."

"It's okay," I said. "I'm just glad you're still talking to me."

"Well, you did have to travel six thousand miles to have this conversation," he reminded me. We both managed a smile. The very same one, in fact. One of those things that makes it weirdly wonderful to be a twin. "Then again," he went on, "you did bring Cassandra with you. That in itself deserves high praise."

"So you guys are getting along pretty well, huh?" My gut twisted slightly at the thought, but I realized it wasn't for him; it was for me. For him I wanted only happiness.

"She's . . . amazing. I think I could spend my whole life talking to her and never get bored. I haven't gotten to see her much today though. We've been really busy running through the scenario. Getting prepped. Lots of last-minute stuff I probably should've taken care of yesterday. I'd like to see her before we go though. Maybe I'll go check on her now."

Holy crap! Dave's about to crash the we-know-you're-the-mole party. May Day! May Day! In my mind I could hear jets crashing and ships exploding. This was not going to be pretty if I couldn't think of a good distraction. And my mind was a sudden and total blank!

I followed Dave out the kitchen door, my jaw working like I'd just bitten into a caramel, but nothing came out. No brilliant delay tactic. Not even a bad joke to give me five seconds to pray for a miracle. As we went past the living room I caught Cam's eye and began to do wild charades. I jumped up and down. Made last-chance-motel faces. Pointed at Dave and then at the closed door toward which he headed. The one behind which Cassandra and Bergman had been laboring all day to develop a device that could remove the Wizard's control from him.

"Yo, boss," Cam called. "Question for you."

"Hold that thought," Dave called. "I've got business."

Jet dropped something. Broke something else. Said, "Shit!" as loud as he could manage. The din would've brought an entire firehouse down the poles to investigate. Dave kept walking. I'll say this for my brother: He's got focus.

I was seriously considering grabbing a bust of Iran's latest president, which was sitting on a pedestal between the bedrooms, and clubbing him over the head with it when Cassandra emerged from the girl's room.

Part of my Sensitivity opens me up to very strong feelings among my fellow humans. Boy was she ever glad to see him. And likewise with my twin. In fact, if the house had been empty, I was pretty sure they'd have greeted each other in an entirely different manner.

"Where have you been all day?" Dave asked, his voice low and, for the first time in a long time, excited.

She smiled. "A little project for Jaz. She's not very pleased with this Seer Vayl has taken up with."

Dave glanced over his shoulder, but I'd already sidled around him. He still managed to catch my eye before I entered the bedroom. "Everything okay with the vamp there, Jazzy?" he asked.

"Nothing I can't handle," I assured him. I shut the door before I could catch a glimpse of them making googly eyes at each other. Yuck.

"Bergman!" I whispered, tiptoeing up to him like Dave might have just thrown Cassandra out of his way and pressed his ear against the door. Hey, I've seen weirder things. Sad. But true.

He looked up from the temporary work station he and Cassandra had set up at the dressing table. They'd left it against the wall so they wouldn't have to worry about disturbing the attached mirror, and scattered their tools across it. Bergman's computer hardware and the gear required to modify it buddied up with Cassandra's herbs and potions, all of which surrounded the Enkyklios.

I sat at the chair beside Bergman's that Cassandra had obviously just vacated. "Any luck?" I asked.

He nodded as he peered through a magnifying glass at an item he held with tweezers. It was about the size of a watch battery, but it glowed the red of the rubies in my ring. "We think this will do the trick," he said.

"Okay." I gulped down another urge to cry. This was so not going to work if I was going to blubber every five minutes. I resolved to have a huge emotional breakdown the second I stepped foot in my apartment. I'd supply myself with chocolate. A gallon of cookie-dough ice cream. Two boxes of Kleenex. And maybe a good tearjerker to get me jump-started. *The Pursuit of Happyness* always did the trick. Yeah, that sounded like a winner.

Having planned ahead, I now felt better. At least, better able to function. "Okay. How does it work?"

Bergman took a while to answer. Finally he admitted, "I'm not completely sure. Cassandra has made it able to follow the path of the ohm."

When my eyebrows shot up he explained. "That's what they call the item a necromancer uses to control his, uh, zombie with." He gave me an apologetic frown. "Cassandra finally got hold of this woman she said you guys tried to talk to before the mission even started. What was her name?" He had to think a second. "Oh yeah. Sister Doshomi. She had a story on her Enkyklios that basically explained Dave to us. He was made the second way, the way Hilda—remember her, the woman whose daughter died—who ended up as the great necromancy professor?" I nodded, feeling a jolt of sympathy for the woman who'd lost everything and still managed to reach across time to help me. "Dave was made the way Hilda suspected. The way she actually discovered before she was murdered."

He cleared his throat. Looked at me sympathetically, like we were at a funeral, which it kind of felt like we were. "Jaz, Dave's not just a regular zombie. He's a zedran. Which is why there's an ohm in the first place. You know, so the Wizard can communicate with him from a distance." Maybe sensing that I was having a hard time digesting all his information without falling off my chair, he rushed on. "The good news is, the ohm has to be made from the Wizard's own flesh. So once we get it out of Dave, actually once the retriever we've built gets it out of him, we can use it to find the Wizard."

"How?"

"Cassandra knows a spell."

That got my attention. I laid my hand on Bergman's forehead. "Are you feeling okay?"

"Yeah, why?"

"Oh, I don't know. Maybe because only three weeks ago if I'd have said the word 'spell' to you, you'd have burst a blood vessel."

He nodded slowly. "It's why I wanted to come." He put everything down and sat back. "I didn't count on meeting Natchez. But I guess I was hoping to find somebody—or something—like him on this trip." He shook his head in amazement. "The man knows how to *live*, Jaz. He's not afraid of anything that I can tell. Not of getting sick. Or working something new into his repertoire. Or trying something totally off the wall. Did you know he once saw a woman on the street that he just loved the looks of, so he asked her out? Just like that! I mean, she could've been psycho. She could've had four different STDs."

"And?"

"She was fine! They went out a few times. Didn't have enough in common for a longer relationship and parted friends. Isn't that amazing?"

"Yeah, it is."

"He's the same age as me, Jaz, and he's lived, like, twenty lives compared to mine."

"Do you really envy him as much as it sounds? I mean, if you'd spent all your time jumping out of airplanes and climbing mountains, you wouldn't have come up with even half your inventions."

He clasped his hands between his knees and slouched in his chair, like I was one of his professors reprimanding him for not handing in his paper its usual two weeks in advance. But when he looked at me it was with a new defiance in his eyes. "I hate being a wimp. Feeling this paranoia so extreme it's burning knots in my chest. Like the world's going to end if I don't protect myself well enough, if I take one step in the wrong direction. You can't imagine how bad it sucks."

Actually I could. After I lost Matt, Jessie, my crew . . . the Agency kept a sharp eye on my sanity. Rightfully so, since I could feel the shards of it slicing against the inside of my skull every single day. And I'd developed a few bizarre habits that were tough to hide. Among them a tendency for my brain to stick on a word like a bad stutter. Also a habit of blacking out at the worst possible moment. Fortunately I'd been able to toe the line long enough to get my head on fairly straight. I said, "So what's your next step? Surfing those massive Australian waves? Skiing the Alps? Exploring the wilds of Burma?"

Bergman cleared his throat. "Actually, I thought I'd just explain how the retriever works. And then, you know, after this mission's over? Maybe take a vacation to Cancun. Buy some funky clothes and tell the girls I'm a musician. You know—see what happens."

I chuckled. "Sounds like an excellent place to start." I scooted my chair forward. "So show me."

He handed me the magnifying glass. "It's the same principal as the bug card. Only with a magical wallop. You introduce it into Dave's body. It zeroes in on the ohm. Attaches to it. Disables it. And then reemerges."

"How does it get in and out?" I pictured it like the killer pill he'd made to zap one of the vamps we'd targeted during our last mission. We'd tried to get him to eat it, so I was seeing Dave wolfing this thing down in a cheeseburger or whatever equivalent we could drum up on short notice. Given our current location it would probably be hidden among some rice-stuffed veggie leaves.

Bergman took off his glasses, cleaned, and reset them on his face. His hands shook slightly as he worked the frames. "Cassandra says, in order for the magic to be effective, the retriever has to take the same route as the ohm." He stopped, waiting for me to figure it out. It took less time than I would've liked. I felt my lips draw back from my teeth in a snarl as I said, "You mean we have to cut Dave's throat?"

Chapter Twenty-Nine

Dave and his crew took off before Vayl woke. The idea, in order to "fool" the Wizard, was for them to leave early, make sure the place was thoroughly scouted and covered before we arrived to carry out the assassination. We'd actually run through the scenario the night before, after Soheil left. Though, with everyone in the know, it seemed an empty exercise. Even the mole understood we'd never join them. Because we would head to the "right" location.

They left the house in twos, with Dave and Amazon Grace in the first pair. That gave me a chance to powwow with the rest of his crew. We met in the living room, Cam, Jet, and Natchez leaning against the back of the couch as I explained about the retriever while Cassandra and Bergman backed me up when they came up with the hard questions.

The guys didn't like the mode of delivery any more than I did.

"Listen, before we slice into the man's throat, isn't there any way we can make one hundred percent sure he's the mole?" asked Natch.

As Bergman threw him a sympathetic look I said grimly, "He's it. And it's not like we're going to jam a dagger into his carotid. It'll just be a little incision. Just enough to insert the thing." *I hope.*

"When?" asked Jet.

"After the mission is over. Vayl and I will handle it."

"Whoa, wait a minute," said Cam. "We're his men. We're going to help get this monkey off his back." Chorus of hell-yeahs from the other guys.

My mind immediately jumped to the mahghul. Would they gather for an event like the one we were planning? I reminded myself to check the roof the next time I stepped outside. I said, "This isn't some kind of intervention where we all sit around and whale on Dave for spazzing on our Monday-night football parties and showing up drunk at our weddings. This is a violent attack on a military officer, during which he will die. Not"—I held up a finger to ward off the slew of questions I could see coming—"because of the cut on his throat. But because as soon as the Wizard's control is released he'll go back to the state he was in before the Wizard took him. Which was dead."

I could hardly bear to look at their faces, tight with pain and despair. It made it nearly impossible to contain my own. Which was why I totally avoided looking at Cassandra. Thank God she kept silent. If I'd have heard one hint of a sob, I'd have lost it. I went on. "If we're lucky, he'll come back. Like I did."

I gave them a brief sketch of my own revival, Raoul's hand in it, and his willingness to take on Dave if my brother made the choice. I hesitated, not wanting to utter the next words, knowing they had to be spoken. *I'm so sorry, Cassandra.* "But you have to know, he may choose to stay gone. In which case, it would suck for you to have touched a superior officer with the intention of harming him. And we all know nobody will believe the Wizard had a hand in his passing, because we won't be able to prove he had control over Dave in the first place."

We wouldn't be able to prove anything about the Wizard, which was why, after all this was over, Danfer would go headhunting and Pete would have to give him mine. I'd be unemployed. Out of the job that had sustained me through the worst tragedy of my life. Dammit! Wasn't there a single bright spot in this whole, muck-ridden mess?

Of course there is, Jazzy, Granny May said from her spot at the bridge game she kept going near the center of my temporal lobe. She set a coaster under Bob Hope's water glass, the game temporarily suspended while Abe Lincoln made popcorn. *As bright as a spotlight, if you'll just look hard enough to see it.*

I'm looking, dammit! But at the moment all I could see was Cam, watching Cassandra, who'd sought the comfort of Bergman's arms at my last pronouncement. "Oh, he's coming back," Dave's right-hand man said confidently, giving our Seer a wink when she finally turned to look at him. The cheerful optimism on his scarred face made her sit up straighter and say, "How can you be sure?"

"Woman, I've seen the way he looks at you. And vice versa. No fully functioning man gives that up willingly." Cam nodded. "He'll be back."

I wished I could feel so sure. Unfortunately I knew how tough his return trip might be. But I kept my mouth shut for once, and in the end I convinced Dave's unit to leave freeing him to us. We said our goodbyes and they left. At which point Vayl emerged from the guys' room.

He wore a button-down shirt of dark purple silk that flowed off his broad shoulders and caressed his chest. His coal-black trousers hugged his lean hips with the help of a matching leather belt, and I was sure his shoes had been crafted by a master cobbler who, like his great-grandfather before him, still plied his trade on the streets of Milan. On one hand I could've scooped that seething mass of masculinity and power into a waffle cone and savored dessert for the next forty-eight hours. On the other, I badly wanted to kick his ass.

Because he'd taken my blood, Vayl was attuned to my emotions.

So he turned to me in surprise, detouring through the living room on his way to the kitchen.

Uh-oh.

I'd been leaning against the couch in the spot Cam had vacated. Now I backed behind the love seat, keeping it and our consultants, who still sat on it, between my boss and me. "Hey, how are you?" I asked, keeping my voice level, trying not to glare. I'd already chosen my fights tonight. Ours wasn't included.

Vayl gave Bergman and Cassandra a nod that they took as dismissal. They helped each other up, stumbling over each other's excuses to leave.

"Wow, look at the time," said Bergman. "I'd better go get the TV van ready for later."

At the same time Cassandra said, "I'm going to work on that spell you'll need to locate the Wizard. Perhaps it will help clear my head. If I could just squeeze one vision out of this fog that will help David . . ." She trailed off and let Bergman help her from the room.

"They're good people," I said as various doors closed behind our consultants. *Too good to be soiled by contact with the likes of us.* I was thinking no more missions for either one for at least six months.

"They are," Vayl agreed. "And yet, the strength of your feelings is not directed toward them just now. And neither are they positive emotions."

I pressed my lips together. Maybe if I did it hard enough this whole unpleasant business would go away and we could get on with the assassinating. Or not.

"I am puzzled," Vayl said with the quirk to his lips that passed for a frown. "I have only just risen. How is it that I have disturbed you so deeply already?"

"Ha, ha, ha." What a lovely little trill of a laugh I have. When

I'm drunk. Otherwise—gag. "You know, I'm just thinking about the, uh, the thing tonight. Getting wound up. Like I usually do. You know me."

"Yes, I do." He approached me slowly. As if I might spook at any sudden moves. His brows slanted down. "You and I should be fine. I have rescinded my agreement with Zarsa. I will not try to meet Badu and Hanzi until I am sure they will not be harmed by our reunion. And yet I sense you would cheerfully slam my head against the wall if you thought you could get away with it. Why is that?"

"Uh." My voice broke. I cleared my throat, which felt far too dry for somebody who'd just downed an entire glass of tea. "Do we really have time for this?" I tapped the face of my watch. "We should be at the café in, like—" I checked the time. *Crap! An hour?* How was I going to put him off that long?

Screw it. I sat down. On the floor. Looked up at him until he sank down in front of me. I was about to rip him a new one over Zarsa. Let him know I didn't appreciate being the other woman. But some part of me knew that wasn't the real problem. And when I opened my mouth, that was the bit that spoke up.

"You need to bury your boys," I said.

Immediately his powers shifted. As if I'd physically threatened him, he raised his abilities the way a boxer will lift his fists. "What do you mean?" he asked, biting off each word as if he wished it were my head. His eyes, which had been their typical relaxed brown, began to darken.

The ghost of my mother rose before me. Not like I'd seen her in hell, but the real-life version. She spread her nicotine-stained fingers like she was holding a plate full of chicken gizzards and screeched, *See? This is why you need to learn to bury your feelings. Never mind how crazy that'll make you. These conversations never turn out well!*

Ignoring her, I plowed on. "You never really grieved. I mean, you went from fury over their deaths, to plotting and pulling off the ultimate revenge. And then, from what I gather, you stepped straight into denial that you might never see them again. You never really mourned. And you definitely never accepted. This whole search has been one long demonstration of how far you'll go to deny the fact that Badu and Hanzi died. That you lost them. And that it feels horrible."

"How do you know what I did and did not do?" he snarled. "You were not there. You did not follow me to their graves every night."

"What did you do there?" I asked mildly. "Did you talk to them about how much you missed them? Or did you promise them vengeance?"

Vayl's powers tightened up another notch. I didn't believe he'd freeze me, but I could tell by the look in his eye I'd pushed him about as far as he was willing to go. So I gave him one last shove.

"I need to be able to trust you. Professionally I know I can. But if you want to be with me . . . you need to be with me all the way."

"This is an ultimatum, then?" he spat, his black eyes sparking red. "Either give up on meeting my boys or forget about us?"

I sighed. "Liliana really did a number on you, didn't she?" At his wide eyes I said, "I don't do ultimatums, Vayl. It's not a this or that deal. You're going to do what you feel is right. So am I. That's why they call us adults. And, frankly, I do think you should try to meet the souls that once lived in the bodies of your boys. Someday. After you've said goodbye to Hanzi and Badu. When you've come to realize that the men you meet in America will not be the teenage Rom you loved beyond words over two hundred years ago. They'll be grown-ups. Who were raised by men other than you. Men they call Dad."

Vayl shook his head. Hard. "No. It must not be like that."

"Why not?"

"Because they are all I have!" He spat the words like they'd been beaten out of him.

"No, Vayl," I said softly. I let my fingers brush across the top of his hand. Just a touch to remind him of what could be. He shuddered. To be honest, I felt the same. I sucked in a breath. Forced myself to concentrate. I said, "They were all you *had*."

Before his eyes could go completely green I held up my hands. "My point is, your obsession has already messed with me. The fact that you took Zarsa's blood. That you did something that intimate with her. That you planned to get even closer. You're right. It makes me want to wrap you up in rubber bands and then just sit next to you and snap them every time I feel annoyed at you. Which at this point would be all night long."

He should have looked remorseful. But I thought my words actually excited him. His voice, always husky and low took on a rich undertone as he said, "Jasmine? Are you jealous?"

"Not quite," I said softly. "But if you belonged to me. Only me. I would be."

He knew exactly what I meant. He ran his hands up my thighs. Oh. So. Slowly. "Soon," he whispered.

I shook my head. "Not until you're ready."

He pulled his hands back. My thighs throbbed, missing their weight, their heat. "My boys," he whispered.

"I love them too," I told him. "Because they were yours." Startling thought. *I wish they'd been mine. I'd have kicked their asses up, down, and sideways before I'd have allowed them to be the kind of hellions who'd steal a farmer's wagon. Then they would never have been in a position for that same farmer to shoot them dead.* "But you're holding them too hard."

He took a while to ponder the palms of his hands. The mask that typically held back every emotion he ever experienced had slid back into place. "I will have to think on it. This is not something I can just . . . do."

"Sure."

I watched him get up, go into the kitchen. I still had to tell him the man we were assigned to take out tonight wasn't the Wizard's henchman, but somebody our country would love to support if only we'd known about him. I sighed. It should be good news. *Guess what, Vayl? We don't have to kill anybody tonight. Let's partaaay!!* Except the uppity-ups wouldn't buy our evidence. It was way too flimsy in light of their particular theory, which took into account everything they'd invested in this project. They wanted results. And since we couldn't promise them that, at least not the kind they could parade across the TV screen, we'd no doubt lose our jobs before we had a chance to pull off the mission as we'd rearranged it.

I went into the kitchen. Vayl was sitting at the counter, pouring blood into a coffee cup. I took the stool beside him. "Is there any way we can avoid contacting Pete and the DOD dudes until our mission's over?"

"Why?"

I explained what I'd learned about FarjAd Daei while he was out of touch. And my suspicions that my little rewrite of the Big Boss's script would be met with either outright hostility—"You're FIRED!"—or surface cooperation—"Well, what you say makes sense"—at which point General Danfer covers the receiver, tells an aide to call Dave on the other line, and orders him to follow through on the assignment Vayl and I inexplicably refuse to complete.

Vayl looked at his cup thoughtfully. "I apologize."

"What?"

"You have shouldered the burden of this entire mission yourself."

"Naw, not really. I mean—"

"Yes. And you must be frantic about David. But you have not said a word to me, your *sverhamin*. To whom you should feel free to reveal any thought. Any wish."

I shrugged. "It's what I do."

He shook his head. "It was what you did before we met. Long before I gave you Cirilai. I have shoved you back into your former life. And you barely even noticed. Were you so comfortable there?"

I shrugged. "No. Horribly, terribly *un*comfortable. But I knew where I stood. Here, it's like I'm never sure of my next step. Nobody tells me the rules until five minutes before I need to know. And you." I shook my head. "Being with you is like riding the highest, longest roller coaster ever made."

When he winced I added, "Don't get me wrong. I love coasters. I'm just explaining why I can transition back to Lonersville so easily."

He wrapped his hands around his cup. I could see the whites of his knuckles, so I was surprised he didn't actually break it. He said, "Then I will have to make sure you come to like your new situation so well you cannot stand to slide back anymore. Not even for a day."

As we stared at each other across the countertop I felt like he'd just made some sort of sacred vow. Especially when Cirilai sent a shot of warmth up my arm. I managed a breathy "Okay," and realized I was considering climbing on top of that smooth flat surface, knowing that if I did he'd meet me halfway and whatever happened would be Guinness World Record material. Then Cole walked into the room.

I tried not to glare. But dammit! He was like a three-year-old. Always interrupting at the worst possible moment! He sauntered in like he was actually welcome, splayed himself across half the counter, and grinned charmingly. "So. What are we doing?"

Sending your ass to Portugal the first chance we get, I thought, my inner bitch snapping her fingers in his face as I spoke. Surprisingly, Vayl was the one who kept his temper. He said, "A great deal of Jasmine's plan tonight rotates on your ability to convince our target that he is a target, but not of our country. That, indeed, we have come to help."

"We don't know much about him beyond the fact that his name is FarjAd Daei," I added. "And that he's sort of the Martin Luther King Jr. for his people. Which would explain why the Wizard wants him dead."

"Why is it the good ones always die young?" Cole wondered.

"Generally it is because the bad ones have been in charge far too long and they are reluctant to release power," Vayl said.

Score another one for the Master of Understatement, I thought. But I gave Vayl a smile. He had a very European way of sliding up on a subject that I'd only recently come to appreciate. Maybe it had something to do with becoming one of those subjects. I said, "Well, look, I don't know how long we can keep this guy *alive*. I don't expect him to stress the retirement system around here, for sure. But we have to, at least, keep him safe until the Wizard is no longer a threat."

"So has the plan changed?" Cole asked.

"Not much," I said. "We set up just like for the assassination. We know the event's not private, so the three of us can enter the café as arranged. Vayl goes to the bathroom early. When FarjAd exits the main room to relieve himself, the two of us follow, bag him without the previously planned fatal blow, hustle him out the window to Asha's waiting car, and hide him at Zarsa's house until it's safe for him to go home."

"And Zarsa's okay with this?" Cole asked, slicing a narrow look at Vayl.

"She's practically frothing at the mouth for a chance to help," I said.

Cole gaped at me. "You *talked* to her? When?"

"Today. She's a mess, you know."

He blew a breath through his teeth. "Well, Christ, who the hell can live here for long and not be? I haven't seen so much pain in one place since I watched that training video on torture."

We were silent, conceding the point. Which was why we heard so clearly the knock at the door. "That'll be Asha," I said. "Everybody ready?"

The guys nodded. Though I didn't expect violence, I'd geared up for it. After leaving Bergman I'd gone back to my room, dug into my weapons bag, and pulled out my usual array of guns and blades. Grief sat in its customary shoulder holster. Grandpa Samuel's bolo was snug in its hip sheath. Since my holy water carrier had been converted to a chew toy, I now wore wrist sheaths for throwing blades on both arms. Knives on the left. Stars on the right.

Since Vayl and I had both been the victims of thrown blades on our last mission, I'd used our downtime to raise my own proficiency in that area as well as swordplay. Now I was confident I'd increased my ability to keep enemies at a distance, which was always my main concern.

Bergman had also outfitted us with his latest improvement on group communication devices. For receiving audio we still had the tiny hearing-aide type devices that fit into our ears. But for transmitting, we'd graduated from mint-style gadgets that stuck to the roofs of our mouths to much smaller stick-on items that looked remarkably like beauty marks. Mine was adorable and went in the crease of my left cheek, à la Marilyn Monroe. Vayl had placed his just above and to the right of his lip. Cole had started with his on the end of his nose which, while hilarious, made you want to recommend a good dermatologist the second you saw him. So in the end he'd put it on his chin. The result—now, instead of hearing our comrades in the woofer range of surround-sound stereo, they sounded more like themselves.

We went to the door and I let Asha in. I expected an überawkward moment when he and Vayl met. But Asha took care of that problem right away. "So you belong to Jasmine," he said in his melancholy voice. It somehow delivered Vayl his deepest condolences without bearing a trace of malice toward me.

Vayl let out a bark of laughter as he shook Asha's hand. "Indeed. I am honored to meet the Amanha Szeya. Your legend is vast."

"And unearned as of late," Asha said. He turned to Cole. "And you, young hero? Do you also belong to Jasmine?"

Though Cole sent me a quick, searching glance, he grinned at Asha and said, "Not even close, buddy. I'm a free spirit. But if you know any beautiful lady Amanha Szeyas who'd like some company . . . point the way."

Asha smiled, lighting up the entire room. I instantly felt better. Surely everything would go according to plan tonight. Just because Asha had smiled.

Chapter Thirty

It did seem at first as if we were charmed. We arrived at the café in plenty of time to get good seats near the bathroom so no one would notice when we slipped away. Vayl sat across from me at a small white table, giving us each a full view of the room. Without hesitation, Cole settled in the seat beside mine. If we'd been in America, I suspected he'd have gone so far as to rest his arm across the back of my chair, give Vayl that challenging stare I'd seen him send a couple of times when he thought I wasn't looking. But Cole knew the rules in Iran. A casual touch in our country could get us jail time in this one. So he kept his hands on the laminate and behaved.

Even more miraculously, most of the people attending the evening's festivities spoke English, so Vayl and I didn't feel lost in a sea of gibberish. They didn't say anything worth overhearing. Asked after each other's families. Commented on the weather. But their nods, their smiles, and that hand gesture I'd first seen at the hanging, all pointed to a bigger, more exciting conversation going on just under the surface.

The evening started to go wrong when the owner and his pals began unrolling the blinds that had been tied at the tops of the windows. Claustrophobia scratched at my skull as, one by one, my portholes to the outside world were blocked. Shortly afterward Asha called.

We'd left him in the car, though he'd protested. "I would like to go in with you. I could help," he'd said. His mournful face held such eagerness I nearly hugged him.

"Dude, you're the getaway driver," said Cole.

"We may need to exit quickly," Vayl agreed. "It would help if you were ready to leave at a moment's notice."

More to make him feel involved than out of a true sense of need, I'd donned my special specs and given him the access number. "Just phone me if you see something fishy," I'd told him.

Now I put my hand over my ear to hide the tiny arm that snaked out to provide me with audio and looked down, so the movement of my lips would be hidden in the folds of my hijab. "Yeah?"

"The mahghul are gathering."

"What? Here?"

"Yes. What is it that you intend?" he asked, his voice strained.

"It's not us, Asha. Somebody else must be looking for trouble tonight."

"Should I come in?"

"Are you sure the source of the danger is inside?"

Long pause. "No. The sidewalks are busy tonight."

"Well, we're already inside. So we'll do what we can from here. Why don't you scout around out there? See what you come up with. Call if you need help, okay?"

"Okay."

I disconnected. "Crap." I told the guys what was happening. Both of them thought we had another assassin in our midst.

"This guy FarjAd's got to have a ton of enemies," Cole reasoned. "In a country full of radicals, his viewpoint is bound to raise alarms. Frankly, I can't believe he's still roaming around free. Either he's one lucky sucker or they've only just started hearing about him."

"Just look at this assemblage," Vayl agreed. "Strangers such as we should not be given such easy access if they wish for FarjAd to live a long life."

"The whole point is freedom," I reminded them. "These people are trying to create an atmosphere where it's okay to just walk in and listen. You know? Like in America?"

"Well, all this freedom is going to get their keynote speaker killed," said Cole.

"Goddammit!" I hissed the word, but it got Vayl and Cole's attention. "Here's an idea. Why don't you two quite vying for coolest agent of the month and help me figure out how to save a guy who's naive enough to think he can run around Iran having open forums?"

Vayl's nod allowed me the point. "People are milling about enough that I believe we can move through the room without causing undue attention. It is Secret Service time."

Even though Cole had only been hanging with us a little while, he knew what Vayl meant. When we're not working, we're training, and Vayl's go-to drill is the Secret Service. The idea is to disguise ourselves and then try to pick one another out of a crowd. It's how we learn to blend so we don't get nailed before—or after—our missions are completed. In this case, we weren't looking for Cole in a ball cap and a flannel shirt or Vayl sporting plastic-rimmed glasses and a briefcase. We wanted the killer Asha had detected.

We got up and spread out. Every computer had a user, as well as two or three onlookers. The tables were all full and small groups of men and women stood in the spaces between, chatting comfortably as they waited for the evening to get underway. The mix of men and women was about even, with the atmosphere equivalent to what you might expect from a crowd waiting to see a much-anticipated play. I had one of those small-world moments I often experience while out-of-country, when I understand that yawning gaps in culture and belief systems are never so huge they can't be bridged. There's always common ground. Like how much we all enjoy the company of people we agree with.

I didn't catch sight of FarjAd at first because he was hidden behind a group of students. I'd thought they were gathered around a computer, because they were laughing every few seconds. A sure sign one of them had found a hilarious Web site. Then the group split, their grinning faces following the subject of their attention as he emerged to greet the rest of the crowd.

He had a presence that made you smile before you realized what you were doing. I'd met so few people like him it was hard to compare. Our secretary, Martha, whose husband was a minister, shared his kindness. But not his immense, almost booming vitality. It crackled through the room like electricity, and I wasn't surprised to find the hairs on my neck standing on end as he came closer to my position.

I tore my eyes from him and scanned the area, concentrating on the people standing closest to him. Vayl and Cole would take care of their zones, and hopefully we'd discover the culprit in time to divert whatever disaster he or she had in mind. I hadn't found anybody suspicious by the time I looked back at FarjAd. To find him beaming amiably at me.

"It is so good of you to come," he said, taking my hands in his and bowing over them. "I have not seen your face before, true?"

"True," I replied, realizing too late I was smiling again. As a general rule, you try not to do that during the Secret Service drill. Throws you off.

"And from where have you traveled to be with us this night?"

I'm a student from Canada studying Farsi, said my brain, just like it had practiced. Repeatedly. I looked into those shrewd brown eyes, only a couple of inches above mine, and realized I couldn't lie. Some people just demand honesty. They're like walking jolts of truth juice. Granny May had been that way. She'd skewer you with her don't-screw-with-me stare and you'd be babbling out a confession before the cookie crumbs had dried on your lips.

"I'm from America," I told him. "My friends and I have come to save your life."

I don't know how I thought he'd react. Maybe like Cole, who squawked in my ear. Or Vayl, who whispered, "You must be joking." But I certainly didn't expect him to lean his head sideways and say, "May I deliver my speech first? These people have risked a great deal to hear me. And I hate to disappoint them."

I found myself nodding. "Okay." I cocked my head at him as his eyes began to twinkle, reminding me oddly of Cam. "Who *are* you?"

He stuck his hands in his pockets. "Do you know how they say the worst kinds of reformers are those who have sinned themselves?"

"You mean, like former smokers are the most rabid antismoking fanatics on earth?"

"Exactly." The twinkle dimmed. "When I was a young man I joined the Ministry of Intelligence." He looked me right in the eye, accepting my shock and disgust as he said, "I have done unspeakable things for which I may never be forgiven. I have scarred my people and my country. This is the only way I can think of to put it right again."

"That must've been one hell of an epiphany," I said.

Still meeting my eyes, his brightened as the memory played through his mind. "You have no idea how the birth of a child will change a man."

I thought of my father, who'd been out of the country the day Dave and I were born. "No," I said, "I don't."

"Then listen," he said. He went to a table near the center of the room and stood on the closest chair. He didn't even have to hold up his arms for quiet. People just stopped and listened. *Holy crap*, my stunned little brain thought, *he'd be great in an E.F. Hutton commercial.*

His message shocked me too. It was so—well—reasonable. Not something I'd expect to hear from a crowd pleaser in the capital city of Iran. As he spoke I studied the faces of his audience. Rapt. Optimistic. Peaceful. Not one of them looked prepared to end his life. These were some true-blue converts. Since I couldn't find the threat in my area of influence, I moved to another spot in the room, occasionally pausing to check on my partners or tune into the talk.

"We must not concede our country to bullies and bandits," FarjAd insisted at one point. "Their club is fear. And they beat us with it constantly. We become like abused women. Convinced we deserve our fates and hoping for nothing better. Content to let our children become inured to the continuous spewing of hatred for free lands from teachers, priests, and government-controlled media. Accepting of the ridiculous notion that our sons and brothers must destroy themselves in order to kill two or three or ten enemy men in the name of some far-flung outrage."

Murmurs of agreement from the crowd. FarjAd held his hands out to them, his eyes wide with passion. "We must stand tall again. We are a blessed people. These are the laws we must live by again: love, forgiveness, fairness, generosity to those who are less fortunate." He lapsed into Farsi.

"Cole," I hissed. "What's he saying?"

"He's quoting a famous Persian poet named Sadi," Cole replied. "I'm not good enough to translate the rhyme. But basically Sadi said all human beings are connected to each other. And therefore, we can't stand idly by while even one of us suffers."

FarjAd had a lot more to say, but I stopped listening. Too distracting for me to be of any use if something violent went down. I retreated to a corner and, using the menu on my nifty glasses, called Asha. "Anything?"

"Just more mahghul," he said. "How about you?"

"Nothing so far. But this guy. Eloquent doesn't even come close to his speaking ability. They're enthralled!"

"His potential to lead this country into peace and prosperity is—how you put it—off the charts. The greatest I have seen in fifty years. You *must* keep him safe."

Asha's urgency fueled my own. How was I supposed to protect him when all I could come up with was a general sense of menace? I hung up, looking at FarjAd with new eyes. Yesterday I'd been planning to kill him. Now I thought maybe he was the leader these people needed to enact the change they were looking for, and I was deeply afraid he wouldn't live through the night.

"Anything, Vayl?" I asked, meeting his eyes across the room. He stood near the bathroom door, leaning against the wall as he surveyed the crowd. "Nothing."

"How about you, Cole?"

He sat at an abandoned Internet station, his back to the computer. "Naw. These people seem pretty stoked for FarjAd. If we were at a pep rally they'd all be cheering like horny teenagers."

You know what? Maybe this is all just coincidence. The mahghul are here because one of these couples is going to get in a huge fight later tonight and end up killing each other. The end.

Still I waited. And watched. And when his speech was over, and FarjAd jumped down from the chair, I began another circuit of the room.

I suppose what first caught my eye was the guy's size. I actually thought Asha had snuck into the room for a second, this man was so tall. Plus, he wore the same sort of turban Asha favored. Also a long white thobe over beige pants, which stood out among the men, most of whom had come dressed in Western-style clothes.

I hadn't caught sight of him before, and he definitely hadn't entered through the main doorway. Which meant he'd come in through the kitchen. A strange way to join the party.

"Guys," I whispered. "Check out the white turban, my six o'clock from FarjAd."

I inched closer. Something about the way he moved seemed eerily familiar. It was the same sensation you get recognizing an actor in a film, but you can't remember what you've seen him in before.

He kept his back to me. Almost like he knew I was there. How could he? Still, he had an uncanny way of turning with the crowd just when I was about to get a good look at his face. And he kept getting closer to FarjAd.

"I don't like this guy," I finally said.

"I agree," said Vayl. "Who has the best angle?"

"I'm totally blocked," said Cole. "Congratulators out the wazoo."

"FarjAd keeps moving between me and the Turban," said Vayl. "It looks like he is yours, Jasmine."

"Okay. And when all hell breaks loose?"

"We grab him and run, as per the original plan," said Vayl.

The crowd around FarjAd was thick. I gave a few people my dazzling Lucille Robinson smile, which allowed me some progress, but not enough to get to the Turban before he reached his target. With mounting worry and frustration, I weighed my options and came up with only one truly workable alternative. I pulled a FarjAd and climbed on a chair.

It made my interest in the Turban obvious if he bothered to turn and look. He didn't. He'd almost reached FarjAd by the time I'd found my new vantage point. And he was solely focused on the man, who smiled and shook hands with an exuberance that somehow lit the room.

The Turban made a move only people in my business should recognize. Which was when I saw the dark glint of metal. The shockingly familiar outline of a weapon I'd never expected to see inside this room.

"Gun!" I yelled.

Instant chaos.

Vayl and Cole surged forward to protect FarjAd as the crowd screamed and scattered. Those nearest the doors ran outside, allowing a steady stream of mahghul in.

I didn't pull Grief. I wanted this assassin alive. So instead I yanked a knife from my wrist sheath and winged it at the attacker's back. I hit the Turban squarely between the shoulder blades, bringing a disappointed shriek from the mahghul. The Turban dropped to his knees. Still he struggled to bring his gun, one of those Bergman had carried all the way from America for the express use of Dave's team, to bear.

Vayl shot the sheath of his cane sword at the Turban's shoulder, knocking his arm off target just as he squeezed the trigger. Bullets peppered an entire row of monitors, shattering glass, leaving behind a mass of dead black screens. It was a miracle no people were hit, but they'd all dropped to the floor as soon as the Manx began its thunderous attack.

I threw another blade, burying it in the meat of the Turban's shoulder. He dropped the gun. Another knife, to the back of the thigh, took him all the way to the floor.

Though the mahghul had crowded toward me at my first throw, none of them had jumped me. As I continued to broadcast a strong, antimurderous intent, they turned to the Turban, swarming him like a mass of gigantic swamp rats.

Vayl grabbed at the single arm he'd managed to swing free and yanked him from the bottom of the writhing pile, snatching off the three or four attached mahghul as he and Cole secured him. As soon as the Turban became a captive the mahghul lost interest and began loping out of the café.

I jumped off the chair, ran to FarjAd, and took his arm. "I thought you were being figurative," he gasped as I pulled him toward the kitchen. With a wounded prisoner in tow, no way were we jumping out any windows. So my next choice was a back door.

"You've been reading too much poetry," I told him. I eyeballed my specs, and seconds later had Asha on the phone. "It's happened," I told him. "But FarjAd's alive. Meet us at the car. You're driving."

Cole picked up the Manx, Vayl hefted the Turban over one shoulder, and they followed FarjAd and me into the cooking area. As I'd feared, we had plenty of witnesses for our escape. Maybe five altogether. But they were all panicked. All headed for the same exit as we were. We let them go first. Hoped they wouldn't think to scope out Asha's BMW or wonder why we were taking the assassin with us. FarjAd, the master storyteller, would have to come up with a whopper to cover this one.

Asha sat in the driver's seat, peering over his shoulder anxiously as we piled in. Cole and FarjAd in the front seat. Vayl, the Turban, and I in the back.

"Go, go, go!" I yelled as a couple of FarjAd's followers belatedly realized he'd been hustled away by absolute strangers and came after us, shouting and waving for us to stop.

Asha peeled out like a drag racer. At which point FarjAd and Cole buckled their seat belts. The Turban moaned. I nodded to Vayl and straightened the assassin in his seat, forcing his face upward so we could both see it better. I yanked the turban off his head. And realized he wasn't a guy at all.

"Grace?" murmured Vayl.

I sat back. Stunned. Everything had pointed to Dave. "Are you insane?" I whispered. "You're an elite officer in the United States military. You have just betrayed, not only your entire country and all of your comrades, but every woman in Iran who stands to gain from FarjAd's survival." I studied her face, trying to fathom her motives. Her stony expression gave nothing away. Not even the immense amount of pain she must be experiencing. Finally I asked, "Why?"

"I was obeying orders."

"From who?"

"My commanding officer."

"Your commanding officer on this mission is Vayl," I told her. "And Vayl expected you to be at the Hotel Sraosa with the rest of your team. Therefore you have disobeyed your commanding officer."

She winced then, her eyes darting to the window, as if she'd had the same thoughts herself and wanted to escape them. "We told you Dave was the mole," I said. "And yet, knowing his orders were coming directly from the Wizard, you still obeyed him. What's the deal with that, Grace?" I asked her.

"Am I going to die?" Her voice had become small. Faint.

"If you're lucky," I said. I know it was cruel. Screw it. She deserved every gob of shit that hit her now. "Tell me exactly what he said to you."

"He just said to come watch you. He suspected that you'd been taken over by the Wizard without your knowledge. He said if you didn't seem to be gearing up for the job that I was supposed to do it."

"And how were you supposed to get away afterward?"

"He made it clear it was my choice. That I'd be caught. Probably tortured. Definitely killed."

"Grace. Think. That's not Dave's MO. He'd never send one of his own into that kind of situation. Not ever. That's a Wizard move."

She began to cry then. Soft, muffled sobs that made her moan with pain every time they shook her. "I loved him so much. I'd have done anything for him. Anything."

Obviously. I looked at Vayl. *Does love make fools of us all? Maybe. Eventually. At least for a little while.*

Chapter Thirty-One

We left FarjAd and Asha with Zarsa and Soheil, who still hadn't gotten over their awe by the time we moved on. Since they didn't know of a doctor who wouldn't blab to the authorities, we took Grace back to the house, stowed her facedown in the girls' room bed, and let Cassandra experiment with her nursing skills, which, while admittedly rusty, were still exceptional.

Before I left I said, "We can't get you to a hospital until this mission is complete, Grace, and it's not done until the Wizard's dead. But that should be tonight. As soon as the guys are back I'll send in the best backup medic. Who is that?"

"David," she said miserably.

I muttered a very bad word under my breath. "Next?"

"Cam."

"Okay." I turned to leave.

"Jaz?"

I nearly snapped at her. But since she still had three of my blades sticking out of her body, I figured enough was probably enough. "Yeah?"

"I'm sorry."

I nodded. "You'd better be."

When Cassandra assured me she had everything she needed, I went to the kitchen. All three of my guys were there, standing around looking like they could use a stiff drink.

"Phase two?" asked Cole.

I nodded, unstrapping the sheath from my right wrist. I chose the knife I wanted. It had a short, thin blade, which I held in the stove burner until it glowed red. While I watched the sanitization process I tried to jump out of myself. Not physically. This was no time to confront the Magistrate. I just needed that separation between action and emotion that would allow me to cut my brother's throat without collapsing into a gibbering heap. At least until later.

The front door slammed. My heart constricted.

"They're back," said Bergman, his voice pitched so high I almost expected to look up and see someone strangling him.

"Jasmine," Vayl said, his voice icy, his powers rising. "Can you do this?"

I nodded, raising my eyes to his. I couldn't explain that only I loved David enough to make this work. That I didn't trust anyone else to be quick. That I thought even Vayl, who was strong enough, cool enough, might be too distracted by the blood to go fast. I suddenly understood the stories I'd heard of families who, during the Middle Ages, had piled wood high on their condemned relative's pyres. Though their loved ones had been consigned to burn at the stake for choosing the wrong religion, or bewitching the wrong husband, their concern in the end had been for as much speed and as little pain as possible. Funny how some things never change.

I turned off the burner. Held the knife behind me and leaned casually against the counter as my brother walked into the room, scratching steadily at the back of his neck. He smiled when my eyes met his. I reminded myself the soul looking out from those deep green orbs was trapped, screaming to be free.

"How'd it go?" he asked.

I gave him Lucille's fake warmth, hoping he wouldn't be able to tell the difference. "Like clockwork. What did you expect, bro? You're working with the best."

Vayl had circled behind him during our conversation. I stepped forward, nodding to him as if giving him his kudos. Dave looked over his shoulder. Started to congratulate Vayl. But he'd already taken his cue and raised his powers, sending ice into David's veins as he grabbed his arms.

We weren't sure how he'd be affected by Vayl's abilities. If he was a Sensitive, like me, he'd be resistant. We had no idea how zedran reacted. But hopefully the cold would slow the bleeding. I know, I know. If Raoul brought him back it wouldn't matter if he puddled all over the floor. Physically he'd be fine. But I didn't want him waking up in a huge pool of his own blood. One less nightmare. At this point, that was all I could give him.

"What the hell are you doing?" Dave demanded, his eyes going wide. Not scared. Not yet.

"You're the mole, Dave."

"What? Are you out of your mind?"

"The Wizard's man, the one who attacked you during questioning? He killed you and inserted a control device in your neck called an ohm." I hated this next part. But the Wizard was listening, so I continued. "I'm sorry. You set me up. Forced me to kill the wrong man tonight. So now I have to kill you."

Now the fear. I faced it, understanding it might be the last expression I ever saw in my brother's eyes. "You've snapped! The Helsingers! Matt! Jessie! It's all jumbled your brains. There's no way I'm a traitor! No way!"

"Goodbye, David. I love you."

Vayl moved his right arm, still clenched under Dave's, higher, so his hand could control his face. He forced Dave to look up. I had the retriever in my left hand. With my right I made a quick incision with my dagger.

Dave roared in protest and tried to throw his head backward. But Vayl had such a tight hold on him he could only flinch.

I slipped the retriever into the opening I'd made near the base of his throat and kept my hand over it, staunching the bleeding, which slowed quickly to a trickle.

"Is it in?" Cole asked a few seconds later.

I dropped my hand. Nodded.

Vayl let go of David's head.

"I'm not dead," David whispered.

I just looked at him, so full of regret I couldn't speak. Never in my life had I wanted more to be a different person. One of those women who cringe at violence. Who are all about healing and mending, birth and rebirth.

Suddenly Dave's head jerked back. His eyes rolled. His mouth began to work at sucking in air he could no longer seem to access.

"Let him go," I said in a low voice.

Vayl released Dave's arms. His hands immediately went to the back of his neck, clawing at it until his fingernails were bloody. He went to his knees. I dropped to mine before him. I wanted to touch him, but I knew it would be of no comfort. I'd brought this horror down on him.

But I stayed with him. Suffered with him as he fell onto his back and went into full-body spasms. Cole moved everything out of the way that might injure him. I knelt on his right. Vayl on his left. We watched helplessly as foam erupted from his lips.

The spasms gave way to convulsions. Not quick, hard shakes, but long, tight moments where his entire back would bow and he would almost stand on his head. I counted one. Two. Three. And on the fourth the retriever appeared.

When I didn't immediately take it, Vayl nodded at me. *You must finish what you started,* his look told me.

I reached out. Took the retriever between my fingers and gently pulled. It resisted one hand's efforts, so I brought the other into play, pulling out Bergman and Cassandra's invention along with the item it had attached itself to. A red plastic tube the length of a toothpick and as big around as my pinky.

As soon as it exited Dave's body he went absolutely still.

I dropped my head and quickly spoke the words Raoul had taught me. Within seconds I felt myself lifting from my body. I heard Cole say, "How long until we know?"

Vayl shook his head. Shrugged.

A shimmer above Dave's body let me know they wouldn't have long to wait. He was rising.

He hesitated when he saw me. "Jazzy?"

"Go on," I urged. "Raoul's waiting for you." I didn't tell him I'd protect him. He never would have left then. But I did follow close behind, watching sharply for the Magistrate as Dave followed the rainbow-colored strand that led to Raoul. If my Spirit Guide and I were right, this would be the moment he'd pounce.

Nothing happened.

Dave made it safely to Raoul's. I was just chastising myself for reading the signs as hieroglyphs when they were, in fact, Roman numerals, when I caught sight of the demons. Three of them, including the Magistrate, winging their way toward one of the cords that bound me to my loved ones. Not Dave's at all. E.J.'s.

"Raoul!" I yelled. "They're after the baby!" But even as I spoke I knew he couldn't help. He was occupied with Dave. Doing the deal. Or not. Which left this battle to me.

I flew at the demons, not knowing how much damage I could actually cause in my noncorporeal state. Not caring. I had to *do* something!

Feeling like a fighter jet, I screamed headfirst into the Magistrate. And right through him. He laughed, waved his hand carelessly. A wind came up out of nowhere, buffeting me backward.

As I rolled and spun, trying desperately to regain my equilibrium, I could see the three of them advancing on E.J.'s cord. The largest of the demons, who had a bluish blotch across half his face that seemed to be growing its own fungi, reached out for the golden cable that connected her to me. His claws touched it, and jerked back as if burned. At his contact E.J.'s cord had flashed. Apparently the kid had some built-in defenses.

"Idiot!" barked the Magistrate. "Why do you think I told you to bring the vine?"

"Aha!" shouted the third demon, a pig-eared, dog-snouted hulk who, even here, smelt of rancid meat and feces. Reaching inside the breastplate of his brown spiked armor he pulled out a braided green rope, complete with black-edged leaves and even a couple of sickly yellow flowers. I'd just managed to halt my tumbling when the Magistrate snatched one end of the vine from the demon and began wrapping it around E.J.'s cord as the demon held the other end still.

"No!" I cried as the vine instantly tightened, sending white thorns into its new support, making it tremble and visibly fade. I rushed back into the fray. The bad guys loved it. They laughed like maniacs as I sped toward them, thinking I'd had another brain fart and decided I liked being tumbled halfway across space. In reality I was pulling a move I'd watched Cam do at the poker table a couple of times the night before, making a small sacrifice now so I could see how they really meant to play their cards.

I tried not to think of my niece, whimpering on the other end of a line that seemed to be strangling under the vine's hold as I watched the demons prepare to whip up on me. Their gestures seemed random, so I dismissed signed magic. But they had to be pulling power from somewhere. I concentrated on the Magistrate. His psychic scent was the strongest, least pleasant, and most familiar.

I let it draw my Sensitivity, what the reavers liked to call my Spirit Eye, into full focus.

"Leave her alone, Magistrate!" I shouted.

He glanced sideways, reached down as if to pluck a blade of grass out of the ground. But now that I was concentrating I could see he'd actually flicked a braid out of one of the shining black cords that bound him and his companions to their own world and snapped it toward me. It struck me square in the chest, numbing my entire untorso, spinning me backward yet again.

I wasn't sure why I hadn't been able to see their cords before. But I thought it had something to do with Raoul saying I needed training if I wanted to fight effectively in this dimension, combined with what I knew about Vayl's ability to camouflage. The Magistrate knew how to disguise his cords so that I wouldn't see them unless I was looking for them. Which made them highly significant.

Problem was, I had no idea how to cut them and very little time to do so. The vine they'd brought was tightening like a boa constrictor. More flowers had begun to bloom. Any minute now I expected E.J.'s cord to go as limp as a drowning victim. The only thing I could think of was to use my cords the way they had theirs.

I flew to Albert's cord, misjudged my speed, and stopped against it so suddenly that it twanged dissonantly. The Magistrate's buddies covered their ears.

"Watch your aim, there, nimrod!" barked the larger one. When his hands came away I saw his earlobes were bloody.

"Don't you like that?" I asked. I grabbed the cord and whacked it, making a harsh noise that caused the smaller demon to wince and stick his stubby fingers in his greenish brown ears. A drop of blood escaped his nose.

The Magistrate lashed at me with his newfound weapon. It

snaked out to sting me, so much like his whip I wondered if that was why he carried one in the first place. At the last moment I dodged, shoving Albert's cord into the gap I'd just vacated. The Magistrate's cord wound around it and immediately began to sizzle. I took a second to watch the shock work its way back up the line, enjoy the clench of the Magistrate's teeth as his body began to twitch. He jerked on his weapon, trying to free it as I raced to Vayl's cord.

I hit it hard, bouncing off and then smacking into it again as the Magistrate's companions howled in protest.

"Stop!" they screamed as blood spurted out of every orifice. They were prone now. Writhing in pain. The vine looked none too healthy either.

Holy crap, I think this might just do the trick!

I ran the circuit of the golden cords that connected me to those I cared for. Evie. Cassandra. Bergman. Cole. Albert. Vayl. Dave's was still missing. But E.J.'s looked brighter every time I slammed into a line, bringing from it a razor-sharp tune that cut into the demons and their cords like broken glass.

When the first cable gave, it split with an unearthly scream, as if it were a living thing and not just a conduit. The largest demon disintegrated. His buddy wasn't far behind. As I slammed into Cole's cord, his exploded, along with his unbody.

Yeah, baby! I felt amazing. Elated. Damn near invincible. Nobody could stop me now that I'd figured out the key to destroying these evil sons of bitches.

I should've known better.

As I moved to strum the Magistrate's death song he broke free. The speed at which he came after me made my movements look like somebody upstairs had hit their remote and consigned me to slow motion for the remainder of the battle.

He'd reached up for another section of his braid while he was struggling. Now he held two whiplike weapons. He snapped one around my waist, pinning me to my current position just three feet shy of E.J.'s shining cord. The other he snaked around my neck. Immediately my vision began to dim, as if he were cutting off blood supply. Which he wasn't. So what the hell?

Exactly, said Granny May as she wound up her bridge game and began packing the snacks. *Name one other place that made you feel this kind of horror. This awful sense of futility.*

So what's your point? I asked her dully.

She snatched a popcorn kernel out of the bamboo bowl she held and poked it at me impatiently. *What? Have you forgotten what we talked about all those Sunday afternoons?*

After church. After lunch. During our long, ambling walks around her farm. We'd talked about everything. But those were usually our get-serious times. When we kids could tell her anything that was on our minds and expect a nugget or two of wisdom in return. Often, however, due to how we'd spent our mornings, our talks had turned to the nature of good and evil, everything that fell between, and how to tell where you stood at any given moment.

"Hell's a real place," she'd informed us. "Don't you let anyone tell you different. And it's not just a destination. It's one of those powerful, sneaky places that will move in next door, wait until you're looking in the other direction, then reach out and grab you if it can."

"How do you fight something like that?" I'd asked.

Granny May had pursed her lips and looked at me sideways, her way of applauding me for asking the question she'd hoped for. "Purity of motive," she'd responded. "Innocence of spirit."

Why, you sly old witch, I thought as the Magistrate loomed over me, his finely sculpted face set in a triumphant smile as he watched me weaken, *you've fought demons before*. Later, when I had time, I'd delve into Granny's past. Right now, I'd just take her advice.

I closed my eyes. And concentrated on the purest, most innocent person I knew.

I could feel her. The same way I often felt Vayl through Cirilai and through my senses. E.J. hung out there at the edge of my psyche like a new star. So fine and bright I could feel the beauty of her being burning away my own darkness.

The Magistrate jumped and squawked. I opened my eyes. His coils had retreated. He'd reared back, rubbing his hands as if they'd been singed.

I reached out. Wrapped my own hands around E.J.'s cord.

As soon as I touched it, the last, wilted vestiges of vine dropped away. I strummed it. Made the music uniquely suited to my niece. It filled the air, loud as a symphony, joyous as a Christmas carol.

"No!" screamed the Magistrate, blocking both of his bleeding ears with his hands. "STOP!"

I played on until the echoes of that fresh, uncorrupted song bounced off all the other cords around us, pulling out harmonies that made me weep with joy. Not so the Magistrate.

He clutched at his black, glistening line. Tried to ride it back to its source. But it began to shred. Then *he* began to crack, like one of Evie's porcelain dolls after a tumble off the shelf. His model's body developed long fissures, as if everything inside it had shifted. His perfect face split. Skull and teeth, muscle and blood, replaced smooth red skin. But I continued to play until the Magistrate's entire unbody shivered into pieces and the cord that bound him finally melted into tiny black globs of horror that fell like black rain back to where they'd begun.

I let my hands drop. God, I was so tired. And my cord was starting to fade. A sure sign my body was weakening. But was it smart to return before I'd talked to Raoul? How vulnerable would that leave E.J.? On the other hand, Dave might need me back at the house. As I debated, I felt myself suddenly pushed—hard—back into physical.

I felt my back bow as the pain of rejoining hit. When I finally regained my breath I only had enough to say, "What the . . ."

Vayl leaned over me. "Is everything all right?"

I shook my head, trying to clear it. *Raoul? What's the word?*

No answer.

Shit!

"Cam!" I yelled. Natchez came running into the kitchen, took one look at me kneeling by David, who still wasn't breathing, and slapped a tear from his cheek. "Where's Cam?" I demanded.

"Working on Grace."

"Get him! Now!"

Natch was back in thirty seconds with the entire team in tow.

"CPR!" I snapped. "Now!"

Without a word Cam went to his knees and started chest compressions.

"I thought you said Raoul—" Cole began.

"I'm not leaving it up to him," I growled. I bent down to give Dave some air.

The door flew open again and Cassandra ran into the room. "Jasmine, I can See again!" she cried. She looked like she'd prefer to remain in Curtainland.

I nodded, saving my breath for Dave.

"You have to leave!" Cassandra said, her voice shaking with barely checked emotion.

"What?"

"A vision. Terrible destruction. Mass murders. Black smoke from fire bombings. Thousands of innocents dead in the rubble. The Wizard will not be stopped unless you go for him now!"

I looked down at my brother, tears blinding me as I struggled to my feet. Jet took my place as Vayl led me out of the kitchen, into the guys' room, where Cassandra had secreted the items she needed for her spell.

She'd explained earlier that it was based on my already heightened abilities to track *others*. So far the only way I could follow a trail was to find its source first. This spell would not only show me the source, it would impress the Wizard's psychic scent on my brain so I could follow it if he moved to another location before we arrived.

Cassandra held out her hand for the ohm, which I was only too glad to get rid of. She took one of Bergman's small hammers, broke open the plastic casing, and pulled from the wreckage a small white bone.

"What is that?" I asked, not even recognizing my own voice. I sounded like a robot. Yeah, somewhere along the line I'd switched to full automatic. There'd be hell to pay when I took back the reins. But until then I could at least do my job.

Cassandra said, "When you locate the Wizard, I believe you will notice he is missing part of a finger."

I nodded. That would be the least of his worries when I found him.

Cole came in.

"Anything yet?" I asked him.

He shook his head.

Goddammit, Raoul, do *something!*

I turned my attention, such as it was, back to Cassandra. She'd laid the finger bone on the floor in the center of a circle of yellow powder. "Now, Jaz," she said tightly. "Lean your head over the circle."

I did as I was told, not much caring what came next. If she'd set the powder on fire and, by proximity, my hair, I wouldn't have muttered a word of protest. Instead she sprinkled a sparkly white substance, like sugar only with bigger crystals, on top of the powder. At the same time she whispered a series of funky words. *"Ayada. Torenia. Terell avatam latem."*

The circle ignited into a sort of mini electric storm, with my head as the locus. Every time I breathed in or swallowed I tasted iron. My eyes felt gritty, and no matter how often I blinked, it seemed like an eyelash the size of a giant redwood was caught inside my contact lenses. My head began to throb, but I welcomed the pain. I deserved no less for what I'd done to my brother. No matter that he'd never have wanted his current existence. He was now lying dead on the kitchen floor because of me.

The storm ended suddenly, leaving me on all fours, panting like a dehydrated hound dog. But I had it. The scent of the Wizard. My lips drew back at its stench. A mix of bloated corpse, stagnant water, and really cheap aftershave. And I'd thought vampires were bad.

"I know where he is," I said. I stood up, swayed dangerously, grabbed on to Vayl and Cole as they straightened me up again. "We're going to need some wheels. And a couple more guns."

The four of us went back into the kitchen.

"David!" Cassandra went to her knees beside my twin. Who was sitting up. Shaking hands. Not smiling. But not ripping anybody a new one either.

I stopped just inside the doorway, my hands clutching Vayl and Cole each by the forearm. Otherwise I definitely would have fallen. The relief took the juice completely out of my legs. But since Cassandra was doing my sobbing for me, I was able to stand dry-eyed. Waiting for his verdict.

He looked into my eyes and the room went silent. "I could never have done what you've done," he finally said. "You're an amazing woman. Thank you."

I bobbed my head, pressing my lips together so I wouldn't start blubbering. Because the next step would definitely be snot bubbles. And I so did not want to ruin this moment with snot bubbles. So I did it with work.

"I can't even tell you how happy I am to have you back. But we have to go," I told him. "Cassandra says if we don't, the Wizard will go free."

"You know where he is?" asked Cam as David's face drained of the little color he'd regained at the mention of his former master.

"Yeah," I said. "We're taking the TV van."

"Then you'll have room for us," said Jet, rising with the sort of try-to-stop-me purpose I'd learned early on not to fight against.

I shrugged and said, "Yeah, okay, whoever wants to come."

"That would be all of us," said Dave. He struggled to his feet. And rather than let him embarrass himself, Cam and Natchez gave him a hand. He looked around. "Where's Grace? We're going to need her too."

"She's been injured," I said shortly, unwilling to take him on that guilt trip for the moment. We all knew better than to try to talk Dave out of coming with us. Still, it was easily the worst idea of all time. I needed him gone. Far away. Preferably in another time zone, where we could only speak via sat phone, our signals kissing cheeks as they met at a dish not unlike the one that sat atop the TV van.

Which gave me the brightest idea ever. Inside my head, Granny May grinned, nodded with approval, and said, *Finally*.

"I need you and Jet at the TV station," I told Dave. "Right now it's being manned by the two remaining reavers who were sent to take me out. You need to either get control of them, so they'll obey your orders, or kill them and then figure out how to receive a live feed from the van and then transmit it out the tower. Just remember, if you do kill them, you'll also have to contend with mahghul." I described the little buggers and briefly explained my own showdown with them in front of the temple.

"It sounds as if you have a plan," said Vayl.

I tried to contain my rising excitement, but as I continued to roll the idea around in my brain and couldn't think of any huge stoppers, I couldn't suppress a small smile. "Maybe," I said. "Just maybe there's a way we can save our asses while we accomplish this one. Bergman? We're going to need your expertise, buddy. Looks like you're really going to earn that vacation tonight."

Fleeting look of fear. Then it was replaced by a new expression. Bergman and determination: I kind of thought they looked good on each other. He nodded sharply. "You've got me."

"Cam, don't you guys all carry first aid kits?"

"Yeah."

"I'm going to need to fake an injury to my left hand." He looked bewildered, but knew better than to ask questions while I was on a roll. As he left to get his supplies I spec-phoned Asha. "How's it going on your end?" I asked.

"Excellent. You would not believe the plans FarjAd and Zarsa have made! I think they have pulled apart the seams of the world and resewn them four different times since they met! Zarsa believes she can use her Gift to help FarjAd survive any future attacks. And he thinks having a woman of her ability and family support will bring even more people to his movement. And you?"

"So far, so good. But I have another favor to ask: We need your wheels one last time." I explained our mission and my plan as well as I could in ten seconds.

"I will be right there," he said. I had to give Asha his pats. When he finally decided to step back into the ring, he did it with both feet.

We all escorted Dave to the living room to wait with Jet for Asha. Cassandra would stay with them too until they left, at which time she'd go back to Grace. The Amazon was definitely getting the short end of the stick on this one. But considering Dave had just died—again—I wasn't wasting any sympathy on her.

"I'll be okay," Dave kept insisting as one by one we asked him if we could get him anything before we left. It just felt wrong to go. We should be celebrating. We should be bouncing off the ceilings, for chrissake! And instead we were deserting the man whose resurrection we had all hoped and prayed for. Not only that. We were allowing him to step back into a life-or-death situation. Despite the fact that we all knew none of us had any other choice, it sucked.

One thing I could do. *Raoul? You are keeping some sort of watch, right? Over him? Over E.J.?*

THEY ARE WELL PROTECTED.

And that would have to do for now. I patted Dave as we finally ran out of excuses not to go. "Be careful, please. If I have to bring you back to life again, Raoul's going to want something major, like a virgin sacrifice. And I need Bergman too badly to give him up at this point."

Dave laughed, as he was meant to. It brought a whole new meaning to the phrase "music to my ears." Then, so suddenly it took my breath away, he swung me into a bear hug, lifting me until my toes barely touched the floor. "I love you," he said. "And about Jessie? I understand. And I forgive you."

I stood back in his arms. Grateful for his words. Certain they came from his heart. But also sure that heart was no longer as comfortable as it once was. I could see it in his eyes. In the way he looked at his men and then quickly at his fists, so they wouldn't catch the flicker of rage. Not at them. At himself, for consorting with their enemy. For endangering their lives and their country. It didn't make sense. Maybe it never would. But I understood. He'd only begun to deal with the realities of what he'd done. And even though he hadn't been responsible, he was still the boss. So he *felt* like he was. Maybe we could talk it through. Later. Right now—it was time to finish the mission.

Chapter Thirty-Two

The Wizard headquartered in the northern part of the city, where the mountains loomed over the rooftops like angry gods. I eyed his house through the rolled-down window of the TV van, charmed by the visual despite knowing its contents. The three-story confection reminded me of a miniature Taj Mahal, a bright white masterpiece complete with turrets and five separate domed roofs. It stood surrounded by a large well-lit yard, securely fenced by a six-foot wall of mauve-tinted concrete. Not a very nondescript home in which to hide the King of Chaos. However the Wizard was also Delir Kazimi, a well-known businessman and community leader. Popular due to his generous contributions to charity. For him the mini mansion, his home away from his Saudi headquarters, fit.

However, its designers had clearly put security first. Cameras perched on the corners of the fence and on strategic points of the house itself. Only one gate allowed access from the front, and that crossed a cement driveway. This led me to assume pedestrian visitors were not welcome at Chez Wiz. While that gate wasn't manned, it was guarded by an intimidating-looking digital lock whose keypad required you to put your hand entirely inside a metal box. I imagined if your fingerprints didn't match the scan a small blade came down and chopped it right off.

As I took a turn around the block my specs notified me of an incoming call. It was Jet.

"Everything's secure here," he said.

"How's Dave?"

"About like you'd expect."

I took that as a tired-but-functioning and decided to be satisfied. "Okay. We'll call when we're ready for you." I broke contact.

As I approached the front of the place again, I reviewed the conversation we'd had on the way to the Wizard's backup stronghold, looking for holes in our admittedly flimsy and alarmingly last-minute plan.

"Jasmine and I will go in alone," Vayl had said as I drove, following the pull of the Wizard's scent, taking as straight a route as I could manage without actually mowing through yards and parks.

"Vayl's got a way of moving unnoticed that even you guys can't match," Bergman had explained. He'd taken one of the four available chairs, with Cole, Cam, and Natchez filling the other three. If they'd pulled them up to the banks of monitors and electronic controls that lined the walls of the van, they could've covered the summer Olympics. As it was they simply belted in and made sure their weapons were ready to fire.

"Fine," said Cam, twirling in his chair so he could see Vayl better. "What's our role?"

"Bait," he said frankly. I glanced in the rearview to see how Bergman would take this morsel. Looked to me like he was forcing himself to chew, fighting his ingrained urge to regurge. *Well, what do you know? He really meant it when he said he was tired of being a wuss.*

As I reworked my perspective of him to include some newfound respect, Vayl went on. "Jasmine and I are betting the Wizard will not be able to resist the lure of this TV truck since he just received an anonymous tip—thanks to Bergman—that Edward Samos has taken control of the station and has sent reavers to initiate the coup Jasmine mentioned to David just after we entered the country. He will send his guards to take it out. It will be up to you four to make sure that does not happen."

"Understood," said Cam, gritting his teeth on his toothpick as he spoke. "We'll have the drop on them, so if we plan well it could even go down without a fight." The rest of the men nodded and put their heads together. Before they could begin formulating a plan, Vayl signaled Cole.

"As soon as you catch sight of them, let us know," he said. "It will mean they have temporarily disabled their security system, which will be our cue to move into the house."

I wished Bergman had brought enough hi-tech instant-communications devices for the whole bunch of us, but he hadn't anticipated such a large group needing to network on our dime. So, while Cole could talk to us through his stick-on transmitter, if anyone else on the team wanted a word, he'd have to use Cole as a relay.

I pulled the van to a stop beside the curb. To our right, darkened houses marched down the street like good little soldiers, all of them built to similar specs, the only difference being the color scheme and the shape of the gate in the obligatory fence/wall that separated sidewalk from courtyard. I wondered what the neighbors would say when they discovered they'd been living across the street from one of the world's most reviled terrorists. I could hear the interviews now.

"You know, maybe we should've been suspicious when the bomb went off in his basement. But we thought he was learning to play the bass drum. And who would we tell anyway? Half the cops on the force are scared to leave their cars and the other half are working for him!"

I looked back at the guys, sharing the smile that can grow right out of your teeth just before battle. It's involuntary. Like breathing.

Or shaking your ass to rap music. Something about the threat of death just makes you feel alive. I know I wouldn't have chosen any other spot than the one I occupied beside these fierce, grinning men tonight.

Okay. We're as ready as we're going to get. I looked a question at Vayl. *Now?* He gave me the slight tilt of his head that passed as a nod. I felt his powers rise once again, like a cool swirling breeze that encased only us.

"Where'd they go?" asked Natchez.

"I told you he was good," said Bergman. I followed Vayl out his side of the van, slamming the door on Bergman's monologue of my boss's known and suspected kills despite a strong urge to crawl into the back, sit absolutely still, and listen like I might never hear again.

With Vayl's camouflage flowing over us we walked boldly across the street, daring the cameras to record us. They might show some movement, but watchers would see it as a blur and think the lenses needed to be cleaned.

A miniscule jerk of Vayl's head told me he wanted to head around back. I followed closely enough to stay within his sphere of influence. Reaching into the compound with my senses, I tried to pick up any information I could. I'm no Cassandra, but I can perceive intense human emotion. And somebody inside was pissed.

"Vayl," I whispered. "We made the Wizard mad."

"Really?" he drawled.

"I'm thinking we can use that to our advantage."

He slanted me an amused look over his shoulder. "Jasmine, if anyone can manipulate someone else's fury to her gain, it is you."

"I'm taking that as a compliment," I warned him.

He made a muffled sound that I interpreted as a chuckle. "I meant it no other way."

The house took up half the block. We turned the corner,

followed it to a private access road. It was blocked by a chained gate upon which hung a sign that might've spelled out why nobody but the owners were allowed to drive past that point—except I couldn't read Farsi, so I was just guessing. For all I knew, it said, *Sick of living? Have we got a job for you! Inquire inside.*

The gate itself was lower than the one in front. Also somewhat in disrepair. In fact, it looked to me like somebody had run into it with their vehicle. Hard. Leaving a buckled-in spot that made it resemble an enormous football player who's just been kicked in the cojones. The resulting fold made a great foothold for us as we climbed to the top of the wall and then gently dropped to the other side.

The lack of outbuildings and absolute void in landscaping meant we could see the entire backyard and rear of the house from our vantage point. The only adornment the architect had given this area was a pool. But there were no lawn chairs. No potted plants. Nothing softened the stark effect of cement-encased water. It looked like a place where people are baptized. Or drowned.

If I'd been a run-of-the-mill assassin, the distance between the gate at which I stood and the back of the house would have seemed to stretch for miles. The Wizard had made it virtually impossible for anyone to sneak up on him while he was at home. But then, he'd never expected to be targeted by a vampire like Vayl.

We had our choice of entrances. As we faced the house, the garage sat to our left. It had four bays, all of them accessed by barn-like closures. A walk led from the driveway to the main door, a windowless white-painted archway with a black metal latch. To our far right, almost at the building's edge, was another entry. A much less imposing white rectangle—definitely reserved for the servants.

Vayl motioned to my gut. *Where is it leading you?* his expression asked me.

I nodded to door number two.

We walked to the corner of the building. Despite our relative safety, it still felt eerie to cross someone's line of sight and realize you might as well be invisible to them. Too bad we didn't have more time. It would be such a blast to make them think they were cursed. I could just see the guards, gathered around the monitors.

"Holy crap, Khorsand!" one of them would shriek. "Look at camera five! The light fixtures have leaped off the garage and are floating around the pool like severed heads! What could it mean?"

"We are obviously being haunted by the souls of all the good men we murdered, NimA," his partner would respond. "The only choice we have left to us is to fall upon our swords!"

I sighed. *Aah, if it were only that easy.*

We took our positions and waited for Cole's signal.

"You smell amazing," said Vayl, standing as close as he could get to me without touching. Apparently that was his definition of professional distance.

"Keep your mind on the job, bub."

"Bub? Is that my new nickname?"

"Sure."

"I hate it," Vayl said decisively. "Give me another."

I looked up at him, his excitement so palpable I could almost reach out and stroke it, like a luscious mink coat I'd feel guilty about petting while I totally grooved on the furry. This job necessarily brings out the worst in us, usually at the same moment. We were feeling the buzz now. That rush of God-power that precedes most kills. Lucky for us, my contrary nature drives me to poke holes in anything that seems overinflated.

"I had a parakeet named Murray once. How about that?" I asked.

His shoulders dropped. "Are you serious? When you look at me you think . . . parakeet?"

"Definitely," I said, warming up to the idea now that I knew he hated it. "Because your eyes turn all kinds of colors like a parakeet's feathers. And your fangs are kind of shaped like its beak. Murray crapped on newspapers. And you read the newspapers while you—" His look stopped me. "Or maybe, being a vampire, that's not a necessary function. But since you eat, and you take the papers, I just thought—"

"Jasmine!"

"You're right. This conversation should definitely wait until we've known each other a while longer."

I didn't catch his entire reply, but it sounded like he might've said, "A hundred years longer."

"Okay," came Cole's voice. "I've had all I can stand without puking. Plus, the bad guys are coming. Repeat, Wizard henchies are on the loose."

I took off the necklace I wore, worked the shark's tooth into the lock, and waited while Bergman's molten metal worked itself into the correct configuration. Within ten seconds we were inside, sans alarm, thanks to our baited TV van. I spared a moment to hope for their success. Then I brought all my concentration back to the task at hand.

We'd walked into a room that seemed too small and far too plain for the rest of the house. It was as if the architect had come to this corner and mused, "Well . . . they are going to need somewhere to throw their bloody clothes."

In America we'd have called it a mud room. It was basically an eight-by-nine dump-your-shoes-and-shawl area, with a row of pegs on the wall opposite the door on which hung a couple of caps. Faded brown tile covered the floor. Two steps led up to another door.

I unzipped the pouch at my waist as Vayl gently inched it open. The dental mirror I carried reflected a large meeting room. Dark and empty, it reminded me of a church basement. Long tables. Folding chairs. And on the other end a kitchen area. Smaller rooms adjoined the large one, but we weren't interested in those. The Wizard was brewing up a storm on one of the upper floors.

I led the way through the kitchen to an alcove that contained a wooden stairway. This led to a second-floor hallway, but it also continued to the third floor.

"He's up there," I whispered. "Now, remember. The idea is *not* to kill him right away. Okay?"

"That is the third time you have reminded me!" Vayl hissed. "I am a professional, you know!"

"Kill him!" Cole yelled suddenly, his voice so loud in my ear I considered removing my receiver and stomping on it.

"Cole, what are you talking about?" I demanded.

"These guys he sent out after us? They're zombies! Our bullets are barely slowing them down. So screw the plan! Kill him!"

Shit! I should've known something weird was up when I didn't see any mahghul gathering. But I'd thought it was because our guys hadn't begun their part of the evening with murderous intent.

As Cole related the story later, they'd all agreed that only one of them really needed to physically stay inside the van and act as bait. And they'd elected Bergman. "You look like a TV geek," Cam had told him genially.

"Hey, Miles," Natch asked, holding up his Manx. "Didn't you tell us this baby has a built-in silencer?"

"Yeah," Bergman said, trying to hang on to his newfound toughness in light of Cam's shocking news. "Just twist the barrel to the right until it won't turn anymore."

Cole clapped him on the shoulder. "Looks like your adventures have already started," he said.

"Heh. Yeah," said Bergman.

His Manx now in stealth mode, Natch unsnapped the holster at his hip, pulled his sidearm, a silenced Beretta M9, and handed it to Bergman. "Aim careful," he said with a big grin as Bergman took the gun and stuttered his thanks. "We don't want anybody down tonight but the bad guys. Got it?" Bergman nodded.

"Ya scared?"

Bergman nodded again. But he said, "No, not at all. Of course, my bowels are so loose if I stood up I'd shit down both legs. But I'm sure it was just something I ate." They looked at each other for a couple of beats. Then they both burst into laughter. Natchez clapped Bergman on the shoulder and followed Cam out of the van.

Cole, already on the sidewalk, gave Bergman thumbs-up and closed the doors. After which they made themselves scarce. While they didn't have Vayl's powers, these guys were damn good at disappearing. Especially when they came prepared, wearing the black body armor that usually went underneath their uniforms, and having already darkened their faces. Except for Natch, of course, who liked to say God created him for night combat. Cole ended up tucked between two cars parked a quarter block up the road. Cam and Natch faded into the shadows provided by the recessed gates of the houses nearest the van.

The Wizard's men didn't even try for sneaky. Almost as soon as our guys had secreted themselves they trooped out the front gate, six in all, headed straight for the van. Once he saw they'd cleared the street, Cole moved in behind them, hugging cover, making his way to the driver's side. The men never even looked over their shoulders. They were that confident. When they realized nobody sat in either of the front seats they all went around to the side and threw open the door.

Cole had figured on getting a jump on the Wizard's men. So

when the bad guys made their move, Cole aimed his Manx through the driver's side window and yelled, "Freeze!"

Except, as walking dead, they only heeded a single command. And that was coming from inside the house.

"Cole, they're zombies!" screamed Bergman.

"Get out now!" Cole shouted as he saw one of them raise his weapon. He riddled the creature with bullets as Bergman grabbed one of the cameras and dove for the back door. He threw it open and jumped out, falling to his knees, but saving the equipment from harm.

"Take cover!" Cam yelled, as the zombies, three of them downed by Cole's quick reaction, began to return fire.

As soon as Bergman was out of the way, Cam and Natch opened up from behind the zombies, ripping into the backs of their heads with rounds designed to leave only fragments in the aftermath.

Bergman joined Cole behind the van as the zombies turned on their attackers. Even though most of them could no longer see through their own eyes, their master could. Cam and Natch vaulted the nearest wall just as they opened up.

"Jasmine, haven't you found the bastard yet?" Cole demanded as he covered his comrades' withdrawal. "We're in some dire straits here!"

"Moving on him now," I whispered. We'd made it up the third flight of stairs. It had led us down a hallway, past a series of rooms clearly used for training purposes. Tables held reams of paper. Maps covered the walls. Other rooms held weights, stationary bicycles, punching bags, mats. I got the feeling not all of the Wizard's men were zombies. Or, at least, not at first. I wondered where they'd gone. Surely he had more than the six he'd sent against our guys. But the rooms were empty.

The hall finally opened to a large circular area accented with a huge rug done in blues and reds. Silk pillows in rich, dark hues were strewn across this in groupings of twelve or fifteen. An indentation in one large red one showed where the Wizard had been resting before we showed up to disturb him.

He stood at the opposite end of the room, staring through one of a large bank of windows, clutching at the sill as if only it was keeping him from falling to his knees. If my knowledge of necromancy was correct, all we had to do was break his concentration, get his eyes off those zombies, and our guys would be able to destroy them.

I looked at Vayl. Got the nod.

"So you're the son of a bitch who killed my brother."

Chapter Thirty-Three

I felt like Clint Eastwood, about to duel it out on the streets of Laredo with the gun-toting bully who'd torched my farm and shot my horse. And, like I said before, killed my brother. Only, since Dave was technically alive, I didn't feel I was bringing quite enough emotion to the role. So I reminded myself of how I'd felt before he'd revived. There. That did it.

I stalked to the middle of the room as the Wizard turned, first his body, then his head, then his eyes. A slow-motion dance step that made him realize belatedly that he faced two attackers.

"They're off us and coming your way!" Cole warned me. "You've got maybe three minutes before they're on you."

Just keep to the plan, I told him silently, knowing he would despite the fact that it looked as if Vayl and I were about to be trapped between six zombies and their pissed-off master.

"I ought to kill you right now, you . . . you monster!" I cried. I kept my expression taut. Fraught with pain. But just behind my eyes calculations were whizzing through my brain like I'd just been handed my college chemistry final. The Wizard, whose resemblance to FarjAd I'd put down to coincidence, I now realized must be familial. It wasn't just looks they shared. It was a way of moving. A sense of one's place in the world. But where FarjAd opened up to include everyone along with him, the Wizard kept out all but a select few. You could see it in his expression, even now forbidding us access though we had him at a huge disadvantage.

"No, Jasmine!" Vayl held up his free hand. The other, holding tight to his cane, pointed at the Wizard as he spoke. "This man must pay. And there is only one way to ensure that justice is served. You promised!"

"Yes," I said, allowing my stance to ease somewhat. "My brother made a specific request of me. And I will honor it." I held up the bone in my right hand, my left securely tucked behind my back. "Do you see this? Do you know what it is?"

He glanced down. His left hand wasn't even bandaged, it had healed so long ago. It just lacked a pinky.

"No!" I yelled. "I destroyed yours the second I took it out of my brother's neck!"

I whipped my left arm into the open. Let him see the fantastic bandaging job Cam had done. A hint of red showed at the "stump" where it sure looked like I'd hacked off my smallest finger.

"You are not a necromancer," the Wizard whispered. But he sounded unsure. He stepped forward, into the pool of light provided by a standing lamp covered by a beaded red and gold shade. Here the resemblance to FarjAd faded beneath the sallow, emaciated look of a man who hadn't slept in weeks and only ate when someone forced him. Running Dave must have taxed him to his limit. I hid my satisfaction behind a surge of anger that my brother had once been spiritually connected to this slime.

"I am *other*," I told him hotly. "And that's enough. Especially when all I want to do is control one. Puny. Zombie."

Vayl slid the sheath off his cane sword. The metallic *whoosh* sent a shiver up my spine. "Just a slit to your throat," Vayl said silkily. "Just enough for Jasmine's ohm to be inserted."

"And then you're mine," I said. "Just like Dave wanted. You'll be my zombie servant forever. Slave to an American assassin. How do you like them apples, Kazimi? And here's the yummiest"—I hugged myself and licked my lips ecstatically—"the most chocolate cream-filled deliciousness part. Before I set you up in my apartment, wearing a frilly white apron, baking bread, dusting, and cleaning the toilet? I'm going to use you to take down the Raptor. That's right. I'm setting your whole network up for an Edward Samos takeover. You're going to lure him right out of the shadows. And when he moves in, the whole network caves. Won't that be lovely?"

As the Wizard's stony facade started to crumble, what I'd just said about Samos and shadows triggered a memory from my trip to hell with Raoul. It was important, but not enough to warrant my attention just now. I tucked it into my Check Later pile and concentrated on the Wizard's face. I'd seen men go gray before. Delightful, as usual.

"What is it that you want?" he whispered. "I'll do anything to avoid . . ."

"Zombie bondage?" I inquired. I got right in his face, mustering all the spite I could gather on short notice. A surprising amount surfaced. If the words on my tongue were venom my whole mouth would've gone numb.

"You know what I want? Nothing," I spat, my voice low and cruel. "My boss, here, has agreed to let me kill you slowly. You've got a lot of lives to answer for, after all. And justice so often looks the other way when it comes to pricks like you. So why would I give up my one chance to make things right? I mean, you've hidden yourself from the world for what? Twenty years? Built a booming real estate business using your legit identity while your shadow self perpetrated the worst sorts of atrocities imaginable on innocent civilians. It was you who released mustard gas into that subway in New York, right? And you planned the murder of three hundred Kurdish schoolgirls. Because we all know what Angra

Mainyu thinks about females who can read. And, yeah, I'm certain I heard the Wizard was behind the bombings of Israeli airliners, British consulates, and Somalian Freedom trains."

"You have no proof!" the Wizard cried.

Bingo. "Give it to me," I said.

"What?" He looked bewildered. Like I'd just dropped him in the middle of the rain forest and ordered him to hitchhike home.

"I've got a TV van outside. Go on camera. Show your face. Admit what you've done. And I'll let you live."

"What kind of life will that be?" he demanded. "To watch my world slowly decay as more and more misguided idiots swallow the rantings of men like—" He bit his lip.

"Your brother?" Vayl asked. Aha, so he'd seen the resemblance too.

"FarjAd Daei," I said as the bitterness on the Wizard's face betrayed him. "You set us up to kill your own brother."

"*Half* brother," Delir corrected. "We share only a mother."

I shook my head. "I gotta say it was a brilliant plan. You couldn't shed your own relative's blood, so you manipulate the Americans into doing your dirty work for you. The bonus being that you cause a huge rift between our country and the only people in Iran who don't want to vaporize us at the moment."

Despite his dire situation, the Wizard grinned. "It was a glorious plan," he said.

"It blew," I told him. "You kill my brother to force me into killing yours? There's no balance in that. You know the universe is going to come back and slap you for even trying it. And tonight, Delir, I am her strong right hand."

"You are nothing!" he spat. "You have so little value that I am surprised every time I blink that you do not suddenly wink out of existence!"

"Oh yeah? Putting me in the garage sale before you even get a look at the goods? Not wise, Wizzy."

"Bah. What good are you . . . you Americans? You strut around spouting rhetoric as if everyone should follow your lead. And yet your sons drive drunk and your daughters idolize whores. You scream that the planet is failing. But you guzzle the world's resources as if they were cheap wine. You pray for peace even as your soldiers fight and die for a purpose they can no longer discern."

"Ah, don't give me that crap," I said, waving off his rant with a careless hand. "You just hate us because you enjoy hating people and we're an easy target. If we weren't around you wouldn't be any different."

"Would too!" he insisted, stomping his foot like a surly three-year-old.

"Would not," I said coldly. "Because the problem isn't us. It's you. You won't talk. You won't compromise. Hell, you won't even come to the table without a big old stick of dynamite strapped across your chest. So screw you."

The Wizard's eyes got so big I wondered for a second if they were going to pop out of his head. "Infidel!" the Wizard screamed, spittle spraying off his lips. "Angra Mainyu let me live a thousand years so I can kill every American on earth!"

"Are you certain Angra Mainyu has any interest in your plans at this point?" Vayl asked. "After all, he did allow us to find you here." When the Wizard had no reply Vayl added, "I should also note, though you cry for American deaths, the one you desire most is that of your brother, who is not."

"He might as well be. Spouting all that rot about peace and tolerance. I should have killed him when we were boys. But I couldn't figure out how to make it seem as if I were innocent. And my blessed mother would never have forgiven me had she known.

'If only he were dead, but everyone else thought he was alive,' I used to think. So I began to study necromancy."

"But the zombie path wasn't your ultimate choice for FarjAd," I said. The Wizard shook his head. "Why not?" I asked.

"He'd be too hard to control. But I couldn't trust myself to kill him. So I had to arrange for you Americans to do it." Kazimi looked at me slyly. "And you have. So, despite the fact that your heart is set on binding me to your yoke indefinitely, I fear I must decline." He directed our attention to the back of the room, where his zombies lined up like a badass bombardment team.

"Um, Wizzy?" I gave him a little wave to get his attention. "Before things get too hectic in here, I'd suggest you take a peek at Channel Fourteen."

Giving me a puzzled look, he grabbed the remote from a low-slung table and keyed the power on his fifty-two-inch plasma. Up came his own snarling face, in five-second delay, announcing that he should've killed his brother when they were kids.

"Of course, not everybody in Iran knows English, so we'll be taking our interpreter to the station later on to provide a translation. I think we'll do a little ticker underneath the video as well. Something like *Real Estate mogul Delir Kazimi revealed to be state's enemy, the Wizard. Housing prices drop accordingly.* What do you think?"

Vayl pointed toward the hallway's end, where you could just see a lens and one pale, trembling hand. "Wave to the camera, Delir." Bergman peered around the corner, gave me a brash grin, and then went back into half hiding. His bodyguards didn't. Cole, Cam, and Natchez stepped out from their secreted spots and aimed their weapons at the Wiz as if daring him to hurt their little buddy.

"You ever heard of character assassination?" I asked. "It can be worse than death, Kazimi. Because you never recover. But you live on. Broke. Friendless. Exiled from your family. Your country—"

"I will always have the dead!" the Wizard cried, holding out his arms to his zombies.

"No. You will not." It was Asha. He'd come. My shoulders slumped with relief as he swept into the room. I handed him the bone. He held it up. "This is the ohm of Delir Kazimi. Let it hold all his power forevermore." The Wizard fell to his knees as a black cloud that buzzed like an angry nest of wasps swirled out of his mouth and into the ohm. For a moment the room filled with pressure. So much that my ears popped. Asha folded the bone into his large hand. Squeezed. And when he opened it, all that was left filtered onto the carpet as harmless white powder. The pressure released. The Wizard's zombies fell to the floor, finally truly dead. And we all stared as Asha laid his hand on Kazimi's forehead.

"I am the Amanha Szeya, and I say you are still too dangerous to live."

"Asha"—I pointed to the windows—"the mahghul." If they were at the glass, they were also trying to find another way in. It wouldn't be long until they joined us in this room.

"Be ready to fight," he told me. I drew Grief and prepped it to fire. Looked to Vayl and the team. *Do you see them?* Vayl nodded, but the others shook their heads. They'd be visible soon enough, however. As soon, in fact, as we made one of them bleed.

"Don't freak when a bunch of nasty little spikey-faced gargoyles seem to appear out of nowhere," I told them. "Just kill them. Okay?"

They nodded.

Asha drew a long crystalline blade from his robe. It looked otherworldly, none too sharp, and I briefly considered offering my bolo for the job. But Asha had started murmuring some ceremonial-sounding words and I hesitated to interrupt.

In the few moments since Vayl and I had stripped him of his veneer and Asha had rescinded his powers, Kazimi seemed to have shriveled. He knelt, unmoving, at Asha's feet, shoulders bowed, eyes staring off into the distance. That look never changed. Not when Asha's chant gained power and he grabbed Delir by the hair. Not when he set the tip of the blade against Kazimi's face five separate times, drawing a sort of star across it. Not even when he cut his throat.

As soon as the body dropped the mahghul came pouring through the doorway. I had just enough time to take a deep, calming breath before they were on me.

I fired both clips and half of a third before I could no longer see. One of the little bastards had covered my face. Remembering how the hanged woman had gone to her death, I holstered Grief, grabbed the mahghul with both hands, and yanked as hard as I could. I lost some hair off the back of my head, but I could see again.

I threw the mahghul against the wall. Heard its neck snap as I pulled my bolo. I skewered the mahghul attached to my right leg, stabbed the one on my left through the side, and then Vayl was there. Pulling them off me. His face a frenzied mask of blood and gore.

"I thought they had you," he gasped as he broke a mahghul's back.

"Me too."

We went to help Asha, whose entire torso was a writhing mass of mahghul. Stabbing, slashing, sometimes just grabbing and punching, we worked him free. On the other side of the room I could see our guys were faring much better. The mahghul didn't appreciate Bergman's weapons a bit. In fact, the Manxes seemed to repel them. They'd leap at Cam or Cole, but as soon as they touched that new alloy they'd jump away, as if singed.

"Asha," I said as the last of his mahghul hit the ground. "Look."

We watched as one of the monsters charged Natchez from the right. He was shooting off to his left, so by the time he swung the Manx around the mahghul was nearly on him. It jumped up, touched the gun barrel, and somersaulted backward.

"What is that?" Asha asked.

"Bergman will never tell you," I said. "But I'll bet I can have him make you some armor out of it."

Asha's eyes gleamed. "How soon?"

"How about right after his vacation?"

"Excellent."

Chapter Thirty-Four

Finally. Celebration. We were all back in that cheery yellow kitchen, drinking tea and wishing it was beer, but happy nonetheless. Somehow fighting the mahghul together had negated their ability to drain us emotionally. Dave and Cassandra stood arm in arm, gazing into each other's eyes every few minutes as if they'd found the world's greatest treasure. And in between we related our adventures.

Dave and Jet had overcome the reavers easily. One of them had been asleep. The other was so engrossed in the movie they were airing he didn't hear them until it was far too late.

"So we duct taped them to some chairs," Jet said. "And man, they did not want to cooperate. But we kept asking them questions, and their third eyes kept straying right to the spots we needed. You could tell they really wanted to bang their heads against the wall before it was all over. It was hilarious!"

As Cole began relating their tales I thought about those eyes. They'd been designed to entrap the souls of a reaver's victim until it could be transported to hell. Where I'd been myself, and had seen another pair of eyes quite unlike those of the reavers. They'd haunted me from the shadows of my psyche for so long, I'd all but given up on identifying their source. But maybe, if I replayed that scene in my head one more time . . .

Just before the demons had seen us, they'd been talking about

Samos trying to make a deal with the Magistrate so he could watch the pound-of-flesh ceremony. But he hadn't been willing to sign the contract allowing him temporary-visitation rights, because it would've required him to give up something precious. I was just getting an image of that something when the demons identified us. All I'd seen were its eyes, glowing, as if in the lights of a vehicle.

Forget about the eyes for a second, Jaz. You're so damn fixated it's nauseating. What else was there? Anything? At all?

I thought hard. It had all happened so fast, it was tough to remember. Just a split second really.

I closed my own eyes. Relaxed. *Don't create anything. Don't try to see. Just be in that moment one more time.*

Demons talking. Gossiping, really. *Did you hear? No, you're kidding!* Their words creating images, like a movie, right in front of me. Yeah, yeah, there were the eyes. And . . . something more. A rough outline, darker than the dark, of a furry body. Four legs. A tail.

"Holy crap!" I opened my eyes, realized the room had gone silent.

"Jasmine?" Vayl crooked an are-you-all-right eyebrow at me.

"I just figured it out! The reason I was willing to go to hell with Raoul. Give up shuffling cards. It was for the chance to find out what is more precious to Samos than anything in the world now that his *avhar*'s dead."

Vayl's eyes glittered with excitement. He knew what this could mean. Leverage of the best kind against our worst enemy. "What is it?" he asked.

"His dog. He wouldn't give it up. Not even to come to hell. Meet with the Magistrate. Maybe arrange himself a real power play." And we all knew how much Samos adored power.

Vayl rubbed his hands together. "How do you put it? This is

major. This is . . . this is very exciting, Jasmine. We could really get to him with this."

"Yeah. So start thinking."

Everybody began talking at once, which gave me the cover I needed to slip out of the room. Asha had offered to take care of the reavers for me, but I felt like I should be the one to deal with them. My actions had brought them to this place, after all. In a roundabout way, okay, but still. As I suited up for one last job, I thought back to my farewell with the Amanha Szeya. He'd come such a long way in the short time I'd known him. The sad-dog look had fallen from his face, to be replaced with a quiet, proud courage. He stood taller, smiled wider, spoke surer than I'd ever known him to before.

"I wish I could do something for you," he'd said as we stood outside the Wizard's compound.

"You've done plenty, Asha."

"And yet I feel incomplete." He stared at me a moment; then his eyes cleared. "There may be something after all." He laid his hand on my forehead. For a second it burned, just as his tears had. Then it was over. "Your Mark is gone," he said.

"How did you do that?" I asked. "I thought—"

He shrugged. "It is within my rights, and so I exercise them."

I smiled up at him. "You're a good guy to know."

"Thank you."

I was just pulling on my manteau when Dave walked into the girls' room. "What're you up to?" he asked.

"Going to get those reavers," I said.

"Why?"

"Well, I can't let them run around loose grabbing stray souls, now, can I?"

"Jaz, I'm working for Raoul now, remember?"

"Um, yeah."

"So . . . it's taken care of."

I looked at him. There were new lines beside his eyes. New depths behind them. A blooming misery I hoped he'd be able to master. "Oh. Thanks."

"No problem."

Long pause. Soon an awkward one. "Jaz?"

"Yeah?" I said quickly. My chest tightened. I knew what he was going to say. He was going to ask me to go back into hell. To rescue our mother. And I couldn't. Wouldn't. There was only so much you could sacrifice. I'd given her my childhood. I'd given the CIA my beloved cards. I'd reached my limit.

Maybe he read it in my eyes, because that wasn't the question he asked. "Do you like Cassandra?"

"She's a jewel."

He nodded. "Good."

He left and I sank onto the bed, mostly because my knees didn't want to hold me anymore. Before I realized what was happening my eyes had strayed to the calling feature on my special specs and I'd dialed Evie's number. "Jaz?"

"Yeah. How's everyone? How's E.J.?"

"Fine. She's right here. She just woke up for the day. I'm feeding her right now."

Crap, I hadn't even thought about the time difference. I checked my watch. Nearly midnight in Iran. Yeah, I guess it was about time for breakfast in Evieland.

"And Albert?"

"Why don't you ask him yourself?"

Before I could stop her, she'd handed the phone to the old man. We talked for a while. Just long enough to exhaust him. We hung up just as Vayl walked into the room.

"I missed you," he said, striding over to sit on the bed beside me.

"Yeah." I handed him my glasses. Didn't want to wear them anymore. They felt too heavy. "I just talked to my dad."

"Oh? That is good, yes? You should tell David."

"Okay. But maybe, you know, just until he's sort of recovered from this whole ordeal, I'll leave out the part about how Albert thinks somebody is trying to kill him."

I leaned my head on Vayl's shoulder as his arm came around me. But I could not feel comforted. A necromancer had enslaved my brother, a demon had tried to steal my niece's soul, and now my father was telling me his motorcycle wreck was no accident. The violence that formed the framework of my life had never before touched my family. But within just a few days it had nearly destroyed it.

I looked into Vayl's eyes. "This shit's hitting too close to home," I whispered.

"What do you want to do about it?"

I didn't even have to think. "Hit back."

EXTRAS

www.orbitbooks.net

About the Author

Jennifer Rardin began writing at the age of twelve, mostly poems to amuse her classmates and short stories featuring her best friends as the heroines. She lives in an old farmhouse in Illinois with her husband and two children. Find out more about Jennifer Rardin at www.JenniferRardin.com.

Find out more about Jennifer and other Orbit authors by registering for the free monthly newsletter at www.orbitbooks.net

If you enjoyed
BITING THE BULLET,
look out for

BITTEN TO DEATH

Book 4 of the Jaz Parks series

by

Jennifer Rardin

I stood in the stone-paved courtyard of a Greek villa so old and refined it would've made me feel like a cave-dweller if I hadn't been so pissed. I'd only just raised Grief, the Walther PPK my former roommate-turned-tech consultant had modified for me, so I had no problem keeping a steady bead on my target. Since he was a vampire, I'd pressed the magic button, transforming Grief into a crossbow. Which said vamp was taking pretty seriously. The only reason he was still pretending to breathe.

Beside me, my boss played his part to perfection. He'd already made the leap from feigned surprise that I'd drawn on one of our hosts, to acceptance that I'd once again dropped him into a socially precarious situation. Maybe he slipped into the role so easily because he was used to it. I did tend to make his existence, well, interesting.

He turned his head slightly; his dark curls indifferent to the steady breeze coming off the bay they were clipped so short. He managed to keep an eye on my target, as well as whatever vamps might come pouring out of the sprawling sand-colored mansion to back him up as he said, "Are you sure you recognize this fellow?"

"I'm telling you, Vayl, he's the one," I insisted. "I just

saw the report on him last week. He's wanted for murder in three different countries. His specialty is families. The pictures were—" *gruesome,* I thought, but I choked on the word. The twitch of Vayl's left eyebrow told me I was on a roll. The thing was, at the moment, I didn't give two craps about our little game. The Vampere world might be all about superiority, which was why we'd needed to make a power play the minute we crossed their threshold, but I'd have popped the vamp in front of me even if it meant we had to fight our way out of a nest of enraged vultures and their human guardians. In fact, that we should personally benefit from his demise made me feel almost . . . dirty. I know, I know. As assistant to the CIA's top assassin, I was hardly in a position to make moral judgments. But I didn't see why that should stop me now.

"You can't prove anything," snarled the vamp, whose shoulder length hair did nothing to hide his enormous bulging forehead.

"I don't *have* to, you idiot!" I snapped, wishing I could objectify the rage I was feeling, hurl it at him like it was an enormous black vase full of cobras. "Much as it often pains me to say so, you *others* have so few official rights they could fit on the back of my driver's license. That leaves me free to smoke you if I feel you are a clear and present danger to society. Which you are."

"What is the meaning of this?" demanded the woman who steamed out one of the villa's blue-framed back doors, all four of which were framed by solar lamps made to resemble antique street lights. The tendrils of her black chiffon gown batted the air behind her, making her resemble a pissed off Homecoming Queen candidate, one whose friends had voted for the other, uglier girl. Though her carefully groomed version of beauty could have landed her in any number of pageants, her psychic scent hit me between the eyes so hard I felt like I'd been drop-kicked into a garbage dump. As a Sensitive, I recognize vampires like hawks sight rabbits. But I'd never before felt so nauseated by the realization. What the hell kind of vamp *was* she?

Vayl turned to intercept her, placing the tiger-carved cane he always carried firmly on the gray rock between them to make sure she kept her distance. She stopped three feet from it, rearing back as if she'd hit an invisible wall. Her eyes, the liquid brown of a beagle pup, widened angrily as a how-dare-you look tried to settle on her face. But it fled almost immediately, as if she'd undergone a recent Botox treatment and couldn't sustain any sort of facial feature that might leave evidence of emotion. I struggled not to stare. I had a job to do after all. But her scent, combined with the way she strafed Vayl with her eyes, made me want to give her a closer look.

I forced my gaze back to my target. He'd taken half a step forward. I smiled at him. *Come on, asshole. Make it easy for me.* He stopped.

"What are *you* doing here?" the woman snarled at Vayl.

For a second I thought he was going to ignore her completely. Then he said, "Where is your *Deyrar*?"

She drew herself up to her full height, which was maybe five-one, and said, "*I* am the *Deyrar*."

Vayl and I don't have a psychic link. But we're tight enough to say a ton of words with one stricken look.

Are we screwed? I asked him with raised eyebrows.

A valid question, Jasmine, his narrowed gaze replied. *We must play this carefully. Obviously she was not expecting us. Which means she knows nothing about the deal.*

Well, shit.

We'd been asked to come to Patras by the vampire who ran Vayl's former Trust, a canny old sleaze named Hamon Eryx, who'd promised us safe passage in return for a shot at Edward Samos, aka The Raptor. Samos had either committed or attempted enough acts of terrorism in the last few years to raise him to the top of our department's hit list.

We had made one great stride in identifying Samos's vulnerabilities, and had been hatching a plan that would draw him into the open when Eryx had contacted Vayl with a thinly disguised plea for help. Samos had contacted him offering an alliance. This was not good news to Eryx, since he wasn't interested in playing. And since he knew that those who refused Samos's advances generally ended up dead, he'd asked Vayl to intervene. After some negotiations that ended with a contract signed in blood—no, I'm not kidding—Vayl got our boss, Pete's, blessing and we were on our way to Greece.

Now the *Deyrar* had apparently been replaced, which meant our whole mission could be junk before it even came out of the box. Plus we were standing in the middle of a Vampere household. Any minute now we could be surrounded by fifteen to twenty pissed off vamps and their human guardians, who would feel they had every right to kill us for trespassing.

As if he'd read my mind, an enormous man burst out of the door the new *Deyrar* had just exited. His appearance, yet even more distracting than that of his mistress, made me seriously consider smoking my target just so I could stand and stare. He went shirtless, though mid-April in Greece is pretty mild and the temperature currently hovered around sixty degrees. I supposed that said something about the man's vanity. Maybe he wanted me to get a load of that sculpted bod and wonder how many hours he worked out a day. It wouldn't have made a difference if he was a vamp. But he wasn't. From what I could tell with my souped-up, *other*-sensing abilities, he was human. The kind photographers love to feature on the covers of books with titles like Forbidden Folly and Wesley's Wench.

"Disa, I came as soon as you called," he said eagerly. He looked at Vayl, starting slightly, as if he'd only just seen him. "Who're you?" he demanded.

"I am Vayl. And this is my *avhar*, Lucille Robinson."

Huh. Hamon Eryx had insisted on using real names, because he said they gave us all a certain power over each other once the deal was signed. Vayl couldn't fake his own identity, because most of the vamps in the Trust would know him. But the fact that he'd given them my favorite fake ID showed me how little faith he had that we'd find anybody we could work with on the inside now that Eryx was gone.

Cover Boy looked at Disa. "Do you want me to kill them?" he asked.

I tried not to gape. After all, I was holding a loaded

weapon. How long did he think it would take me to swing it in his direction? Could he *be* that stupid?

Disa's fleeting expression seemed to wonder the same. "Get the rest of the Trust," she snapped. As he bobbed his head obediently and went back inside, she turned her glare to me. "So you are Vayl's *avhar*." She made it sound like a criminal sentence. *Guilty, as charged. Hang her from the highest tree, boys!*

I gave her one, hopefully, emotionless look, said, "Yeah," and then sent my attention back to my target. He was beginning to relax. Starting to believe his *Deyrar* would get him out of this pickle. So I shot him in the shoulder.

His hands went immediately to the wound as he looked at me in shock. "What did you do that for?"

"Hair-trigger," I said, though my eyes told him different. I'd read the reports. He liked to torture his victims before he killed them, half of whom had been under the age of twelve. The more I thought about it, the less control my brain seemed to have over my hand. "I suggest you stand very still. Wouldn't want you to have a bad accident before I decide your fate." In the deep silence that followed all I could hear was the whir of well-oiled machinery as Grief automatically loaded another bolt into my crossbow.

FOR THE LATEST NEWS AND THE HOTTEST EXCLUSIVES ON ALL YOUR FAVOURITE SF AND FANTASY STARS, SIGN UP FOR:

ORBIT'S FREE MONTHLY E-ZINE

PACKED WITH

BREAKING NEWS
THE LATEST REVIEWS
EXCLUSIVE INTERVIEWS
STUNNING EXTRACTS
SPECIAL OFFERS
BRILLIANT COMPETITIONS

AND A GALAXY OF
NEW AND ESTABLISHED SFF STARS!

TO GET A DELICIOUS SLICE OF SFF IN YOUR INBOX EVERY MONTH, SEND YOUR DETAILS BY EMAIL TO: ORBIT@LITTLEBROWN.CO.UK OR VISIT:

WWW.ORBITBOOKS.NET

THE HOME OF SFF ONLINE